More By The Author

The Raven's Journey

Book 1: See Me
Book 2: See Me Revealed
Book 3: See Me Go
Book 4: See Me Believe
Book 5: See Me Overcome
Book 6: Hawk
Book 7: Ronan
Book 8: Stolas

Looking Through The Shadows

The Underbelly
After the Wreckage
We Always Fight

I S.P.I.

I S.P.I. Mischievous Magic (Volume 1)
I S.P.I. Spicy Sorcery (Volume 2)

Short Stories & More

Where Realms Collide
Unnerving Descent
Unnerving Eclipse
Unnerving Wicked
Super: Unexpected Heroes Arise
Rise Reflection
Rise Resurrection
Rise Revolution
Rise Recreation
The Space Between Us
The Pulse (The Haunting of Orchard House)

Michelle Lee on the Web

Michelle on Facebook at
tiny.cc/MichelleLeeWrites

or write to
MichelleLeeWrites@gmail.com

THE RAVEN'S JOURNEY
BOOK TWO

SEE ME REVEALED

Michelle Lee

BLUE FORGE PRESS
Port Orchard, Washington

See Me Revealed
Copyright 2019, 2022
by Michelle Lee

First eBook Edition February 2020
First Print Edition February 2020
Second eBook Edition May 2022
Second Print Edition May 2022

Cover photograph by Michelle Lee
Cover design by Brianne DiMarco
Interior design by Brianne DiMarco

ISBN 978-1-59092-886-8

For information about film, reprint or other subsidiary rights, contact: blueforgegroup@gmail.com

Blue Forge Press is the print division of the volunteer-run, federal 501(c)3 nonprofit company, Blue Forge Group, founded in 1989 and dedicated to bringing light to the shadows and voice to the silence. We strive to empower storytellers across all walks of life with our four divisions: Blue Forge Press, Blue Forge Films, Blue Forge Gaming, and Blue Forge Records. Find out more at www.BlueForgeGroup.org

Blue Forge Press
7419 Ebbert Drive Southeast
Port Orchard, Washington 98367
blueforgepress@gmail.com
360-550-2071 ph.txt

For my Dad,
who taught me that
I can solve problems
by breaking them down.

For Nicole,
who sometimes knows me
better than I know myself.

SEE ME REVEALED

Michelle Lee

Chapter One

Jax woke up feeling disoriented and with a headache. Like he had been out drinking all night then got into a fight and lost. Badly. His whole body was sore and he couldn't remember where he was or how he got here. As he sat up and looked around, he saw Ronnie asleep in a chair over by a window.

That's when reality crashed back down around him. He'd flipped out in the observation room! He tried to throw a chair through the glass because that girl, Airiella, had pissed him off. To be fair, he didn't think it was him that was pissed off, she made the darkness inside him mad. He hadn't been in control at all and had just wanted to get out into the conference room to choke her.

He paled as he remembered. He had wanted to do physical harm to her. He had tried. If not for Ronnie and Aedan, he would have. He covered his face with his hands and rocked back and forth in the bed. That's why Ronnie was still here, it was making sense now. She had told Ronnie to restrain him. To her credit, she hadn't been wrong.

He got up quietly and went to the bathroom to hop

in a cold shower to try and jolt his body awake. He didn't understand why he felt sore, yet at the same time, he felt lighter too. He closed the bathroom door behind him as softly as possible because he didn't want to wake Ronnie up, nor did he lock the door, in case he needed Ronnie's help.

He stripped and then stepped beneath the icy spray of the shower that pelted his skin like thousands of little tiny needles. The cold helped wash away the fog that was clouding his head. He turned it to warm and finished up while he mentally went over everything again with a clearer mind.

She—Airiella, he reminded himself—had pulled some of the darkness from him. That's why he felt lighter. Holy shit, she's the real deal. He felt hopeful for the first time. He got dressed and saw Ronnie stirring in the chair.

"Good morning, sunshine!" Jax called to him in a sing song voice.

"You are just going to start the day off with being weird then?" Ronnie shot off as he stretched.

"I feel lighter today," Jax said seriously.

"Well you should, Airiella damn near killed herself with that display, between you and Dr. Stone," Ronnie muttered sleepily.

"What?" Was there something that Jax was still missing?

"You passed the fuck out! Dr. Stone crumbled like an old building, you passed out, and she dropped to the floor to be rushed out by Smitty and Father Roarke. Tak, Tama and Oni followed. Word is she was pretty bad off. They are all closed up about it too," Ronnie filled him in.

"Airiella is bad off?" Jax felt dumb because he wasn't understanding.

"Smitty said she is exactly what we asked for, but doing what she does comes at a heavy price for her. He wouldn't go into details, but I've never heard Smitty rattled like that before, man. He was crying," Ronnie ground out in frustration.

"Smitty?" All Jax was doing was repeating words back to Ronnie. His brain wasn't catching up.

"Yes, Smitty." Ronnie turned to glare at Jax.

"He's not back to his room yet?" Jax shook his head trying jar thoughts into place.

"No, neither of them are."

"Them? You mean Airiella?" Jax was so confused.

"Yes. Father Roarke kept them down in the chapel. Taklishim stopped by to say he was making more blends for Airiella, and he looked bad. Wouldn't tell me anything other than he was there for the whole thing and he'd never experienced something so terrifying." Ronnie's voice had dropped. Jax knew he felt guilty.

"Is this all because of me?" Jax caught on finally.

Ronnie nodded, his green eyes dimmed with sadness. "Smitty told me that Taklishim said you don't have much time before it's consumed everything in you."

"Not possible, she pulled it from me," Jax argued blandly.

"She pulled enough from you to save you," Ronnie clarified.

"Shit." Jax sat down with a thud.

"Father Roarke wants to meet with you before you go," Ronnie told him as he walked to the bathroom.

Jax watched him come back out, running a wet washcloth over his face. "I'll do it."

"I wasn't going to give you a choice, bro," Ronnie told him. "I gotta go change. I'll meet you downstairs in the dining room."

Jax stood and walked with Ronnie to the hall. The elevator dinged across the corridor and he looked over to see Smitty walking out, carrying Airiella's still form. Blood streaked across her face, and arms. Smitty looked no better.

"Oh my God!" Ronnie cried. He started to run towards Smitty, but Smitty shook his head, stopping Ronnie in his tracks; the look on his face making Jax's heart clench as he looked at the still form. Something dark in him was happy to see it, but the newly lighter side felt the horror that was in Smitty's eyes.

"Just open the door for me please, her key is in my pocket," Smitty said, his voice scratchy. Ronnie hadn't moved so Jax walked over and grabbed the key, opening the door so Smitty could go in.

"Will she be okay?" Jax asked, fear in his voice.

"I hope so," was Smitty's weak reply.

Jax tossed the key on the table inside the door, pulling it gently closed behind him and pushed Ronnie towards his own room. "Snap out of it, change, and meet me downstairs."

Jax was afraid of what he had seen of Airiella. That was because of him. She didn't even look alive. He took the stairs instead of the elevator and gave himself a moment to sit there and gather his thoughts. His fear was that he wasn't strong enough to fight this. The look on Smitty's face would be haunting Jax for a while.

Winnie stayed out of sight from Smitty, thinking he couldn't handle any more than what had been thrown at him so far. She watched him take care of Airiella in a tender way and Winnie's heart hurt. Smitty had always been pretty unshakable and steadfast, and now he looked shattered. His normally light blue eyes a darker color that hinted at the depths this experience had taken him to.

When Airiella had woken up screaming, she had nearly given Smitty and Father Roarke a heart attack. And she had just kept screaming. Father Roarke had run out of the chapel and called Taklishim who must have still been in the building somewhere, because they both came running back in five minutes later.

Smitty was just rocking Airiella back and forth trying to soothe her. Her big brown eyes were wide open but seeing nothing, and that scream was just bouncing off the walls in a bone chilling sound. Taklishim had tipped her head back and poured something down her throat, rubbing it to get her to swallow. It knocked her out quickly, and Winnie jumped back over to the spirit plane to make sure she hadn't gone back there.

She hadn't. She was just unconscious. Her body had gone completely limp against Smitty. Winnie was worried. She went to the altar and prayed; she didn't know what else to do. She asked God for protection for all of them, help to guide them through all this, and peace for when they slept. It didn't feel adequate, but it was all she could do. She was a ghost.

Smitty was standing up now, stretching and covered Airiella with the blanket. He pulled out his phone and had called someone, her guess was Ronnie. While Smitty was on the phone, Winnie curled up to Airiella and stroked her hair knowing she liked that.

She was going to stay here until Smitty came back, she didn't want Airiella to be alone. She heard Smitty talking quietly to Father Roarke now, and Winnie started singing Amazing Grace to Airy's still body. Winnie had loved that song; it always made her feel. So, she sang and stroked her hair, never noticing that Father Roarke was looking right at her.

Aedan packed up his clothes while Mags still slept and checked in with Ronnie, he still hadn't heard from Smitty and was a little concerned. Ronnie was in the dining room with Jax, so he kissed Mags on the forehead and went down to join them.

They both looked shook up, and their greeting was subdued. "What's going on?"

"Just passed Smitty in the hall on the way here," Jax said solemnly. "He was carrying Airiella, she was covered in blood and not moving at all." Jax choked up. "Smitty... he..."

Ronnie laid his hand on Jax's arm. "Smitty looks like an empty shell right now."

That concerned Aedan more than he cared to admit. "Is she okay?"

"No idea. It looks bad," Jax replied, his voice steady again. "She looked dead."

"Don't even think that," Ronnie spit out, his face darkening.

Aedan put his hand on Ronnie this time. "Let's not jump to conclusions. Has anyone talked to Smitty?"

Ronnie nodded. "He wouldn't talk about it. Said it was bad. He was crying when he called me. After seeing her, I get it."

"I have a hard time even thinking about what we saw yesterday, I can't imagine what Smitty saw," Aedan confessed. "I'll check on him, did he go back to his room?"

"He's in hers," Ronnie said, his eyes vacant.

"As far as I know, Mags and I are still planning to fly out to Seattle with her," Aedan said thoughtfully.

"Is that where she is from?" Jax asked, curious.

"I don't think the city itself, but somewhere over there," Aedan told him.

"I like it there." Jax's mind wandered off.

"Well it can't be you that goes with her," Ronnie snapped.

Aedan stepped in, not wanting the tension to rebuild between them. "Mags and I are going; I'll get her as prepped as possible. You two will need to get the house ready."

"We going straight to Cali then?" Ronnie looked at Aedan.

"That's where we'll fly from Seattle," Aedan confirmed. "I think you guys can go home first, do what you need to do. After the show in the conference room yesterday, Dave told me to plan on being in Washington for about a week."

"What do you want us to prepare?" Jax asked.

"Make sure she has her own room, and at least try to make it comfortable for her," Aedan replied. "She's going to be there for a bit."

"Aedan, are you concerned about how this will work at all? I mean, come on, I wasn't even in the same room with her and that energy took over me before I even had a chance to fight it. I wanted to kill her, well the thing in me did, not me personally."

"It concerns *me*," was Ronnie's hot reply. He'd barely touched the food on his plate.

"Ronnie," Aedan warned. "Yeah, Jax, it concerns me. We all felt the energy coming off you then, it for sure wasn't you. I'm going to try to talk to the council today to see if there is anything we can do in that type of situation again."

"Dude," Ronnie started, "I'm bigger than you. I outweigh you. I'm stronger than you, have more fighting skills than you, and *I* could barely contain you. Aedan had to help me. That's how strong whatever is inside you is."

"If you hadn't passed out when she pulled it from you," Aedan joined in, "I don't think we would have been able to hold you."

"Yet you still want to bring an unknown female into the group and place her in danger like that?" Jax was getting angry. "I can't take much more guilt, and if I hurt her, I don't know what I'll do."

"My impression is she can handle you," Ronnie said flatly. "I don't like it, but I don't think she is afraid of you."

Aedan looked pensive. "I don't like it either, but she helped you. By the way, do you feel differently today?" He lowered his voice because others in the dining room were watching them at this point.

Jax deflated a little, "Yeah. I noticed when I woke up I felt lighter. Also felt like I had a hangover and had been fighting too, though. I'm sore."

Aedan looked at Ronnie. "He didn't drink, did he?"

"No, he was out cold all night," Ronnie said, finishing his breakfast finally.

Aedan frowned. "Jax, when we flew in, did you talk to anyone other than us?"

"Just that homeless guy who came up to me and said he watched our show all the time," Jax thought out loud. "I shook his hand and took a photo with him."

Aedan frantically scrolled through something on his phone, then held it out to Jax. "Was it that guy?"

Confused, Jax looked at the photo and then nodded. "Yep, but that's not the picture, it's on my phone, I told him I'd print it and sign it for him." Jax pulled his phone out and handed it to Aedan. "That's the picture."

Aedan looked at Jax with his arm around the guy smiling for the picture. "Shit."

"What?" Ronnie grabbed the phone and looked at the picture too. "Shit is right."

"Jax, you can't be around people," Aedan said gently. "Not sure why it doesn't affect us, but that guy is the guy who was all over the news for kidnapping that kid and was going to murder him. Airiella stopped it from happening during her test with Asher."

Jax paled and dropped his phone as it was handed back to him. "Are you fucking serious?"

"Look it up," Ronnie said. "He's right."

"Were you with Dr. Stone yesterday at all?" Aedan asked, his voice faint.

Jax nodded slowly. "He was asking me how I was feeling..." he trailed off. "Shit. It really is my fault."

"Not directly, it hasn't done anything to us." Aedan pushed back his chair. "I'm going to speak to the council. Jax, research the locations the producers gave us in your room."

"Wait, Father Roarke said he wanted to talk to me," Jax started.

"Let me talk to him first," Aedan said and walked away. He didn't want to argue with Jax, but now his concern was through the roof. He sent Mags a text telling her he was going to try to talk to the council and would be back later.

He called Tom, one of the producers, and asked him to gather the council so he could meet with them and ask their advice. That done, he headed out feeling like a cloud was hanging over his head.

Smitty was exhausted. Airiella was on the bed at least now, and back in her room instead of laying on the cold floor. She still hadn't moved after she stopped screaming. He paced the room and grabbed a bottle of water from the fridge, downing it in a few gulps.

He pulled out his phone and called Jillian. "Hey babe," she said as she answered the phone.

Smitty smiled, "Hey Jilly, how you doing?"

"Good. Miss you though. Met a new girl last night, she was fun," she said with a laugh.

"A girl this time?" Smitty chuckled. "Actually, me too," he told her.

He heard a sharp intake of breath from her, "Really?" Her voice was quiet.

"Yeah," he admitted.

"It's your first time." Her tone was unreadable over the phone.

"It was. You are okay with it, right?" he asked, suddenly worried.

"Of course, I am. It makes me feel less guilty now since I was the only one doing it," she confessed.

"Jilly, we talked about it, I'm okay with it. I'm not like the others, sex is just sex," he assured, his voice calm.

"Does that mean you have no emotional attachment to her?" she carefully asked him.

"I think in this case it's different, maybe that's why I slept with her. I haven't felt the desire or need to since we've been together. I can't explain it. I don't feel for her the way I do for you, but I feel something for her. Maybe love, but again, not in the same way as you," his words came out in a rushed jumble.

Jillian was quiet. "Are we through?"

Smitty laughed softly. "Not even close, babe. I told you, it's different with her. You'll just have to meet her."

"Wait, you are bringing her home?" Jilly asked, her voice going up in pitch.

"She works with us now," Smitty explained.

"You slept with someone you work with? That's never a good idea," she cautioned.

"Babe, you wouldn't believe me if I tried to explain anything that's happened here. Just trust me on this. You'll understand when you meet her."

"I do trust you," she breathed out. "I just don't want to lose you."

"You aren't losing me, I love you," his voice warm.

"You just said you might love her too," she returned.

"Yeah, I did. It's really not the same though. There's this draw to her, to be near her, to protect her. Something about her that just feels right when you are with her," he tried explaining and realized that what he said sounded bad. He couldn't tell her Airiella was an angel.

"Sounds an awful lot like love to me, Art." Jillian's voice had gotten hard.

"To be fair, all the guys in the group feel that way too," he argued.

"Even Jax?"

"Well, not that he has admitted, but we can see he is affected as well. Even Mags feels the same way. You just have to trust me on this," he pleaded.

"I do," she softened. "It was just harder to hear than I thought it would be."

"What we have works, babe. I know we aren't conventional, but for us, it works. I love coming home to you," he said.

He could hear the smile in her voice, and then, "I love that, too. When will you be home?"

"Probably tomorrow; things went sideways yesterday, and I think there will be some follow up on our end with the council to help better understand what's going on with Jax," he said carefully. He didn't want Jillian involved in this mix.

"Okay baby, see you then. I gotta run." She made a kissing sound and then hung up.

Smitty looked over at Airiella laying exactly the same as he left her. It had been twenty-four hours now. He wanted to clean the blood off her, it didn't feel right to leave her laying like that. He walked into the bathroom and noted she had one of the really large jetted tubs. If he got in with her, he could get her cleaned off and still have a skin connection to her.

He texted Ronnie. "I need your help, come to Airiella's room."

Smitty picked her up enough to get her clothes off her and threw them in a pile on the floor. He'd call room service to come get them to wash them up for her. He added his bloody shirt to the mix and waited for Ronnie.

He pulled open the door before Ronnie knocked and pulled him in quickly. "I need your help to get her in the tub with me. I need to get all this blood off her," Smitty told him, leading him over to the bed.

"What the fuck happened, dude?" Ronnie looked shell shocked at the sight.

"I can't talk about it right now. Just, trust me, you wouldn't have wanted to be there," Smitty admitted, still feeling shattered by everything that happened.

"Can't say I've ever seen you look this bad before, so I'm just going to agree with you on that." Ronnie leaned over and picked Airiella up. "She's like a noodle. A beautiful one, but still a noodle."

"She's been deathly still for a full twenty-four hours now," Smitty said. He walked in the bathroom and turned the tub on making the water a bit on the hotter side. He stripped off the rest of his clothes and then threw them out to the pile on the floor. "Can you call room service and have them send up food and take those clothes to be washed?"

"She hasn't moved for twenty-four hours?" Ronnie stared down at her in his arms, his face pale and shocked. "Is she okay?"

Smitty sat on the edge of the tub, not caring that he was naked, they'd all been around each other naked. Tears fell and his voice was thick, "I hope so. She had no heartbeat for about five minutes. Father Roarke kept telling me she was okay, but man," Smitty choked, "she was dead.

Blood coming out of her mouth, her nose, her ears. Her body fucking broke, I heard her bones snap."

Ronnie paled even more, his green eyes bright with fear, cradling her to his chest. "She's breathing right now; I have to believe she will be okay."

Smitty angrily wiped the tears away, grabbed a couple of washcloths and got in the water, hissing at the heat, but dealing with it anyway. "I just need to see her not bloody; I need to get her clean." He sat down and let his body adjust before holding out his arms.

"I get it, I'd want to do the same," Ronnie agreed, understanding and leaned over to lower her down to Smitty. "Is that where all these bruises came from?"

"Some were already there," Smitty said softly. "She told me about everything that happened to her while she was here. She told me about her life, she let me in," his voice got thick again and he fought back against the tears. "She did this voluntarily, to save the others."

Ronnie sat down on the floor facing away from Smitty, leaning against the side of the tub. "Is she what they think she is?"

"I wholly believe she is an angel. But seeing it in front of your face is something else entirely," Smitty whispered.

Ronnie nodded, at a loss for words. "I'll be out there, if you need me."

Smitty heard him call and order food and someone to come grab the clothes. He soaked the washcloth and got it lathered up with soap. She was facing forward away from him, her weight supported against his body and his legs holding her in place.

He pushed her forward and used his left arm as a brace in front of her to keep her from falling face forward and he washed her back, taking care not to push hard against the bruises that marred her skin. In the well-lit bathroom, he saw all the scars he hadn't seen before and he recalled her story.

He traced each scar he found with his finger, and

lost count soon enough. Her body was a map of her life. He felt awed by her. He also felt honored that she trusted him enough to be there yesterday while she lived through the horror of having to do what she did.

He finished washing the blood off her body and got her all cleaned up. He quickly washed himself off, the water turning a color he'd rather not see and he drained the tub and pulled the shower head down to wash her hair and his own.

He filled the tub back up with clean water and cradled her in his arms as he turned the jets on and hoped she woke up soon. He soaked them both for about an hour and then called Ronnie back in to help get her out of the tub. Between them they got her dressed in a night gown she had brought and put her back in the freshly cleaned room.

Ronnie laid with her as Smitty ate some food, trying to restore energy, and then he climbed in on the other side and immediately fell asleep.

Chapter Two

edan's phone chirped as he waited in one of the other conference rooms for the council to arrive. It was a picture from Ronnie, a pile of bloody clothes. He cringed when he saw they were Smitty's and Airiella's. Ronnie's caption said, "We need answers."

That didn't look good. "Trying," he wrote back.

Father Roarke walked in alone and sat across from him. He looked haggard and a lot older than he had yesterday. "I can't tell you what happened," he started.

Aedan jumped in, "How can we prepare, then? How can we help her?"

"It's up to her if she wants to tell you or not. Besides the fact that I'm not in her, I can't tell you what was going on inside." Father Roarke sighed. "I will tell you that this was so much worse than the first time she came to me, after that man in the park." His eyes were haunted in a way that sent a shiver through Aedan.

"How can we prepare? On location, what if something like this happens?" Aedan pushed despite the growing fear in him.

"I've been thinking about exactly that, but I can't say I came up with any good answers. In all my years of doing this, working with demons and evil spirits, I have never encountered something like this before. Frankly, it terrifies my cold Irish heart."

Aedan closed his eyes. "I don't want to lose Jax," he whispered. "I know these actions aren't him. I just want him back."

Father Roarke reached across the table to clasp Aedan's hand. "As much as it pains me to say this, she *is* the way you get him back. I wouldn't wish what that lass goes through on anyone, she does it anyway knowing what it costs her."

"What does it cost her?" Aedan asked.

"Life. She clinically dies each time. She suffers greatly with the pain it causes. When she told me what happens to her, I understood her words and took her at face value. What she *doesn't* tell you is what catches you off guard. Nothing could have prepared me for what I saw. What I felt. This young lass *is* some sort of angel. I do not say this lightly." The serious look on the priest's face was absolute.

"But you won't tell me any details of what happens," Aedan said, his voice flat.

"The two times I was a part of it, it was different, so I don't know what will happen next. She dies, she is reborn, she suffers unimaginable pain. Yet her capacity to come out of it with her humor intact and her ability to still love is something to behold." Father Roarke rubbed his eyes, his motions slow.

"Father, I don't know what to think right now. Ronnie said Smitty is pretty much a shell of a man after that, I don't know how to help him. Ronnie sent me a picture of bloody clothes. Jax has this thing living inside him that kills her from what you say, and I'm supposed to be okay with all of this and just go along with it?" Aedan's voice started to raise.

"No son, I don't expect you to be okay with any of this. I do plan on sending you with large amounts of holy water, since I do know that it kills off this manifestation. But my suggestion is to utilize the rest of the council, and with the combined beliefs of others, maybe an answer will emerge. It will take all of our knowledge, but only she can kill it." Father Roarke's head sunk down to the table.

"Will Jax survive?" Aedan hesitated, but asked it anyway. Fear crept up his spine.

"I don't know. If Airiella has any say in it, he will. She's the physical embodiment of love. Of life. I do, however, believe that when she needs to release this energy again, she will need as many of you with her as possible. It was only when Art was touching her that her body settled down. The others may know more of that than I do. They are waiting in the hall, I asked for a few minutes alone with you."

"Will holy water help Jax?" Aedan wanted something to hold on to for hope.

"I don't know the answer to that either. I sent word that I'd like to see him and I will try a blessing on him, but I have no idea how that thing will react. You need to be prepared for violence," Father Roarke said and stood.

"Wait. I think this thing, Jax calls it the darkness, I think it's spreading from him. Jax encountered the park guy outside the airport, and he was with Dr. Stone before yesterday's explosion of whatever that was." Aedan wanted to believe it wasn't true, but it was pretty damning evidence.

"You could very well be right, and Tama said the same thing to me. Give me a moment and I'll go get them." Father Roarke turned and left the room, his shoulders slumping forward.

Aedan nodded weakly. He knew he was in way over his head, but Jax was his brother, one of his best friends. He had to dive into this to help him however he could. And Mags, she had been beside herself with worry about Airiella. Aedan was desperate, and he knew it.

Taklishim and Tama walked in, followed by Onida who was talking quietly with Kalisha. Then Degataga came last with Father Roarke.

"No Aminda, Asher or Dr. Fields?" Aedan asked, surprised.

"They didn't feel that they had anything they could add," Father Roarke said apologetically.

Aedan shrugged, nothing he could do about it anyway. "So, who here can tell me what the hell is going on?"

Onida smiled at him. "Tam, Tak and I were with her yesterday with Father Roarke." Aedan nodded; he knew that much. "Us three, we watched from the spirit side of things while in that chapel. But in here, the room upstairs, I think only Tak was looking."

Aedan glanced over at Taklishim, who nodded briefly. "Do you know what this is?"

"No, I'm sorry," Onida said. "I've never seen anything like it before. It wants to consume anything in its path and it tries. It thinks, and it adapts. The spirits won't go near it, but they voice their fear for Airiella."

"The spirits flock to Airiella," Tama said, jumping in. "When she doesn't have that energy in her, that is. She's a beacon for them, but she can't see them. What is interesting though, is she does see, and feel this energy."

"She felt a void when I was with her," Degataga added, joining the conversation. "I noticed it too, but I assumed it was a spot where something died. Sometimes nature reflects blank spaces if something loses its life in certain spots. To me it felt blank, but to her, she felt a void. It was one of the first things she noticed."

"She felt it when it came for us while we were in our animal forms," Onida said. Tama nodded. "I felt a sinister presence and took to flight to see more as a whole. Tama knocked Airiella over right as this thing shot a gun."

Startled, Aedan said, "Someone shot at her?"

Tama spoke up, "I don't think it was a someone. It was a something, not a person. And yes, it shot at her twice, the second time, it hit me."

Taklishim flinched at those words, but leaned forward. "I heard their calls and flew in. It was not human, not on either side. On the spirit side it does show as a black hole, or void, but it's not blank. It consumes. It's not a demon, nor is it a ghost. Maybe it's a hybrid of the two, I don't know what it is. It was reacting to Airiella's movements, tracking her and adjusting."

"That girl is incredible in her abilities," Degataga said. "Lightning struck while I was with her, and I knew it had to be her, but I couldn't be sure because I didn't feel it."

Tama nodded. "It was her. In my animal sight, which is different than either spirit or here, she had these colors wash over her when she saw I was shot. The emotion that flew out of her carried weight and power, and her soul became this pure white. She called lightning to her like it was nothing. She wielded it, and struck the thing, turning it to ash. The gun actually melted."

Onida piped in, "I watched from above and saw the same thing."

"Impossible," Aedan whispered.

"Her very being is impossible," Taklishim added, "but here she is. I know Father Roarke calls her an angel, in Zuni she is a Raven. Essentially the same thing for different beliefs. She is very rare, one of her nature hasn't walked the earth in centuries."

"It is true," Degataga said. "Though she is not immortal as Father Roarke thinks. She can easily die."

"She comes back though," Father Roarke argued weakly.

"She does, but as Degataga said, I don't think it's actually death that you see happening," Taklishim said, thoughtful. "I think she is stepping out of her body into the spirit plane. I saw her there yesterday. Her ghost friend was yelling at her."

"She stops breathing though." Father Roarke looked confused.

"Yes, and she glowed and lifted off the ground,"

Onida added. "I think that is the divine light healing her. It may be that the healing is too painful and she needs to leave her body. I don't understand that part yet."

"What you guys are describing isn't scientifically possible," Aedan said, his voice panicky at the images their words were painting. It stretched his beliefs too far.

"Think with your heart and your spirit," Degataga told him. "Have you spent any time with her yet?"

"No, not really," Aedan admitted.

"You will feel differently after you do," Degataga said plainly.

Kalisha finally spoke up and asked, "Did she use the stones?"

Father Roarke shook his head no. "I don't think she had time, she passed out in the conference room and in the chapel. I think she was only aware once but she was so filled with pain, I don't think she was able to think clearly."

Kalisha sat forward and looked at Aedan. "I am going to make protective amulets for each of your team, I think you will need them."

"Will wearing one hurt Jax?" Aedan asked, skeptical.

"No, it should help him keep control better," she responded. "But I may add a bit more to his to see if it will help Airiella."

"I am also going to make a tea blend for you and the rest of the team to drink every day to help fortify your spirit in repelling the bad energies," Degataga added. "Airiella has a raven I sculpted for her, that will help her."

Tama and Onida looked at each other, then Onida said, "Tama and I are the best help to you in finding out what it is. We plan on digging more into the spirit plane and sending out messages. We will keep in contact."

Taklishim looked Aedan straight in the eyes. "I have several mixes ready for Airiella for healing, for pain and for sleep. My skills are best used on her, not the team. Don't misunderstand me with that. My helping her, will help your team. She battles this on our plane here, and in the spirit plane."

"None of your skills will help the team?" Aedan asked.

"Not any more than what the others are doing for you. Kalisha's amulets will be the best bet for you all. Airiella needs to heal her soul before she can fight more effectively. Help her do that, and you will be giving your team a huge fighting chance."

"What do you mean?" Aedan asked for clarification.

"Hers is her story for her to tell you, but like everyone else, she has wounds on her soul that have not healed. They act as a block to her abilities. When that block is removed, nothing can stop her. Even death does not stand in the way of that kind of love." If Aedan wasn't mistaken, Taklishim sounded awed.

"This is challenging for me on so many levels," Aedan muttered.

"You work on a show that hunts ghosts and demons, and this is a stretch for you?" Father Roarke asked, amazed.

Flustered, Aedan didn't have a response. Father Roarke wasn't wrong. He'd seen Airiella do something he had no hope of explaining so he wasn't sure why he was having a hard time with this. He'd seen it with his own eyes.

Taklishim spoke up again. "We do think this energy is invasive. I think it looks for weaknesses in people that it can penetrate and splits itself, attaching to that person and growing. We know that holy water works, but it's painful for her. I believe that salt water will help as well. By that, I mean an actual body of water, a sea or ocean, possibly even a large salt water lake. It's untested of course, but it's an avenue worth exploring."

"I agree," Tama said. "We know she has used nature before to release what she calls the bad energy she gathers from people and takes on. If she had a spot with that kind of energy that was near a body of salt water, it might be easier than drinking holy water."

"Wait, she drank the holy water?!" Aedan practically shouted, his mind snapping hard.

"Well this last time it was thrown on her, and then she drank some," Onida added.

Aedan stared at Father Roarke, but he wouldn't look at Aedan. "Isn't that just for demons?"

"No, I think it's reacting to the blessing that is bestowed up on the water, combined with the blessing of her life and love that flows in her blood. She herself is a blessing, add holy water to divine light and it's hard to beat that," Degataga said.

"Salt water is a purifying element," Onida jumped in.

"Yes, it cleanses bad spirits releasing clean energy back into the earth," Kalisha added.

"If all this is true, why can't we just try this stuff on Jax to see if it can help him?" Aedan was genuinely curious.

"He doesn't have the blessing in his blood to help him fight. Honestly Aedan, I think it would kill him. After what I saw with Airiella, I don't think any human could survive that," Taklishim said gently.

"Is that why he slept the rest of the day yesterday until this morning?" Aedan asked, a puzzle piece falling into place.

"Most likely. From what I witnessed in the conference room, it's painful to whoever is having the energy pulled from them. Dr. Stone isn't awake yet either and the doctors don't know why," Onida said.

"So even though Airiella can help him, it's going to hurt them both," Aedan stated. He got nods all around. "Great. That's fantastic. We hire someone to help, and she gets the benefit of being purposely hurt."

"She was made for this, she does it of her own free will," Degataga told him. "Don't disrespect that."

"There's one more piece to this you will need," Taklishim said cautiously looking at Tama. She nodded. "For some people, in their beliefs or way of life, there is something called a bond."

Aedan nodded; he'd heard of bonds before. This was something they'd come across on other investigations, a lot having to do with sacred native American tribes and beliefs.

"It is true of her," Taklishim went on. "She has bonds in place with several of you, is what she told me. She can feel them when she touches the person." A weird feeling settled in the pit of Aedan's stomach.

"Go on," he told Taklishim.

"The bonds will help her, as they provide her with something needed. In my case with Tama, our bond allows me to feel when she needs me, or if she is in danger. She feels when I need something from her. She can call on some of my abilities when connected with me skin to skin."

"For the bonds to work we need to be touching her?" Aedan asked for clarification.

"No," Tama said. "They work without that, but at a much slower rate and not as effective. What Tak is trying to say gently, but not well, is that to make these bonds work for your team, you'll need to have sex. It's the seed, so to speak, that cements the bond in place and provides an unbreakable connection."

Aedan blushed. "We all need to have sex with her?" he asked flatly, recalling Mags's reaction to Airiella.

Onida laughed. "For best results, shake well."

"Who are these bonds with?" Aedan tentatively asked.

"All of you," Taklishim answered bluntly. "It's not something to be ashamed of. I can assure you that she felt the same way. She has made one connection already and I can tell you that it made a huge difference in how yesterday went."

"Smitty," Aedan breathed out.

Taklishim nodded, but Tama spoke. "With Airiella being what she is, it's remarkable really that she has multiple connections. If she is here for the reasons we believe, you all play a part. We aren't telling you to sleep with her," Tama said gently. "We are just telling you the knowledge you need to understand a larger picture."

"I'm married," Aedan said. Mags' words playing through his mind that she thought Airiella was the one she wanted to experiment with. His face heated at the memory.

"From what she said when she was with me, your wife is one of the connections," Taklishim added.

"Um, this is a lot to take in," Aedan mumbled, his face burning red.

"Imagine how she feels," Onida fired back in defense of Airiella.

Ashamed, Aedan nodded. "I get it. I really do. I just want my brother back," he added.

"Help her, you help him," Father Roarke said, a voice of reason in a room full of people with paranormal powers and abilities Aedan had no hope of understanding.

"Anything else?" Aedan said guardedly.

"One thing occurred to me after I went back to the hotel last night," Onida brought up. "The doctor part of my brain was thinking, and when a person is host to a disease, a carrier is what I call them; anyway, when a carrier is patient zero, the infection he carries is potent, though he himself is somewhat immune. I was thinking maybe that is why you say it is worse than the last time." She looked at Father Roarke. "She pulled some of that from the carrier. Maybe what is in him is the patient zero, and each person he infects it just mutates? Just a theory, but it keeps popping up in my head."

Taklishim shifted. "You might be on to something. Even diseases are sentient to a degree, they adapt to survive. Worth thinking about."

"Should I keep Jax away from people?" Aedan was worried.

"As much as possible until we can learn more," Onida suggested.

"I'll have the amulets to you at the hotel tonight," Kalisha added, a sense of urgency to her tone. "Not sure if the immunity to this extends to you all because of the connection Airiella feels to you, but I'd rather be safe. With the amulet on, he should be okay to be around others."

Aedan nodded. "Well, thanks, I think. I have more information now, but I also have a shit ton more questions too." He stood. "I appreciate the time you gave me."

"We will be in touch Aedan," Father Roarke said. Aedan nodded once more and left, his brain a train wreck, but stuck on the thought that he had to tell Mags that they should sleep with Airiella for safety reasons. He had to laugh at that. It was the only thing there was to laugh about.

Chapter Three

I woke up and groaned, my body feeling like I had been crushed in a vice. I was also stifling hot. I peeked out one of my eye lids and saw Smitty staring right back at me, worry written all over his face. His blue eyes tired and bruised looking. Oh no. I remembered everything in a flash.

I tried to sit up but felt pinned, and then I became aware of another body behind me. Had to be Ronnie. Smitty shook his head at me and pushed me back gently.

"Stay put, baby girl," he said softly but it sounded like a shout in my ears.

I winced. I tried to talk but my throat was raw and dry. Like he read my mind, Ronnie's hand came from behind me holding a cup with a straw in it in front of my face. I took a drink slowly savoring the feel of the cool liquid making its way down my irritated throat. I sucked down about half the cup before he pulled it away and Smitty held another in front of me.

"Soda, has sugar and calories to give you a little fuel," he told me. I could have cried I felt so grateful. "Take it easy, it's been almost two days."

My eyes bugged out. "What?!" I whispered.

"Baby girl," Smitty started but his voice cracked and to my horror his eyes teared up, "that was pretty traumatic."

I agreed with him, that little episode had not been fun in the slightest. I felt Ronnie lightly rubbing my back, my skin still feeling highly sensitive, I pulled away a bit. "Sorry, angel."

"You know that connection we share now? I felt it. I felt the pain, I felt you die," he told her as tears fell from his eyes. "I know it was barely even a shadow of what you felt, but holy shit, Airiella," his voice trailed off.

Ronnie stilled his movements behind me. "I know I wasn't there, angel, I wish I had been. Well, a part of me does, the other part thinks I wouldn't be able to handle it. But, you see this man in front of you? He doesn't cry. Ever. Maybe it's not a good idea for you to be here, doing this," he said carefully.

"No," I rasped out. "I'm where I'm supposed to be. I know that. I'm just sorry you had to get sucked up into this. I'd change it if I could, take it back. You don't need to feel that shit."

Smitty exploded up from the bed and I shifted, Ronnie pulling me back up against him and sitting me up. "Smitty..." Ronnie said, his voice a warning.

"No!" Smitty shouted. "No! Ronnie, I'm sorry but you weren't there. You need to leave now."

"Not when you are like this. Dude, chill out a minute," Ronnie tried to reason with Smitty.

"Ronnie. Go. Now."

"Smitty, you're unhinged if you think I'm leaving when you are acting like this," Ronnie said, his teeth gritting.

"This is a conversation between me, and baby girl, right here. You know damn well I won't hurt her." Smitty's eyes flashed with a fire that felt cold.

"Look in the mirror at yourself and tell me you wouldn't react the same way," Ronnie argued, his arm tight around me.

Smitty looked at me, pointing to the connection between us. "This is a two-way street, baby girl." He pointed at his chest. "I can now feel you like you feel everyone else." He ran his fingers along the tether, making me gasp. "I can read you like a book, just like you can read everyone else. Feel me, tell him I am not going to hurt you."

Smitty could use my empath ability now? He nodded at me like he understood my thoughts. His eyes were wild, the blue sparking vividly, and he looked like a crazy person but I knew he wouldn't hurt me. I nodded at him, he'd been with me when I was at my most vulnerable and he took care of me. I reached up and put my hand over Ronnie's arm where he was holding me.

"It's okay, Ronnie. He's not going to hurt me." My whispered words hurt my throat.

"Don't angel, don't let him control you like this. You may have a connection now," he said it with jealousy, "but he's not acting right."

"Ronnie. Don't. You weren't there!" Smitty shouted, losing his grip on sanity. "You don't know! You don't get it. I need to talk to her. Alone. I can say over and over again that you don't get it, but it won't do any good. I hope to whatever God is out there listening that you never have to see what I did, but I know without a doubt that you will. And there is nothing I can say that will prepare you for it. Nothing! Not a damn thing!"

I pulled away from Ronnie, the anguish coming off Smitty propelling me to my feet. "Ronnie, it's okay, I promise."

Smitty threw his hands up in the air, "Look, I get that you are worried. When—if," he amended, "the time comes for you and her to connect, I'm not going to stand in your way when you need a moment with her because something flipped you the fuck out! Give me this please!" He shouted, his eyes shining with tears.

I looked back at Ronnie who was close to coming unglued as well. "I will tell you everything later. You'll know what happened. I'm not hiding anything. But he needs this right now, and I probably need to hear what he has to say, even if I don't like it."

Ronnie nodded at me, gave a warning look to Smitty and left. Smitty cleared the space between us in one step and hauled me into his body, crushing me to him. Still not over the pain yet, I groaned trying to stifle the sound but he heard me anyway and released me in the next second.

"Baby girl, I'm so sorry. Fuck. I'm so damn sorry." He broke down falling to his knees before me. "You don't ever get to tell me what I do, or don't need to feel. Never. If you hurt, I hurt. I learned that the hard way."

"Smitty," I whispered, moving towards him, but he held his hands up to stop me.

"I don't understand any of this," he choked out. "I don't know how I have your powers to feel things now, how I can see Winnie, how to explain what happened in that chapel, or how you did any of what you did. I don't get any of it," he spoke fast.

"That's why I'm sorry," I touched his arm, sitting in front of him on the floor.

"I don't want you to be sorry. I want to know how to not have that happen again, and I know it will. I fucking know it, because Jax still has this shit inside him!" He sucked in air through his teeth. "I fucking watched you die, felt the connection with you wither to almost nothing, saw Winnie screaming at you. I felt a shadow of the pain that you did, and it damn near broke me! How are you here?" The wild look was back in his eyes.

"I don't know," I said honestly, absorbing his distress.

"I want to wrap you up and stick you somewhere safe so that never happens again," he admitted, his voice cracking again.

"Sadly, it would still happen," I told him, lifting his face so he looked at me. "It's what I'm supposed to do."

"Father Roarke wouldn't let me go to you," he said brokenly. "I had to stay back and watch while it looked like your body was shattering. Your screams tore me open and I felt like I was dying. Taklishim had to hold me back. You were covered in blood and the air in the room was fucking vibrating. But you know when it was the worst?" He looked at me, his eyes the color of aqua and shimmering with tears, shattered, as he relived it. "When you went silent. The screaming stopped, and you were gone. You don't know what it felt like to lose you."

I knew from personal experience how it felt, but there was nothing I could say that would take this from him. I could pull his emotions, but the memory would still be there. It would haunt him as I knew it did me. I just held his hand. "I do know what it's like to lose though," I said, my voice soft. I cupped his cheek in my hand, using my thumb to wipe his tears.

"He wouldn't let me near you, said it wasn't finished. The energy was still there in the room and I knew he was right because I could feel it. I have never seen those three Indians scared before, and they were just as terrified as I was. Something in me broke watching all of that. It broke in a way I didn't know was possible. And when I saw you glowing and lifting off the ground, something in me knitted together."

I looked in his eyes, letting him in. There was nothing I could hide from him now. I was tired of hiding anyway. I put his hand on my chest, over my heart and held it there. The connection between us flaring to life.

"There was little doubt in my mind that I was in the presence of some sort of higher power. We all saw it, we all felt it, we all cried. We all fucking broke. It wasn't just me. The sound of your bones snapping back into place after hearing the sound of them breaking made me weak. I knew somewhere inside me; I wasn't good enough to be even anywhere near you. I wasn't worthy of you, of your love, of being in the same room as you."

"That's not true Smitty," I started, but he cut me off.

"It is true, baby girl. It's true of all of us. You've done this what, three times now?" I nodded slowly. "You died three times for other people. To save other people. None of us can say that. I don't think any of us would even do it! You do it voluntarily, knowing the pain it causes you. You knew what would happen when you told me you needed my help. You knew then and you did it anyway." His voice was so raw and emotional that I just wanted to curl around him and hold him.

"When you finally stopped glowing and were back on the ground, there was nothing Father Roarke could do to keep me away from you. I haven't left your side since. I took a bath with you, I hope that's okay." Smitty was just rambling now. "I needed to get that blood off you. I couldn't keep seeing it knowing how it got there. I can't sleep for long, it's on replay in my head, and the chorus of 'you aren't good enough to be her friend' plays in my head."

I didn't care what he thought. I climbed in his lap and wrapped myself around him. Both of us crying big, fat and ugly tears. "Watching someone go through something horrible doesn't make you unworthy. I know how powerless it makes you feel though. Smitty, do you know why I chose you to be my first connection?"

I felt him shake his head no. He tightened his arms around me. "Don't feed me a line of bullshit to make me feel better, baby girl," he whispered in my ear.

"Smitty, use those abilities of mine, right now. Just picture yourself opening a box and all your senses are in it, and fly free," I said gently. I could feel the exact moment he did it too. "Now listen to my voice and you will know it's not bullshit. Feel the words." I spoke from my heart into his ear. "I chose you because of how calm, relaxed and logical you are. You are the voice of reason in my head. You ground me when I feel out of control. All this I noticed from you in a couple of days. Trust me, I've never been wrong in my instincts about people. I didn't choose you because you were available. If you weren't there and it was one of the others, I wouldn't have taken it where I did with you. I chose you. I believe in you; in the strength you bring into my heart and soul. I trust you. I respect you."

He crushed me into him again and cried hard. "You said our connection wasn't as strong as the one you had with Ronnie."

"It's a different connection," I amended. I fed love into the connection I had with him and he relaxed under me. "Ronnie wouldn't have gotten me through that night. We both know that. His connection to me is more emotional. That doesn't mean I don't have strong emotions for you, it just means they are on different wavelengths. You were what I needed."

"Fuck, you destroy me, baby girl." He shook under me.

"I never want to destroy you. I don't like that you had to see what you did, and I wish that no one else would have to see it. I know you are right, in that they will. It's inevitable." I leaned back from him so he could look in my eyes. "I need you to understand this, even though it makes no sense to either of us, I love you. I feel it deep inside. If I have to die again to save any one of you, and I'm pretty sure I will, I will do it with zero hesitation as many times as needed."

He buried his face in my neck. "This is exactly why none of us are good enough for you."

"There's a purpose for everything," I told him quietly. "We don't know what it is, but there is a purpose for it. Maybe yours was to see something unbelievable to broaden your knowledge. Maybe it was just to be there to hold me afterwards. Maybe it's something neither of us can see right now. I don't know. It sucks big fat hairy monkey balls, don't get me wrong, I just know it's something I have to do."

"You have no idea how incredible you are," he said reverently.

I didn't know what to say to that since it's obvious to everyone I don't see myself that way. "It's just the way it is," I said vaguely.

Smitty scooted out from under me and pulled my legs straight out in front of me, bruises all over. I tried to cover them up but he stopped me and gave me a sad smile. "Stop hiding yourself. I saw every single bit of you when I bathed you. I touched every scar on your body. Every bruise."

Shame lit my face and I couldn't look at him. He was in the territory Degataga told me I needed to heal, and I wasn't sure I was ready for that. "Don't go there, Smitty."

"It's something I have to do, baby girl," he pushed my words back at me. "Why are you ashamed?"

"Look at me!" I cried.

"I am," he said gently. He traced the scars on my knee. "I may not know how these got here, but I do know your story. You told me, remember?"

He ran his fingers in a feather light caress over the bruises on my legs and down to one of the tattoos on my feet. He traced the pattern. "While I know what this symbol means, you didn't specifically tell me why you got this, and what it means to you, but I still know. Every mark on your body is a road map, it tells me where you've been, it shows me how beautiful the different landscapes can be. Maps are meant to be read. The curves and valleys followed and explored."

I sucked in my breath and stared at him. "I..." I wasn't even sure what I had been planning to say, but he silenced me.

"I even see the scars you hide inside. I can see them clearly now," he touched the connection between us. "Not one of those scars disgusted me. I may hold grudges against the people that caused them, but to me, they make you more beautiful than you can know. Beauty is flawed, by nature. Anyone can look at a burned forest and see the devastation, destruction and loss of life. But it takes someone like you to see the new life beginning under it, to see that beauty exists despite the travesty that others cause. It takes you, to show that love is determined to win and push through the ashes of what once was."

A crack inside me filled with his words as every one of them rang true in my ears, in the look on his face, in the nature of his touch. He wholly believed what he was saying.

"It takes someone like you to pick up that discarded item someone tossed aside and breathe new life into it, give it love and watch it become something else coveted by others. It takes you, only you, to make the broken pieces inside me mend, pieces that no one else even knows exist. No one can see them but you, and you glued them together in a way that has changed me. I love Jillian with all my heart, but even she didn't fix what's in here." He tapped his chest.

"I..." I tried to drop my eyes, but he wouldn't let me.

"No, you keep your eyes on me. It took you screaming in excruciating pain that I will never come close to understanding, your body breaking before my eyes, and then healing again for me to be put back together. I told you something in me mended, and while I can't name it, it's fixed. That is because of you and the unspeakable horrors you put yourself through for the love you have for others that don't even deserve your time. You need to see you the way I see you."

"Smitty, that's not me," I said weakly.

"It is you. Every person on that council knows it and saw it. What will it take to make you believe me?" he demanded gently.

"I'm just me," I argued.

"Well, you are damn incredible, stronger than any person I have ever known, absolutely fearless and brave, beautiful in ways that only the lucky will get to experience, and such a rare gift that I can't even find words to describe it. There's a fire in you that burns true and once someone knows you, they can see that fire, the beautiful flames that reach out and touch your soul, marked forever. Plus, you've got a fantastic rack."

"I'm not fearless," I said, latching on to the argument I thought I could win. "I'm terrified all the time!"

"Fearless doesn't mean you have no fear," he started, and I interrupted him this time.

"That is the very definition of the word!" I cried.

"Okay yes, that is the literal definition, but fearless is someone that keeps going despite the fear."

"That's brave," I said quietly hoping he wouldn't pick up on it. But he did.

"Fearless and brave are synonyms of each other," he chucked me under the chin. "Stop arguing with me."

I didn't say anything, I just crawled back over to him and curled up between his legs. He had me feeling vulnerable again. He hugged me to him. "What now?" I was afraid to ask, but I was trying to fill the silence. "And really? You had to throw in fantastic rack?"

He chuckled knowing what I was doing. He squeezed a boob and said, "Yes, I did. Now, you go home with Aedan and Mags and get ready to jump in the crazy shit hole of filming a TV show, I guess. I don't know Airiella, I don't think it's going to be an easy ride, and I'm not ashamed to admit that I am petrified now of what could possibly happen." He took a shaky breath in, "I can't un-see what happened, but I am so damn thankful you are still here and trusted me enough to be with you."

"Me too, on both counts," I admitted.

"I'm sorry I fucking lost my shit." He kissed me on the top of my head.

"Don't be, you needed to vent."

"Simply amazing," he said his breath warming my ear. "Want to make a wager that Ronnie is laying on the floor outside your door?"

"He is not! I would have felt him," I said in his defense, but wondering at the same time if he was right.

Smitty threw his head back and laughed. The sound was music to my ears and I smiled and snuggled into him again. "I can't wait for you to meet Jillian," he said. "I told her about you while you were still out."

I tensed up a bit. "Stop, it's okay, I told you. We have an open relationship," he admonished me. He stood and lifted me to my feet. "Let's order some food, I'm hungry."

"Did I tell you Mags propositioned me?" I said,

going for shock value as a payback.

He turned and looked at me as I grinned. "You're kidding me, right?"

"Nope," I laughed.

"Shit." He adjusted himself. "That will give me a whole different type of dream." Perfect, I thought.

"This here," I pointed between us again, "this banter, the sarcasm, the jokes, this is me. This is who I am. Anyone is worthy of that. I'm not special. I'm just me."

"You are special, even without all the other stuff, you are special. That is what I need you to see. I need you to work on that with me. Your confidence in yourself. Please."

"Fine. I'm a fucking unicorn in a world of plain horses." I snapped, still reeling from all that he just threw at me.

Smitty howled again. "You may just have given yourself a new nickname."

I threw a pillow at him. "Where's my damn food? Jeez, make a girl cry and get her all messy and worked up then starve her and shit. Feed me!" I demanded, stomping my feet in a mock tantrum.

"And this is why I love you, baby girl unicorn."

"Definitely not going to be my new nickname," I told him. "I'll tell Ronnie you were mean and made me cry."

He chuckled at that, "He doesn't scare me."

"Smitty, come here please," I called him over to me. When he sat next to me on the bed, I straddled him and gave him a piece of my heart and soul in a kiss that left him breathless and wanting more. I was happy to oblige, food forgotten for a little bit.

Aedan looked at his wife, "I'm scared Mags. The council painted a grim picture with Jax as the star villain."

She sat down next to him on the end of the bed. "I'd say nothing is set in stone. It's a pretty fantastical path we've been set on for sure." She stroked his face. "I'm choosing to look at it as an adventure. Life is constantly throwing plot twists at us. But if I'm honest, I'm scared too."

"You aren't acting scared," Aedan said. "You are acting like a horny teenager."

Mags laughed. "Maybe, but you like it."

Aedan smiled, "Okay, I do. I gotta say though, after all that stuff the council told me, I'm feeling a bit hesitant."

"I get it. I've been around Airy, and I believe she is everything they think she is. Just a feeling I get inside when I'm around her. Something in me settles and I feel like I'm in the presence of something greater."

"Should I be jealous?" Aedan was serious.

"No, I belong with you, you giant ass. Why would you even think that would change?"

"They said you were one of her connections," he worried.

"So are you, but you don't see me freaking out about it," Mags fired back at him.

"Why aren't you?" he asked, seriously.

"I'm just not. It feels right. Something in me tells me that it will bring you and I closer together. I love the idea of that."

"What about Jax?" Aedan threw in for good measure.

"What about him?" Mags asked confused. "I don't want to have sex with your brother."

"What if he doesn't make it through this?" Aedan clarified in an exasperated tone.

"Stop that thought in its tracks. He will. I do think he will need to fight for himself instead of relying on the rest of you to pick him up and clean up after him. That will be a real challenge for him. Airiella has this strength and fire in her soul that demands to be noticed. Jax is going to have to bend to it." Mags grinned wickedly.

"Smitty, Ronnie and you are all in love with this chic. It worries me."

"It should comfort you!" Mags replied.

"Why the hell would it comfort me?" Aedan was confused and worried, both.

"If all three of us feel the same way about her, then it should tell you that there is truth to what we say and feel," Mags responded. "When have you ever seen Smitty tumble like that? Even with Jillian it was gradual." Mags paused, "Hell, even Ronnie has never acted that way towards a female. He's the wham, bam, thank you ma'am type."

"I think that concerns me too. How is Ronnie, or even Jax for that matter, going to feel about sleeping with someone the rest of us have slept with?"

"Didn't you say that the council said it doesn't need to go there?"

"Yeah, I guess. But they were quick to point out that it wouldn't be as effective if sex didn't happen. Well, really, they implied that it was the coming that sealed the deal."

"I'm lost," Mags said.

"They said seed." Aedan was embarrassed.

"I don't have seed," Mags pointed out.

"I think you have to come though, or make her come. I didn't ask. In my case, it would be me coming." Aedan blushed madly again.

Mags laughed. "We have talked about this so much that it truly shocks me that you are embarrassed about this!"

"I know," he said glumly. "I guess there is still a part of me that feel like it's a betrayal to you to have penetration."

"Ah," Mags said, understanding. "There are others ways you can come."

Aedan shifted again, his body betraying him. Mags of course noticed right away. "I know. Maybe it will get easier after I have spent some time with her."

Mags pointed at his crotch, "That won't get easier. There's just something about her."

"Well at least we know she is conscious now. I'll have the producers get us a flight out and arrange a car rental. Might as well get going on this." Aedan tried to guide his wife into easier territory.

"Nice change of subject Aedan." Mags laughed. "You'll see. Just keep an open mind."

"I'm trying, but after witnessing what happened in the conference room, my mind is just chaos."

Mags leaned over and kissed him deep, winding her arms around his neck. "Just go with it, love."

Jax wondered how was he supposed to talk to Father Roarke if he wasn't supposed to be around people? He shuddered as he remembered throwing the chair at the glass. His reaction to Airiella was so visceral, he couldn't tell if it was love or hate. Or both.

He knew the darkness in him hated her. That was obvious to him. He struggled for control of his own body against it every time he was near her. Shame washed through him as he thought about it, because it wasn't his nature to be that way. He wasn't violent, he wasn't rage filled. Selfish, yes for sure. Arrogant, yes.

He paced around his room, feeling caged and on edge. He even went on the balcony for a bit to get some fresh air, but he panicked when his thoughts turned to jumping off the balcony. He admitted to himself that he was scared, and he even admitted that he had hope that this new girl could help him. He just didn't know if he could live with the guilt of what it cost her to do so.

There was a knock on his door and it caught Jax off guard for a few seconds. He didn't know if he should open it. He looked through the little peephole and saw Father Roarke standing there. Surely, he could let the priest in? As he opened the door, that darkness in him stirred to life and Jax froze.

"It's okay son, let me in," Father Roarke said seeing the look on Jax's face. When Jax didn't move Father Roarke pushed him out of the way and walked in on his own. "The energy in you doesn't like me, does it?"

Jax shook his head no, afraid to speak. Afraid that

nasty words would come flying out of his mouth cementing his spot in Hell. The old Irish priest had never been anything but kind to Jax and he didn't want to hurt the old man.

"I have a couple of things I want to talk to you about, sit down. You can sit across the room if it makes you feel better," Father Roarke told him with a smile. Jax walked across the room and leaned in the farthest corner possible from him.

"Kalisha will be here shortly with an amulet she has made for you to wear. It will have a protection spell on it, a blessing from whatever god she is asking for help from and whatever else she feels will help keep you and others around you safe."

Jax nodded, that made sense. "What about the others?"

"She is making them amulets too. But that is not why I am here." Father Roarke looked at Jax for signs of the energy.

"Then what is it Father?" Jax absently rubbed the Celtic cross tattoo he had on his ring finger that he got after Winnie died.

"I want to bless you with holy water," Father Roarke started.

"Why would I have a problem with that?" Jax asked confused.

"The energy in you doesn't like holy water," he explained to Jax.

Understanding lit Jax's eyes. "You think I will react badly? Is it a demon in me? She pulled some of it from me, didn't she?"

"It's not a demon. At least not one I can identify, nor is it a spirit. It's been suggested it might be a hybrid of the two, or something that you manifested on your own. It acts in ways that we don't understand, and it's intelligent. It adapts itself the more we kill it. It's frightening in that way, and in what it's doing to you." Father Roarke looked wiped out.

"If I am understanding you right, it acts like a cold virus?" Jax was flummoxed.

"Essentially, yes. I *do* think you will react badly. I'd rather do this in the chapel, but we also believe that this energy is intelligent enough to break pieces of itself off and jump into others it senses weakness in. Airiella did pull some from you, though from my understanding it wasn't very much considering what she said she felt in you. I do know that it is quite painful for her."

"I remember the pain when she pulled it, but I don't remember anything after that since I blacked out. Can she stop this?" Jax dared to hope.

"I believe with all my heart and soul that she can. It will take work on your part though. Jax, this has to start with you." The priest's words confused Jax.

"Didn't you just say that you believe she can fix this?" He was missing some information, he was sure.

"She can't do it alone. If this is something that you manifested in yourself, you have to change the way you act, behave, and think. It's feeding off you. Even if it isn't something you brought into creation, it's still feeding off you," Father Roarke calmly explained.

Jax sunk to the floor resting his head on his knees. "Father, I don't think I'm strong enough."

"Nonsense Jax. Utter nonsense. How many shows have I seen where you get aggressive with demons and spirits? Do the same thing with this one," his Irish voice gentled.

"What if the darkness inside me is the reason I am aggressive with the other things I encounter?" Jax asked weakly.

Father Roarke caught his breath. "I don't know, son. That thought never occurred to me."

"I wasn't aggressive when I was younger," Jax admitted. "Foolish, arrogant, selfish, but never aggressive."

"If that's the case, then you just work on it. You have to be open and honest with the rest of your team. I know you don't want them hurt, the only way to help ensure that is to tell them." Father Roarke's guidance never failed to help Jax, until now.

"I'm so scared, Father. I don't recognize myself anymore." Jax cowered in the corner.

"Turn it around. You can do this. Turn that fear into an advantage. If you don't recognize yourself, then rebuild the way you want to be. That will make you strong. Fear is natural, everyone has it. Don't hide behind it though. Don't let it be your excuse. Let me ask you, do you want to live?" the blunt words had a sharp edge to them.

"Of course, I do," Jax retorted, but his voice was flat.

"But?" Father Roarke prodded.

"I keep thinking about stupid things. Earlier I was on the balcony because I needed air, and I kept thinking of jumping off." Shame colored his face.

"Jax, however you have changed, whatever you see in yourself, I know enough to believe that you don't want to do that. You have to fight this." Father Roarke drew a gulp of air in. "Will you let me bless you with holy water?"

"It's not the first time I've been blessed, but sure," Jax agreed. He didn't see why the priest was so nervous about this. "Why do you think this will hurt me?"

"From what I have witnessed with my own eyes happening to Airiella," he told Jax softly.

Fear flashed across Jax's eyes and Father Roarke could see Jax fighting internally. "My stomach is cramping," he bit out.

"It knows, Jax. I don't know how you will react though." Father Roarke sounded nervous to Jax which amped up his fear.

"Just do it," he ground out. Standing up he walked closer to the priest and saw him hesitate. Jax's nerves were strung tight. "Should someone else be here?"

"No, I'd rather have minimal damage," the priest said cryptically. He pulled out a vial of water and moistened his fingers, stepping up to Jax.

His entire body was rigid with fear and tension and

as the priest touched his fingers to Jax's head speaking a prayer, Jax roared in pain, his eyes immediately going bloodshot. His fists were clenched so tightly that his nails dug into his palms breaking open the stitches there once again.

Father Roarke continued to pray but didn't touch Jax with more holy water, he just stepped back out of arms reach. The veins in Jax's body were bulging out and the more Jax yelled the redder his eyes got. Father Roarke heard pounding on the door behind him, but fear for the safety of others kept him from opening it.

He took the vial of holy water and splashed it across Jax, watching steam rise from the exposed skin that it touched. Then Jax dropped as if there were no bones in his body and the room became still. Father Roarke opened the door and a flushed and worried Ronnie fell inside.

"Jax?" Ronnie whispered. "What happened?" he asked the priest.

"He allowed me to try a blessing with holy water," Father Roarke said, his face paler than normal. "I'm not sure how it turned out. You heard the yells, then he dropped." He pointed to Jax.

"Jax?" Ronnie said, walking over to him and crouching down. He smacked his face a little bit. "Jax? Open your damn eyes!" Ronnie shouted, smacking him.

Jax shot to his feet, his eyes red and tortured looking. "Don't touch me!" he hissed, sounding nothing like himself.

"Snap out of it, man!" Ronnie didn't back down.

"Get him out of here!" he shouted pointing at Father Roarke, who had stepped closer to Jax.

Ronnie looked at the priest and back at Jax. "He's here to help you, so calm your shit!" Ronnie shoved Jax making his step backwards. "If you want to hit me, then hit me!"

Jax deflated, himself again. "I don't want to hit you."

"Jax, what happened?" Father Roarke asked.

"It took over me when you touched me. Felt like someone stuck a live wire right into my brain. Intense pain."

"Tell me how this thing feels, what it does to you," the priest pushed.

"The instant switch like that has only happened a few times, all of them related to Airiella. There's no warning, it's just like I am out of my body watching, I have no control. I guess when it's out of energy or something, I'm back in my body and shame washes over me. It's so dark, like hate, rage, evil and it's crawling inside me, seeping into everything. Other times, I can feel it build inside me, and I try to fight it back. I haven't won, but I can overcome it for little moments of time. It's awful. I feel sick."

"You have to work at it Jax. Rebuild. It has to start with you," Father Roarke reminded him.

At that moment, Kalisha popped her head in the open door, "Can I come in?"

Jax nodded. She walked over to him and held out a silver chain with a stone wrapped in wire on it. "This is for you to wear at all times." She slid it over his head and he felt caged again. Nervous energy making his muscles vibrate.

Ronnie noticed and pulled Kalisha back away from Jax. "Buddy? You under control?"

"I feel trapped," Jax whispered, his eyes frantically looking around as if he were wanting to escape.

"It is the amulet. I put a binding spell on it. When you wear this, that energy can't leave your body."

"Then how will Airiella help me?"

"You will have to take it off. I don't know if it will adapt itself to find a way from under the spell, but for now, you can be around people. It's also blessed with a protection spell, though I am unsure if it will work. I asked for it to keep you from losing more of yourself. We don't know what this is, neither do the loa. This was the best I could come up with."

"Thanks, Kalisha," Ronnie told her. She placed one around his neck too, but he just felt the warmth of the stone.

"Protection for you," she told him.

Jax paced since he didn't know what else to do. "Thank you," he said tightly to Kalisha who just nodded at him with narrowed eyes.

"Do not remove it Jax," she warned, then left. Father Roarke following her out.

"It's a start," Ronnie told Jax carefully.

"Yeah, right." Suddenly tired, Jax sat on the bed and then flopped backwards. "Don't let this kill me, Ronnie," he pleaded.

"Not my goal man, but you heard Roarke. Fight it. Show me that teenager that was so worried about his friend that he found a way around the bullshit to save him. There's a fighting spirit in you Jax, you just have to want it."

"I do want it gone, I'm just scared." He rolled on his side away from Ronnie so he couldn't see his face.

"We all are. Fight Jax." Ronnie patted him on the back and then left the room quietly leaving Jax to his thoughts.

They had just finished eating and Smitty was helping Airiella gather the last of her stuff up to leave in the morning when someone knocked at her hotel room door. Smitty assumed it was Ronnie and flung it open ready with a smart-ass comment, but froze at seeing two cops standing there.

"Is Airiella Raven here?" the shorter of the two asked. Smitty looked at the uniform for a name, saw Reynolds. He nodded and looked over his shoulder at her as she came out of the bathroom with her hands full of her toiletries.

"Is everything okay?" she asked timidly.

"Airiella Raven?" Reynolds asked again. She nodded.

"We have some questions about the attack in the park," he told her and stepped around Smitty.

"Smitty." She gave him a look and he walked over to her side.

"You aren't in trouble ma'am," the taller one replied. Smitty saw his name was Black. "We just need to ask a few more questions and we wanted to catch you before you left."

She nodded, "Okay."

"The man in the park claims that you did something to him," Black started. Smitty felt her back tense up under his hand and he rubbed soothing circles.

"Well, I fought back, but I am not sure what you are getting at." She shifted her stance to a more even one. Smitty felt a change in her energy and he couldn't identify what it was, but he was on guard now.

"He has a history of mental illness that is well documented, as well as previous run ins with the law," Reynolds added. "Though when we ran another psych evaluation on him, he passed everything with flying colors. He said you changed him."

"I'm not sure how that is possible. He didn't even talk to me; he was just swearing at me. I was in plain sight the whole time. What does he think I did to him?"

"He said you showed him God," Black said bluntly.

Airiella barked in laughter. "Well that's a new one."

"We don't think there is any truth to his claims, that's not why we are here, we just wanted to check the facts again and consider this closed." Reynolds shot a look at his partner. Smitty caught it. "Can you walk us through the attack again?"

Airiella told them everything again, and Smitty listened to the tones of the officers. They were fishing for something, but he didn't know what. Airiella finished and crossed her arms over her chest. Smitty moved slightly behind her so she was leaning on him.

"You didn't give him a drug, or chant anything?" Black asked again.

"You think I'm a witch?" she sounded dumbfounded.

"You were in the presence of a well-known self-professed medium, I'm not ruling anything out," Black responded.

"No, I didn't chant or give him any drugs. I don't even have any drugs. I'm not a witch," Airiella retorted hotly.

Smitty felt something click in his head, and he pulled out his phone and shot a text to Aedan. "Find out if her blood can change people." Then he slid it back in his pocket.

"Here's the kicker, he had cancer. He doesn't have it now," Reynolds put in.

"How would fighting with me in a public park after he kidnapped a child that I risked my life to get back have anything to do with that?" Airiella was getting angry.

"We have no idea. He is just claiming that you fixed him," Reynolds stated.

"Well, if I had the cure for cancer, I would have saved myself a lot of fucking heartache and trouble." She swore swinging around and continued packing.

"I understand, ma'am. I'm just doing my job. We'll be on our way. Thank you for your help and time. Safe travels," Reynolds said, turning away. Black stood there glaring for a moment then followed his partner out of the room.

"What the fuck?" she asked Smitty.

"No idea, little unicorn." He tried to make her smile. "I did text Aedan and told him to ask about your blood though. You said you bled on him. Maybe there is something in your blood that's healing?"

"I don't want to become a science experiment," she said sadly.

"You won't. It was just a theory I told him to look into. Chances are he will relay it to the council and they will research it." Smitty pushed a lock of hair out of her face.

"I feel like the biggest freak to have ever walked the

face of the earth," she said sullenly.

"Oh, not even close." Smitty smiled. "You've got moves, but I dated this girl once who only wanted me to jack off all over her. She never touched me."

She finally laughed and the tension bled out of the air.

Chapter Four

Mags couldn't help but feel a thrill of excitement as she boarded the plane to Seattle. She'd never been to Washington before, plus she had the opportunity to learn more about Airiella and her life. She also was looking forward to the possibility of exploring her three-way fantasy.

Mags almost felt bad about being excited because of the reason behind all of this, though the excitement won out. No use in focusing on the bad and worry, it would only weigh her down and she loved life and trying new things. Besides, Airiella was the one who requested that she come along.

Their tickets had been for business class and as they settled in their seats Mags noticed that one of the flight attendants was talking intently with Airiella. Soon enough they were reseated in first class the flight attendant enamored with Airiella.

Mags saw the plane wasn't even close to being full which she thought was weird, because Seattle was one of the major hubs, though she didn't care because she was now seated in first class in a window seat. She almost squealed in happiness at the thought of getting to see one of the world's most dangerous volcanos as they flew over it.

She glanced over at Aedan sitting next to her, who was watching Airiella intently. She didn't need to be an empath to know that he was feeling conflicted. She held his hand and whispered in his ear, "Go sit next to her and talk to her."

"What? No." He looked at her quizzically. "Why?"

"So you can move past whatever block you've stumbled on." Mags smiled at her husband. "Man up cowboy. Just go do it. Trust me."

"It's just your hormones talking," he shot back at her, but his eyes were smiling.

"If you want mine to listen to yours then you better get to talking," she threatened him.

Aedan groaned. "That was hitting low."

Mags laughed knowing she won that one. "She is so far beyond special. You need to get to know her anyway. You have to get her up to speed on the show stuff."

"Talking to her about that is easy though, asking her to trust me with the other stuff is a little harder," he argued.

"Shut up, man of mine. Go." Mags pushed him out of his seat.

He gave her a nasty look but went and sat down next to Airiella. Her voice was a naturally low and husky tone that didn't carry, especially above the noise of the plane. The few other people that were up here wouldn't hear them. Mags sat back in her seat and just enjoyed being.

She looked over at Aedan and Airiella every so often, the position of Aedan's body giving away how intently he was focused on the conversation. Mags smiled; he'd be under the same spell she was soon enough. She couldn't wait.

Normally Mags wasn't a part of the investigations they went on, and she was sure she still wouldn't be. A part of her felt like she was included though because of the connection she kept hearing about. It made her feel needed and that was something she felt was missing from her life.

Aedan didn't need her. She often felt like she was cumbersome to him because she was so free spirited. She constantly pushed his boundaries and comfort zones but he never complained about it. When she heard that she was part of this connection with Airiella it lifted her soul and made her giddy.

She must have dozed off for a bit and woke up to turbulence. She looked out the windows but didn't see anything yet. She felt someone sit next to her and she looked up, seeing Airiella.

"Wait, the plane will turn and you will see," she said softly. Mags glanced over and saw Aedan glued to the window.

Mags felt the plane turn and she saw snowcapped mountain ranges stretching across the landscape. She followed Airiella's pointing finger to a peak. "Mt. St. Helens," Airiella told her.

It was gorgeous, Mag's breath caught in her throat as she scanned. Airiella pointed again, "Mt. Adams," then she pointed to the largest one. "Mt. Rainier. That's the one I live closest to."

It towered majestically above the range below it, covered in snow, it's ridges gleaming against the bright sun. Mags was captivated by the sheer size and beauty of the mountain so many called dangerous. "It doesn't look dangerous," Mags whispered.

"Well unless you are hiking it, climbing it, or skiing it in the wrong gear it really isn't. It is active though which is why they call it dangerous. If she blows it would be devastating to a lot of people."

"You hike there?" Mags asked, unable to look away from it.

"Sometimes. The trails are more aggressive than I normally hike, but the beauty is unparalleled. Mt. St. Helens feels like another planet in comparison due to the decimated landscape from when she blew, but still quite amazing. It's one of the reasons I haven't left here, it has everything I want. Mountains, ocean, desert, rainforests, valleys, clean rivers and lakes. The overpopulation is ruining it, but for now, this is my home," she said, her eyes bright.

Mags had looked away from the mountains at the tone of Airy's voice. Wistful, and in awe as she described the places she loved. "I wish we had time to see it all." Mags sighed.

"Maybe once the filming is finished for the season we can come back and I can show you around," she suggested to Mags.

"I'm in 100%," Mags gushed in enthusiasm. Airy smiled at her and went back to her seat so Aedan could come back.

"Pretty incredible isn't it?" he said nodding to the mountains. "I never get tired of seeing that every time I've flown in here."

"It looks so small from up here but at the same time like it's looming above everything," she breathed, then looked back at Aedan. "How was your talk?"

Aedan searched her eyes, a little glint sparking his own. "You were right," was all he gave her.

Mags clapped her hands, "I knew it!"

"I think she misses being here," he said looking over at Airy. She was sitting in the window seat looking off into the distance, one of her knees up to her chest.

"I think it's more that her mind is overwhelmed and she's trying to wrap her head around it all," Mags told him.

"Why do you think that? I mean it's true, but how can you tell?" Aedan asked, perplexed.

"For someone like her, that is a defensive posture. See how she is holding her leg tight to herself? Her limbs close to her body? She feels unprotected and lost, she's pulled within, vulnerable," Mags explained. "Think about it Aed, her whole life has been turned on its side."

"Shit Mags, I didn't even think of that." He exhaled

and looked at her. "I don't think we can protect her."

"I'm going to damn well try," Mags huffed. "She told me her story, and even though she's undeniably strong, right now she looks totally fragile to me."

"She does. Thanks for pointing it out to me Mags. Love you." He kissed her on the nose.

Home. My heart beat rapidly in my chest as the plane landed and I thought about all the stuff I had to do and figure out in such a short time period. I desperately wanted to go to the coast and bury my feet in the sand before I left, but doubted that I would have time to make that journey.

I've been in a constant state of having to prove myself to strangers, expose my secrets that I purposely hide, fight against an unknown enemy, fight myself, and put my trust in people that I don't know. It's no wonder the ocean called to me. Physically I was tired, mentally, I was on fumes.

I spent two hours baring my life and soul to another person that I was just supposed to blindly trust and it took a toll. I knew Aedan wasn't the biggest of my concerns, that Jax was, but it was still hard for me to open up to him. Mags was much easier. The connection with Aedan was there, but he didn't like it, and it was not something I would ever force on anyone.

I stood and grabbed my bag to depart, lost in my own thoughts completely unaware of my surroundings. When Aedan's hand grabbed my arm, it startled me and I reacted out of instinct swinging my bag. Too late to stop it when I realized it was him, it slammed into his stomach doubling him over.

Mags' mouth formed a perfect O as she bent to help him. "Idiot," I heard her tell him. "Don't grab women like that." I hid a smile and looked away while he gathered himself.

"Sorry Airiella, I was trying to get your attention." His voice warbled a bit.

"It's okay," I told him.

"We've got a rental to pick up," he told me, so I headed in the direction of where we needed to go. I hung back while he did the paperwork for the rental car and when he was finished, I held out my hand for the keys.

"What?" he asked, confused.

"I know where I'm going, I'll drive," I insisted.

"I have GPS," he argued.

"I live here," I shot back, my hand still out. He sighed and gave me the keys. "An SUV?"

"They said we would be in the mountains," he muttered, shrugging his shoulders.

I cracked up laughing. "Doesn't matter, we will still get there, even driving a tank."

"It's mid-sized at least," he said.

I hopped in the driver's seat and took off once they were in the car. "You weren't joking, there's a ton of traffic," Mags said.

"Always," I replied dryly.

As we came up the highway when I got close to home, I told them both to keep their eyes in front of them. "For an urban drive in traffic, on clear days like this you can't beat the view as you crest this hill." They watched as Mt. Rainier came into view looking gigantic from the angle we were at.

"Now watch, as we drive towards it, it looks like it moves farther away." I smiled at the look on Mags' face. "She's my view on my way home from work every day if she's out."

"If she's out?" Aedan asked.

"Haven't you been here?"

"Not this city, but in Seattle," he said.

"When?"

"It was summer, I think, or early fall."

"Well mountains like this are known for crazy weather. You know how everyone says it's always raining here? That's not true, we aren't even in the top 20 for rainfall amounts. But it does get overcast a lot. Especially around the mountain. If you weren't familiar with this area and didn't know the mountain was there, you'd never see it."

"How can you not see something that big?" Mags asked in awe.

"Cloud cover," I said simply.

"Doesn't seem possible," she breathed.

I pulled up to my house minutes later, happy to be home. I texted my family to let them know I was back and that we needed to get together for dinner in the next couple of days, that I had news to share. "I'm going to have to have dinner with my family one of these nights, did you want to join or would you rather do your own thing?"

"I want to go!" Mags said jumping up and down. "I'd love to meet them."

"She's the boss," Aedan said smiling.

"Alright." I led them upstairs and showed them their room and left them alone. Checking on the cats I put my stuff down and went to lay on the floor with them. I felt safe here, and for a moment I let the fear of all the unknown hit me and plague me with the "what if's".

I needed to call work, but I had questions for Aedan before I could think about what I was going to do about that. I needed to either find someone to take my cats or live here for a while. As I was running through a list in my head of possibilities Aedan walked in and sat on the floor in front of me.

"I feel like I owe you an apology." He held out his hand to me. I took it thinking he was going to shake it but instead he held it. "Not only for myself, but for Jax and this whole mess. It wasn't until Mags pointed it out to me that I understood just how much you were giving up and taken on in doing this. For that I am truly sorry."

"You don't need to apologize Aedan," I said, carefully opening my senses a little to get a read on how he was feeling. This was an unexpected display of sensitivity and emotion from him. I also hadn't failed to notice he still held my hand and that my skin tingled where he touched it.

"I really do, Airiella," he replied, looking at our hands. "Is that the connection I am feeling?" he asked sidetracked. I nodded in response. "Fascinating. Oh, um, sorry. It's distracting," he said but didn't drop my hand. "I know things are going to get ugly with Jax. I just hope you know that what you've seen so far isn't him."

"I understand." I tried to pull my hand back, but he held tight.

"Um," he hedged, blushing and then I felt the lust roll off him and almost laughed. "I know Mags talked to you about something she's been wanting to try..."

He was so uncomfortable that I pushed a little calm into him and he looked at me with his wide hazel eyes. A lock of his light brown hair fell across his forehead when he leaned his head towards me. "Wow, that felt great."

"Aedan, please talk freely with me, there is no judgement here. You are one of four people alive that know my whole story. I'm the last person who would ever judge you or Mags. Sex doesn't make me uncomfortable despite what people think after learning about my past. Nor am I ashamed to admit my own curiosity."

He huffed out the breath he had been holding. "It just feels awkward talking like this with someone who isn't Mags."

"I get that too. Yes, the connection is there, you can feel it as well as I can, but no one is going to make you sleep with me. I won't force that on anyone. That's no better than rape."

"It's not that I don't want to do it, though, I feel shame for admitting I want someone else than my wife. It's that I think there should be boundaries. I'm making a fool of myself right now, I know." He let go of my hand.

"Talk to me. The worst either of us can say is no. Right?" I went for casual, trying to ease him.

"Mags thinks I'm being stuffy," he said with a half-smile.

"I think I see it as you are just being who you are. She is your wife." I smiled.

He laughed. "How many people can say that their wife wants you to sleep with someone else?"

"I think you'd be surprised by that answer," I told him truthfully.

He sobered up. "Right. Maybe I'm just old fashioned."

"Aedan, be you. No one else can do it better."

"I totally see why Mags is in love with you." He leaned back on his elbows, the cats smelling him cautiously. "I want to do this, but I need to know if you are okay with no actual penetration between you and I?"

"Wait, so you both really want this to happen?" Color me surprised. One more thing to add to the what the fuck just happened list that started a couple of weeks ago.

"Yeah." His voice was faint but held a tremor of excitement. "She's so open and free, a curious soul and I love that about her. She keeps me from being boring. I'd do anything to keep her happy," he said, his tone pure love.

"I hope someday someone loves me like that." I kicked my legs up in the air behind me. "Whatever you feel like doing or not doing is fine with me."

He looked relieved. "You seem awfully relaxed about this."

That sent me into a fit of laughter that bubbled right up from my belly. I literally rolled around on the floor while he smiled a sexy crooked smile at me. When I calmed down, I looked at him, "I haven't been relaxed at all! It's hilarious to me that you think I have been."

"You certainly don't show it," he mused.

I tapped my head, "Walls. I'm good at hiding things. Wait, you should know something." I remembered Smitty suddenly could feel stuff. "After, um, well, the connection is made, you might suddenly be feeling me."

"Not sure I follow," he said.

"Smitty said he had empath abilities afterwards and he could feel what I felt." I sounded crazy. "Something to be aware of at least if we do this. He wasn't okay after the energy release."

He looked thoughtful, "Ronnie mentioned something to that effect. How not okay are we talking? This is Smitty, he's as laid back as they come."

I felt suddenly uncomfortable talking about this. "You need to talk to him about that."

He gave me a curious look. "Okay, fair enough. That leads me to this next question, is what happens between us, just between us?"

"You mean like do I kiss and tell details?" He nodded. "No. I am fine with joking around about it, but you won't ever get any details about what happened between me and Smitty, or anyone else for that matter. The connection I share with him, is for him and I alone."

He relaxed, then grinned, "So I don't have to tell Smitty that my dick is bigger than his?"

Mags walked in then and looked between us and replied with a straight face, "Oh his is way bigger than yours."

I laughed so hard and loud that the cats ran away. The look on Aedan's face was priceless. Mags was giggling madly. While they were both so carefree at the moment, I wanted to test out the connection and I took up both of their hands and like it had with Ronnie and Smitty, electricity zinged fast between us.

They both looked at me in silence, their mouths hanging open. "It's stronger when you are together," I said thoughtfully. "Interesting."

Aedan's eyes were unreadable at the moment, but Mags were heavy with lust. I stood up and said to Aedan, "I am trying to figure out what to do about my job. A week isn't really enough time to give them to find someone else. Do you think that if I were to do my work for them remotely, I'd have time to do what I need to do for the show?"

"Hmmm, what do you do?" he mused.

"Marketing, mostly reports, some creation of marketing materials," I replied.

"Do you have deadlines?" he wondered.

"If they need something made for a meeting then yes, for the reporting, not really. I log into other systems and pull data," I explained.

"It could probably work for a while, but it does get busy. You'll be burning the candle at both ends so to speak." Aedan looked thoughtful, then worried.

I wanted to give them options rather than leave them high and dry, but I really didn't know anything about what they needed me to do for the show. "I think we need to discuss how you think my role will play out then."

Mags slipped out of the room saying she wanted to shower. I pulled her back and led her into my room and showed her my big tub. "Yes! Can I use it?"

"Go ahead. Here's towels, bath salts, bubble bath, soap, body wash, body butter and whatever else you need."

"Damn, you've got your own spa." She looked happy.

"Kind of. The only thing I didn't make was the towels, the rest are all-natural products I make here when I have time."

She pulled me in and gave me a huge hug and brushed her lips across mine then pushed me out. "Go talk shop, I've got things do to." She winked closing the door.

"Tub?" Aedan asked as I walked out.

"Yeah, a soaking one." I smiled.

"She'll be there a couple hours then." He walked back downstairs with a notebook in his hand.

"Aedan, one more thing. I don't want awkwardness, so if you think you will regret anything the next morning, let's not go through with it," I felt the need to say as I followed him.

"Understood, thank you."

My phone went off with a text message, dinner would be tomorrow with my parents. That didn't leave me a lot of time to figure this shit out. "Okay, hit me with it. We don't have a lot of time."

"On location they will want you to check out an area before sending Jax in right now. After your demonstration with them, they will fully take advantage of you. Be prepared. If you sense that bad energy, or any bad things, really, then we can assume it will trigger Jax."

"Okay, I'm following."

"During the investigation while filming you'll be on standby outside with the crew. If something happens, you'll be sent in to calm the situation down. I don't know what that will look like, if you will have to do what you did the other day, or if it will be something minor that you can kind of soothe out." Aedan fidgeted nervously.

I closed my eyes and thought about options. "That will definitely be something that is an unknown," I agreed.

"Each location is different, and we never really know what will happen, who will react, that kind of thing. It could be any of us that reacts, not just Jax," he threw out as a cautionary warning.

"I understand," I told him. "I watch the show, been a fan for years."

"We often arrive during the day or the night before and at least a day is spent interviewing people, walking the location, doing local research. They will want you on hand for any interactions Jax has with anyone." Aedan glanced down at his notes.

"It's looking like the days and nights will be full." I mulled it over.

"They will. But still that being said, while you are on standby there is nothing saying you couldn't have a computer and be doing your own thing." He tapped the notepad, lost in thought.

I frowned. "I don't think that would be a good idea. I am sure that I can do it, but my attention will be divided, and if I am trying to read emotions at the same time, I don't think my reaction time will be the same. With what I have seen so far that could potentially be dangerous."

"Good point." He thought for a few minutes, tapping a pen against his notepad now. "I think really, that this is going to be a call you will have to make after a few weeks of doing this."

I nodded, not liking my options. "How bad were the last locations?"

"You saw the one where he went after Smitty?" I nodded. "They were like that. He was completely unpredictable. Hence, you being here. They wanted to fire him. Ronnie and I argued with them for days about that."

I thought about that, the show wouldn't be the same without him. "Well now I need to figure out what to tell my boss. I can't obviously tell them I was told that I'm an angel and need to help a ghost show keep their star from going bat shit crazy."

Aedan laughed at that. "You could, but I wouldn't recommend it. Are you going to try to work remotely?"

"I think I will give them two weeks for that option. I will leave it up to them if they want to take it or not. As for the reason I quit, I can't think of anything to say." I hated doing this to them.

"You can use the old fall back of family situation," he suggested.

"Am I going to be on camera?" I asked.

"Not that I am aware of, but it is a possibility." Aedan frowned as he thought about it.

"Then I can't use that excuse, because a few of my coworkers watch the show."

"Then just tell the truth, say you applied for a position and were hired. Call it a research position," he suggested.

"I guess." I didn't like any of my options, but the truth was better than a lie. "Now I need to figure out what I am going to tell my family."

"That one is a bit harder," he agreed. "They know about your empath stuff?"

"Oh yes. I grew up with calling them out on their emotions when they tried to hide it. I always knew what everyone was feeling. Didn't make for an easy childhood in some ways."

"Then I suggest going with a simpler version of the truth without telling them about the shit storm involved."

He grinned lightly.

"You make it sound easy," I said wryly.

"It's only as hard as you make it," he told me bluntly.

"What's your faith?" I asked him out of the blue.

"I was raised Christian I guess, non-denomination." He gave me an odd look.

"You went to church?" I asked.

"Sometimes. It gave me a sense of peace when I needed it," he said fondly.

"The whole angel thing is kind of hard to take, isn't it?" I went for simple honesty.

He leaned back in the chair and studied me. "I'm not sure where this is headed, but hearing it only, yes, it was hard to take. Seeing you in action is a whole different story. It's not something that can be explained away by science. It makes you believe there is a higher power at work. It's both awe inspiring and terrifying at the same time."

"I was raised Catholic. My mom's side of the family is strong in their faith. They are all Italian. While my parents didn't raise my brother and I in a strict Catholic way, I still went to Catholic school and classes that teach Catholic ways when I was a kid. My own faith is just what I call spirituality. I don't follow a religion, but I don't denounce them the way others do either," I explained softly.

"A ghost show hiring you would sound pretty weird to them, right?" Aedan guessed.

I nodded. "To say the least. That doesn't mean I won't tell them that, it will just be hard for them to understand. As well as the moving away for longer than a week at a time. We are a close-knit family and all live relatively close to each other. The holidays and birthdays are all spent together, that kind of thing. See where I'm going with this?"

"I do. You are saying you will meet resistance."

"Not really resistance. They won't understand. I've

always marched to my own beat, and they all accept that. Since I had cancer, they tend to try to hold me closer. I'm the one of the group that they rely on to help them through things, they need the quiet strength I have, whether they know it or not. I'm the one they call when they need something. Me not being here and available will be hard, not only on them, but on me as well." I sighed.

Understanding lit his face. "You feel like you are letting them down by leaving."

I nodded. "I do. And I haven't even left yet."

"Damn it. Mags was right again. You are incredible." He studied me. "Do you ever do anything just for yourself?"

I smirked at him. "All the time. I hike, do yoga, read, swim, watch movies, write."

"That's called taking care of yourself," Aedan pointed out.

I waved him off. "Are you going to do dinner with my family?"

"Mags wants to, it could be fun."

"Fun for you, not me. You'll hear all sorts of interesting stories about me, I am sure. Fair warning though, they are high energy people." He had no idea what he would be walking into and it made me smile.

"I work on a TV show Airiella, I'm used to high energy. And, well, you met Jax." His offhanded comment made my smile even wider.

"Oh, I might have forgotten to mention, my mom and brother are bi-polar." He sunk lower in his chair. I smiled again and got up. "I've got to call work now, possibly drive out to meet with the owner today instead of tomorrow. You good on your own?"

"Yeah, I'm good." He sounded a little glum.

"See you in a while then." I waved and walked off leaving him to his thoughts, while I took the time to sort through my own. I had no idea how to come out on the other side of this whole. Every step I took was pushing me farther and farther from who I had thought I was.

Chapter Five

Jax pulled up to the house in California and stared at the gated monstrosity wondering if he was going to survive this. He missed the guys being around him and Mags bossing him around though he would never admit that to her. He didn't see Ronnie yet, so he entered the code and waited for the gate to open.

The house was huge, stucco with a red tiled roof common in this area. The drive way had a circular entrance with a fountain in the middle and he scoffed at the ostentation it presented. He parked and pulled out his suitcases scrolling through his phone for the code to open the front door.

Once he got in and silenced the alarm, he checked out the downstairs, noting the movie room, giant kitchen they would probably never use, three bathrooms, dining room, a library, an office, a living room and big winding staircase going up. Everything was white, stainless steel, glass and dark cherry wood. The wood was the only color. Even the artwork on the walls had a cold feel to them.

He pulled his suitcases behind him as he went up

the stairs. Six bedrooms, all with their own bathrooms in varying sizes. Normally he would pick the biggest room, but right now he just wanted to be in the farthest corner away from everyone. He was acting like a child and he knew it.

He failed to notice that his room connected to the one next to it, not that it mattered to him and he put his clothes away. He then packed a go bag he would take to locations. With that finished, he figured he would go look for something to make Airiella feel comfortable. Nothing in the house really screamed comfort to him, and based off what he had seen in the short time he'd been around her, she was color and life.

He looked in the other rooms and tried to think like a female. He figured she would like the one across from him the best as it had the best unobstructed view. It was too close to his, but anything in the house was too close right now.

Mags had texted him a list of things to get for the house, as well as Airiella. Since Ronnie wasn't here yet, he decided to go do it on his own. As he got back in the car, he saw a delivery truck outside the gate and drove down to open it. He signed for the packages and threw them in the back of his car and went out.

She occupied a big chunk of his mind. He kept thinking about when she touched his face and the feelings he got from that. As much as he didn't want to accept any of this, he had to admit they both felt something when she touched him. The real him, not the darkness, wanted to explore it and see what it was, the darkness wanted to kill any chance of him getting close.

He was tired of the constant battle raging inside him, and he thought hard about everything Father Roarke said to him. He'd always held him in the highest respect, and it was hard to disagree with his assessment. Jax just didn't know how to make it a reality.

Self-reflection was a tricky thing to Jax. He knew he was a coward in a lot of ways and facing those parts of himself created obstacles he couldn't mentally get around without a big push. A bitter laugh boiled up in him, like the evil shit growing inside him wasn't a good enough reason to change. It could cost him his life if he didn't. Possibly the lives of others as well.

Jax wandered down aisles grabbing items from the list and he stopped in front of a wall full of throw pillows in vibrant colors and textures. Each of them made him think of Airiella. He ran his hands over a lime green pillow that had the softest fabric. When his fingers touched it, he thought of the way her fingers felt against his face and he snatched the pillow from the bunch and threw it in his cart.

He then found an oversized pillow in a coppery orange color that made him think of sunsets and her hair when light hit it. He grabbed that one too without thinking about it and made his way to the front of the store. He refused to acknowledge the part of him that immediately thought of her at seeing the colorful display.

He passed a display of lotions and once again his brain was immediately on Airiella. He swore under his breath and added one of those to the cart and put mental blinders on and checked out. His phone dinged as he was putting the bags in the car and he saw a message from Ronnie that he had arrived.

Good, Jax thought, maybe he'd be able to distract his mind away from thoughts of her. He was so scared to put his hope in her, though he knew he didn't have a lot of choices. And every time she popped up in his mind, the darkness in him counter attacked with vile thoughts of strangling her. Maybe they'd hit up a club. Jax could find a fan to forget himself with for a night. Sex was a good distraction.

He pulled up to the gate at the same time as a cab and saw Smitty in the back. He nodded a hello and opened the gate for them both. He'd overheard Ronnie and knew Smitty had hooked up with Airiella. He refused to acknowledge the twisting jealousy that tore through him when he heard. He knew Ronnie was jealous too. He'd wanted to punch Smitty.

Fuck, he needed to get laid. Deciding that was his plan for the night he unloaded the bags and dropped them all in the entrance as Smitty dragged his bags in dropping them too. "Get the location list?"

Smitty nodded, "Yeah it's in the bag. Some good spots. Live one is in Washington," he said, his voice taking on an edge that set Jax's gut churning.

"State or DC?" Jax asked. He knew now that Airiella lived in Washington.

"State. I think they purposely did it so she could visit her family." Smitty's tone was too easy for Jax's liking.

"How nice for her," Jax sneered.

Smitty settled a cold gaze on him and Jax felt something shrivel under the intense look. "Get over it fast before she gets here," he warned Jax. "I won't put up with you trying to hurt her."

Jax knew something major had happened when he blacked out and Smitty went with Airiella. He'd seen her battered and bloody body, heard that she'd died. They were all being very tight lipped about it though, but Jax could see a change in Smitty and it left him feeling unsettled. "I'm working on it," he bit out.

"See that you do." Smitty walked off leaving Jax standing there alone. He remembered the boxes that had been delivered and went back out to get them. One for him and one for Airiella. He grabbed the bags and boxes and went back upstairs. He dropped off the box and orange pillow in the room he thought she would like and took the rest to his room.

He'd sort through the bags later. He sat on the bed and opened the box, seeing a tin and a note. Suddenly his closet door opened and he shouted dropping both the tin and the note as Ronnie walked through. "What the fuck, why are you in the closet?"

"It's a connecting door, you dumb ass," Ronnie mouthed off.

"Whatever, what do you want?" Jax tried to control his racing heart.

"These." He grabbed the bags and went through them, pulling stuff out and leaving Jax's things. He held up the green pillow, "Um, who's is this?"

"Mine, got a problem with that?" Jax was combative and defensive suddenly.

"No, not really your style, but whatever floats your boat, dude." Ronnie threw it at him and went back through the door closing it behind him.

Jax grabbed the pillow and stuck it behind his head as he laid back and opened the note.

Jax,

This is a mix that will help you see the areas of your life that are out of balance. Mix it in with some water and drink it like a tea before going to bed. It will make you dream, but the dream will be about what you need to fix. They may look like nightmares, but you need to pay close attention to them. With what is inside you, I fear it won't be an easy process to go through; though I can assure you it is a necessary one. My gut says this is something you created that has taken on its own life force. You must heal what is broken inside you to beat this. Good luck. —Degataga

He looked at the tin and gingerly set it aside. He didn't know when he was going to tackle this task, but he knew that he would drink it as he was told. He rolled on his side and let the pillow brush against his cheek and he closed his eyes and pretended that it was her. That she was with him and nothing was inside him trying to destroy his life. He fell asleep remembering the touch of her fingers, and the enticing smell of her skin.

Ronnie was sitting down in the movie room with Smitty going over the location list and making lists of equipment to bring on each. "Does Jax seem off to you? I mean more than normal?"

Smitty looked up from his computer at Ronnie. "He seemed to be wavering when I saw him. To be honest though, since the event with Airiella, I am different. I might not be the best judge of character on that."

"No, you nailed it. He was having moments when he seemed like who he used to be before Winnie died, and then this new asshole with the darkness inside him. Maybe he's starting to fight it? Am I looking too much into this?" Ronnie desperately wanted him to be fighting it.

"Well if we both saw something, maybe there's something to it," Smitty said hopefully.

"Okay, so this is really odd even for Jax. When I went into his room through the connecting door, he flipped out, but I saw a very green soft pillow that he got defensive about having. Also, on Airiella's bed was a huge soft pillow he had gotten for her." Ronnie rubbed his chin. "It just sticks out in my mind for whatever reason. He's never been the thoughtful type for a female. Other than Winnie, really."

"He did something nice? For Airiella?" Smitty asked, shocked.

"Yeah. There was lotion on her bed too," Ronnie recalled.

"Think she got under his skin the way she snuck right under ours?" Smitty sounded hopeful again.

"No clue. He's just off. She pulled some of that shit out of him, right? Maybe that allowed him to be him more? Does that even make any sense?" Ronnie looked down at the list, unsure what to think.

"I get what you are saying, but I don't have an answer for it. It's a possibility, so let's just keep a close eye on him for the next couple of days. Even with as much of an asshole as he's been, it's got to be hard on him. There are times I don't want to feel sorry for him, and others that I'm ready to defend him to the death." Smitty leaned back in his chair and closed his eyes. "I won't let him get away with treating her like shit though. I draw the line there."

"I agree. I'm going to hold out hope that he's

starting to come around. He's still my best friend and brother, even if I want to kick him in the balls. Which I will do if he's mean to her," Ronnie growled.

Smitty snorted, "Do it. He deserves it."

Ronnie picked back up the list he'd been working on and looked up more info on the live show location. "The live show, we haven't been there before, have we?"

"No, the last time we were in Seattle; in the downtown area, and before that we were over on the peninsula at that hotel," Smitty said. "I've found a few obscure articles that mention some witch rituals that were supposedly happening out there, and one that mentions a voodoo group."

"Something keeps tickling my brain about that location and I can't figure it out," Ronnie said, his tone puzzled.

"Focus on something else instead, it will come to you." Smitty shrugged.

Ronnie put all the papers down. "I'm going to go for a run. Want to come?"

"Nah, I need some down time before all the crazy starts. Take Jax, he needs the exercise." Smitty went back to what he was doing.

"I'll ask, doubt he will go, though." Ronnie headed upstairs to the room that connected with Jax's.

He didn't hear any noise coming from his room and he wondered if he left and they just hadn't noticed. He poked his head in and froze. Jax was asleep, clutching the green pillow, his body quaking. Ronnie thought at first that he was having a seizure and as he walked closer, he saw that Jax was in the grips of a nightmare.

Shit. Ronnie didn't know if he should wake him up or not. He wasn't sure which Jax it would be if he woke him up. He snuck back into his room and ran down the stairs to find Smitty. "Jax is having a nightmare."

Smitty jolted up and they flew back up the stairs. Ronnie motioned for them to be quiet and went back in through the connecting door. Jax was exactly how Ronnie had left him, only now he had tears rolling down his cheeks on to the green pillow.

Ronnie looked at Smitty who could only raise his eyebrows and shrug. Smitty pulled him back into the other room. "Just leave him. I hate to say it, but maybe you are right. Something is different."

"Right? I'm half tempted to call the council," Ronnie said, concern lacing his voice.

"Let's just watch him, see how this plays out," Smitty advised and left.

Ronnie changed, but left that door open so he could hear if anything changed, and instead of going for a run, he decided to work out in his room. At least that way he could be close by if Jax needed him.

Winnie didn't know what was happening, but her energy levels had been the lowest they had ever been. She felt like she was trapped in this endless gray without being able to go anywhere. She could still feel Jax and Airy. And now Smitty could see her.

She was having a hard time popping in anywhere though. She'd been trying to pop in on Jax, but it felt like there was a block around him. Something felt different with him, and she didn't know what it meant. It concerned her because sometimes his life force felt like it was weakening.

She focused all her energy on Airiella and was able to pop in on her, but she couldn't make herself seen. Airiella was in bed, but she was crying and shaking. What was going on? She knew Aedan and Mags were here with Airy, but neither of them could see her.

She focused again, this time on Smitty, and she popped in on him going over paperwork. Hoping he could still see her, she put all her energy in calling his name, "Smitty!" Judging by the way he jumped and dropped everything, it worked, but it didn't look like he could see her.

Lowering her voice so she wasn't yelling, "Smitty, it's Winnie, can you hear me?"

"Um... yeah," he was looking frantically around the room, his voice tinted with unease.

"I don't know what's changed, I can't appear now. I can't even get to Jax. Airy needs help, can you text Aedan or Mags to go check on her?" she said frantically.

His voice was alert now, "What's wrong with her?"

"I don't know, she's shaking and crying in bed," Winnie replied quickly.

"What? Jax is doing the same exact thing." Smitty looked confused.

"Something has changed. Please text, at least tell one of them to look in on her," Winnie begged.

"I will. Thanks for the heads-up Winnie." Smitty already had his phone out and was texting. Winnie let go of the energy she was holding on to in order to stay there and she was back in the gray floating somewhere between worlds, feeling lost.

Mags was curled up into his side reading a book she took from Airiella's office and he was researching angel blood, without a whole lot of success. His phone vibrated and he ignored it. A few minutes later it rang.

Mags looked up at him and he answered mouthing Smitty to her. "What's up?"

"I just had a close encounter of the Winnie kind," Smitty answered. "She said someone needs to go check on Airiella. Before you go, I gotta tell you, that Jax is in the same condition Airiella is. Winnie said that she was in bed crying and shaking. Ronnie and I just checked on Jax who is asleep doing the same exact thing."

"They are connected?" Aedan's mind raced trying to figure it out.

"Somehow, though not like her and I are," Smitty said worriedly.

"Is he having a nightmare?" Aedan worried out loud.

"I think so, so does Ronnie." Smitty's tone was

cautious.

"He's sharing it with her? Maybe? Could this be related to her pulling some of that shit from him?" Aedan took a wild stab in the dark.

"That was my thought too," Smitty admitted.

"I'll go check on her," Aedan told him. "Thanks for the call."

"Let me know she's okay please?" Smitty asked softly, his voice filled with concern.

"You got it." Aedan hung up and saw Mags watching him.

"Should we go in there?" she asked him.

He nodded, getting up. "If she is somehow seeing his nightmare it can't be good. I don't think we should wake her up though. When we wake Jax, it's always bad."

Mags stood up and held out her hand. "Then let's go take care of our girl."

Aedan took it and then went down the hall, trying to ease quietly in her room, but the door stuck and made a racket. They paused to see if she would wake, but she was just how Smitty said she was. Directly in the middle of the bed, on her side, her eyes closed, entire body shaking and tears soaking the pillow under her head. It struck him in the chest how alone she looked.

Mags didn't hesitate, she pulled the covers back and slid in right in front of Airiella, forming her body so Airiella was spooning her. Mags pulled Airiella's arm across her body and held it over her belly. "She's ice cold Aedan," he heard Mags whisper.

Aedan grabbed his phone and sent a text asking Smitty to check if Jax was cold too. He shut the bedroom door and then slid in behind Airiella so he was spooning her. Mags was right, she was frozen from head to toe. None of the movement or noise they had made had woken her either. She almost felt hypothermic.

His phone buzzed and he checked to see a message from Smitty confirming Jax was ice cold too. There was some link between the two they didn't understand yet.

They'd barely been in the same room with each other and his best guess was it had something to do with when she pulled some of that darkness from him.

"Aedan, she isn't warming up," hissed Mags.

"I noticed," he whispered back. "Shit, pull off your clothes, treat it like hypothermia." Aedan reached down to grab the hem of the shirt she had on and pulled it up her body as far as he could. "We need to lift her to get this off her. Help me, I'll lift you pull it off." Aedan slipped his arms under her body and lifted her off the bed, noticing she was completely rigid.

"Not how I imagined getting naked with her for the first time." Mags teeth chattered.

"Hang tight babe, I'm going to stick a blanket in the dryer to heat it up, I'll be right back." He pulled the fuzzy throw off the bed and beelined for the laundry room. The dryer going on high, he went back to the bedroom and pulled his clothes off and climbed in behind her once again. Throwing his arm over the both of them he pulled it tight. "Smitty said Jax was cold too."

"This is more than cold," Mags muttered. He could feel her rubbing Airiella's arm that she had pulled around her.

"Good idea on the rubbing her, maybe we can get circulation flowing." Aedan started rubbing his hand up and down her side and hip, down her leg. "She's shaking so much."

"If I put her hands between my legs, she'd be a nice vibrator," Mags joked, but her voice was filled with worry.

Aedan laughed. "Totally inappropriate right now, but that was funny as hell." He heard the dryer buzz and he jumped out to get the blanket. He pulled the covers down and put the now hot blanket over Mags and Airiella and then pulled the blankets back up over them and crawled in. The heat from the blanket was delicious.

Much slower than Aedan would like, Airiella started to warm back up. Mags had fallen asleep, and as soon as Airiella stopped shaking Aedan relaxed. Her body was still rigid, but starting to loosen up. Aedan put his arm back around the two women and held them tight, it was the only thing he could do.

Jax woke up to see Smitty asleep in the chair by the window. His head was foggy feeling and he had a pile of blankets on him. No wonder he was so hot. He pushed the blankets off him and sat up wincing. His body hurt.

Smitty must have been sleeping light because that little noise woke him. "How are you feeling?"

Jax thought about it before answering. "Foggy brain, and body hurts. Did something happen?"

"You don't remember anything?" Smitty stretched.

"Just tell me, don't play games," Jax said, losing patience.

"I don't know what happened, that's why I'm asking. Don't be a dick." Smitty stood, his face stormy. "I didn't kill my back sleeping in this stupid chair for nothing."

"Sorry." Jax actually sounded contrite. "I vaguely remember a nightmare, but it wasn't the same as they usually are."

Smitty nodded, sitting back down, his gaze hard. "You were crying in your sleep, body stiff as a board, and ice cold. Like cold enough we turned the heat on and piled blankets on you."

"That explains the blankets and why you are in here then," Jax said, searching his memory trying to remember the nightmare.

"Here's the kicker." Smitty smirked and Jax got the feeling he wasn't going to like whatever came out of his mouth. "A thousand miles away Airiella was in an identical state as you."

A chill went down Jax's spine as he remembered what was different about this nightmare. He wasn't alone in it. "What does that mean?"

"No idea. Is this the first nightmare you've had since she pulled that darkness from you?" Smitty asked.

Jax nodded vaguely, trying to recall the details of the nightmare but he couldn't. It was just fog. "I don't get it."

"Neither do I. Just another question to add on to the thousands of others piling up." Smitty stood. "Ronnie mentioned something about having you help him set up a gym or workout room out in the detached garage behind us."

"Sure, fine." Jax stretched his aching body. Smitty left and Jax ran his hands over the green pillow and another chill hit him. He pulled his hand back and tried to grasp the thought that was tugging at his mind. Shaking his head, he gave up and went to shower.

I woke up with a jolt and immediately was aware that I was naked again and not alone. This was becoming normal to me. I was flat on my back and Mags was sprawled out half on top of me and Aedan was on the other side, his leg thrown over mine, a hand on my boob and a morning wood erection pressed into my hip.

A little awkward to me, but I had to admit I wasn't uncomfortable, and I really wanted to wiggle my hips around just to be bad. Right as that thought hit me, his hand moved on my boob and my nipple pebbled under his fingers as he pinched it. I held absolutely still completely certain he thought I was Mags. I swallowed a moan as tingles shot straight down between my legs.

I looked over at Mags to see her smiling at me. "We are both awake Airy, good morning beautiful." I flushed as Aedan shifted, rubbing his cock along my hip.

"Oh," I breathed, "so this is happening." She gave me a wicked grin and brushed a kiss against my lips.

"Do you want us to stop?" She licked down my neck and bit me lightly.

I honestly had no idea if I wanted them to stop or not. My brain was screaming stop, my body was saying something entirely different. Aedan pinched my nipple and a groan slipped from my lips. "Sounds like a no to me," he said roughly in my ear.

Mags slid up on to me and straddled me while bending over to kiss Aedan hotly. My body was lit up with the contact of my skin between the two of them. Sensations rolling over me and numbing my brain as I gave in to the feelings. "I have no idea what to do right now," I whispered helplessly.

"Just feel," Mags said pulling my hand to rub my fingers against her wet swollen flesh. Holy shit, I was touching a woman. Aedan groaned this time as he watched me play with his wife. Mags tugged my other hand and wrapped it around Aedan's cock and stroked him with me.

Okay, my lust filled brain enjoyed that. It was hot. His eyes were heavy lidded as together Mags and I stroked him slowly. She let go of my hand and cupped his balls, doing something to make his hips jerk. Always got me when that happened. I loved that feeling guys got when totally in the moment and were enjoying the touch.

I was fully engaged now and my curiosity got the better of me with Mags, while I absently stroked Aedan, I dipped my fingers into Mags and dragged them over her, up and down as she threw her head back and ground herself down on me.

"Fuck this is hot," Aedan growled and sealed his mouth on my boob and moved his fingers to my folds. His tongue rolling across my nipple and his fingers smearing the wetness around the incredibly sensitive bud, he took his wet finger and ran it over Mags nipple and then sucked it clean. She went crazy.

"Will you lick me, Airy?" she gasped, bucking under my hand. Suddenly shy, I didn't know how to respond. She leaned forward and kissed me hard, then said against my lips, "I'll eat you at the same time."

Aedan jerked hard in my hand at hearing that and a groan tore from him. Mags flipped around on me and suddenly I was staring right at her crotch over my face. Her tongue flicked against me and electricity exploded inside me and my hips jammed up into her face as she sucked, licked and nibbled.

I licked up her tentatively and her body shuddered on top of me, her hips spasming. Feeling encouraged I mimicked the movements that she was doing to me and head a muffled, "Oh fuck, I'm gonna come!" and she exploded over my tongue. Instantly I felt the connection snap into place with her, the sensations multiplying across my body sending me over the edge as I came under her.

"Oh my God Airy," she moaned into me, "the connection, holy shit, I'm coming again!" she screamed sucking on me hard. I bucked under her, so sensitive now that tears came out of my eyes. She rolled off me and played with my nipples. "Aedan, you need to feel this. Please baby, fuck her," she groaned, her body still trembling.

It was easy for me to see how on edge Aedan was as he looked at me with a burning question in his eyes. I nodded feeling like a slave to these feelings. "I want you both though, can I finish in you Airiella for the connection?" I nodded again and he yanked Mags around so she was on all fours and he slammed into her from behind, his hips jackhammering fast. "I'm too close," he growled and pulled out of her and slowly slid into me.

I moaned loud, Mags fingered me as he slid in and out in a maddeningly slow pace. "Faster." I lifted my hips into him. Mags kissed me and flicked her finger faster on me. I came hard, clenching around Aedan as he ground his teeth together and fell over the edge with me. The connection between him and I snapped into place causing me to arch up into him.

His body shook at the force that hit him and he grabbed Mags, all three of us touching each other now, the connection humming between us like a live wire. Aedan dropped, slipping out of me and rolled over, pulling Mags into his chest as he sobbed. Mags tugged me into her arms and we lay there, letting our bodies come down.

"Damn, Airy," Mags said, still breathing heavy. "I'm

surprised Smitty let you leave if that was what it was like for you two." Aedan grunted his agreement. "Poor Ronnie," she giggled.

"Why poor Ronnie?" I asked, confused, my brain still in a sex fog.

"More like poor Airiella," Aedan said.

"Why poor me?" I parroted.

"He's going to tie you to a bed," Aedan mumbled into Mags's shoulder. "I'm not asking for details, more out of curiosity, was this connection like that with Smitty?"

I shook my head no. "They are different from each other, even without the sex."

Mags played with my hair. "Different how? That was mind blowing."

"From what I can tell by touch alone, each person brings a different feel to me, like an added strength to something that is a weakness in me. I don't think I'm explaining this well, my head isn't working yet." I blinked slowly.

"You are glowing," Aedan said. "Holy shit! There's a line between us." His voice was pure amazement."

"That's the connection between us," I said gently. "You'll probably be able to see Winnie now too."

"Really?" Mags squealed.

I nodded. Mags put her fingers out and touched the tether between her and I. A groan escaped me at the touch and her body shifted, her eyes wide in fascination. She stroked her hand over it and sensations ripped through my body of curiosity and a wild energy. It was a heady feeling.

"What do you feel?" she asked me.

"Wild energy, like a free feeling and an insatiable curiosity," I answered, my body responding with lust again.

"I feel love," Mags said. "Bright encompassing love that has no end. It's warm and settled on my skin like a blanket but feels sensual too. Like chocolate melting on my tongue." She licked her lips.

"You're killing me babe," Aedan groaned. "I feel horny."

She turned to look at him, "The connection makes you feel horny?"

"No, you talking like that does, combined with the feeling of touching the both of you and the electric feel that's on my skin." Aedan looked a little wild.

Mags got up and walked into the bathroom, wet a washcloth and came back out, cleaned all three of us up, and said, "So let's do that again."

Aedan smiled. "I'm not going to say no."

Mags pushed him back on the bed and sat on his face, his hands wrapped around her hips. "Airy, suck on him."

I changed positions, too wrapped up in the feelings to think about saying no, and licked him up and down, again loving the feel of how his hips jerked and moved under my mouth. It wasn't long before he pushed Mags off him and moved me. He put her on all fours again and slid in, his hand working her from the front.

"Don't think you are getting left out," she moaned as Aedan hit a sweet spot. "Lay in front of me," she demanded. I lay down without questions, and she worked me with her tongue until we all came in an explosion of electricity and tangled limbs.

"Aedan, honey, what do you feel from the connection?" Mags asked in curiosity after we came down again.

"Strength and love," he said plainly.

"What do you get from him?" she asked me.

"A sense of solace and acceptance." I spoke softly, my voice barely heard.

"I have a lot of emotions going through me," Mags said. "Is that normal?"

"Smitty said he gained my empath abilities to a degree afterwards, so maybe that is what you are feeling," I said, feeling a little bad.

"It's wonderful," she sighed. "I love it. I can feel every part of Aedan now, and you too." She looked at me. "Stop feeling bad, it's the best gift I could have ever gotten."

"She's right Airiella, it's amazing to feel what Mags is feeling. I didn't think I could love her more than I already do, but you've taken it to a whole new level, brought us even closer. It's a damn great gift." At least he wasn't so unsure about it now.

That feeling of total acceptance washed through me again, and it made me understand that there was nothing to regret about anything that happened. Aedan might not understand all of this stuff happening, but he accepted me into the group and his life.

Aedan came down from the high he was on and stared across the table at Airiella as she picked at an orange. "What happened last night?"

Her head jerked up and her eyes met his, fear flickered across her face, and he felt her put walls up around her mind. "What do you mean?" her voice held a tremor.

"Why are you hiding now?" he sat forward and took the orange from her, peeled it and handed it back.

"I don't know." She shoved the fruit in her mouth so she didn't have to answer.

"Did something happen when you pulled that darkness from Jax?" Aedan pushed. She shrugged in response, not meeting his eyes. "Airiella, level with me."

"Tonight, is the dinner with my family, are you both still wanting to come with?" she asked, avoiding the question.

Mags looked at Aedan and nodded. "We already said we were, now talk to me," he said, his voice gruff.

"I don't really know," she admitted finally.

"You know something or you wouldn't be avoiding me," Aedan went on, crossing his arms as he leaned back in the chair. "I can't help if I don't know," he added.

"I don't think anyone can help," she said quietly.

"Bullshit. Knowledge is power, the more we know, the better we can counteract whatever this is," he argued. "I got a text from Smitty who said to check on you. When we came in you were totally still, hypothermic cold, and crying."

"I was?" she looked at me in disbelief.

"Even stranger, Jax was in the same exact condition you were in. So I'll ask again, what happened last night?" Aedan repeated.

"I truly don't know," she blathered. "I want to say it was a nightmare, but I can't recall any of the details of it. Nothing at all. The only thing I remember is that I wasn't alone in it."

"I'm assuming you were in Jax's nightmare. Since you've barely spoken three sentences to each other I can only guess that something happened when you pulled that energy," he hypothesized.

"It would make sense," she hedged. "I don't like talking about it though. It does something to me inside, and when I release it, it's even worse. I'm not avoiding telling you, it's just something that unfortunately you would have to witness to understand what I mean. Believe me, I'm not wanting that to happen either. Being vulnerable in front of people like that doesn't sit well with me. Aside from the fact that I can't really tell you what happens anyway since all I feel or know is pain."

"Father Roarke wouldn't give me any details either. Smitty won't say a word. I feel like I'm walking blind here." Mags touched his arm and shook her head at him. "Okay, I get it, leave this part alone. Why do you think we will see it happen?"

"Jax still has it inside him," she responded dully.

"Why didn't you pull more?" he asked, curious and trying to understand.

His gut clenched tight as he saw her shudder under the force weighing on her and her eyes fill. "I couldn't. I tried, but I couldn't hold any more of it. Not after pulling it from Dr. Stone. It's so potent and, revolting. I wasn't even gentle with either of them, I just ripped it out."

"Is that why he blacked out?" he asked in an easier tone.

"I think so. I only know what it feels like when I have to get rid of it. And it's painful to the extreme. I would guess it's the same when I pull it from them. It's consuming and vile, slimy feeling, like I'm being violated in every way possible. Dark thoughts try to take over my head but they can't. It looks for cracks in my walls, trying to get in anyway it can." Her voice quaked at the memory of it.

Aedan felt like the world's biggest jerk. "You told Smitty you needed him before you even did it, why is that?"

"I knew it would take me down, the tiny bit I had pulled from Winnie was awful. Then when I pulled it from the guy in the park, it was worse. I was hoping that the connection we shared would make it easier, and if it did, I don't know. It wants me exposed. It wants to see me revealed, to take me apart piece by piece. It has no good intention, pure black evil." She stood and walked to the kitchen sink.

Aedan saw her hands shaking as she washed them just to busy them with something. "It can't get through your walls?"

"Not yet. I don't know how much more they will hold. I know that the force of it leaving me brings my walls down. Or they come down when it's fighting me, I'm not sure. Smitty would be able to tell you better since he was on the other end of it." She paused as she dried her hands off. "It's the worse horror show you can ever see." The blunt truth of her words hit him hard. "He doesn't talk about it for a reason. He changed because of it. Please understand I am not hiding things from you; all I know is pain. If he doesn't tell you, then it's probably because he is trying to protect you. It was intensely personal to him. For myself as well. Vulnerability isn't something I am comfortable with and doing that renders me completely vulnerable and at the mercy of others."

Stunned silent, Aedan let her walk away. He glanced at Mags who sat quietly through it and saw her face pale. She knew more than she was telling him. "Do you know?"

She shook her head. "Not really, I was there for the

aftermath of the guy in the park. She gave me an overview like you just got, but the aftermath is hard on her. She was pretty shattered." Mags took his hand in hers. "I totally understand where you are coming from and I agree with you in needing to know more, especially if you have to be part of it. You aren't going to get answers from her though. Don't push. Talk to Smitty."

Aedan squeezed her hand. "What now?" He was in over his head on this and felt lost.

She pointed to the connections that they saw. "Learn about these instead. If they exist for us to help her, let's figure out how."

"Wise beyond your years, little lady." Aedan kissed the back of her hand. "Now tell me how we do that?"

Mags smiled, "What else? We experiment. We aren't only connected to her, we are connected to each other." She pointed and touched it. Aedan felt the jolt it sent through him and grinned.

"This could be fun," he told her, doing the same to her.

Chapter Six

I left Aedan and Mags at the house and went to meet with the owner of my company after my phone call with him the day before. The sex had done wonders for me, but the conversation that followed had taken it away and I felt drained.

I mentally made my list as I drove, one of my friends agreed to stay at my place for a while since she was going through a divorce and needed a place to stay anyway, so the cats and house would be taken care of. One less thing to worry about.

The guilt at leaving the company I loved ripped away at me, they were the most wonderful people I had ever worked with and I hated leaving them in the lurch like this. I'd given him the option of me working remotely for a bit and he said he'd talk with the executive team about it and let me know today.

I pulled up to the office and saw more cars than usual, but my brain was distracted by an inordinate amount of other shit so I didn't pay attention. As I walked in the office I froze, he had gathered everyone in a goodbye party.

My heart was overjoyed at the kindness and broke because I was leaving.

He had brought in caterers for a lunch for us all and we talked about what I would be doing, in vague terms on my part, and they all wanted to know how I had found out about the position. Friend of a friend was the only response I could think of as I flashed on the thought of wondering where Winnie was, not for the first time.

They decided that they would use me as an independent contributor with the understanding that I would have time constraints. The owner gave me a brand-new laptop as a parting gift and said that he had already had my work e-mail address set up on there as a way to contact me. I sobbed like a baby.

He told me to let him know when my contract was up and they would see if they could work me back into the company. The kindness of others always humbles me and I knew that I would miss this team more than I had any other job in my life. They had become like family to me. As we said our teary goodbyes, I left fast, the hold on my own emotions tremulous.

I headed back home to start packing and wondered again why Winnie had been so absent. I turned my music on to drown out everything else as I drove. One of the last things I had in my life that felt normal to me.

Winnie could pop in on Airiella, but it was too hard for her to stay for long. She heard portions of the conversation she had with Aedan, she saw the party with her co-workers and felt the emotions that were tumbling around inside her. She even knew Airiella was wondering about her.

She also knew that Aedan and Mags would be able to see or at least hear her now, which she found helpful if she needed to get help for Airiella again. She just couldn't piece together why she was unable to really be there like she was before.

She tried Smitty again and was surprised when she

popped right in on him in the shower. "Looking good Smitty!" she cat called to him and laughed as he freaked out.

"What the fuck, Winnie!" he shouted at her.

"Why can you see me now, and Airiella can't?" she asked aloud.

"What do you mean she can't see you?" he covered himself with a towel and shot a glare at her.

"I'm not that dead that I can't appreciate a fine man like you," she giggled at him.

He shot her a look and slid a necklace back on his neck and she found herself back in the gray again. It clicked; it was the necklace. There was some sort of spell on it to protect them against spirits. Winnie laughed now that it made sense to her.

She focused back on Smitty with all her energy and said, "The necklace keeps me from you!"

Then she was back as he held it out in his hand, the stone away from his skin. He looked at her in wonder. "We all have them, Kalisha made them to protect us."

"That's why I can't get through to Airiella now, or even see Jax. Seeing you naked really helped me figure it out!" she laughed again when he made a face at her.

"I'm not telling her to take it off," he warned Winnie.

"I don't want you to, right now." She looked thoughtful. "I just couldn't understand why I couldn't get through. Is she okay?"

"I don't know," Smitty admitted honestly. "I'm different. I don't know how she couldn't be."

"That last time was really bad Smitty," Winnie worried her hair.

"Fuck, I don't want to ever see that again." He paled even thinking about it. "On the other hand, no way would I let her be there alone for that."

"Take care of them Smitty, I gotta go," Winnie said and disappeared back into the gray to think.

Ronnie watched while Jax stood on the ladder and hooked the top of the punching bag to the ceiling while Ronnie held it in place. They had gotten mats on the floor, 3 different bags hung, a bench weight set they pulled out of storage and the mini fridge they stocked with water for work outs, all set up and ready to go.

Ronnie unpacked the gloves and wraps for their hands and hung them on hooks on the walls and took a look around. It would have to do for now. Jax folded up the ladder and hung it on the back wall where he had found it and sprawled out on the floor.

"Why am I so tired?" he asked Ronnie.

"Cause you're getting old?" Ronnie fired back.

"Ha ha. You're the same age as me," he said flatly.

"Yeah, but look at me, I'm perfection." He laughed at the look on Jax's face. "Okay, I'm being serious. You not feeling right?"

Jax shook his head, "I'm not. I feel caged, trapped. I have memory lapses, my body hurts, zero energy unless this shit in me takes over and rage comes on. Sometimes I feel like who I should be tries to come through only to have it suffocated by this violent hatred in me."

Ronnie was worried. It was exactly what he had seen happening with Jax. "What was with that nightmare last night?"

"I don't remember any details other than I felt like someone was with me in it. Smitty thinks it's that altruistic girl." His tone grew an edge and Ronnie's spine stiffened in response.

"Jax," he warned, "don't. I think I'm in love with her." He stood up and put some pads on his hands. "Stand up, hit the pads."

"I can't." He paled. "I don't ever want to take a swing at you again."

"Jax!" Ronnie snapped at him. "I have pads on, this is for you, get off your ass now."

Ronnie watched him stagger to his feet like he was

drunk. He narrowed his eyes, taking in the movements of his closest friend. That was the real Jax he was seeing, the sensitive side not many others knew. He wanted to see if the violence of hitting brought out the darkness.

Jax walked over woodenly and swung at the pad. "Fucking snap out of it man. Hit!" Jax took another swing with more effort this time and Ronnie watched something flash across his face and he braced himself. The next swing had weight behind it, but no malice.

Ronnie wasn't worried. This was his playground and he knew he could put Jax flat on his back in a matter of seconds if he had to. He hoped it didn't come to that, but the time for going easy on him had come to an end. Ronnie worked him for almost two hours until Jax couldn't even stand anymore and was drenched in sweat, his body shaking with the adrenaline flooding him.

"How do you feel now?" he asked Jax.

"Still trapped, but I feel more myself now than when I started," he admitted, panting.

Ronnie handed him a bottle of water and watched him suck it down. "Maybe you need to make this a part of your daily routine," he suggested.

Jax shook his head. "I can feel the aggression wanting to surface, it's close, but right now with just us here I can keep it down. Adding more people to the house will make me feel like I'm out of control."

Ronnie thought about it. "Energy expenditure seems to help you keep it in control."

"It does feel like that, but I don't want it to be fighting. Maybe I'll run with you, or swim. Something. There's hoops in the back, I can drag Aedan into a basketball game..." Jax listed off different activities other than fighting.

"Maybe. Those are all things we've done before and still seen you flip out. What if it's the aggressive nature of fighting that keeps it in check?" Ronnie probed.

"Feels like a slippery slope," Jax said, his breathing slowing down a bit.

"Think on it," Ronnie told him and got up. "Thanks for the workout."

Jax huffed, "I think I worked harder than you did."

"That's because I'm in better shape than you." Ronnie chuckled and ducked the empty water bottle thrown at his head. However brief of a moment it was, Ronnie was glad to see Jax more of himself.

I got changed for dinner at my parent's house and put on a little makeup. If I knew my family at all, my mom had taken my words that I needed to talk with them and invited everyone she could. I winced, granted the last time I had said that, I had to tell them I had cancer. I was prepared for an invasion.

I headed downstairs and found Mags looking like she stepped off a magazine cover. "Damn girl, you clean up nice," I told her. She sauntered up and down the hallway like she was on a catwalk, twirling and sashaying her hips.

She came up to me and gave me a hug, "You're looking pretty hot yourself."

I blushed. I never knew how to take compliments. "I gotta warn you, my mom probably invited half my family over, so it will be loud, crazy and probably obnoxious. Not to mention intrusive."

"Perfect, just the way I love it," Mags declared as Aedan walked down. I bit back a whistle. Now that I knew what was under those clothes, it was impressive. He was smaller in stature than the others, but still cut and toned, with muscles most guys would be envious of. Mags smiled at me again like she could read my mind, and then she winked.

Blushing again, I grabbed my coat and held out my hand for the keys again. "Wait, never mind, we can take my car."

"No." Aedan handed me the keys. "Take the rental, put the miles on that."

"At the very least, you will eat well. My mom is one hell of a cook, and she usually caters to my brothers tastes of meats. I'm the salad and vegetable one," I told them as I locked up.

"Italian, you said, right?" Aedan asked as he climbed in.

"Yep." I pulled out of the driveway.

"My favorite!" came Mags's enthusiastic reply.

Aedan laughed, "All food is your favorite." She smacked him on the back of the head.

"Do you think we will have time for you to show us around anywhere before we head out?" Mags asked.

"When do we leave?" I asked.

"Two days," Aedan said.

"Sure, what do you want to see?" I asked her.

"The mountain," was the immediate answer. I thought about places we'd be able to get to as I drove on autopilot, the way ingrained into my head.

We pulled up and I saw my brother's car, my grandparent's car and one aunt's car. Not as many as it could be, nonetheless still a lot of people. "Maybe a few more tips before we go in. They are nosy, they will ask numerous personal questions. My dad and grandpa are fairly quiet, some think it's intimidating because my dad was a SEAL. He's just quiet. You may think my brother doesn't like you, that's just him. He's not a warm person unless he knows you well. Please take no offense at anything said."

"Relax Airy, we will be fine," Mags said with a smile and jumped out.

"Right," I murmured, "best of luck to you." Aedan laughed and got out to join Mags in waiting for me to get out of the car.

"It's not like we haven't dealt with intrusive people before," he told me as I reluctantly got out.

"I'll just apologize now." I gave them both a tight smile and headed to the door.

I heard my mom's dog going crazy, so they knew we were here. At least I had warned my parents that people would be with me so that she could try and keep my nanie in line. Mentally bracing myself I opened the front door and walked in, Mags and Aedan trailing behind me.

My cousin appeared in the hallway to my surprise, I hadn't known she would be here. She froze, a look of pure astonishment on her face. "Oh my God! That's... that's... oh my God!"

I shot forward to stop her from throwing herself at Aedan. "Gabby calm down. This is Aedan and his wife Mags. Aedan, Mags, this is my cousin Gabriella."

"It's okay Airiella, I'm used to it," Aedan said softly as he walked up to me, Mags stifling a laugh behind him. "Hi Gabby, it's nice to meet you."

"You're my favorite one on that show!" she gushed.

"Well that's always nice to hear. Usually it's Jax," he said kindly.

"He's a jerk," she said bluntly, looking him up and down.

"Gabby," I sighed, "his wife is right here, and Jax is his brother."

"I don't care, your brother is a jerk too." She stepped closer to Aedan.

Mags burst out laughing, "Hi Gabby, I'm Mags. I have to say that I agree with you, Aedan is my favorite too, and Jax is a jerk."

"See?" Gabby smirked at me. "What are they doing here?"

"Let us past so I can tell the family all at once, I don't want to repeat myself over and over," I said, tired already.

We walked into the kitchen and family room to see my mom and nanie in the kitchen, my dad, grandpa and brother at the kitchen table, my aunt, uncle and sister-in-law in the family room with my nieces playing on the floor. "Hi everyone." I made my voice cheery.

My brother had a look on his face of suspicion as he eyed Aedan and Mags. The rest just looked curious. "Hi Ells!" my sister-in-law called out to me. My nieces came running up to me and I swung them around, not faking my happiness with them.

"Ells?" Aedan asked in my ear.

"My family calls me Ella, or Ells. My friends call me Airy," I explained. "These two little monkeys call me auntie."

Mags squatted down, "Well hello! My name is Mags," she told them as they stared at her. "You two are cute as bugs!"

"I not a bug," said Amanda, my youngest niece. "I a girl," she said totally serious.

"Her name is Amanda," Grace, my other niece said shyly. "I'm Grace."

"Well it's very nice to meet you both," Mags said with a genuine smile.

I turned around to see everyone looking at me expectantly. Here goes nothing. "Everyone this is Aedan and his wife Mags," I introduced them. "Aedan, Mags, this is my mom Mariana, my nanie Florence," I said pointing to the stove where they stood. "My dad Spencer, my grandpa Giuseppe, my brother Nick." I looked over into the living room. "You've met Gabby, Grace and Amanda. That is my aunt Elena, my sister in law Samantha, and my uncle Joe."

They all welcomed Mags and Aedan, but still had an expectant look on all their faces. After my mom offered them something to drink and my dad handed them each a beer, I went on. "Aedan works for a cable TV show that I watch, and through word of mouth, I applied for a job with them." At this my brother gave me a surprised look.

"That's the interview you went on?" he asked. I nodded. "What show?"

"Shadow Seekers," I told him. "You wouldn't know it."

"It's the best show on TV!" Gabby piped up.

"What kind of job?" My mom asked, an odd look on her face. "You don't like the lime light."

"Well," I began, but Aedan interrupted, Mags putting her hand on my arm.

"If I may?" They nodded at him. "Airiella told us

that she has always had this gift of being able to tell people's emotions." Once again, my brother shot me a look. "We had just put in a request for someone with that skill set to help us on filming location."

"How will that be useful?" my brother, the skeptic, asked. "That's not something she advertises to people."

"She will be able to tell us if there are negative emotions in a particular spot to help warn us if we are treading somewhere we shouldn't be," Aedan explained vaguely, but he had their undivided attention. "It will help us stay out of danger. It will also help us know if something is affecting one of us and she can alert the crew to have us stop or be pulled out."

"Do you believe in this shit?" my brother fired off at Aedan.

Mags squeezed my arm before I interrupted, so I stayed quiet. "I'm the skeptic of the group. I have a degree in business and my background is in sciences. I joined with my brother to start this crew when we lost a very dear person to us. My brother, Jax, wanted to prove that life after death exists, that ghosts are real. I agreed to front half the money to be the devil's advocate to his believer role. I can honestly say that I have seen things that I cannot explain away with science, and I have also seen things that can easily be explained away. While I am no longer a complete skeptic, I look deeper into what is going on for other possibilities than a ghost, demon, spirit or whatever you want to call it. Now I have an open mind while I research all possible explanations."

"It's what makes that show so great," Gabby added, clapping her hands. I tried not to laugh and bit my lip.

"That's what I am here to tell you," I said breaking in before it got out of hand. "I accepted the job when it was offered to me. I'll be living out of state for at least half the year and travelling quite a bit. I'll be leaving in a few days," I added a little quieter.

"What?" my mom's voice went shrill. "Where will you live?"

"With the crew in a rented house near the studio during filming season," I answered, looking to Aedan in case more detail is needed.

"That's right. It's a new house this year, so I'm not sure it's exact location, but it's in the L.A. area in California. We stay there between locations so we can work on the editing between shoots, and that's where we fly out of."

"Ells, you have to live in a house with strangers?" my mom asked. You'd think I was a teenager, not thirty-four.

"You are so lucky," Gabby breathed.

"It's fine Mom. A great opportunity for me to use the skills that have been a pain in my ass for so long," I said carefully. "I wanted you to meet at least one of the people I'd be working with. His wife, Mags, will be in the house as well. I'll get to help with researching locations and help keep people safe."

"What about your house and cats?" my dad asked.

"Mel, one of my friends, is going to live in the house while I am gone and take care of the cats for me. She's going through a divorce and needs a place to stay, so it works out great." My dad was one that liked to ensure all bases were covered.

"She will also be able to come home when she wants," Aedan added. "She won't be unavailable or out of reach."

My dad nodded, and my mom just looked stricken. Samantha looked kind of excited, and Gabby was Gabby. The rest hadn't said anything and sat there in silence. "Look, it's already decided I am going, so save the arguments," I told them gently. "You know I like exploring new places and this is a great way to do that and get paid to do it."

Ever logical, my dad agreed. My mom went back to furiously stirring whatever was on the stove. I let her be and got down on the floor with my nieces and Mags joined me. We sat there playing with the girls while Aedan sat at the table and talked history with my grandpa, brother and dad.

"It'll be okay," Mags said quietly. "Aedan is good with people. They will come around before we leave."

"Auntie are you leaving?" Grace asked and crawled on me as she usually did. She was seven and way too smart for her age. I loved this kid beyond reason.

"Just for a little while, but I'll be back. I couldn't stay away from you," I said and tickled her.

"Will you take me to the beach when you get back?" she asked between giggles.

"Sure, if that's what you want," I told her and saw Gabby moving closer to Aedan. I nodded in that direction at Mags. She just shrugged and smiled.

"Dinner," my mom yelled, a little too loudly, a sign that she was still struggling with my decision.

We filed into the dining room and Gabby managed to sit herself by Aedan, so Mags sat by me. "Sorry about my cousin," I said to her.

"Don't be. I'm not worried about it. Aedan can handle himself and he has my utter trust. She hasn't tried to molest him or anything, which, by the way, I would laugh hysterically about." Mags gave me a small smile.

I smiled, feeling lucky this amazing woman was now in my life. As usual my mom had made enough food to feed the entire neighborhood. We got through dinner pretty easily, my nanie, mom and aunt telling childhood stories about the exploits my brother and I pulled, which delighted Mags and Aedan. I was less enthusiastic about it.

After dinner Mags sat with the females of my family while I cleaned up and did the dishes. Mags wormed her way into my mom's graces and by the time we left, my mom was on board with it all, rather reluctantly, but still on board. Mags had exchanged numbers with my mom and promised to stay in touch.

It felt bittersweet leaving. I was worried about not being close by if they needed me, but also felt a sense of freedom I hadn't expected. My cousin had weaseled an invitation to join us on our mountain excursion the next day and came home with us.

I didn't say much about anything we were dealing with, neither did Mags or Aedan, thankfully. My cousin tended to have a hard time keeping things quiet and some things my family didn't need to know. The protest they would stage at my leaving if they knew the nature of it all would put the civil rights war marches to shame.

Gabby followed Aedan around like a lost puppy when I got home, and I left her and went to pack up clothes. Mags followed with to give advice on what types of clothes to bring. I turned on my music to random and started pulling out clothes which Mags either agreed with or set off to the side.

Once the clothes were packed, she went through my lingerie drawer and added some things to my embarrassment. "What?" she asked me innocently. "Ronnie will like these, Jax would like these."

Blushing, "Jax can't even stand the sight of me. And well, Ronnie..." I trailed off.

"You know you will eventually get there with both of them, might as well be prepared." She winked.

I stuffed them in the suitcase, choosing not to argue with her, I wouldn't win. She settled back on my bed. "What's with the music?"

I shrugged. "Music is a way to calm me, distract my brain when needed, or helps me focus. It speaks emotions for me when I can't. I need music like I need air," I said. "I breathe it."

"It's quite the mix you have going on, you don't have a favorite?" she asked, scrolling through the songs.

"Not really. I choose my songs based off the lyrics, and the beat. If I like the lyrics, but not the music that goes with, I don't buy the song. Same with the reverse. But when both speak to me, I buy it, regardless of the genre. My tastes run more towards rock, but there's music on there from all genre's, I believe."

"No favorite artist or song?" she pushed, still scrolling.

"No. It all depends on my mood," I said honestly.

"You've got some fantastic songs on here," she said as she scrolled through some more then set it aside. "Your family is great. You are lucky."

"I really am. They can be overbearing, but at least it's out of love," I admitted.

"This will work out, Airy. I believe that with all my heart," she said, her voice rich with honesty.

"You ready for the mountain tomorrow?" I asked, changing the subject as I set the suitcases on the floor.

"Hell yes!" she exclaimed. "Will it be snowy?"

I laughed. "Yeah it will. It's winter and it's a mountain. You can wear my extra snow boots. We will swing by my brothers on the way out so Aedan can borrow his."

"Can we build a snowman? I've never gotten to do that," she said, which surprised me.

"It's fine with me. We can even ambush Aedan with a snowball fight," I told her mischievously.

"Oh my God, yes!" Mags cried delightfully.

"Let's go save Aedan," I said, standing up.

"No, let him suffer. It's peaceful here in your room," she told me dreamily. "It suits you perfectly."

I settled back on my pillows and she laid her head on my stomach and positioned herself to look out the windows. We laid there in an easy companionship until Gabby walked in and joined us. "Aedan said he was tired and going to bed. He didn't invite me," she joked.

Mags laughed. "He's boring like that," she said winking at me.

Gabby latched on to that wink, "Why is she winking? Did you sleep with Aedan? What's going on?"

"For fucks sake Gabby, relax. Aedan is married, happily, to Mags," I bit out.

"A girl can dream," she said. Mags laughed harder and got up.

"Well that's my cue to head off to a night of sin with my sexy man," she said giggling.

"So lucky," Gabby said as she walked out closing the door behind her.

"Early day tomorrow Gabby, I'm going to sleep. You can either sleep in here with me, or on the couch, your choice but make it quick," I told her.

"I'll stay here, bed is better than a couch. Lend me a shirt to sleep in." I threw one at her and went to take a shower.

Chapter Seven

The trip to the mountain was fantastic if I do say so myself. I was having a blast and when it was time to head home, I felt like I was leaving a part of myself behind. A sadness had overcome me the closer to home I got. I know that both Mags and Aedan felt it too due to the connection we now shared. Thankfully they didn't push me to talk about it.

I dropped Gabby off at home and asked if it was okay if I turned on some music after I watched to make sure she was safely in the house. Aedan countered with he didn't care as long as he got to drive. Wordlessly I got out and switched seats with him.

I plugged in my old iPod and flipped through songs playing the ones that spoke to my suddenly melancholic mood. I didn't play the music as loud as I normally did because Aedan needed to hear the GPS direct him back to my house.

When we pulled up, I still hadn't spoken really and they both took their cues from me and let me be. I went about the kitchen and made up an easy dinner trying to find a peace in the routine, but I was still stuck in the mood, so I popped my ear buds in and listened to more songs.

I brought my suitcases down to get them loaded in the car and since they weren't watching TV, I did some yoga while dinner cooked. We ate dinner and cleaned up, they talked to each other, leaving me to my thoughts.

I cleaned up and went and sat on my front porch in the dark. A wind had kicked up and I wrapped my arms around my legs and listened to it blow through the trees. I knew I would be back here, however, I knew the me that was coming back wouldn't be the same me I was now. Change is inevitable but not always easy. It never bothered me, though it did sometimes leave scars. I was certain that was going to be the case this time.

Mel was coming tomorrow to go over everything with me and get the lay of the land and we were leaving the following morning. I wasn't really good with goodbyes, and I didn't want to say goodbye to my home or my cats. I was uneasy about having let so many people into my life, and feeling vulnerable all the time because of it.

I got up and decided to walk around for a bit, something that usually brought me comfort. It wasn't to be found for me this night though. The unsettled feeling just followed me around, the wind swirling it around me with every step I took.

A few strong gusts blew through and the power went out. The neighborhood was plunged into darkness and silence, a weird feeling crept up my back and clung to my neck like an invisible hand choking me with its icy fingers.

I turned back to go back home and found myself face to face with a man wearing all black. Fear didn't hit me, but anger did. It slammed into me in unfamiliar waves trying to find a foothold inside me and my instincts had me take a step back. It wasn't *my* anger I was feeling.

I heard Mags call for me, her voice uncertain and I opened my senses so they knew I was alright. I reached out to read the man in front of me but only felt the anger. None of that awful energy I'd been plagued with in Colorado. Whatever this man's problem was it had nothing to do with me.

I stepped around him and his body turned as if he was going to follow me, but he didn't move. Just watched me. My own anger spiked, sensing he wanted to start a conflict. I wouldn't give in to it and I kept walking back towards home, disappearing from his line of sight as I rounded the corner. I hurried my pace in case he decided to follow, I didn't want him to know which house mine was.

Mags was on the porch waiting for me and I motioned her inside and locked up behind me, peeking out the blinds to see if he had followed, but it was too dark for me to tell. "Everything okay?" she asked, concerned.

"Just feeling off," I answered. "I'm going to go to bed. I'll see you in the morning." She gave me a hug and didn't push. I crawled into bed, not bothering to shower, not even closing my curtains. I watched the trees bend and sway in the wind, feeling like it was prophetic of my life. Fear was normal in this entire situation, right?

Smitty picked up his phone to see who had texted. "Airy is having a hard time," Mags had texted him. "I think she is worried about leaving."

"Understandable," he wrote back.

"Any suggestions on how to make it better?"

"Not really," he texted. "She's close with her family, right?"

"Very," came the response.

"Maybe bring a picture of them with for her room?"

"Have you talked to her?" Mags asked.

"No. I'm a little scared to," Smitty admitted.

"You? Why on earth would you be scared to talk to her?" was Mags immediate reply.

"I just am, leave it alone," Smitty answered.

"We connected with her too, just FYI." It had taken a longer to receive the response that time.

"Good to know. I'm not asking," he responded, but he wanted to ask questions. It wasn't his business, so he wouldn't.

"Jax doing okay? Aedan hasn't said anything."

"Something is different, but he's otherwise okay," Smitty informed her.

"We will see you in a couple of days then."

Smitty put his phone down. He thought for a minute then picked it back up. "What are her hobbies? Or what things does she do to decompress?"

"Music," Mags responded instantly. "She turns to music when she's struggling with something."

"She has a mp3 player, right?" Smitty's brain whirled with thoughts.

"Yes."

"Okay, when you get here, can you steal it long enough for me to clone it?" Smitty texted.

"I'll do my best. Care to share your idea?" Mags replied.

"I'm going to look through the music she has on there and create a playlist for her of songs that show her how I think of her." It sounded cheesy when he read over it again.

"That's sweet. Using the songs she has on there, right?"

"Yes," he wrote.

"I think she would really like that," Mags assured him.

Smitty smiled. It felt kind of childish to him, but if music was her go to then it might cheer her up. He knew she liked to read too, so he'd get her a gift card for some ebooks. He also knew she liked the little gestures from the time he had spent with her.

Winnie knew Airy was struggling and she also knew there wasn't anything she could do to ease it. Winnie knew it was her fault that Airy was in this position, so she kept her distance on purpose. Maybe it was the wrong choice, she didn't really know. Her own life experience was short lived and had been nowhere near as complicated as Airy's was.

Winnie figured she could at least try to keep the nightmares or dreams away from Airy for a night. Sitting in this gray had given her a lot of time to think about how to get around things and she felt like she had enough energy to be a block for her of sorts while she was asleep.

Jax was afraid to sleep. He had pulled out one of his empty notebooks he used for ideas on locations with the thought that maybe he would journal some of these things that were bothering him. He hoped doing that would help him learn to fight this darkness.

Or at least possibly it would help him figure out his feelings that were so conflicted about Airiella. He opened the book and set it on his lap and tried to clear his mind for a meditation. The darkness inside him was unusually quiet, so he hoped this would work. Journaling wasn't really his thing.

He mediated for fifteen minutes and was feeling quite at peace when he grabbed the pen and started to write in the notebook.

The first time she touched me in the dining room of that hotel, I saw my life flash in front of my eyes. It was a life with her in it. The feel of her fingers on my face was seared into my soul like I was being branded, and in that moment, I didn't care, she was all I wanted. I felt the air between us moving like it had an energy of its own. I want to feel her touching me again. I can't get it out of my head. She's magic. And I'm terrified I'm going to kill her. That this darkness in me will try to take from me what matters most. I don't know how I know this, but she is what matters most to me. Without her, I am nothing. With her, I can breathe. I know all this from that single moment, that one touch. How can it work when the darkness in me wants to consume her and the part of my soul that lives wants to love her?

He put the journal away, no wanting to read what he wrote, because it didn't make sense to him, these feelings that kept popping up in his head. The haunting feel of her fingers on his skin that held the promise of salvation. He knew that was why he bought the green pillow. It made him think of her. Hope was a scary thing for him to have right now with the darkness living inside him, but he was just selfish enough to hold on to it like it was a lifeline.

Jax laid back on the bed, his mind still at peace and he closed his eyes. Something happened though. His eyes were closed, but he was seeing out a window. Watching trees bend and sway in the wind. He smelled the crisp cold air wash over his face and he realized the window he was looking out was open.

He was awake, even though his eyes were closed. He knew this wasn't a dream. He was looking from someone else's eyes. He could feel the feeling of being alone, feeling lost, even fear. What hit him the hardest though was the feeling of love. He saw an arm move across the field of vision and he knew for sure it wasn't his own. It was feminine.

Something clicked inside him, he was connected with her. With Airiella. He was seeing through her eyes, feeling what she felt. The love she was feeling was for them. For him. So was the fear. "I'm so sorry," he whispered, wondering if she could hear him, if she knew he could see what she was seeing.

"Don't be sorry." Her voice floated through his head, warming parts of his heart he thought had been long dead. "Just don't give up." She knew he was there! Terrified she could see inside him, he forced his eyes open, losing the connection and he found himself breathing hard and sweating.

Longing washed over him. He had to push it away,

she didn't deserve to be stuck with someone like him. He wanted it though, no matter how much he lied to himself, she was it for him. That scared him most of all. Was he even capable of loving someone?

I woke up feeling a sense of rejection that hurt me deep inside and I couldn't pinpoint where it came from. I remembered feeling someone else with me last night as I watched the storm from out of my bedroom windows, and how when I no longer felt them with me it left me bereft.

I didn't have time for this. I still had a lot to do to get ready for walking away from the only life I've ever known. I got up and put on some yoga clothes and made a note to myself to wash and pack them to bring with.

I quietly went downstairs and did yoga for an hour until I felt like jelly and then got ready for my day. Mel would be here shortly. I laid on the floor and my cats came to sit with me and I snuggled with them, apologizing for leaving them and hoped they didn't hate me for it.

Aedan and Mags came down as Mel was pulling up, I introduced them, and showed Mel where everything was. Brought the cats with me and her into the office and closed the door so that they could get used to her and understand she was safe.

Mel sensed my discomfort with everything and gave me a hug like only she could. Tight and full of acceptance. I finished my chores, packed the last of my stuff and the rest of the day went in a blur. Mel slept with me that night, we stayed up late talking, she filled me in on the mess her life had become. For a while, my life felt normal.

At least I was happy that she had someplace to go during this, and she loved animals so it worked out well. All I'd have to do is call her when I was coming home and she would arrange somewhere else to stay until I left again. That way I still had my space. She had my trust; she'd been one of my longest friendships.

The alarm rang all too early and I found myself back in the rental car doing my best not to cry as all that was familiar to me was left behind. I felt like a zombie, just going through the motions. Before I knew it, the plane had taken off and it was done. That chapter of my life ended, and now on to the next. I hated goodbyes.

Ronnie was so excited! Airiella was going to be here today. He had made up a training schedule for her which guaranteed him alone time with her every day they weren't on location. Smitty had told him about the song idea he had to make her feel more welcome and relaxed and he was all in.

He planned to make a workout list out of the songs she liked. Maybe he'd also do a playlist for her of songs that made him think of her like Smitty was doing. He had told Ronnie that Mags had shared Airiella was struggling. He knew it couldn't be easy, especially jumping into the volatile situation she was diving into.

He planned to make it as easy for her as possible, and he desperately wanted that connection with her like Smitty had. Not just because of sex either, he wanted to feel connected to someone, not just endless flings to scratch an itch. He knew Jax needed it too, but he didn't want to think about that right now.

He just wanted to be around her again, she made him feel whole and light. He was so looking forward to training her it was ridiculous. It gave him a feeling of accomplishment to think that he was skilled enough to be trusted with the task of her safety.

He checked his watch for about the thousandth time much to Smitty's amusement. Ronnie knew he was excited to see her again too; he was just able to keep it contained a lot better than Ronnie was. He believed Jax was looking forward to it too in his own way, but he hadn't even shown himself today yet.

I was still numb feeling, even after we landed in L.A. and picked up Aedan's car from airport parking. It was weird for me, feeling like this. Like I was a passenger on a ride at an amusement park, but not finding it fun.

Mags was trying to fill me in on what life was like at the house, though I wasn't really listening. I kept giving her the grunts of acknowledgement, but she knew I wasn't really there. She eventually fell quiet and I saw more than a few concerned looks from Aedan in the rearview mirror. I felt like an ass and I needed to snap out of it.

I could feel their concern bleeding through the connection even, but I kept my walls locked up tight not letting anything slip from me. This concerned them as well, but it wasn't their burden to carry my sudden sadness and feeling of being alone.

We pulled up to a gated mansion. It was way too big to be called a house. It had a separate garage and giant circular driveway complete with a fountain. I got slowly out of the car and saw Ronnie barreling out of the front door at a full-on dead run towards me. He plowed into me with the force of a train and I was swept up in his arms as he twirled me around.

That got a smile out of me. He managed to break through the clouds that boxed me in and his exuberance washed over me. With his crushing hug I didn't feel alone anymore. Suddenly I was passed off into another set of arms, this one that I was intimately familiar with and I buried my face in his chest and soaked him up.

Who knew this was exactly what I had needed? "Baby girl, I'm so happy to see you," Smitty whispered into my ear. Then I was sandwiched between him and Ronnie and I felt my heart soar. I was right where I was supposed to be. It didn't make me miss home or my family any less, though it cemented the fleeting thought that this group was also my family now and that I had a home with them too.

Ronnie had grabbed my suitcases and was jabbering to me about a training schedule and Smitty held my hand and they led me into the house and up the stairs not even giving me a chance to look around. They brought me to the end of a long hallway with doors on either side.

"This one here is my room," Ronnie said, shooting

me a look I could only describe as one filled with anticipation. He pointed to the one at the end next to his, "This is Jax." The one directly across from Jax he pointed to next, "This is yours. Jax thought it had the best view and that you would like it."

My heart did a little trip at that and something pulsed strong in my blood that I didn't want to think about. "This one here is mine," Smitty said pointing to the one next to mine. "The one at the top of the stairs on the left is Aedan and Mags."

I nodded and pushed past Ronnie into the room Jax picked out for me, curious to see. The color scheme of everything I had seen so far was bland. Everything white. But on the bed in my room I found splashes of surprising colors in different textures that I wanted to surround myself with. I ran my hands over an oversized orange toned pillow that was silky soft against my fingers. I loved it.

There was also rich green and brown patterned throw on the bed in a fuzzy fabric that spoke of pure comfort. "Jax picked those out for you," Ronnie said quietly, leaning against the doorframe. I had thought for sure that they were from Smitty and Ronnie.

I sat on the bed and rubbed my hands over the two gifts and felt that pulse in my blood again and a pull so strong to go to him that I wanted Ronnie to sit on me to keep me in place. Forcing myself on him wouldn't do any of us any good. He'd come to me when he was ready, or at least I hoped he would.

"We've been kind of rough on him the past couple of days," Smitty said, sitting next to me as Ronnie closed the door so we'd have privacy. "Been drumming into him that the attitude that pops up when you are around won't be tolerated."

"Something changed in him," Ronnie added. "Sometimes I can see the Jax he used to be before Winnie died. And other times, he's not him at all. But since you came into the picture, he's been different. Noticeably different."

I didn't know if this was good or not. I ran my hands over the gifts on my bed and hoped like crazy it was a good thing. I had enough hope for all of us in that sense. He had nailed my colors, textures and style that I liked. I also saw a body lotion that was the scent of jasmine, my favorite. I picked it up and smelled it, the scent soothing to me.

"He picked that out too. Like I said, all this was from him." Smitty motioned to the several bags I hadn't looked through yet.

"He was spot on." I smiled. "I love it all." My heart was flip-flopping madly in my chest. Even though I knew from the first touch of my fingers on his face that he was my future, his reaction to me spoke otherwise. Now that spark lit up again where he was concerned, maybe all wasn't as lost as I had thought it to be.

"He's still struggling, where you are concerned, angel," Ronnie cautioned.

"I get it, but I'm allowed to have hope," I said gently but firmly. Smitty laughed.

"I'd be worried if you didn't." Smitty smiled and leaned over to give me a kiss.

Not to be left out, Ronnie swooped in with one of his own so filled with longing that he left me wet. "We have one week here before we fly out to the first location," Ronnie said, getting down to business. "This week is going to consist of you and I training for 2 hours every day."

"Two hours? Of what?" I said cringing.

"Strength, cardio, resistance, stretching," he named off. "They want you to be able to physically defend yourself, which I want too. There is also the fact that on location, we ourselves are lugging around all the equipment and you'll be helping us. We need to make sure you will be able to physically carry stuff without injuring yourself or dropping the equipment."

"I get it," I sighed, resigned to the torture I was sure was going to be inflicted upon me.

"You'll also spend at least two hours of every day with Smitty learning the equipment, what it does, how it's used and how we decide which location will be using which equipment," Ronnie continued. "After that, you'll spend time with Aedan going over the locations and what types of things he will have you research so when we get there, you'll know what to expect, kind of."

I nodded, my days would be full. "If Jax is up to it, we will have you spend time with him as well," Smitty put in. "Though this time with Jax would not be time alone with you. One of us will always be there as a buffer, and also as a safety precaution."

I swallowed. There was the challenge. The time with Jax. I desperately wanted it, craved it if I was honest, but also was terrified by it. "I think alone time with him would be beneficial to us all," I said cautiously.

"It would," Ronnie agreed. "But not yet. He's not ready yet. Hell, I'm not ready to trust him with you yet."

"Me neither, baby girl. He's not used to unicorns." Smitty gave me a crooked smile.

"Unicorns?" Ronnie looked perplexed, like Smitty had given him a puzzle to figure out.

"Nothing," I said quickly, trying not to blush. "Okay so the Jax thing we will play by ear."

"The rest of the time will be free time, do what you need to do. Think of it just as a regular work day, it will just be spaced out inconsistently at first," Ronnie said.

"Do we start today then?" I asked.

"If you want." Ronnie shrugged. "I was going to give you a day to settle in."

I pulled open one of the suitcases and pulled out my yoga clothes. "I'd rather get started with the training; I need to kill off some nervous energy."

Smitty pulled me down on his lap. "Don't be nervous. You've got me, you've got Ronnie, and also Aedan and Mags. Jax will just take time."

I let him hold me for a minute to calm my insides down, using the connection we had and felt him sigh in my ear as the feeling washed over us both. "Thank you, I needed that."

Ronnie watched us, and I felt the jealousy. God only knows I wanted him just as much as I had wanted the others, if not more. The timing just wasn't right yet. Doesn't mean I couldn't enjoy hugging him though, or having my skin on his. I stood up from Smitty and went to lean on Ronnie.

His arms came around me like it was natural, and I laid my head on his chest, my ear over his heart and found solace in the steady rhythm it beat out. "Go easy on me," I said, his shirt muffling my words.

Smitty stood up and laughed. "Good luck with that, he's never gone easy on me," he fired off as he walked out of my room.

"You trust me, don't you?" Ronnie said into the top of my head, planting his lips on my scalp. I nodded. "Good. Get changed. I'll meet you at the bottom of the stairs." He let me go and closed the door behind him.

I picked up the pillow Jax had gotten me and clutched it to me, tears stinging my eyes. Saving him not only meant a lot to the people in this house with me, it was beginning to mean a lot to me too.

Jax knew she was here, he felt her. The moment she walked in a part of his blackened soul lit up, and the darkness in him started to battle it. The sick feeling coming over him and sending him racing for the bathroom in time to hurl. He wiped his mouth off and drank some water straight out of the tap.

He heard Ronnie chattering non-stop as he led her to her room and Jax felt nerves hit him. What if she didn't like the room, or the things he picked out for her? Insecurities flooded through him and disappointment bubbled up and he crawled onto his bed and curled himself into a ball around that green pillow.

He didn't know how much time passed, but he heard his door open and close and out of the corner of his eye he saw Smitty. His demeanor was stiff, but Jax caught something flit across Smitty's face that wasn't unkind.

"She loved the things you picked out. Thanks for doing that. I think you made her day." Smitty squatted down in front of Jax so they were eye level. "You can do this Jax. That was a good start. Ronnie is going to go start training with her today."

Jax gave a slight nod of his head so Smitty knew that he understood. Smitty patted him on the arm as he walked out of the room closing the door softly behind him. Jax released his death grip on the pillow and sat up slowly.

He could watch them, in the gym, he thought. He could get closer to her without being in the same room or presenting harm to her. He wanted to test himself because if he stopped lying to himself and everyone else, he wanted to be able to be around her.

He waited until he saw them enter the garage they had set up as a gym, spying through his window. He grabbed a coat and headed down as quietly as possible, so the others didn't know what he was doing. He crept around the side of the house and ran to the garage wall that hid him from sight. He eased forward to the window but saw he didn't have a good line of sight from this angle, so he moved to another one and sat there, staring.

He wasn't aware that Smitty, Aedan and Mags were watching him closely from the house. He also didn't know that Airiella had felt him approach. He thought his presence was a secret, never knowing that Smitty told him about the plans for a reason.

His body was having a visceral reaction to her again, and he was glad he was on the other side of the wall. Heat pooled in his belly in a need so strong within him that he wanted to throw himself at her feet and beg her to love him. The darkness in him recoiled violently and wanted to destroy her. Rip her apart and kill the light that shone from her soul.

He forced it back knowing that he could never hurt Ronnie in the way it would hurt him to destroy her. He knew himself that if she was gone, he would cease to be as well. He felt it in his heart that she was the reason he was alive. He crossed his arms to stop from splitting open the stitches in his palms again.

Standing there watching, he felt like two separate people, the one filled with hate, and the other desperately needing love. It was driving him mad. He watched Ronnie show her how to throw a punch and he wished it was him she was hitting. Shame driving him to his knees outside the window. He felt a wild cry ripping through his body though it only came out as a pathetic mewl.

He felt hands on him. It was her. Shit. Her skin was on his, and at the contact sobs tore out of his chest in agony. Her touch both giving him a reason to live and one to die. He didn't have the strength to pull away from her, and he also knew that her touch was keeping the darkness at bay even though it wanted to take over.

She pulled him off the ground his upper body resting against her and held him while he sobbed. He desperately wanted to run away, embarrassed to have this happening. When it came to her touch though, he was powerless. He felt the purity of her soul and he was terrified he would ruin it. Mar the perfection of that light.

"Ssshhh, Jax. I've got you," she murmured to him. Her voice the only sound he wanted to hear for the rest of his life. "I'm not letting this beat you, I've got you." She kissed his head, and the love he felt her filling him with, flared to life and he squeezed her to him. The next second pushing her away and shooting to his feet as he scrambled to get away before the darkness took over.

He didn't make it far, stumbling over his own feet and felt the darkness creep in. "Oh, I don't fucking think so," Jax heard Airiella yell.

"Baby girl, no!" Smitty shouted running out of the house. "Don't pull it!"

Jax felt himself losing control, snarling as he brought himself upright again, then found himself on the ground as the most intoxicating feeling of love swamped through his body rendering him useless. It was pure light. It hurt, and it healed, and it fought against the darkness and Jax surrendered to it.

I looked back at Ronnie whose face was open in shock at the scene before him. "I told you he was out here."

"What happened to him?" he asked as I sagged from the energy loss.

"He tried to fight it, but it hates me," I said, recalling the emotions as they tumbled around in him. "He doesn't believe in himself enough to hold it back."

"Sounds a little like you," Smitty said carefully.

"Don't." I warned. "In answer to your unasked question, no I didn't pull anything from him. I fed him my energy instead, and I really need to sit down now."

Ronnie picked me up ignoring my protestations that I could walk just fine and carried me back into the gym and sat me down in the one chair in the room. "Are you okay?" he asked me as he checked me over.

"I am, it just took more energy than I thought it would to stop him," I answered. Remembering the disturbing feeling of the darkness fighting me. "It's all still there in him, but I'm in there too. For now, at least, until he wakes up. That was just a stop gap, I think. It's what I will have to do on locations where that happens. If I pull it on a filming location, then we will need to get me somewhere fast to get it out of me. I do not want that filmed."

Smitty paled at the thought. "Hell no. No."

Ronnie looked between the two of us. "Anyone going to tell me about that?"

I looked at him sadly. "Not right now. Can we call it a day with this? Resume tomorrow? Jax needs to be brought back inside and probably laid down somewhere comfortable."

"Aedan and I will get him to his room," Smitty said walking out of the gym fast.

"How'd you know he was out there?" Ronnie finally asked me.

"I felt him. I felt the energy inside him. I knew what was happening. Ronnie, this is hard for him. I know it's hard for you guys too, but he's literally at war with himself in there. This thing he calls darkness wants to destroy him as much as it wants to destroy me." I struggled to explain what I had felt.

He nodded at me. "I know. We were hoping the tough love angle would make him more inclined to fight it. He's shown more change since we started that, but now I'm afraid we will push him over the edge."

"I don't have an answer for that. It's potent though. Like a hopeless situation that was given more devastating news. It's physically hurting him too." I mentally sorted through it all.

"Father Roarke put holy water on his head," Ronnie told me. "It was ugly."

I couldn't hold my reaction in at the thought of the holy water and my skin broke out in goosebumps making me shiver. "When I open my senses and I look for ways to help people, I see all these strands of emotions, they show in different colors, different shades for different people, and I can feel what each emotion is. For example, right now, looking at you, I see love, fear, hope, anger, pain, confusion, lust and just a strand that is pure energy. The thickest strand right now is fear." I pulled on it and saw his eyes widen. "I just took a little of it from you, did you feel it?"

"Yeah," he said in wonder. "It didn't hurt though."

"It wouldn't, it's not a permanent emotion embedded in you. It comes and goes with events." I tugged on the energy and he shook a little. "What did that feel like?"

"There was a little pain, but nothing awful," he said.

"That was a permanent one for you. I just call it your energy, it's there every time I've looked at you like this. I think that would be similar to what this darkness is in Jax. It's cemented itself to him, though because it has bad intentions, it would hurt a lot worse." I switched the flow of energy and fed into the strand of lust.

His eyes went dark and pupils dilated, and his body

reacted. "Um, whatever you did had a particular reaction in me," he stammered.

"I fed the lust strand I saw," I explained. I switched and fed my own love into his love strand. I smiled as a dopey look flooded his face and everything else faded away.

"That's fucking amazing," he breathed and moved to pull me down onto him. "Do more of that."

I laughed. "That's what I just did to Jax and he blacked out. I showed you this so you understand just how I can help and what it feels like to you. It will feel differently for the others. What I just gave you, was my own love. It's the only thing I think I can fight that darkness with."

"Well, no shit. Everything else went away when you did that, the only thing I felt was overwhelming love, light, warmth. It like, I don't know, filled all the corners with this pure feeling. I can't even find words for it. Why would a feeling like that make him black out?" Ronnie shook his head.

"Because of that dark energy in him. It fights back. It's warring against what I am feeding to Jax and pulls all his energy to fight it. I think all I did was shove so much in there that it just suppressed it. He may very well wake up in a complete rage, I don't know. That's why I think it's just a stop-gap. It will work on sight when filming, but if I have to feed as much into him as I just did, he will pass out. That's my best guess anyway." I really had no idea what else to do other than pull it.

"If you had started sooner than you did, do you think it would have had a different outcome?" Ronnie asked thoughtfully.

"Possibly. It will take me being around him more to know for sure, and I'd feel better about it if he knew what we were doing. The last thing he needs right now is to feel like a science experiment. I know how awful that feels. He already doesn't feel like he has worth," I admitted to Ronnie. "I know that feeling too."

Ronnie's face clouded up, "How can he feel like that

though? We are all still here with him.”

“It's what that stuff in him is doing to him. It's toxic. It is quite literally killing off the humanity in him. Destroying who he is.” I spoke the harsh words as gently as I could.

“Smitty said to not pull when he came running out, what would have happened if you had?” Ronnie gazed at me intently.

I tried to find a way to answer that as vaguely as possible while still being honest. “I don't know. I can say with certainty that it would have physically hurt him. For him, it would have been okay for the short term as he probably would have felt more like himself, but I don't know how fast it's multiplying in him, so it could be for nothing. For myself, well, it would have been bad, and I don't think I'm quite ready yet to go through it again. I need a couple more days of rest.”

Ronnie eyed me with suspicion. “You are holding back. I know it's bad based off Smitty's reaction in your hotel room, and the tone of voice he used out here.”

“Give it time Ronnie,” I said and leaned into him.

He held me to him. “I'm not going to like it, am I?”

“No,” I said truthfully. “I'm fairly sure it will change you like it has Smitty. How, I don't know yet, but it will.”

“Does it change you?” he asked softly.

I nodded. “I don't know the long term affects yet; we'll see. Short, easy answer is yes.”

He studied me carefully, penetrating green eyes probing my face. “It changes you, but does it cost you?”

I considered the question. “It's one and the same, I think.” I brushed the hair back from his forehead. “Pulling energy comes at a price for me no matter what type it is. The release isn't always painful for me though, like with the stuff Jax has. On a normal release for me, it's freeing. Just letting go. The cost comes for me if I hold on to it for too long. It starts to affect me. I lose sleep, become irritable, joints hurt, things like that. The first time I pulled that energy from Winnie, it made me sick. It didn't happen as fast as it did this last go around. Winnie told me that if I didn't get it out of me, I would become fallen. That what she calls my glow was turning gray. I haven't pieced it all together yet, but I am getting a better picture of it all." He sat quietly and rubbed my arm.

The tingle of his skin on mine reminded me that at some point I would have to talk to him about this connection too. Right now, I just wanted to enjoy being held, so I snuggled into him. "Let's go back to the house," he suggested, his voice strained.

"What's wrong?" I pulled away.

"Nothing wrong, per se, just, um, rather uncomfortable," he stammered looking at his crotch.

I bit back a smile and stood up, holding my hand out to him. He grabbed it and almost pulled me off balance as he leveraged himself up. "Let me rest before I tackle that," I joked.

The grin on his face as he threw his arm around my shoulder and we walked out of the gym had me feeling a lot better. The connection with him was definitely a lot more emotional than the one I had with the others. The one with Jax was on a whole different planet.

By the time they got Jax back to his bed he had started to wake up. Smitty checked him over for any injuries but didn't see any. He checked his hands, the stitches still held. Mentally though, Jax was in rough shape and Smitty knew it.

"What did she do to me?" Jax asked roughly. His eyes lighter than Smitty had seen them in years, though it was fading before his eyes.

"I'm not sure exactly, but she didn't pull anything from you," Smitty told him.

"You know how the story of the Grinch says his heart grew three sizes? That's what it felt like. I was overcome with love like I had never felt before." Jax's voice held awe.

"I'd consider that a blessing then," Smitty said a

little harshly, biting back the need to tell him he didn't deserve her love.

"It was and it wasn't. The darkness was pushed back by it, but it's so angry in me that I feel like I'm going to puke again. Is she okay?" Jax rubbed his hands over his face.

"Are you asking out of concern because you care, or because you are hoping she isn't?" Smitty asked slowly.

"Concern. I'm still riding high on what she did to me, slowly coming down now. I don't want to hurt her, please believe me, Art," Jax said solemnly, his brown eyes holding truth in them.

Surprised by Jax calling him Art, Smitty accepted the statement as true. "Want to eat some dinner?"

"No, I think I should stay alone for a bit to see how this will play out. Do we have any snacks you can bring up? I'd rather keep this on the safe side."

Impressed with the sudden clarity Jax was showing, Smitty just got up and went to the kitchen to grab a handful of things to bring up. He grabbed a few waters and a soda for him as well. He saw Ronnie leading Airiella back to the house and he let out a sigh of relief he didn't know he'd been holding back.

Smitty dropped the snacks off for Jax and closed the door behind him as he headed back down. He met Airiella at the bottom of the stairs and gave her a bone crushing hug, happy that she hadn't pulled that energy and had to go through that horror show again.

"I'm going to order pizza for dinner, any special requests?" Smitty asked.

"Can you order from somewhere that has a salad too? If Ronnie is going to be torturing me, I need clean food." She smiled gently, and Ronnie laughed.

"You got it, babe. Ronnie? Any requests? Aedan," he yelled up the stairs.

"Meat for me," Ronnie said.

"What is your problem now?" Aedan popped up at the top of the stairs.

"I'm ordering pizza, you guys want anything special?" Smitty asked.

"We're easy, we'll eat whatever," Aedan responded and disappeared back into his room.

"Meat pizza it is then," Smitty said, pulling out his phone and ordering online. "Any particular dressing you want, baby girl?"

"Hmmm, vinaigrette please," she said.

"Done deal, it'll be here in about forty minutes," Smitty said. "Plenty of time for you to de-sweat."

"I thought you liked me sweaty," she joked as she headed up the stairs.

Smitty let a gruff laugh out, "I do, I just like the sweat I cause better than the Ronnie sweat. His just stinks."

He headed back to the kitchen as their laughter faded up the stairs. He was thankful, this little experiment could have ended so much worse than it had. It gave him hope.

Ronnie showered quickly, his mind going over everything Airiella had told him, and remembering the way it felt when she did her thing. Gave him a new respect for what Jax was dealing with, especially after feeling pain when she pulled on his energy.

It was concerning and a little scary, he admitted to himself. While he didn't know many details of what happened when she released the energy the last time, the fact that it cost her made him pause. He had a big desire to protect her, and logic told him that nothing he could do would help with this. The haunted look he remembered on Smitty's face still hung in his mind.

He needed to read some legends about angels and their abilities and find the common thread among them. He knew the commonality between stories would likely be rooted in fact. Fact would help him learn what he and the others could do to make this easier on both her and Jax.

He remained preoccupied throughout dinner with trying to come up with a plan of action and missed a lot of the jokes that got flung around the table, from Aedan and Mags having dinner with Airiella's family.

He excused himself after eating and went to his room to start researching the stories he had found about angels. He lost himself in the work and the stories, fascinated in what he was reading. If even a fraction of it was true, she was more than remarkable. Hours after he started, he fell asleep, his head rolling to the side as the battery in his laptop drained.

Chapter Eight

I settled into bed alone, a little grateful for the chance to just settle. I was bone weary. The boxing moves Ronnie had shown me wore me out fast, but also ignited a sense of satisfaction as I did them. The episode with Jax could have been so much worse than it was, but my brain latched on to the way he had held on to me. The way it had felt touching him, being close to him.

I got up and opened my window, needing air all of a sudden. Aedan had called the breeze the Santa Ana winds. Whatever it was, it was nice. I sucked in big lungful's of the air and settled back on the bed, on top of the blankets, my body flushed from thinking about how Jax held me.

I drifted off and felt a chill enter the room. It reminded me of when I was at home and in that gray nightmare. The difference was that I could see this time though. Jax was there, looking all around him, but he couldn't see me. He was being stalked by a figure all in black. I didn't want to call it a person because the shape was shifting as it moved, only vaguely resembling a person.

I didn't know where we were, a street somewhere,

could be anywhere. The landscape fading into the background, trees on the side of the road we were on. No other sign of life, no sky, no moon, no stars. The air was still and the sound dampened, though the only sounds I could hear were that of Jax's footsteps and both of us breathing. The dark mass was menacing in feeling, and Jax kept backing away from it, a look of revulsion on his face. I kept calling to him, though he never glanced my way once. I didn't think he could hear me, or even knew that I was there.

With a start, I realized that the mass was the darkness inside him, coming to life in his nightmares. It didn't appear to be solid, just a swirling shape that emanated evil intentions. I stepped between Jax and the mass, hoping to save Jax from whatever it had planned for him. Though Jax couldn't see me, the mass could. I didn't know if it had eyes, but it knew I was there. The wave of hate that hit me staggered my steps, and I almost tripped, but I managed to keep my eyes glued to its movements.

Foreboding feelings of sickness tried to take root in me, but couldn't get past my walls. It just rolled over my skin feeling like it was coating me in tar. Jax still backed away even though the mass hadn't moved towards me again. It couldn't get around me and its focus was still on Jax. I could feel it's need to take him down and make him suffer. It was sickening.

The vile, black oily feeling was creeping across my skin, feeling like it was leaving tracks. I had no idea how to stop this, or get Jax out of here without opening my senses and filling him with love again. The thought of taking my walls down though, set my instincts on edge and I didn't think it was safe for either of us.

The sound of Jax moving away behind me stopped, and I didn't feel like I could take my eyes off this sinister thing in front of me. I felt the energy shift from behind me as Jax weakened against the emotional onslaught taking place against him. It was almost as if this mass was feeling glee as Jax faltered again.

"No! Jax, fight it!" I shouted, hoping like mad that he could hear me. No response. My vision swam and I dared to glance behind me and saw him on his knees, his face showing agony. That was all it took for it to get around me. That split second I took my attention off of it, it slid around me and surrounded Jax.

I watched in horror as it consumed him. Its arms reaching into Jax and pulling out pieces of his soul and shredding it like an old piece of paper, the tatters falling to the ground around him, his life force fading from each little piece. A scream tore through my body as I bolted to him. "No! You can't have him!" I screamed, my throat feeling like it was bleeding at the power of my screams. I thrust my hand through the vile mass, its icy form wrapping around my arm as I reached desperately for Jax and grasping at his shirt to pull towards me. "He doesn't belong to you!" I yelled as I retched violently at the feelings trying to overpower me, take my will from me.

A force blasted through me as my skin made contact with Jax and I was thrown backwards, my head slamming into the ground hard enough to make my ears ring as the mass was pushed away and Jax saw me, terror etched in the lines on his gray face. "No!" he screamed.

I bolted awake at the sound of my door crashing open and Ronnie and Smitty bolting into my room. "It's a nightmare, angel, it's a nightmare." Ronnie grabbed my hand and pressed it against his face, his stubble rubbing my palm.

My body was still held in the grip of the nightmare and I yanked my hand away and tore across the hall to Jax's room where I could hear him yelling in fear. I pushed the door open and flew over to the bed where he was thrashing around, his movements wild and frantic. "She's mine, get away from her!" he shouted. Shit, he was fighting for me.

Ronnie pushed his way into the room, "Angel, don't get near him, it's not safe when he's like that. He'll be okay," Ronnie said gently. I pushed him back.

"Get out," I told them both, my tone raw. "Just go. I was in there with him, I know what he is seeing," my voice thick with emotion as I watched Jax flail around, while feeling like I failed him for not protecting him.

I reached out and caught his hand on a backswing and held it tight between my own. The feeling of our skin touching stilled his movements but didn't bring him out. I heard Ronnie and Smitty leave the room, and I held on to his hand tightly. I leaned against the bed, out of reach of his limbs in case he moved again and familiarized myself with the darkness in here.

His pulse was racing, his hand had its own heartbeat pulsing against his stitches. He was still crying out, but after a few minutes he started to calm down. His voice was getting softer and the tension bleeding out of him, bit by bit. I risked opening my senses and grabbed for that strand of love and fed as much as I could into it until he slipped into an easy sleep, his body now quiet and still.

I couldn't risk pulling the fear from him, much less the energy that simmered there in plain sight. It knew I was here, and it's hate for me was a living, breathing thing. Jax had full control of himself now, and I stayed right where I was, holding his hand until I drifted off to sleep too, holding his hand against me in case that shit tried to take him again. I was prepared to fight this thing even if Jax couldn't.

I woke up as the sun was starting to rise and turned to check on Jax, seeing him clutching a green pillow in his free hand. He was still sleeping peacefully, and I did a quick scan with my senses to get a read on his emotions to see if that darkness was just waiting to rear its ugly head. He was calm, so I reluctantly let him go and snuck out of his room, my body protesting at the movement I introduced after being in suck an awkward position for so long.

I dropped into my bed and hoped for a couple hours of sleep before I had to be up again. An uneasy feeling lay in the pit of my stomach as I drifted off. I wasn't used to being hated with such force.

Ronnie hadn't been able to go back to sleep after the screams he had heard from Airiella while she had been in the grips of that nightmare. The sounds coming out of her flat out haunted him. He had almost crashed into Smitty as he ran out of his room and the look on Smitty's face was pure terror. It told him he had heard those screams before.

Neither of them wanted to leave her in there with Jax, but her tone of voice left no room for argument and she was fierce. They sat outside the door until all was quiet and they thought she was out of danger, also a little impressed at how quickly she was able to calm him down. He'd never calmed before when they tried it.

He decided to go through the songs that Smitty had copied from her iPod and he made a workout list for her. She had some damn good music on there, though it was quite an eclectic mix. The playlist was about 3 hours' worth of songs which was plenty of time, and he chose songs that had a good pace and rhythm to them. He created a cool down list of some more relaxing ones and it looked like she already had a meditation play list, and one for yoga.

He snuck though the connecting door to Jax's room to check on them and saw her out cold, bunched up on the floor against the bed holding his hand to her face. Jax was gripping that green pillow in his other hand, but both were quiet and asleep. She was going to be sore when she woke up from sleeping like that.

Ronnie went back to his room and tried to sleep, and instead just tossed and turned. Every time his eyes drifted shut his brain replayed those screams and it jarred him awake and set his pulse rate racing. He paused to think about how he reacted to her, the feelings she brought out in him. He hadn't questioned them once, even though he was not a love at first sight type of person. In her case, that's exactly what it had been.

Finally, at dawn, he heard Airiella go back to her

room, and then he heard Smitty follow after her. Ronnie waited a few minutes then followed. He opened the door and saw Smitty curled up behind her, so Ronnie crawled over them both and sandwiched her between them. With Airiella near, he fell into a deep sleep.

I woke up snug between two gorgeous men. I can't complain about that. Both were still asleep and I couldn't move without waking them so I chose to stay right where I was. It wasn't a hardship. I had gotten about three hours of a good deep sleep, probably because of these two and I hoped that Jax was still doing okay.

My body still ached and I needed to stretch. I tried to do it carefully, though they hadn't left me much room. Smitty had his arm wrapped around my belly and curled his body into mine. Ronnie had pushed himself into the front of me and wrapped my arm around him. My palm was resting flat against his magnificent abs under his shirt.

I slowly moved my fingers letting them trace his muscles, I mean come on, what's a girl to do? He was beautiful, a work of art. And the way he felt under my hand was intoxicating. His hand moved and stilled mine and his low voice warned me, "Keep that up, and you will be getting a different type of work out this morning."

I grinned and wiggled, momentarily forgetting the man behind me until his arm tightened around me, "I second that, baby girl."

I pushed myself up and climbed over them since they were both now awake, and couldn't help myself. "Show me, use each other as the examples of what I can expect."

The incredulous looks on their faces had me doubled over in laughter and I ran for the bathroom before I peed myself. I was met at the door with a smoldering Smitty as he leaned down and kissed me breathless. "Sorry for crowding you. Those screams last night wreaked havoc on me." He kissed me again and went in to the bathroom closing the door behind him.

"Put the seat down when you are done," I called

after him.

Ronnie was sitting on the edge of my bed sulking. "Where's my kiss?"

I gave him a crooked smile, "He's in the bathroom."

Ronnie tackled me backwards and planted a big wet sloppy kiss on me. "That's what you get for those comments. Be ready in thirty minutes for your workout." He left going back to his own room.

I was wiping my face off when Smitty came back out. "You doing okay?"

I nodded at him. "Sore from sleeping in the position I was in, but I'm fine."

He misunderstood me. "I'm sorry, I was just worried."

"No, not here, in Jax's room," I corrected him. "I fell asleep sitting against his bed."

"Give him space today," he cautioned me. I'd already planned on that. I'd leave it up to him if he wanted to be around me or not.

"I'm planning on it. I have to go be tortured by Ronnie anyway. Then is it you or Aedan?"

"I'll check with him. Maybe both. Did you know that Winnie can't get through because of these necklaces from Kalisha?" he pointed to his neck.

"No. I guess I didn't really think about that. She's a spirit, so it makes sense." Her disappearance made a lot more sense to me now.

"I don't really want to take it off too much," Smitty mused. "I can hear her sometimes, but from what she said when she was spying on me in the shower, that was hard for her."

I giggled. "She was spying on you?"

"Scared the shit out of me!" he said laughing.

"It's kinda funny," I told him. "I don't blame her for looking." I winked at him and started to change. He ran his hands over my bare skin and our connection sparked.

"Every time I touch you, I am filled with the most incredible feeling of love," he said into my ear, his stubble scraping my ear and sending chills down my spine.

"Oh yeah?" I purred. These men and their sexiness were going to be the death of me.

"It's weird, because I'm not a very emotional person. I feel love of course, I'm not a robot. I'm more led by logic. Then comes you, and every time I am around you, I'm fighting this fear that I could lose you. I could lose this feeling that you give me that is not like anything I've ever felt before. Chases all logic right out of my head." He nuzzled my neck.

Speechless, I could only stare at him. His voice shaky as he spoke his fear. I loved the feeling of stubble on men and I stroked my palm over his face trying to soothe him.

"Baby girl, I'm having a hard time with this. Since that chapel, all I can think of is the fear I had when I lost you. It controls me at times, and last night, those screams..." he trailed off. "I wanted to snatch you up and just run. Walking out of Jax's room and leaving you there took me to a dark place. Then when I crawled into bed with you and touched you, it was gone."

"Smitty," I started but had no idea what to follow with.

He shook his head at me. "I'll be okay. It's just going to take some getting used to. This emotion thing isn't easy for me."

I pulled my clothes on before my body decided on a different plan of action and hugged him. "I'm sorry."

"I'm not. It's a different world you opened my eyes to. Adjustment will happen, just bear with me if I act like a caveman." I nodded into his chest and he dropped a kiss on my head. "Go get sweaty."

I smiled a half smile and pulled him out of my room behind me and headed to the kitchen. Ronnie had made me a smoothie that didn't look all that appetizing. Smitty laughed and poured himself a cup of coffee. I smelled the smoothie and took a tentative sip. It wasn't bad.

"He knows his stuff, you'll be in good hands," he

told me and walked back upstairs. His ginger hair glinting in the morning sun. I wanted to follow him and undress him.

I drank it up fast and headed out to the garage before I gave in to my desire. Ronnie met me halfway. "I'm going to have you do whatever yoga routine you do to stretch out first. You'll probably be sore from sleeping on the floor the way you did."

Yoga. That I could easily do. I put myself through the poses to my own chosen yoga music playing through the docking station that was in there and went through five minutes of meditation. Ronnie threw me a bottle of water telling me to drink it up.

He came over to me and wrapped both my hands and then helped me into boxing gloves. He walked over to the docking station and switched the music to a different playlist with a more up-tempo beat. Surprisingly, all songs that I loved. He took me through the different punches and kicks and then started me working on combos of the two, hitting pads that he had on. He switched me to one of the bags and had me go harder and harder.

I was dripping sweat like a faucet. My body was screaming. He then took me through some resistance exercises and weight training. By the end of two hours my entire body was vibrating, and adrenaline was coursing through my veins, but I couldn't have stood even if I wanted to.

"You did good," he told me as he forced more water on me.

"Good? I can't even stand," I panted.

He laughed, "Give it a minute. You've got good muscle tone. Your legs are strong as hell," he said and ran his hand down my sweaty thighs. I think even my nipples were sweating.

"I feel like a salt lick," I groaned. His touch felt too good, but I felt absolutely gross I was so sweaty.

"Keep drinking water, you are going to be sore tomorrow."

"I'm sore now!" I argued.

"No whining, I could have worked you harder," he chuckled.

"Oh God, no. Please no," I whimpered.

He pulled me up and smacked me on my ass. "Go shower, salt lick."

"That means I have to walk up the stairs, can't you just hose me off," I pleaded, and he burst out laughing. I thought he was actually going to do it, so I headed to the house.

I passed Mags on the stairs and she just laughed at the sight of me. "I'm going to make some sandwiches for lunch, you want one?"

I nodded mutely and managed to get to my room and stripped the soaking wet clothes off me. Gross. The hot shower felt good and I was hungry. Ravenously hungry. I took some anti-inflammatories and headed down to the kitchen, seeing Jax for the first time. Mags placed plates in front of us both.

I gave a hesitant smile though he didn't respond. He looked okay, if somewhat blank. Aedan gave a slight shake of his head, so I left it alone and used my remaining energy to chew. "Smitty and I are going to team up today and we are going to go over the locations with you and sort of take you through what we do."

"Sounds good to me. I can sit, right?" I asked with a mouthful of food.

Mags laughed. "Ronnie's a good trainer, but he's tough."

"No shit." I swallowed and drank another full bottle of water.

"Ronnie worked with you today?" Jax asked. I nodded. "Fighting?" I nodded again.

He went back to eating, so I drank my next bottle of water down and didn't say anything. Jax finished and got up and left. "He doesn't remember," Aedan said softly so his voice didn't carry.

Ah. I understood now. That was fine. Smitty came

down and we got to work, three hours later my brain was full to the brim and I was struggling to keep up after not much sleep and an intense workout. They took pity on me and we called it a day.

I trudged back up to my room and curled up on the bed with the orange pillow Jax picked out for me and pulled the throw over my legs. That was all it took for me to nod off.

The week passed by me in a blaze of the same routine. Nightmares, sleeping either on the floor of Jax's room holding his hand, or curled up behind him touching him and sneaking out before he woke up. Getting a few hours of sleep before Ronnie worked me into the ground, then learning from Smitty and Aedan.

Jax popped up here and there and hung around in the background a bit, he added a few things when he thought Aedan or Smitty left things out, but for the most part he remained uninvolved and didn't remember the nightmares. He knew he had them, however, my part in them stayed blank for him. I was no stranger to nightmares, so I understood how he felt. I wasn't sure how I felt about him not knowing I was a part of that with him though.

Chapter Nine

Jax yawned again. The nightmares were relentless for him this past week. He was exhausted. He'd trailed after Airiella and the guys as they trained her, but he didn't get too close. She had that magnetism that kept him in the vicinity. Needing to be close to her.

He noticed when he got too close, that the darkness in him fought to take over and his rude comments had caused both Smitty and Ronnie to get pissed. Aedan hadn't spoken much to him at all, nor had Mags. It bothered him, so he made more effort to be relaxed around them. He knew he was on a slippery slope.

Aedan only asked about the nightmares once. Jax knew he'd screamed while in them, because his throat hurt. They had to have heard him. Usually, when that happened, he found one of them in his room keeping watch. Not this week. He'd been alone every morning. He feared that was his future, alone.

While he knew that something within the nightmares had changed, he didn't know what. He couldn't remember them in the morning. He did take that as a blessing in disguise. There were only two days left until they flew out for their first shoot on location, and Jax admitted to himself that he was nervous.

He had joined Airiella and Ronnie in the gym for their workout, but he kept to the other side to give them space. He admired the strength she showed as Ronnie put her through the routine that wore Jax out. She held up, and even though her form wasn't perfect, she displayed more than passable skills in holding her own. It was impressive.

Jax noticed how tired she'd been looking, though she didn't let it slow her down. Maybe Ronnie was working her too hard? He'd ask, and he was sure Ronnie would get pissed since he hadn't shown any interest in her wellbeing since she'd gotten here. Well, not to the others anyway.

Jax switched to pushups as Ronnie led her through a punch and kick combo, her hits thudding against Ronnie's pads with force. She was flushed and dripping with sweat, the humidity on her body causing her hair to curl in a wild mess around her face. He knew he was staring; he couldn't help it.

Jax changed to dead lifts as Ronnie now switched it up and had her doing jumping jacks. Which Jax found thoroughly distracting, the way her breasts bounced with each jump. He craved her touch again and found himself moving closer to them. With each small step, the darkness grew.

Jax slammed his hand into a bag in anger, catching Ronnie off guard who spun around to look at him. Jax hit the bag again, his eyes glued to Airiella, so he didn't notice Ronnie come up alongside of him and yank him backwards. Pulling him farther away from Airiella, who called to him on some deep base level.

Fury rolled through him, but Ronnie ignored it, and started wrapping Jax's hands and then angrily shoved gloves on his hand. "Don't be an ass." Ronnie's voice took on a sharp edge.

Jax unleashed his tenuous hold on the anger and took it out on the bag, his eyes shifting from the bag to

Airiella and back again. He grew angrier as he watched her step closer to Ronnie and say something quietly into his ear. He'd never been jealous like this before. He wasn't sure at first where the anger came from, but the closer she got to Ronnie, the angrier he got.

Ronnie was shaking his head hard at her, but she didn't want to accept it. Jax saw her pull the pads off Ronnie's hand and he shook in anger as Ronnie put them on her. Jax froze as she walked up to him, violent emotions clashing inside and his ears buzzing as Ronnie took up a position behind her.

She was talking to him, what was she saying? "What?" Jax asked.

"Battle me," she challenged.

"What?" Jax repeated stupidly. "You want to spar with me?"

"Yes," she told him, smirking.

The darkness rose to the challenge and as she held up the pads, Jax lost control. He hit hard, but she just absorbed it, rooted in place, Ronnie standing guard, his face furious. The darkness clawed at him, trying to take over, seeing its chance to end this.

Jax stepped back, his body preparing to kick, when she lashed out with her legs, catching him off guard in a side kick followed by a roundhouse. He staggered back, shocked at the force she displayed. She easily ducked his jabs and followed through with more kicks that he was certain would leave bruises. With each kick she landed, he was able to fight back the darkness in him.

"I can see it behind your eyes," she taunted him. The darkness swelling inside him responded, pushing Jax right out of the way. "You think I am going to let you beat him?" she snarled, her own anger a match for what he was feeling. "Go back to hell!" she shouted and kicked so hard she knocked him down.

The last kick jarred something in Jax and he snapped back to himself pushing the darkness away. "Are you fighting for me?" he asked stunned as he tried to stand up.

"Of course, I am." She stopped and looked at him. "Is it you right now?" she stepped closer, but Ronnie hauled her back away.

"Look in my eyes and tell me what you see," Jax said carefully, getting to his feet. He was desperately trying to show her his need for her, he wanted that to be what she saw. He wanted her to understand. He didn't want her to see the parts of him that wanted to kill her. "Can you see me? Can you see me revealed beneath this other shit?" his voice was rough, and he swallowed trying to ease it.

"Jax," she said softly and stepped to him again, pulling away from Ronnie, her eyes riveted on his. "I see you, and I see it." She reached for him and the darkness snapped into place as he roared, hatred washing over his body. Whatever progress he thought he'd made, disappearing in a blink.

Ronnie flung himself at her knocking her to the ground as Jax's fist sailed over their heads, the punch missing and throwing him off balance. He'd thrown a punch at her. Sickness rose up in him at the thought. She shoved Ronnie off her and launched to her feet and kicked him hard in the solar plexus.

The air whooshed out of Jax's lungs and she shouted, "Get out of him, you fucking bastard! I will take you down and kill you!"

Something must have changed on Jax's face, because Ronnie stood and flung her over his shoulder and marched her right out of the garage, as Jax lost all control of his body and in a fit of violence, raged against the bags.

He came to with a furious Smitty standing in the corner shooting him a look of death. "You done?"

Jax nodded and silently held up his hands for Smitty to pull the gloves off him. Smitty did and whacked him in the head with each one. "Yeah, I know. I'm a fucking jerk."

"You're lucky Ronnie didn't go after you," Smitty spit out, still glaring.

"It wasn't me," Jax said weakly.

"That's the only reason he didn't. I'd steer clear for an hour or so until he calms down. To be fair, he's just as angry at Airiella," Smitty said with a hint of a smile. "He's being more generous than I would have been."

"I don't want to hurt her. Did she really challenge that darkness in me?" Jax felt the urge to break down in tears as he remembered swinging at her.

At that, Smitty did laugh. "That's what Ronnie said. He said it damn near gave him a heart attack. She's brave."

"She's fucking fierce," Jax said. "That took some serious work on my part to fight that back, but it still took over me a couple times," he said, his tone sad that he'd lost once again.

"You'll have bruises," Smitty pointed out to the darkening spots on his torso.

"She's got a damn strong kick," Jax agreed, looking down.

"Go get changed, you and I are disappearing today. Give her some space. We'll go to the studio and get the equipment packed up and ready." Smitty walked back to the house with him.

Jax agreed and went and did what he was told. Shame and revulsion at his actions pulling him apart.

I was so angry for losing control of my emotions like that, and I was even more pissed that Ronnie took me away the he did. He couldn't feel the emotions that had been tearing though Jax like I could. It pissed me off how much he was hurting. I saw the way he was fighting it.

Whatever. I tore my clothes off and got in bath needing to soak and hoping it would calm me down. Jax would be my undoing. He got to me in a way no one else could, and I didn't want to feel anything for him. I wanted to be indifferent to him. For him to just be another person I helped. He wasn't though, and I knew it with every fiber of my being. But I didn't like it.

I turned the jets of the tub on and let my head rest

on the edge, thankful for this added little bonus to my bathroom. The jasmine oil I added to the water was soothing, just as much as the jets were. Happy to be alone for a bit I allowed myself to relax.

Only to have that peace disturbed by the sudden yelling of a ghost that had been missing out of my life. "Airy!" Winnie shouted, making me jump and slosh water all over the floor. "You finally took that damn necklace off!"

"Hi Winnie, nice to see you too. How are you? How you've been? Where have you been?!" I snarled at her in frustration.

"The last time you released that energy, when you were out, Kalisha made necklaces for the team. She had taken yours back to trade it out for one similar to what the others have, but yours is extra. It's been touched by Degataga, Taklishim, Aminda, Tama, Onida, Father Roarke, and Kalisha. They all added to it. Those necklaces have been keeping me away. I can get through, but only if I use all my energy, and that's just my voice. The stones are activated by touching your skin, and they only work for those who they were made for," Winnie said in a rush of words.

"Huh," I said. "The thought never even occurred to me that it would keep you away too, at least not until Smitty told me."

"You need to keep it on if you are outside the house. I think you are safe here; they all keep theirs on. Do you believe now in what you are?" Winnie sat on the counter.

"Are you really going to talk about that? That's why you are here?" I felt my irritation grow.

"No, I'm here because I can be. I've missed you. Being stuck in this gray fog has been no fun at all. While I can't see Jax or get through to him, I can still feel his emotions. They've been all over the place, what's been going on?" She ignored my facial expression as she peppered me with questions.

"I don't want to talk about him either," I told her wearily. "In case you haven't noticed, I'm in the bath, trying to relax. Our first shooting location is in a couple of days, Ronnie has been training me and I'm worn out. Not sleeping well because at night I get stuck in the nightmares Jax has, and I have to sneak in there until he calms down, but he doesn't know it."

"Oh. Well, uh, I'm not sure what to say to that. Father Roarke and Taklishim have been working closely to see if they can come up with a better way to help your release. So far, holy water and salt water are their best guesses, and within a circle since it's seeming to get more violent." Winnie filled me in.

"Literally, nothing new then," I said, my tone snarky.

"You are in a mood!" Winnie's eyes got wide.

"Can you blame me?" I closed my eyes, tired of the emotions beating at me.

"No," she said quietly. "Would a movie cheer you up?"

I sighed. "Sure Winnie, if that's what you want."

"I'm trying to think of ways to make you in a better mood." Her face took on a glum look.

"Can it wait until after my bath?"

"Yes!" she sounded more excited now. "Just don't put that necklace back on."

H oney, let's get out of the house awhile," Mags suggested.

"And do what?" Aedan asked, distracted.

"I don't know. Not be here. Grab Ronnie and let's go eat lunch somewhere. He needs to be out of the house too. Airy is pissed as hell at him and he's pouting. She's taking a bath and could probably use some alone time." Mags stroked his back absently.

"Can we go eat teriyaki? I've been craving that." Aedan looked up from his tablet.

Mags laughed. "I don't care as long as it's not inside this house."

"I'll go grab him." Aedan walked out of the office

and upstairs to get Ronnie.

Mags snatched up her purse and the keys ready for a change of scenery. The tension these guys were putting off was suffocating her. Smitty had Jax out for a bit, she wanted out too. Aedan came back down with a mopey Ronnie and she set out to make him smile. Taking their arms, she pulled them out the door.

I spent about an hour in that tub and I think it boiled my brains. Feeling like jelly I dried off and threw on some sweats and an old t-shirt I sometimes slept in. Total comfort. "Winnie!" I called. "I'm ready." She popped in as I headed down the stairs to the kitchen.

I hoped there was microwave popcorn in there somewhere. I wasn't a big popcorn fan, but it sounded like exactly what I wanted. I searched through the closet sized pantry and found a box of the good stuff. Loaded with salt and oil, guilty pleasure here I come. I fished out a Diet Coke from the fridge and was almost on cloud nine.

"Can we watch something with that guy you said was so hot?" Winnie asked.

"What guy, there's a lot of hot ones." I laughed.

"Whoever you said Ronnie had a body like..." She trailed of as she tried to remember.

"Jason Momoa," I said salivating. "Sounds good to me." I pulled the bag of popcorn out of the microwave and dumped it in a bowl, grabbed my soda and headed to the TV room.

"Oh yay!" Winnie's enthusiasm was catching.

I had the TV room to myself, for once, since everyone was gone, so I settled in to indulge my eyes on some unattainable man candy. Plus, Winnie had no idea who Jason Momoa was, and that was just unacceptable that she be denied views of that very delicious, lick-able man. Girl time.

I scrolled through Netflix until I found Justice League. "Okay Winnie, sit back and feast your eyes on yum," I said to get her attention. She came over and sat down next to me eyeballing my popcorn jealously and I started watching the movie. As his scene in the beginning came on, her eyes got wide and she shifted closer to the TV. I stifled a laugh. "And that is Jason Momoa!"

Winnie squealed and I laughed at her. "He's hot!" She exclaimed, practically drooling.

"It's Jason Momoa, of course he's hot! Yum, the things I'd do to that man," I sighed.

"Airy, who are you talking to?" Mags asked walking in and sitting in the chair across the room. Guess I wasn't alone in the house anymore. Damn it.

"Um... myself," I stuttered, as Winnie cackled in laughter every time this happened. Mags and the rest still had their necklaces on so Winnie wasn't visible or audible unless she threw all her energy into it. "It's Jason Momoa, doesn't he send your brain a little squirrelly?"

Mags hummed her approval, "I wouldn't kick him out of bed."

"I would even make it to the bed, I'd climb him like a tree before the door even closed," I admitted with zero shame.

"Aw hell, angel. Not you too." Ronnie groaned as he walked in and hung over the back of the couch.

"You're telling me you don't think he's sexy? Your body is ridiculously similar to his, seems hypocritical to me." I looked sideways at Ronnie. Mags nodded along with me from across the room, her eyes glued to the magnificent man on the screen. I looked at Winnie and laughed because she was just as enamored as the rest of us girls.

"I don't get it. If I'm gonna go bi, I'd pick Thor over Aquaman," Ronnie said. Mags raised her eyes at me, wiggling her eyebrows in a silent question that asked when I was going to make my connection with him. I pulled him down over the back of the couch making him land next to me. He threw his arm around me and I leaned my head on his shoulder.

"If it's possible, you just got sexier after that statement, Ronnie," I said as Mags laughed. "Aquaman and

Thor sandwich with Airiella in the middle, that's my dream."

"I agree," both Mags and Winnie said, though only I heard Winnie.

"Really? That's what would make you do a three way?" Ronnie asked me.

"Fuck yeah, my freak side would come screaming to the surface," I quipped, remembering he didn't know about my time with Mags and Aedan yet.

"Think about it, Ronnie, she's slept with all of us already," Mags joked, letting him in on the secret.

Ronnie looked at me with his eyebrows raised, "You slept with Mags and Aedan?"

"She was right between us the whole night," Mags said laughing. "Look at her, I wouldn't kick her out of bed either. Hell, what am I saying? I didn't kick her out of bed."

"Fuck, Smitty needs to put a hidden camera in your room," Ronnie muttered to me.

The rest of the guys walked in then. Fucking great. "Which room am I putting a spy cam in?" Smitty asked, settling on the other side of me. "And do we really need to watch pretty boy Momoa?"

A resounding, "YES!" came from the females in the room.

"In whatever room Airy is sleeping with Mags in," Ronnie deadpanned.

"Yeah, I'd be down to watch that," Smitty replied, earning glares from Aedan and Jax. Jax's response threw me a bit.

"You haven't slept with me, so don't go spreading those rumors Princess," Jax snarled. He was heading into darkness mode, though not fully there yet. I'd already had enough of that darkness in him for the day.

Ronnie and Smitty both stiffened next to me, but I put my hand on each of their arms to calm them, and then stood up and walked slowly over to Jax, swinging my hips. Now everyone was watching me and not the movie. I smiled sweetly, and he missed the edge my smiled hid.

Using my best phone sex voice, I looked in his eyes and said, "Guess what, asshole, I have slept with you. Quite a few times now. Who do you think pulls you safely out of those nightmares? It's me. Who crawls in your bed and holds you until you stop shaking and screaming out? Yep, me again. Who lays there touching you until fall back into a peaceful sleep? Do I need to say it?" I paused, his face registering shock. "Well okay, it's me." I paused again, seeing if he would say anything. "The nights where you are kicking out, I sleep sitting up, propped against your bed, holding your hand until it's all better. Then I sneak out before you wake up, trying to avoid the accusations that I am after something from you. Because guess what else asshole? I'm the only one able to calm you down and pull you out." I stopped, and turned to walk away, then went on, "But honestly, after all the women I've heard talking about how good you were in bed, I wasn't that impressed." I snapped out at him, pushing my hand into his chest, and walked out of the room. Stunned silence the only reply. I smiled as I heard Winnie laughing, calling out after me.

"I wish I had a picture of his face right now!" Can't believe he ruined Jason Momoa for me. Asshole.

No one has to tell me, I know I fucked that up," Jax said, hanging his head. "It just comes out of me with no warning sometimes."

"Well, join me in the club of stupid ass men that pissed off Airiella today," Ronnie said with a smile. "By the way, if we were keeping score, she beat you twice today. In the gym earlier, and just now."

Jax ignored Ronnie. "Was anyone going to tell me about the nightmare thing?"

"You mean that she is the only reason that you are still as much you as you are? She thought it was best to not say anything since you didn't remember. She didn't want you getting mad," Aedan said.

"Is that why she looks so damn tired?" Guilt ate him. That's why he's been feeling more himself lately, he put it together quickly. Damn it. World's biggest selfish asshole, right here.

"Bingo. Good guess," Smitty replied caustically.

"If I ask her out to dinner to talk to her are you guys going to freak out and follow me?" Jax asked grimly.

"Nailed that one too," Ronnie answered with a raised eyebrow.

"Do it here, we'll be somewhere else," Mags volunteered.

"Excuse me?" Smitty interrupted. "He can't be alone with her. It's not safe. For either of them."

"I'll be fine if she does her thing and fills me with that energy first," Jax suggested. "I can fight it off when she does that."

"It also drains her energy," Ronnie informed him.

Mags stepped up, "Let him ask, and let her decide. He's making an effort to mend some fences. If they stay here, we are all close by. We all know she can knock his ass out fast too if she needs to. Airy is not helpless. At all."

Jax rubbed the big bruise on his chest. "No, she's badass without you monkeys helping her."

Ronnie laughed, remembering the kick she delivered. "She got you good."

Jax lifted his shirt to show the bruise. "I'm not arguing. She fought *for* me today, not just fought me. I'd like a chance to at least talk with her without chaperones riding my ass for anything they might misconstrue as something they don't like."

Jax knew that Ronnie would give in, and that Smitty was going to be the hard sell. "You hurt her, I'll hurt you." Smitty glared at Jax.

"Give him a chance," Ronnie said, true to form. "But that statement is true for me too."

"Any advice on how to approach her?" Jax asked hesitantly.

"Don't be a dick would be a start," Aedan put in.

"Helpful. Thanks." Jax shot them all looks before walking out.

Winnie wanted to stay and watch the movie but she felt like Airy needed her, so she followed her out of the house into the backyard where she found Airy sitting in a garden spot on a bench. "Airy," Winnie said gently, feeling the rush of emotions rolling through her friend.

"Winnie," Airy responded trying to be sarcastic but it fell short. She just sounded defeated. "Sorry about that. Something about him always pushes me over the edge I seem to be teetering on lately."

"Personally, I think you handled that beautifully. He truly didn't know that you had been doing that with the nightmares. Nor does he even begin to understand, I don't think anyway, that the reason he hasn't lost himself to this is because of you." Winnie wished she could hug Airy.

"Why do I care?" Airy cried, her tone a mix of frustration and pain.

"Because that's who you are." Winnie stroked her hair.

"It's different with him," Airy argued.

"He's yours, that's why," Winnie whispered, the secret coming out.

Airy shuddered. "He can't be. He hates me."

Winnie laughed. "He doesn't hate you. Not even a little. He's so far gone in love with you the boy is lost."

"Winnie, I know you've been gone a while but I have to believe that in the past twelve years the definition of love hasn't changed. That's not love." Airy closed her eyes.

"Oh Airy, for someone with such an astounding capacity for love you sure are blind when it's looking right at you." Winnie tried some blunt honesty.

"Ronnie loves me. Smitty loves me. Aedan and Mags love me. Jax, despises the sight of me. I know the difference," she insisted.

Winnie moved around in front of her and put her icy hand under Airy's chin. "What if he's just as good at hiding his true feelings as you are?"

Taken aback, Airy flinched. "I don't hide love from people."

"Maybe not love, but you hide everything else," Winnie said gently. "You keep people at an arm's length so you don't have to let them in."

"That's not true, Winnie," she said, her voice lined with raw emotion. "I let Smitty in, trusted him, and it's now changed him forever. I let in Aedan and Mags. I let you dive in my head."

"Smitty's change isn't a bad thing Airy. Ronnie and Jax are the two most emotional connections that you will have. The most powerful." Winnie gentled her tone.

"Yeah, those are the ones that will be able to destroy me in a heartbeat." Jax was doing a good job of it already and they hadn't ever been alone together.

"You don't think Smitty could?" Winnie deciding to keep pushing her.

"I think he could, I just don't think he would," Airy clarified.

"Why don't you want to think that Jax is yours?" Winnie pushed harder.

"Fear maybe. I don't know." This, Winnie knew to be true.

"At some point, for all this to work, you will have to believe. Trust yourself, trust him," Winnie went for broke.

"Stop pushing me Winnie. It's not the time. That's not something you can force. I need to be alone right now. Please understand this isn't personal, I just need some space."

Winnie winced as she saw Airy pull out the necklace that would block her and put it on. She popped back into the gray and prayed. She prayed for Airy to get the answers she needed to move forward, and that she would be okay. She prayed for Jax to find the fortitude to fight this darkness and let her go. She prayed for them both to come through this whole. It was too much to hope that they would come through unscathed.

Jax knew deep in his bones that nothing about this was going to be easy. He also knew that he didn't deserve easy. He was mostly in control of himself right now, so it was better to attempt it while he could. He looked out his window again and saw her on the bench in the garden.

The sun was starting to set and the colors made her look like a celestial being. She had ear buds in, figured that she was listening to music. She was laid out across the bench, and he couldn't tell if her eyes were open or not. He swallowed back the fear that rose up in him and instead focused on the feelings he felt when she touched him.

He buried his face in the green pillow until he felt strong enough to move, and he left his room. Destination, the bench in the garden. Forcing his feet to keep moving he made it outside and stopped. He could see her chest moving as she breathed, but it had a hitch in it. Fuck.

The darkness in him liked seeing that, but Jax pushed it down hard. He didn't like it. He moved forward again and as he got closer, he could see her eyes were closed and her face was streaked with tears. Giant sucker punch to the heart. He knew it was his fault.

He hadn't said anything to announce his presence, but she pulled hear ear buds out and with her eyes still closed and her voice thick she said, "I may have wished for someone to come and save me for once, instead of it always being me that's the one who saves everyone else, but I don't think that person can be you Jax."

Knife to the heart. His knees went weak and he fought for control of his emotions that were a complete shit storm inside him. All of it solidifying the feeling in him that he was no good for her. "I'm willing to try," he said, his voice sounding harsher than he intended.

She let out a bitter laugh and swung her legs off the bench and sat up, opening her eyes that were shining with tears, the sunset reflecting the beauty that was already there. Her hair glowing the same color as her eyes. Jax's breath caught in his throat. "Jax, you are the one person who has the complete power to utterly destroy me. No one else but me can save me, or would probably even try."

His legs gave out with the weight of her words and he fell to his knees on the ground, facing her, but not within touching distance. His every cell wanted to gather her in his arms and he knew that was a very bad idea right now. "I don't want to destroy you," he whispered brokenly.

"Maybe it's not you, I don't know. I don't trust my reasoning around you. Maybe it's both you and that vile energy in you, maybe it's just the energy, but for sure it wants me destroyed in every way possible." Defeat lined her tone.

"I don't want to destroy you," he repeated. "I'm me right now. I don't want to destroy you. While I'm being honest, you have the same power over me." Admitting it felt right, but the energy in him shifted with it.

"I'm here to save you," she told him sadly. "It's what I do, or am supposed to do. Or why I was created. Whatever."

Jax scooted closer to her and she stiffened. "Are you using your empath abilities right now?" he asked her, his voice filled with need.

"No," she said tiredly. "It's too much around you, and leaves me vulnerable in a way I'm not ready for."

Jax shook with understanding at that. She made him, not the darkness, but him, totally vulnerable. "Can you use it so you can see what I'm feeling right now?"

"Why?" she hiccupped on a sob. "I believe you. It's you."

"So you can feel the truth to my words." His tone was pleading, and he hated it, but he desperately wanted her to see him.

"I lose a little more of myself each time I'm around you and I do that," she whispered, tearing him wide open. "If I lose myself, I've failed once again."

Jax's eyes pooled with tears that matched hers and rested his forehead on his knees, muffling his voice, "Your eyes have flecks of gold in them, and right now with the sunset reflecting off them it makes me think of the Northern Lights. Majestic and beautiful in an ethereal way that only God could explain. The curls of your hair are catching the breeze and with the sunlight hitting them, those curls become just as colorful as the sunset, and it makes you look like an angel. Your voice and your smell are more potent than any drug could ever be, it's like a siren song that holds me in a trance, buried and etched in my soul. Haunting me every time I'm not near you." Jax choked on a cry, "Your touch, so fucking amazing that it makes me believe in life again. Makes my heart believe in things I don't want to."

He looked up and saw her shaking, her arms wrapped around her body like she was trying to hold herself together. Jax let his mask down and let her see the raw emotion she ignited in him. "I'm so wrapped up in fear around you, that the feeling you are afraid of, that feeling of losing yourself, it happens when you are near me. I lose myself, and that vulnerability allows that shit in me to take over and it lashes out to hurt you. I'm the tool it's using to hurt you, and it kills me. You are fucking unbelievable and I'm trying to hurt you. I don't know what to do. I want you to shine your light on me, shine it so that I see nothing else but you."

She slipped off the bench and sat closer to him, but she didn't touch him, and he was both devastated by that and grateful for it. He felt like he would shatter if she touched him right now. "Jax, I know it's not you that's trying to hurt me. I've never believed any of those words or thoughts were from you."

"You still think I could destroy you though?" confusion tinting his words.

She sucked in a breath and it caught, then she expelled all her words in a rush, "This thing between us? This feeling you just described in the most beautiful words anyone has ever said to me? That feeling? That's what has the power to destroy me. Despite what all the others think, I'm still broken inside and you aren't the only one scared by this. It feels like it's ripping me apart sometimes. I don't understand much of this and I'm afraid to believe in the things people have told me. Because if it's not true, or if I fail, I lose everything. Everything. What if that cost is too high for me?" She sobbed. "What if I lose you?" she whispered.

Hope bloomed so bright in his chest that he threw himself forward and wrapped his arms around her in the way that he wanted to since the first time she touched him. His tear-soaked cheek pressed up against hers and that feeling he'd been chasing exploded around them as they clung together for a moment, the emotions too encompassing to ignore.

She pushed him away and sat back, but didn't move out of his reach. "Jax, we have to fix us inside before this goes any further. You deserve someone whole. I deserve someone whole. If we don't, we both lose. There are a lot of people counting on me to bring you back to them."

"What if you are what makes me whole?" he croaked. The truth of that statement burning in his eyes and in his chest, hanging in the air between them.

"I don't know that I believe that," she said softly.

Jax looked away and watched the brilliant colors of the sunset and knew he would forever associate the setting sun with the woman in front of him. "You are wrong about one thing," he said carefully.

"What's that?" she asked timidly.

"Smitty, Ronnie, Aedan and Mags, they all would jump at the chance to save you. Even if I want to be the one to do it." Jax knew the truth of those words down to the deepest parts of his heart.

She reached for his hand and held it, "Maybe you'll surprise me."

"Ronnie is in love with you," Jax told her. "I can't compete with him."

"You'd never have to." She tugged on his hand to get him to look at her. "Love isn't finite. My feelings for him aren't the same as the ones I have for you. I don't feel the same about any person."

"I heard Mags though, you've slept with all of them," he said jealously.

"Sex and love aren't the same thing, and I haven't had sex with all of them. Even if I had, it's a physical release only compounded by the emotions I feel for that person, which aren't the same as I feel with anyone else. For me, on a personal level, I find sex and love are very fluid. Meaning it's always moving, always evolving. You don't have to be single for me to love you. I love you for you, not your status, your bank account, your clothes, your job, none of that matters to me. With sex, I will admit curiosity about things I haven't experienced and if the right situation presents itself and I felt safe, I would do it. If I'm in a committed relationship that we both agree is monogamous then that's what it is."

"I already kept Winnie from Ronnie, I can't do the same with you." Guilt ate at him and the darkness stirred, wanting to come to life within him.

"Look at me please," she demanded. "This feeling when we touch? It's called a connection. Most people have one in their life. Some lucky ones have more. I happen to have five that I know of. It's different with each person. It binds me to them. I don't know what to do about this one between us, but I can't ignore it." She opened her senses and Jax felt the minute she did. He was swamped with her feelings, the strength and weight of them dizzying to him. "By far, this connection thing we have, is the strongest I have ever had with anyone. It's so strong that every time that energy in you takes over I lose control and go ape shit with the need to pull you back."

His fingers tightened on hers. "You fought for me today. You challenged it." Jax's voice wavered.

"Damn right I did. That's what happens when I'm near you. We don't ever have to do anything about this connection, it's a choice you have to make based off what you feel is right for you. Not that shit inside you, for you." She tapped his chest. "You need to understand, I will fight for you and I won't give up. I'm damn sure it will cost me, but I'm willing to pay the price."

"Why?" he was afraid to ask.

"I feel you in here." She put her hand over her heart. "I can't walk away without fighting for that. I want to sometimes, but I know it's real. I can take the stupid shit you say and do, I even have experience taking the abuse. I can't take failing you though."

"This energy hates you," Jax warned. She nodded. "It's going to make me hurt you." She nodded sadly again. "That makes me hate myself," he admitted.

"You have to figure out what is worth fighting for. No one can answer that but you. You need to believe you are worth your own effort. It's always got to start with you." Those words carried a heavy weight to them, one that hinted of battles she's faced down.

"Degataga told me that too, so did Father Roarke. Degataga actually sent me a tin of stuff to mix with water to help me heal," Jax said, relishing the warmth of her hand in his.

"I have the same stuff," she admitted.

Jax startled at that admission. "You do?"

"Yeah, I just haven't felt ready to face those nightmares yet. I'm trying to fight yours too," she said wryly.

"You've really been in them, haven't you?" Her eyes held the pain he wanted to avoid. "I'm so sorry, Airiella."

"No one is immune to pain and loss Jax, it's a part of life. You just have to face it and learn from it, then let it go."

He felt the fear coil up inside him at the thought of facing it all, and he pulled away from her because he knew the darkness would feed on it. He felt her close herself off again and he immediately missed her presence. "I gotta go," he stammered.

"Later, Jax," she said, her voice betraying her emotions. He was the one failing her. He fled, shame flaming under his skin, his eyes burning red hot as he tore into the house and into the safety of his room, clutching his lifeline of the green pillow to his chest. He knew she was right.

I didn't know how to feel. Each time I'd been around Jax had left me feeling vulnerable and overwhelmed with emotion I didn't want. I didn't lie to him. It all came at a cost to me. I wasn't honest with him either in that I kept a lot of stuff from him. I didn't think he was ready for it.

I also couldn't help feeling like he was chasing a high with the connection. I craved it too, especially his, but I wanted to be more than just that for someone. Some needs never change. I guess we all want that at some point. I wiped the tears away.

His words had a profound effect on me though, and it made me want him. I wanted all of him. I wanted to be buried in his heart and soul, to feel everything he did, to share everything I was with him. Each of those beautiful words he said to me ripped something wide open in me and left me exposed.

I was honest about my feelings for the others, it wasn't the same as it was with Jax, as much as I wanted it to be. It would be so easy to be with Ronnie. I even tried to lie to myself and say it was the same as it was with Jax, but my heart knew. Damn it all, anyway.

I hated crying. I rarely ever cry and it feels like for the past month that is all I've done. I could have filled a lake with all the stupid tears. I stood up, angry with myself for not being more open with Jax, angry for falling in love with someone that would most likely destroy me, angry for crying, even angry for being angry.

I stomped back to the house lost in thoughts and failed to see the reason for my ire in front of me and crashed right into him. Even through layers of clothes, that connection slammed into me like a runaway freight train. Worried it wasn't him, I stepped back fast and lost the direction my thoughts had been heading.

His eyes glimmered and were so deep my heart

tumbled a bit more. Chestnuts, his eyes were the color of chestnuts. I wanted to taste him, to be lost in him. Fuck, Airy! I yelled at myself. Snap out of it! "Airiella," Jax rasped, "can we talk more?"

Hot need tore through me, and helplessly I nodded. His smile shut down all sensible thoughts and I just followed him into the kitchen. I was going to have wet dreams about that smile. "I thought I could grill us up some dinner. I'm not much of a cook, but I can grill a mean chicken breast."

"Sure," I said numbly. My brain and mouth not connected. "Jax, are you just chasing this because of the feeling you get when we touch?" Oh no, I did not just say that. Shit.

Things were so fragile between us already. "I wondered that too." He spoke honestly. "But no, I don't think so. I've been balls deep in so many women it's sad, and not one of them made me feel even a fraction of what I do in your presence alone."

I coughed, not quite sure what to do with that. "Um, okay."

"You said sex was sex, so I was just being honest. I fucked anything I could to try to get away from everything else. Even the people that I thought maybe there could be something with, it never eased anything inside me. No one ever brought that darkness out like you do either. I'm not going to lie, it scares the hell out of me." Jax gave me the brutal and honest truth.

"Doesn't that make you think that maybe this isn't real? That this connection is only temporary?" My voice was dull as I said that because I knew it wasn't temporary, but I felt like I needed to give him an out.

"No, Airiella. The fear of not being around you again is bigger than the fear of the darkness. To me, that says it's more than temporary. Granted, I'm not the best judge of anything right now, I am speaking from the heart though," he replied easily.

He worked in silence for a moment seasoning the

chicken breasts, put them on a plate and headed out into the backyard again. I followed mutely hoping nothing else damning would come out of my mouth. He was so beautiful, my brain fogged.

I stood there and stared at the stars just starting to show themselves in the night sky, looking for constellations. I felt him come up next to me, though he didn't touch me. "You make me think of starlight," he remarked, his voice calm and soothing for the first time.

"How is that?" My heart stuttered.

"I don't know. Sometimes you're millions of miles away, yet still shining bright, offering hope to those who need something to wish for. Then sometimes you seem so close and in reach, a beacon of the heavens." The timber of his voice resonated in my soul, I fell so hard.

"Jax," I breathed. "That was beautiful. Thank you." Damn tears.

"Why are you broken?" He shifted back to the grill, asking casually like it wasn't a loaded question. "I'd tell you why I was, but you've been in my nightmares. You know why I am." A shadow crossed his face.

I backed up to a patio chair and sat down, putting a little distance between us. Vaguely, I answered, "Everyone is broken at some point. Everyone has a story. I know parts of yours, yes. It doesn't mean I know your thoughts, or why you think the way you do. I can feel your emotions, and they don't always match the expression on your face or your body language. Even though I've been in your nightmares, it doesn't necessarily mean those are why you are broken. Nightmares are movie reels of our fears usually."

"Not just fears, Airiella. Real events from my past," he said, guarded.

"Maybe our stories aren't something we should talk about right now," I suggested gently. "I don't want to play with that energy right now, and maybe talking about some of that stuff flirts too closely with the emotions that will bring it out."

"It might," he agreed. "I still want to know."

"Give it time," I told him.

"I feel like I don't have much of that left," he told me in another moment of brutal honesty.

Fear skittered across my spine. "Why?"

"Because it's all still in me, and while you may be temporarily holding it back, it's still there and I feel myself getting lost to it." He didn't turn around when he said it, but he didn't need to for me to hear the very real fear.

"Fight it, Jax," I reminded him.

He flipped the chicken. "What if I'm not strong enough?"

"What if you are? What happens then? You might find that you can amaze yourself," I countered.

He stood absolutely still. "Are you a witch?"

Well I wasn't expecting that response. "Excuse me?"

"Are you putting spells on me?" He still hadn't turned around.

I laughed at that, and then felt bad because he was serious. "No, I don't know how to perform magic or spells."

"This feeling of wanting to be better, to prove myself, is just a result of what then?" Jax turned to me then.

"You. Jax, try believing in yourself," I pushed gently.

"Rich words coming from you, baby girl," I heard Smitty say from the doorway. I tensed up, because he did know my story.

Jax flew around and narrowed his eyes at Smitty. "What do you mean?"

"She needs to practice what she preaches," he told Jax. "Guess that answers my question on whether you guys want some dinner or not. I was going to go out and grab something."

"Thanks for the offer." I gave him a beseeching look. He just shrugged at me and walked back in the house.

"I'm smart enough to figure out I'm not going to get any details on your past out of you. So how about I ask a question that will tell me without you having to divulge anything. Think of it like a game," he challenged me.

"What?" I asked warily.

"Name a song that talks about past relationships," he said.

He was tricky. Any song I could name would tell him a lot more than I was comfortable with. Maybe it was worth the risk. I couldn't tell. His emotions were pinging around like crazy right now. "Do you want me to calm you a little?" I asked him suddenly.

"I kind of do, I feel like I'm barely balanced on an edge, but I also don't want you to think that is why I am doing this. I wanted to spend time with you. We'll be working closely together in the next few months and we need some sort of relationship where I'm not always an asshole, but I don't want it to be because you have to make me that way." He looked ashamed with himself.

"I get it Jax. I don't hold it against you." I sifted through his emotions and pulled out one that I could feed into instead of pulling from him as I didn't trust that just yet. I pushed my calm into him and watched him visibly relax. I didn't overdo it, just enough to soothe the bee bee in a box car effect of his emotions.

"About that song." He leaned against the grill. His smile was lethal. Smoking hot.

"Better Man," I answered automatically and wishing I had thought more about it. That one revealed a lot about me. Too much, perhaps.

"Pearl Jam?" he asked, confused and pulling out his phone.

"No," I said so quietly he could barely hear me. "Though that fits too."

"I see three songs with that title," he scrolled through his phone.

"Well I guess then you are just going to have to figure it out later." I smiled tightly.

"Fair enough." He pulled the chicken from the grill and we went back in the kitchen. He pulled a bag of lettuce from the fridge, one of the premade salad kits. "I hope you like Caesar salad, and packaged mashed potatoes." He pointed to a pan on the stove I hadn't seen.

"I'm fine with both. Want me to mix the salad?" I offered.

He shook his head no. "I've got it. Grab a couple of plates and silverware."

I dug through the cupboards and drawers until I found what I needed and we sat at the island. "Shouldn't you answer the same question now?"

"I could, but you already know my past," he said passing me the salad bowl.

"Yes, but I don't know how you would define it," I pushed.

"Depends on the day," he said truthfully. "Sometimes its Bulletproof, sometimes it's Something I Can Never Have."

Tingles went through my body again. Both songs I identified with and loved. "You're right, you do a great grilled chicken," I said taking a bite.

"I haven't done a lot that I'm proud of," he told me. "Especially in the relationship area."

"You were young Jax, being stupid is kind of a rite of passage." I gave him an out.

"Why do you make excuses for me?" he asked, seeing right through me.

"It's not an excuse. It was a tragic accident. Yes, you made a mistake. I don't know anyone who hasn't. Nor do I know anyone who hasn't made a selfish mistake. At some point, you have to forgive yourself." I played it straight.

"Have you?" his pointed question hitting its mark.

I shifted uncomfortably. I desperately wanted to be vague on this. "In some cases, yes I have."

"Are we on dangerous ground here?" Caution crept into his voice.

"I don't know about dangerous, depends on how much control you have. For me, it's not dangerous, but it's not something I like to talk about." I despised talking about it.

"Can I ask why? It's in the past, right? Or is there someone waiting for you somewhere?"

Just him. I couldn't tell him that though. "I don't like talking about it because some wounds might scab over, but they don't heal. Some wounds heal, but the scar is fragile and can be opened easily, like the stitches on your palm."

"That's telling in itself." He grinned at his little victory, then quickly sobered. "But, it also tells me that it's something pretty significant."

"Here's something safe, I have two cats. Alpha and Omega," I volunteered.

He chuckled, and thank God I was sitting down or I would have swooned. "Interesting names."

"They are cats, they think they are gods." I shrugged.

"Animals are fantastic. I'd save them all if I could," he said.

I understood that feeling. I'd do the same. I couldn't help it, I reached out and touched the cross he had tattooed on his ring finger. His eyes spoke of grief, and the sparks of our skin touching spoke of a way to forget that grief.

I pulled away. "I got it after Winnie died." I'd figured as much. It was Celtic. "You don't trust easily do you?" he asked me cautiously like he was afraid I was going to bolt.

"I trust way too easily," I blurted out, "and believe people to be inherently good even though time and time again I am proven wrong. If you are referring to my heart, then no. I don't trust easily anymore, or have an easy time letting them in."

He leaned forward resting his elbows on the countertop. His biceps flexed and heat washed through me. Fuck, this was the last thing I needed right now. Sleeping with Jax would be amazing, but also a mistake I couldn't afford to make yet. I wanted to strip that tight t-shirt off him though, and trace every tattoo I saw peeking out with my fingers and my tongue.

"I'm not going to be that cheesy asshole that tells you that you can trust him. I'm not remotely stable enough to say that. I can't even say that I won't hurt you, because we both know I will. I *can* tell you, from within the deepest and truest parts of me, that it will never be my intent. I'm not that kind of person. I hope that one day we can trust each other." The sincerity in his voice almost undid me.

I said goodbye to another little piece of me that he just stole and wasn't aware of. "Don't take it personally." I shifted to look at him. "It's exceedingly rare that I let people in. Even those that have known me for years."

"Seems like you let the others in." His voice took on an edge. I hazarded a look at his emotions and saw that energy trying to push through.

"Don't judge what you don't know," was my warning and I fed him a little more of the calm. "Some situations, like this one, dictate that I divulge more information than I am happy with in order for me to be most effective."

"Will you ever see me as more than a job?" he had relaxed but his insecurities were close to the surface.

"I don't see you as a job," I replied. "I see you. A beyond complicated mess of a man, that has yet to see the beauty in his scars. I see it, even if you can't. I may be here because of a job, but that's not why I stayed."

His voice was rough and fatigued. "Why did you stay?"

I touched him, letting that connection flood our senses. "I didn't stay because of that either." I touched his chest then. "When I first met you, your emotions barreled over me. A tangled web similar to my own. What stuck out to me though, was the unhappiness that you felt with yourself for this thing inside you. Jax, that could easily happen to anyone. We can't control life. We can only control our reactions. That emotion in you told me so much about who you are underneath this. That you can feel a love so powerful that you withstood this growing mass inside you for this long. That's why I stayed." I stroked his arm to reignite the connection again. "This is a happy little bonus."

"I don't know that I loved Winnie as much as you think you saw," he admitted.

"It wasn't your love for Winnie I was talking about. It's your love for Ronnie," I said quietly.

Stunned would have been an understatement for the expression on his face. "Are you sure it isn't shame or guilt?"

I shrugged, "Those are there too, but that isn't what I saw. You asked, and I gave you my honest answer. I can't make you accept it."

His voice broke. "The urge to run right now is so powerful in me." His body shook. "You see too much."

"It's there for anyone who cares to look. You aren't hiding it, Jax."

"I feel like an exposed nerve right now," he trembled.

"I'm well acquainted with the feeling," I said dryly. "Sadly, it's part of the healing process."

A few tears slid down his cheeks. Overcome by the display of emotion I swiped my thumb across his cheeks to catch the tears. His eyes were glued to my thumb. I couldn't think of anything else to do, so I wiped my thumb across my lips rubbing his tears into them. His breath caught and his deep eyes were so intense on me that heat pooled in me again.

"I'll willingly share in the pain you feel Jax. You are part of me," I told him licking my lips.

He pulled me off the stool I was sitting on and crushed me to him in the span of a second. He buried his face in my hair and was breathing me in, swallowing gulps of air. Pure, raw and intense emotions washing over me. "I think it's you who will destroy me, witch." His voice was low and husky but the words were not harmful.

He moved away enough to capture my lips in the most soul burning kiss I have ever had. Tender, filled with a passion I have never felt, yet at the same time violent in the emotions it triggered inside me. I was on fire and would gladly burn forever to stay in that kiss. I put everything I had in me back into it.

He let me go just as abruptly as he grabbed me. Running his tongue over his swollen lips he backed up away from me and I felt the pang of the loss. Shadows danced across his eyes and his jaw tensed.

I sensed the danger before he did and moved to the other side of the island. Whatever fates were on my side chose that moment to have Ronnie and Smitty walk into the kitchen. Jax fled, and I deflated against the counter knowing he would blame himself.

"Angel are you okay?" Ronnie at my side in an instant while Smitty looked between me and the direction Jax had gone.

"I'm fine. Smitty, chill, it's okay," I told them weakly. I cleared the dishes and loaded up the dishwasher.

"Yeah baby girl, you look fine. What did he do?" His tone was even but I heard the dangerous undercurrent.

"We were just talking, Smitty." I leaned against Ronnie, his solid body beneath me giving me a sense of stability.

Neither of them believed me and kept a close watch on me until I excused myself to go to bed. I stared at his closed door wondering if I would be in there tonight for another nightmare, and if I was, I wondered if I'd be able to keep my hands to myself.

I closed my door behind me and fell upon the bed. The tin that Degataga sent me staring at me in a reminder that I needed to do as Smitty said and practice what I preached. Would I have the strength to do that tonight? I doubted it. Not alone anyway. I'd need Smitty or Ronnie, but again, that left me open and vulnerable to them during some dark times.

Chapter Ten

Aedan was in the backyard with Mags on the patio enjoying the night sky when he got a text from Airiella.

"Are you in the house?" He showed Mags.

"Yeah, we are in the back yard if you want to join us," he replied.

"Be down in a minute," she wrote back.

"Think everything went okay with Jax?" Mags worried.

"I guess we'll find out when she gets here," he said into her ear.

They were sharing a chair, Aedan wrapped around Mags making a cozy picture. He was trying to get as much time in with his wife as possible before the crazy schedule started. She'd be staying here in the house while they were on location.

She went with to local shoots, but it wasn't often they had many of those and he missed her when he was gone. She was his balance. They snuggled under the starry sky waiting for Airiella.

They weren't waiting long when she appeared with Ronnie and Smitty in tow. He saw Airiella glance up at an open window that he knew was Jax's room. If Jax was in there, he would be able to hear them, and by the look on her face she knew it too.

"Okay guys, I need a favor," she said simply, not lowering her voice. Whatever she said she wanted Jax to hear. Aedan's curiosity peaked even further.

"Whatever you need, it's yours," Mags said.

"What she said," Aedan said with a smile, tightening his arms around Mags.

"Smitty called me out earlier, and he was right to do it," Airiella stated.

Ronnie shot Smitty a dark look, and Aedan sat very still hoping he wouldn't have to break up a fight between them. That would be physically painful.

Smitty shrugged in response. "He told me to practice what I preach. I was telling Jax that he needed to believe in himself."

"Kinda harsh, Art," Ronnie growled.

"He was right, Ronnie," Airiella said gently and Aedan was struck again by the strength of this woman.

"Smitty knows what Taklishim and Degataga told me about healing myself, and I have the tin of the herbs that he sent me. If I'm going to do this, then I need to get it done, or at least started," she said, hesitating.

Aedan saw then how much this was costing her. She was warning them in a way that it was going to be hard. He knew her story, but maybe not as much about the scars that hadn't healed. He's assumed they were there, and he saw moments where they flashed across her face. Raw and exposed.

"What do you need, sweets?" Mags asked leaning forward.

"Help," she said, her voice wavering.

"Tell me how," Aedan replied.

"Take care of Jax tonight if he needs it. I know you can't do what I can do." Her voice was strong when she said that. "But you can repeat to him to fight it."

"I can do that," Aedan said, glancing at the window.

"I'll help," Mags said with a smile. "I like nagging him."

Aedan thought he heard a snort from the window but didn't look up. "He needs to believe he has the strength to do this. I know he does, but he needs to believe it," she said on a shaky breath. "Shit, I need to believe it myself." She looked at Ronnie and Smitty. "That's where you come in."

"I'm there, angel," Ronnie said gently.

"That's what I need. I need you two to be there. I want to say in case of something, but I don't know what. Degataga told me it was going to be brutal on me, and I have no idea what will happen. I know it will make me relive things I don't want to. I also know that I need to in order to fix whatever is broken in there. Or at least make it scab up." She chewed nervously on her lip.

Once again, her voice had strength to it, but her eyes held fear. Aedan watched her carefully to see how she dealt with it. They could all learn from her.

She took a deep breath in. "No joke, guys. I'm flat out terrified."

Smitty hadn't said anything yet, but he paled significantly. "What did he said would happen?" Aedan took notice of the fear in his voice, it wasn't often he heard that in Smitty.

Airiella crossed to him, "It's not that."

Not what? Aedan wondered. He saw Smitty relax a bit at that news. "I'm missing something."

"Remember, we aren't going to talk about that." Airiella looked at Aedan as she said that, her tone unyielding. Oh. He looked back at Smitty who had a closed off look on his face now.

She moved again and looked back up at the window. She was doing this for him. He got it now. Lead by example. If it was going to be as bad as she thought it was, he hoped Jax understood what she was doing for him.

Her voice quieted as it all hit her. "I may need you all close to me tomorrow. Remember, you might feel it too, and I'm sorry for that."

Mags was up and out of the chair and holding Airiella before he could blink. Ronnie and Smitty circled her too and Aedan felt left out. He hoped Jax was looking out the window and seeing this.

"We'll take care of Jax, don't worry," Aedan reassured her.

Airiella let loose with her emotions and fully engaged the connection they all shared, except Ronnie. He didn't think she had gone there yet. He still felt it though. She drew strength from it and they all gave it freely.

Jax settled back against his bed and held his own tin of nightmares from Degataga. He couldn't do it yet. He was fully aware of what she was sacrificing to do this, and he also knew she wanted him to hear her willingness to do it.

He wanted to stay awake to bear witness to her pain. He couldn't be in her room though. Hell, he might be better off not being in the house. The darkness in him might like it too much. He touched his lips remembering the feel of that kiss. The power of the emotions that ripped right through him and bared his tarnished soul.

He'd stay. He'd deal with it. He'd do it for her, for another chance to feel that kind of love. He hit replay on the song Better Man. He'd figured out which one it was after reading the lyrics to all of them. He wasn't going to be the man in the song, he was going to be the better one she wanted.

The lyrics told him so much that she wouldn't, and he knew that someone, maybe more than one, had hurt her badly. His imagination went wild with scenarios that woke a rage in him, and he understood why she didn't want to tell him. He wanted to know anyway, but she was right. Not yet.

Smitty damn near had a panic attack when he heard the fear in her voice and her willingness to just walk head first into shit that hurt her. The memory of her screams haunting him, her body breaking. What was going to happen in those nightmares? What was she going to face? He remembered her story of her past, and knew that she had understated some of it. Which of those still bled? He wouldn't be surprised if they all did.

He worried about how Ronnie would react to seeing her tormented. He didn't know any of it yet. Or if he did, he didn't know the worst of it, or Jax would never have gotten in the same room as her. He didn't even know if he could handle it. That was a lie. He knew he could, it couldn't be as bad as what he saw happen to her.

He didn't think he'd be able to watch horror movies anymore after seeing that. She knew he was worried. He also knew she trusted him, and that mattered more than anything else. They'd get her through it. Even without Ronnie having a connection yet.

Maybe that was why she was doing it now, so he didn't feel it the way Smitty would. The suffering she would go through ate at him. The suffering Jax was going through did too. His own life issues paling in comparison. If nothing else, it put things in perspective for him.

Ronnie watched her walk away and fought the impulse to cart her off somewhere safe. He knew better than most you couldn't hide from your own demons. He'd been slightly grateful that they didn't have the connection the others had, if it meant he wouldn't have to feel it. Though he also wished he did, so he could share her burden.

He also wanted a drink. Badly. Airiella astounded him on a daily basis with her ability to adapt to the everchanging landscape life threw at her. He looked up at the open window she kept glancing at and knew she wanted him to hear. He had his own tin of the shit to take.

He hoped that whatever was in him didn't react to

the energy she would throw off in her sleep. He didn't think Aedan and Mags would be able to contain that beast if it reared its head. Maybe it should be him in there with Jax instead of Aedan and Mags. Ronnie knew he could take it.

He looked at Smitty, "Should I swap places with Aedan and Mags? You three all have a connection."

"Who am I to question her decision? She asked us for a reason. I'll admit, I had the same thought as you. I also don't think Jax would ever hurt Mags," Smitty replied loud enough to be heard through the open window, his voice holding a warning.

"No, I don't think he would either," Ronnie said. "I just worry. I want my brother back." Ronnie spoke quietly, but his words carried a weight that would reach Jax. He sat back and checked his watch. They'd promised her an hour before they would head up.

Winnie appeared, "Oh there you are," she said snidely to Airy after she had taken the necklace off.

"Sorry, Winnie. I needed time." Airy didn't sound apologetic though.

Winnie softened. "I know. Did something happen with Jax?"

Airiella nodded to her, but didn't add anything to it. "I'm going to put the necklace back on tonight, but it's because I am going to drink the stuff Degataga sent me."

"Airy, I can help you deal with that. You don't need to face that alone," Winnie pleaded.

"I do, Winnie. If you are my crutch in there, I won't really heal. If you want me to have something with Jax, it's something we both have to do. We each deserve someone whole. I don't care if he has cracks, but I can't fix him." Her plaintive tone hurt.

"Will you take your necklace off tomorrow for me? I'd like to help pick up the pieces." Winnie stroked her hair.

Airy wiped tears from her face. "I wish you were alive. I think we'd have been best friends."

Winnie's heart swelled. "You're still my best friend, even in death, you beautiful girl."

"I asked Smitty and Ronnie to be in here with me. I just get the feeling I'll need them close," she explained weakly.

"Airy, it's okay to need people. It's okay to ask for help." Winnie stroked her hair some more.

"It's not something I am used to. I'm trying, though." Airy slumped over. "I just want him to see that I'm willing to take the hard steps so that he can too."

"Jax is many things, but he isn't dumb. He knows. If the feelings rolling through me are any indication, he is well aware," Winnie replied cryptically.

"If I tell Mags to take her necklace off, can you help her? I'm worried that energy will get to her."

"She needs to keep it on, they all do, until you are able to take more of it from him. And after he makes an effort." Winnie used both hands to stroke Airy's hair. "He will be fine for a night. You do you."

"I love you Winnie."

"Oh Airy, I love you too." Winnie was worried, though. She knew from what she had seen in Airiella's head that this road was going to be tough and her night was going to be filled with her own personal horrors and ugly demons. "Just take your necklace off tomorrow. Write a note and leave it here so everyone can see that you are supposed to take it off. Please."

Airy smiled a half smile and did as she was told. "Thank you, Winnie."

Winnie nodded and just sat with her for a bit offering any comfort that she could. She was so brave. Winnie wished that while she had been alive, she'd even had a fraction of the bravery that Airy had. Things might have been different then.

I opened my window to let a breeze come through, thinking that since that relaxed me, it might help me get through this. I got ready for bed and put on some shorts and a tank top and went to make tea out of this stuff. It didn't smell bad, but it didn't smell good either.

Smitty followed me and leaned against the counter while I heated up the water. "You sure you want to do this now?"

I half-smiled at him. "No. You were right to call me out though. I can't expect to fight Jax on this and not do it myself."

"The difference is you aren't carrying that crap inside you, making you a psycho." Smitty ran his hand down my back.

"My perspective of myself is different than yours. I've got plenty of baggage. Don't coddle me," I reminded him.

"I'm not coddling you. I just can't get it out of my head... you know." He shrugged and looked down.

"You don't have to be in there with me if you are worried what will happen. I'm scared, yes, but I'll still face it. Don't make yourself uncomfortable, Smitty. I understand, I really do." I turned to face him.

"Of course, I'm going to be there." He locked his soulful gaze on mine. "I can still worry." He tugged on me and I leaned against him.

"I really am scared," I said into his chest. "The thought of reliving any of the shit from my past is enough to send me running for the hills. Some of it wouldn't even be that bad, by other's standards, but it still reduces me to useless." My hands shook as I moved away to pour the heated water in the cup.

"Again, the difference between you and others, you'll face it. You do it again, and again." Smitty's confidence in me was firm.

"I have no idea how this will work, how fast, what it will do to me, or make happen. You've been warned. I've seen enough abnormal things recently to not discount anything. That said, I'm going to drink it in my room and read to settle my nerves. You guys don't have to come in yet, I know it's still early." I held the warm cup in my hands, letting it heat my fingers.

"I'm ready whenever you are. I'll just bring my computer with and do work. Who knows, maybe nothing will happen. Maybe you are so badass already that you've conquered everything and all you will see is you sitting on top of a mountain." The corners of his mouth turned up in a smile.

That got a laugh out of me. "Right. Nice thought, but I'm thinking no, that isn't what will happen."

Smitty kissed the top of my head, "I still think you are pretty badass," he said as I walked in front of him carrying the smelly tea. "That smells like dirt."

"Yes, it kind of does. Minty dirt." I grimaced. "Tastes like it too."

I settled in bed and grabbed my iPad to read and Smitty and Ronnie both trailed in. Smitty with his computer and Ronnie with a tablet. They parked on either side of me and went about whatever they were doing before. I relaxed some, knowing they weren't going to hover over me.

I drank the tea down as fast as I could and then chased it with some water to get the taste out of my mouth. I laid back and read a few pages and noticed my eyes weren't focusing very well on the words. I think Ronnie caught my iPad before it hit my face, because I didn't feel the impact, but I was not in the room with them.

At least in my head I wasn't. I felt fairly sure my body was still there. I heard the flapping of wings and saw a giant raven in front of me. Was this me, or was this another one bringing me this sight? It cawed at me softly and as I looked in its eyes, I saw my own. Then it began.

Ronnie saw the iPad falling at her face and grabbed it in time. Moments later on the window sill came the caws of a raven and a flurry of flapping wings. Both he and Smitty jumped a little and then gave each other a weird look.

Ronnie looked down at Airiella, whose body was

relaxed at the moment, though her eyes were flicking madly under her closed lids and her face was a little pale. "What do we do?"

"Just let her be," Smitty said cautiously. "That happened fast."

"Think the raven is her?" Ronnie asked, staring at the bird that watched him carefully from the thin screen that separated them. "Look at its eyes, they look just like hers."

Smitty's face had a shocked look. He swallowed a lump of fear. "Yeah, I think that's her. Or part of her."

"Ever wondered lately that we could be on our own show right now?" Ronnie asked wryly.

Smitty chuckled, "Yep. I hate thinking about Jax being a demon though, so I don't want to go there."

"Agreed." Ronnie went back to playing with his tablet.

J ax couldn't fight it, he felt himself falling asleep and he kept trying to keep himself awake, but it was too strong. He was pulled under before he could even turn the light out, but not before hearing the sound of wings flapping.

This wasn't his usual nightmare. He didn't know where he was. He saw a raven looking at him, one with the most incredible eyes. They looked so much like hers, wait, was it her? Hadn't the guys told him that Tak called her a raven?

His mind was fuzzy. He felt like he was in a movie theater, but it was empty except for him. Then he saw her. This wasn't right. "Airiella?" he called out to her softly. She didn't hear him though. Then it hit him. He was watching what she was dreaming.

Oh no. He needed to get out of here. This felt like a huge violation of her. She didn't want him here; he didn't even think he was supposed to be here. He pinched himself repeatedly, but nothing changed other than his arm hurt.

The raven sat in front of him and cawed and Jax felt raw fear. How did this happen? What if the darkness came out while he was in here with her? This was supposed to help her be able to heal herself, not fight this shit. The raven cawed at him again and Jax stopped struggling to get up when he couldn't. He closed his eyes, he wouldn't watch, this wasn't for him to see.

He heard the sound of a thump, then she cried out. His eyes flew open to see her getting punched. Fuck! He needed to get out of here, but as the beating played out in front of his stricken eyes, he was frozen in place, the lyrics to Better Man playing in his head as his fists clenched in rage at what he saw. Blood dripping out of his palms.

Smitty saw Airiella jerk and heard a mewling sound come from the back of her throat and he watched in horror as mark appeared on her face. His blood froze. Calm, he told himself. She needs us to be calm.

He said it out loud, "Stay calm. We have to stay calm. It's in the past," he said quietly hoping Ronnie didn't lose his shit. "She needs us calm. You knew this was in her past, she flat out said it in the interview we watched."

Ronnie nodded, his jaw ticking as he ground his teeth together. "I didn't know I'd have to see it happen."

"The marks are fading," Smitty said, aching to touch her face where the marks had been.

"They don't go away inside, Smitty. They are always there," Ronnie said. He knew. His hands shook as he set the tablet on the nightstand so he didn't throw it.

Tears tracked down her cheeks and something in Smitty broke again, knowing there was nothing he could do to stop this. The look on Ronnie's face, echoing his own. This was going to be a long night.

The blows rained down, alternating between my belly and my face. He spewed words at me in Japanese, words that I never learned what they meant. I tried holding back the cries, but they came anyway. He switched to English, "It's your fault, bitch! If I hadn't had to worry about what time I got home, I would have won!"

I cowered in bed, woken up by violence once again. Which told me he lost at the casino again.
The scene changed again.

My body slammed against the wall as he shoved me back and swung the golf cub at me, my ribs breaking under the onslaught.

The raven appeared and the scene froze. My bloody and broken body was on display for me to remember and feel. The bird stared at me with my own eyes, his cruel words echoing in my ears, each one leaving a scar that never went away. There was a message here the bird was trying to get me to see.

I'd been over this for years, what hadn't I figured out from my three years of this relationship hell? I'd been so young then. I didn't know the signs like I do now. I sensed the bird getting frustrated with my lack of understanding and the scene rewound.

"Fucking cunt! You're worthless! Why am I with you? I could do so much better than your fat ass." He *shouted with each swing of the golf club. Even as I passed out, he kept yelling. Broken blood vessels staining my arms black as I bled under my skin.*

"The words?" I asked the bird as the scene froze again. It cawed softly again. "What about them?" I cringed remembering every cruel thing he ever said, repeated over three years until I believed them all. Then I got it. I needed to forgive myself for believing the things he said to me. Easier said than done. I shook my head at the bird, "I don't know how."

I was being wheeled away on a gurney, the face of the man I would soon divorce watching me get taken back for surgery. His face cold, as I wondered if I would ever see my parents again. I woke up in the hospital room to him asking if I was awake, before he up and left because he wanted to go home. Leaving me there alone after having cancerous tumors removed from my body. Body parts gone I knew would change me forever, wondering what I had done to make this happen.

Tears coursed down my cheeks as I faced myself. I knew I had done nothing to deserve cancer. The fear of that day still hadn't left me though six years later. It was only through my conversation with Tama and Onida, that I understood that I wasn't made to have children. I was supposed to save them. In this moment, watching myself face this alone after my parents went home, hours after my husband had left because they didn't want to leave me by myself, I felt sadness. I watched as the nurses came in and sat with me, so many of them telling me their life stories because they sensed the empath in me. The sadness I was feeling turned to love for myself. I understood why I needed to see this again.

The raven hopped on my shoulder and ruffled its wings like it was giving me a hug. I understood watching it this time, instead of a nightmare reel, I got that the person who sat there awake after surgery and listened to all the nurses, consoled them, helped them feel better about themselves even though her life was hell, was worthy of love. The raven cawed.

"Freak! Weirdo!" came the taunts of the kids who didn't understand that being different is okay. It still hurt my feelings to have very few friends and to try to help the ones I knew needed help, even if they didn't like me. I tried so hard to make them all happy.

I was thankful it was this memory. I understood that the raven wanted me to know that it doesn't matter what others think of me. I was part way there, but I still felt awful when shunned and blamed myself for it. It wasn't my fault. Nothing is wrong with me.

"Fucking whore! I should kill you here right now and save the world from your slut ways and lies. The world is better off without you in it anyway!" My stepson had a loaded pistol shoved in my face while I was out on a walk in the neighborhood. He'd followed me and stopped in the middle of the street. Spit flying from his mouth as he screamed and drew the attention of all that could hear

him. *My husband standing behind him, the smell of alcohol permeating his pores and clothes. Because I couldn't get pregnant.*

Another scene started.

His hands wrapped around my throat squeezing tighter and tighter, fueled by delusions created by harmful words of those that were supposed to love me. My vision was blackening, head ringing at being slammed against the wall while he screamed at me that I was nothing but a whore. The words following me into the darkness that swallowed me whole.

I didn't want to see more of this, I knew how it played out. What was this supposed to show me? This was just another blow to an already shattered self-esteem. The lesson I had learned at the time was one about addictions. The alcoholism my husband had, the dope problem my stepson had. Much like the abusive boyfriend scene it showed me, I didn't know how to fix this one. I knew it tied to that one, I knew they all tied together.

"You changed. I don't like how you changed. You don't allow me to have opinions. You have no self-esteem. I don't want to be responsible. Why can you go do this now? Why couldn't you go do this with me? You are too picky." My last boyfriend listed off the reasons he didn't want to be with me, after breaking up with me over e-mail, then sending a text telling me to read that e-mail. Every insecurity I had he hurled at me. Each landing with concise precision to cause maximum damage. All the work I had done to change how I felt about myself crumbling into dust around me.

While I was out, he had moved all of what he considered his things out of our place, even though he brought nothing in. I came home as he was loading his stuff in his mother's car. "I heard you were out with some guy already." I had been with my dad, who was worried about me.

The wounds he inflicted were the most damaging out of all who came before him. I had trusted him. I had given him all of me. I kept nothing back. He turned it all against me, made it my fault. I wasn't good enough. Nights spent laying in an empty bathtub, crying because I gave my best, and was told it wasn't good enough. I had wanted to die. This one had broken me, shattered the fragile shell that was barely held together.

"I know why you are showing me this. I'm aware I'm still broken by this. But again, I don't know how to fix it. I wish you could talk." Scene after scene was shown to me of all the times I was ashamed of myself, belittled, or broken down by those who professed to love me. Then came the worst physical attack.

I felt the crack of the bat against my head. I had been in my parking lot at home. Someone was taking me. He had a foreign accent. I didn't know him, he kept calling me his. He shoved me in a truck, tied my arms and legs then covered me with a tarp. He drove for a while, my bleeding head slamming hard into the bed of truck over every bump. When he stopped, he pulled me out and dropped me on the ground and tied my hands around the trunk of a tree. He used a knife to cut my clothes off.

Shame flooded my body, saturating everything. Then I felt Jax; the raven cawed loudly as I spun around. "No! Jax wake up! You have to wake up! You can't see this! No! Jax! Wake up!" I started yelling loudly. Fear rushing through my veins.

He tied my legs apart and tied each leg to something so I couldn't fight back. He beat me, calling me his, and he raped me, over and over. I kept telling him to stop, he didn't have to do this, I fought with my words until he shoved something in my mouth, putting a cigarette out over my heart and laughing cruelly.

Ronnie jolted hard. "Is this what I think it is?" Ronnie choked on tears.

"The rape," Smitty said, his voice dead, his emotions tattered.

"No! Jax wake up! You have to wake up! You can't

see this! No! Jax! Wake up!" Airiella started screaming.

Ronnie jumped up. "Shit! Jax is in there?!"

Just then they all heard an inhuman sounding howl coming from Jax's room. "Fuck!" Ronnie bolted out the door and pushed an equally frantic Mags behind him. "You can't go in there!"

Ronnie pushed the door open and the blood in his body turned to ice. Jax was fighting the darkness, but his face was pure anguish, he was sobbing, his eyes wild, hands pulling at his hair making it stick out at odd angles all over his head. Ronnie did the only thing he could think of doing. He wrapped him in a bear hug and held tight.

If Jax had seen Airiella get raped it would destroy him. He hated violence against women. The darkness in him probably loved it, Ronnie thought. He was more Jax right now than darkness though, or he wouldn't be sobbing. "Jax, buddy, I got you. I got you. Fight this. Fight it man. I need you back. I need Jax. I need my brother. I got you, bro," Ronnie chanted, holding him tight as Aedan pushed his way in.

Aedan hugged him from the other side and chanted along with Ronnie. When Jax dropped his head on Ronnie's shoulder, he knew they beat it back. Barely, but he needed to keep him away from Airiella.

"Keep him awake Aedan, or take him on a drive or something. He was in Airiella's dream," Ronnie begged.

"Guessing it was a bad part?" Aedan asked unnecessarily.

"She was beat, humiliated, stalked, left alone to fight cancer, raped." Jax's voice was strangled and Ronnie hugged him tighter as Jax broke down in sobs again listing the offenses he had witnessed.

"Aw, shit," Aedan growled. "You saw it all?"

Jax nodded. "It's not safe for me to be here right now."

Ronnie handed him off to Aedan and went back to Airiella's room and closed the door, leaning against it as his heart thudded in a painful rhythm in his chest. Smitty sitting there hanging his head in his hands, crying silently. "Is it over?" Ronnie asked quietly.

"I don't know. She stopped moving, now, she's just crying." Smitty sounded destroyed.

"Is this worse than whatever happened in that chapel?" Ronnie asked, scared.

"Trauma wise, it's probably the same, just in very different ways. Thankfully she doesn't remember a whole lot about what happens during the other. This? She remembers this shit every day." His raw words grated.

"You gonna be okay?" Ronnie laid a hand on his shoulder sympathetically.

"Jax won't be if he saw it happen, I only saw this end of it, not the crime itself. That was brutal enough." Smitty trembled.

"How is she still alive?" Ronnie cleared his throat trying to stem the tears.

The raven cawed softly at me. "Yeah, I'm supposed to know how to fix this stuff?" I thought this was going to guide me in learning how to fix myself. All I'd seen is the same holes I already knew were there. "I need Tama."

A cougar appeared, "That's all you had to say. You need help, we come. Watch."

Jax talking to me comparing me to the northern lights, starlight.

Ronnie telling me I'm an angel. How amazing I am.

Smitty telling me how beautiful I am. Winnie telling me how beautiful I am.

Mags telling me she loved me, Aedan saying I'm incredible.

Jax's kiss.

"Are you seeing a pattern? For all the bad things you heard and believed about yourself, from people who had known you years no less, here are people who have known you weeks, telling you all the good and you don't believe them," Tama said.

"I need to start believing in myself. That's how I fix these broken spots?" I asked honestly.

"It's a start. But you have to actually believe in yourself. What happened to you, happened for a reason. Who else but a raven, or an angel, whatever they want to call you, can survive those things, move past them and then take their own ugly experience and use their pain to help another over theirs? You do it willingly and selflessly. Airiella Raven, you are magnificent." Tama's voice was kind.

"I forgive myself for believing the worst things about myself. For not believing that I was worth fighting for, I forgive myself. For wanting to take an easy way out and die, I forgive myself. I'm proud of myself for continuing to move forward despite the obstacles put in my way." My voice was cracking, breaking and wavering, but I said it. More importantly I believed it. I kept repeating it, over and over.

"These people were put in my life to try and destroy me in the worst ways possible, and the people in my life now are the people who are showing me all the beauty in my life that can be used to make things better for others." A small feeling of relief started to fill my body.

"You are catching on Ms. Raven. You also need to learn that you've never been alone in this, you just never asked for help, or let people in. I know what happened in the past was a block in letting that happen, but you've started the process now. You are healing. Scars will remain, but the hole that was there before is now a filled in crack. Once you can see that, you'll see the true beauty of a restored piece of art. Beauty is flaws, not flawless." The cougar circled my legs, butting her head on my knees.

"How did Jax get in here?" I thought to ask.

"He's got a very powerful connection to you, even without the sex. This may have set him back some by seeing it. You will need to use your gifts wisely; he can be saved. In saving him, you are opening up a world that you can use to teach others. These new friends of yours have an important role to play for the world, and in assisting you with yours." Tama pushed me a little with her body.

"I'm exhausted. Can I sleep?" I needed it desperately at this point.

"Yes, Ms. Raven, you can sleep. Just remember, the healing only just began, it is not complete. You will hurt tomorrow. Ask for help. Share your life. It's quite incredible."

"Thank you, Tama. The raven is quite beautiful," I told her graciously.

"She is you. Sleep now." The large feline stalked off into the darkness.

I closed my eyes, felt the tears still falling, and let them wash through me, washing away some of those things I should have let go of. In the real world, I felt Smitty and Ronnie settle down around me and hold me. Filling these cracks of mine with a love that was amazing, and for so long I had thought unattainable.

Aedan drove aimlessly, pushing coffee on Jax every chance he got, and his heart broke every time he saw the haunted and shattered look on his face. Dark circles smudged beneath his eyes that were dark with pain. He leaned his head against the window which fogged when the tears started again.

Aedan knew that Jax had seen the beatings that Ronnie's mom had gotten from his dad. They all had seen what Ronnie got. Over the past twelve years that they had been doing the show, Jax had made an effort to help every female that was a victim of abuse, though not many knew that.

Him seeing what Airiella had lived through was a giant blow to an already overwhelmed mind and Aedan was beyond worried at Jax's mental state. No matter how many times he had tried to start a conversation, Jax remained catatonic, sitting there in a state of shock. Robotically drinking the coffee Aedan thrusted at him.

The only good thing was that Jax hadn't given in to

the darkness that Aedan felt simmering below the surface, and he was starting to believe that there was hope in this after all. His feelings for Airiella were stronger than that darkness in him. At least they had been tonight.

Which also told him that Airiella had understated the things she had been through, and that didn't surprise him in the least. The love that woman felt for people defied all logic and reasoning. Love that Jax needed to feel again.

He looked over again as he heard Jax's breathing hitch again. More tears. He needed Mags. Her nurturing personality was able to penetrate Jax's moods sometimes. He kept driving until he got the text that it was safe to return and pulled into the house right as dawn started to break the sky.

He led Jax back to his room where Mags met them and he watched as she tucked him in bed and laid there with him while he cried. Please God, Aedan prayed, let me get my brother back. This broken spirit was not his brother.

Chapter Eleven

I woke up with my body feeling battered, but I was nestled between two sexy men that took care of me voluntarily. I turned my head slowly to look at Smitty. He was asleep, but he had dark half-moons under his eyes. He was so stoic and good. I turned my body towards him and ran a finger over his face, his stubble rough against my skin.

He opened his eyes and I gave him a kiss. A soulful one full of thanks and love. He stayed quiet so he didn't wake Ronnie but he pulled me into him tightly and hugged me close. I could see how tired he was, so I pushed my love through the connection to ease his mind and then opened my senses to feed him some calm.

He sat up and mouthed that he was going to his room. I nodded at him and kissed him again, our tongues sliding against each other in sinuous motions. He gave me a tired smile and rested his forehead against mine for a moment then left quietly.

I moved over to give more room to Ronnie who still hadn't budged, but had the same exhausted look that

Smitty wore. I felt around his emotions, the most prominent being worry, but it was a close tie with love. He was a beautiful man who wore his heart on his sleeve.

I didn't want to wake him up, but I had to touch him. The connection was there, though not strengthened the way it should be. I knew it would happen. I also knew that despite the feelings I had for him, they were a shadow compared to what I felt for Jax.

It made me sad in a way because it would be so easy with Ronnie. His humor and love felt so comfortable and the way he wanted to protect me all the time filled a need I had deep within me that so many others put there.

I shifted so I could kiss his jaw. His stubble scraping my lips in a way that pooled heat in my belly. He was still asleep but he rolled when I kissed him and pulled me to him and buried his face in my hair. He was exactly what I needed after the trauma of seeing all that shit from my past last night.

His very being was balm for my soul. I loved it. I loved all of them. I needed all of them, it no longer scared me to admit it. Jax and Ronnie were my two most powerful connections and I hadn't even made them permanent yet. The only thing stronger was when we all touched like when they hugged me last night in the backyard.

I laid there with Ronnie wrapped around me and felt around inside. I still felt raw, but I felt more whole than I had before. I had a way to go yet. As I remembered what Tama showed me with these guys and their words that I wanted to believe so badly, something healed within and I believed them. I believed the way they felt when they talked about me.

I heard the flapping of wings in my head and dared to think just maybe I could do this, be what everyone said I was. The powers they said I hadn't even realized I had yet, starting to show themselves in how I was feeling the life around me, the love within me, the strength I had to share. I smiled.

"Angel, can we not do that again, please?" Ronnie

whispered roughly in my ear.

I rolled to look at him and cupped his face with my hands and put all my love into a kiss for him. I wanted this beautiful man to feel how he made me feel. I stroked his lips with my tongue and he groaned and opened his mouth letting me in. I pushed my love at him, his breath caught and he looked at me, raw emotion all over his face and shining in his eyes.

"Do you have any idea how much I love you?" I told him. He shook his head at me, tears pooling in his gorgeous green eyes. "Enough to tell you that without you, my life would suffer. I need you, Ronnie. You fill so many holes in my heart."

He sat up and hauled me to him, pulling me up into his lap and wrapping my legs around him as he wound himself around me. It wasn't sexual, it was an emotional need. I held him as he cried silently into my neck, my hair covering his head. "You have such a beautiful soul, Ronnie."

"Angel..." he sighed tightening his arms around me. "Are you okay?"

"I am, but only if you stay with me today," I said in his ear.

"What about Jax?" he shifted so he could look at my face.

"He asked me the same thing about you." I scooted back far enough that my heels rested over his legs against his finely sculpted ass. "I think part of what caused this darkness is the way he feels about you. He loves you so much."

"What about you and him?" Ronnie specified.

"My feelings for him are separate from my feelings for you, we talked about this." I touched his face and he rubbed his face on my palm.

"He loves you," Ronnie told me.

"Maybe," I admitted. "I have no shortage of love to give, don't worry about that."

"Angel, you *are* love." I rested my forehead against

his chest as my inclination to dismiss his claim rose in me and I fought it back. He lifted my chin so I had to look in his eyes. "Do you disagree?"

"I'm trying not to. God knows I've harbored enough hate in my heart to believe I can't be love like you suggest. I will admit that I have a good capacity for it though," I attempted.

"It's a start." He smiled and brushed his lips across mine with a feather light touch. "You are so beautiful." He was purposely challenging me.

"Baby steps, please. But, thank you." I blushed.

"Someday the world is going to know your name. They may not know you saved them from self-destruction, but they will know your name." Ronnie's promise rang loudly in the room, even though his tone was soft.

"I don't want people to know my name. I just want to love, and be loved. Simple as that." I laid back down. "Is he okay?" my voice a whisper.

"I don't know. He saw everything," Ronnie offered.

"What?!" Alarm blared through me.

"You didn't know he was there?" He looked confused as he studied my reaction.

"Only when... only at the end. I felt him." My thoughts raced madly.

"You can talk about it, you know. I know it happened, you announced it in the interview." He laid beside me and held my hand.

"I'd been sexually assaulted before that one. Date rape in the sense that I kept saying no, but he decided that he was going to get it anyway, because that's how you make up after a fight. That last time though, it was different. I know I'm supposed to heal and whatnot, but that attack was brutal. I had hoped that you would get him out before he saw it." My voice caught.

"My dad used to beat my mother, then when she was broken and bloody, he'd force her to have sex because it was owed to him." Ronnie shifted uncomfortably. "The house we lived in was small, I knew exactly what was happening. When I got into high school, I tried to stop him. The beatings turned to me. He was thorough in it too.”

I rolled over to him and put my head on his shoulder. “I tried to find excuses for why people did that when it happened to me. There's never a good enough reason to excuse it.”

“Jax saw me busted up so many times. It hurt him that he couldn't change it. He saw my mom battered, heard the fights when he was over. He loved my mom. He doesn't do well with physical violence against women. Any abuse really, verbal, mental, emotional, physical, it all affects him. Last night something broke in him. When I got into the room, the sounds he was making didn't even sound human. Angel, he was shattered.” Ronnie sounded small.

I braced myself when I heard the flapping of wings again. I knew that I shouldn't feel guilty or that I done something wrong. I totally got why he felt that way and I made myself focus instead on ways I could help him through it.

“I know you don't believe this yet, and I understand, but I know the way he feels about you. I know him so well that he couldn't ever hide that from me. It's in his eyes when he sees you. Him knowing this stuff is one thing, seeing it is entirely another ball game. I honestly don't know what will happen with him. I know you haven't told me your story yet, and you don't ever have to. You said in the vaguest terms what you had dealt with in that interview. It's more than most have had to deal with. I consider myself fairly strong, however, angel, I don't think I could have handled seeing it like he did.” Ronnie kissed my forehead to ease my pain.

“What can I do?” I asked dully.

“Tread carefully. Don't push him, he needs to see you okay, acting normal.” Ronnie's suggestions were reasonable.

“I don't want to be treated differently because of what I've been through. It's one of the biggest reasons I don't tell people. They change the way they act around you, the way they treat you after they know. It bothers me on a deep level, because nothing else changed, other than they now know I was abused. It may have shaped who I have become, but at no point did it or will it define me," I said more firmly.

"Did you know that your body showed the marks left on you while you went through that shit last night?" He leaned up on his elbow to look down at me. His eyes soft, yet penetrating. He stroked his hand over my face and neck.

"No, though it explains why I'm so sore today," I answered hesitantly, realizing just how much they saw without being there.

"Not gonna lie, it hit me hard, it affected me. But it doesn't change how I feel about you. Smitty and I both cried, shamelessly. Jax broke down completely. It's our nature to want to shelter those we love, protect them, fight their demons for them. I know you don't need that, but it's who we are. You'll have to give us a little leeway there."

"One of my biggest challenges is letting people in, it hasn't worked out so well for me in the past, you know? In order for me to move past all that, I need to keep doing it, even though it's my nature not to. Leeway goes both ways, okay?" My voice was firm, but soft.

"Understood."

I sighed deeply. "That being said, feel free to ask anything you want about my past and I will tell you however much you can handle."

His eyes searched mine for a catch, though there wasn't one, I was serious. "Tell me why letting people in hasn't worked out for you."

"How about I give you the most recent example which also happens to be the wound that won't heal in me? The cause of the biggest holes in me." A huge challenge for me to talk about, too.

"Hit me with it, baby." He sat up propping his back against the headboard and pulled me over to sit between his legs with my back resting against his solid chest. I leaned my head back against his shoulder and he settled his arms around my waist.

"His name is Michael. I was with him for five years. He was the first relationship after my divorce. We were friends in high school, I'd known him for years, so it was comfortable to be around him. Thinking back on it now, there were signs I should have seen, but I was so damaged already, I didn't. I needed love."

"What signs?" he asked against my ear.

"He'd never lived on his own, he'd only ever held one job that he was fired from and started working with his dad after that. He spouted off all the lies you want to believe, like he'd always fight for me, I was the best thing that ever happened to him, I changed his life, blah blah blah."

"Some of those may be true, angel," Ronnie said.

I choked up. "I know. It's sad that I still want to believe the best, even though I know otherwise. He'd already known so much about me as a person, it was easy to open up. I told him about my past, the bad things that happened, what my triggers were. What my hot button issues were, my insecurities, the problems I had in my marriage. I told him everything in the spirit of wanting to be better. Truthfully, I still blamed myself for most of the things that I had been through, and I desperately wanted to break the pattern, to have something that felt good."

Pain blossomed in my chest. "Angel, you are safe right now."

"I laid my soul bare for him. I also did everything. That was a sign that I always overlooked. I was desperate to make people happy, for validation that they liked me. I can see the failures now. I did all the cooking because he didn't know how. I did all the cleaning in our shared apartment because he went back and did stuff at his dad's house. I did all the meal planning, the planning of vacations, or things to do. I did all the laundry, I put him first before everything else. He never made any effort."

"Idiot," Ronnie muttered.

"Yes, I was," I admitted, though I knew he wasn't talking about me. I didn't give him a chance to correct me though, or I would have stopped because it still hurt. "I should have noticed it before I did, but love blinded me. I willingly fought for him, went out of my way to make him feel special, did things that only benefited him. In five years, he maybe went down on me six times. He never even made any effort at sex. Still, I pushed away the thoughts that were creeping in that maybe this wasn't a good relationship."

I leaned forward and hugged my knees to me. "He started arguing more when I started to make an effort to improve myself. Even though he knew my weaknesses, he used them as tools in his arguments. Denting the progress I made. He had a way of turning things around on me that made me feel like that was what I was doing to him. I was so willing to believe all the bad things he implied, it sickens me. I gave him so much ammunition to use, never once suspecting that he would do that. He had my trust."

Ronnie pulled me back against him and I sunk into his embrace, grateful for the warmth he provided because I was shaking now. "The rape that Jax saw happened while I was with him. It wasn't him, he was too busy complaining about only getting it in one position, while the times I tried to make him do others he just complained that it was too complicated, or it hurt his knees, or his back, or his calves. Anyway, after the attack, the arguments got worse. I know how hard I am on myself; I freely admit that. But when I start feeling worse about myself because of what he says, then it compounds by my own bar, it starts this domino effect. I started to see signs that paradise wasn't what I thought it was."

I paused because Ronnie was tense and I stroked his arms until he relaxed. "His taunts and jokes were starting to be personal attacks at me. He made fun of me in front of his family because I don't drink, due to the alcoholism of my ex-husband. I don't do drugs because of the things I saw happen to those around me who did. Those became points of arguments and opportunities to break me down. It just kept escalating. Finally, after I cut my hair the last time to donate it, I was at lunch with my cousin who had told me I was an inspiration to her. I had been doing a positivity campaign to find something each day that made me happy. He also made fun of that. Anyway, at that lunch she had asked me how Michael and I were doing. I was surprised by my own answer. I told her I felt like he was holding me back."

"He was gaslighting you," Ronnie broke in, his voice strangled.

"I know that now, I didn't then. He seemed to stop for a couple of weeks, then out of the blue, two weeks before Christmas, I get a text from him telling me to read my e-mail. He had sent an e-mail to me breaking up with me. While he was at work. Listing out all these things I had said in defense of myself and saying that those comments hurt him more than anything because I couldn't see how hard he had tried to convince himself he loved me. Every insecurity I had, he used. Every bad thought I had about myself he voiced. When he got home, he got pissed off at me because I was upset, then told me over and over again it always had to be my way and he wasn't allowed to have his own thoughts. Not once did he ever try to sit down and talk to me about anything, he never shared his feelings, let me know what he was thinking, never. He always got mad when I pushed him."

Hot tears fell on Ronnie's arm and I tried to wipe them away. "Leave them, they are a part of you," he told me gruffly.

"He told me I had changed; he didn't like who I was. The only changes I had made was to start believing in myself. He told me I put too much responsibility on him, his example: asking him to stop at the store on his way home from work to pick up an ingredient I thought I had for making his dinner. He told me he liked being single. I would have accepted it had he sat down and told me he wasn't happy, but he didn't. He took every opportunity he could to destroy me. I called in sick the next day because I wasn't safe to drive. In a moment of weakness, I called my mom to tell her he broke up with me, and she got worried and called my dad. He came and picked me up and carted me around while he did errands."

I sniffled, remembering how broken I was. "You have to understand, despite the time that you have known me, I'm not a crier. I rarely cried. They freaked out because I couldn't stop. When my dad dropped me off, Michael was there loading his mother's car. He had left work early to move out while I wasn't there. Me showing up when I did, ruined his plans and he took the opportunity to once again flay me wide open. I argued out of fear, but let him go. He moved back in with his parents, of course. But the next week I ended up sleeping in the bath tub where I cried myself to sleep every night. Why the tub? I don't know, for some reason it felt safe to me."

"Angel, baby..."

I broke in, "I started noticing weird things after that. Noises that woke me up in the night. I didn't put it together until after I had to move out, and was temporarily homeless. He had been coming in there while I was sleeping. I don't know why, but he did. I had started feeling very unsafe, watched. Then he started texting me, sending me emails about reasons relationships failed, told me that when he looked at me he saw someone who was raped. Never mind it wasn't the first time that happened, and he knew that, but he said I was dirty." I took a deep breath in as those wounds bled freely now. "Ronnie, he broke me. He broke everything about me. Never in my life had I let someone in as much as I let him in. There was nothing he didn't use against me. Every step I had made to feel better about myself was totally gone. I would have rather been raped again. I had to fight to find reasons to live."

Ronnie crushed me to him again and cried with me. "Let it out, angel, I've got you."

"It was emotional warfare of the worst sort. The pain I get when I think of him is enough to stop me in my tracks, but I don't let it because he doesn't deserve that power over me."

"He doesn't deserve to even set eyes upon you," Ronnie growled.

"After everything else I'd been through that was just the last straw. I stopped letting people in unless I felt like something in my story would help them, and even then, they only got that part. Trust isn't something I am generous with when it comes to myself." I gave him a tremulous smile, "You are the first one I've told that stuff too."

"Angel, there isn't anyone in this house that even at their worst, would do those things to you. Jax is an asshole, but he would never do those things to you. Even if that shit in him took over, I think he'd kill himself before taking those steps. Hopefully I don't eat those words, but I believe in my heart he wouldn't." Ronnie was angry and adamant.

"I'm not afraid of him Ronnie. I'm just afraid to let people in. I trust you all with my life, trusting someone with my heart is a different story. This piece of me I told you is an olive branch, saying I'm willing to work on it," I told him quietly.

He gave me a soft kiss on the forehead. "Winnie told me about you before she died, did you know that?"

"She told me in part of her story that she told me. She said she saw me, with you guys," I remembered.

"Did she come clean and tell you that she saw you with Jax? That she said he was yours? That's how she knew to push him to agree they were broken up." He kept his voice even, but I felt an undercurrent of something there.

"She told me she saw that he belonged to someone else. I've pieced together through bits and pieces she's let slip that she believes it's me. Some of the council have alluded to the same thing. I can't lie to you, the connection I feel with him is overwhelming. Also, when I touched him, I saw glimpses of a future with him which unnerved me. I don't like the thought that I don't have control over something like that in my life." I looked at him to see how he took that. He looked thoughtful and melancholy.

"Did she ever say if she saw me with someone?" There was the undercurrent. It was longing.

"Not in so many words. I can tell you that when I first touched you, I knew in my heart that you were meant for someone else, not me. I will admit to feeling disappointment in that because, damn, you are one piece of sexy man candy." I gave him a lascivious look.

He threw his head back and laughed a deep belly laugh. It was music to my ears. "I needed to hear that after all this!" He poked me in the side. "That doesn't mean we can't play."

I used my phone sex voice. "Oh, don't you worry your pretty little head, I fully plan on playing."

His eyes darkened with lust. "Should we start now?"

"No, sadly, I don't think I'm ready at the moment. My body still hurts." I sobered as I remembered the reason why. His face softened and concern filled his gaze.

"Shit, sorry angel, that voice does something to me." He winked.

"Good! It's supposed to!" I gave him my best grin.

"Let's go get some food." He stood up and pulled me up with him. "I need to put something in my mouth, if it's not going to be you, it might as well be food." He grabbed my ass and then pushed me in front of him. "Walk ahead of me so I can stare at your ass without you know it."

I swayed my hips. "How's that?"

He groaned a low throaty groan. "A little too effective."

"Oh, take my necklace! I promised Winnie I'd take it off," I remembered as I swung around. He went back in and placed it on my nightstand.

Winnie shouted, "It's about time! Are you okay?"

"I'm fine Winnie, it wasn't fun, but I survived it."

Ronnie gave Airy a sideways look, not used to the open conversation with her yet.

Winnie looked her over carefully. She didn't know what she was looking for, but she felt better checking anyway. She thought Ronnie looked tense. "What's wrong with Ronnie?"

"Nothing is wrong with Ronnie." Airy looked over at Ronnie with a question on her face.

"Just a long night, Winnie," Ronnie said to the open air, not sure where to direct his statement.

Winnie giggled. "You didn't tell him where I was. That was funny. For a paranormal investigator he looks awfully uncomfortable."

Winnie watched Ronnie's face as Airy relayed the message and he gave a goofy smile. "Where's she at?" Airy gestured to her left. "You're a shit Winnie."

"When are you going to sleep with him so he can see me?" Winnie asked with a laugh.

"Not now Winnie." Airy gave a frustrated sigh.

"What's she saying?" Ronnie was curious.

"Nothing important, don't worry about it," Airy hedged.

"You're mean. If you leave the house, put the necklace back on," Winnie cautioned. "Something feels off."

"I think it's Jax," Airy told her. "He was in the dream state with me, I didn't notice until too late."

Winnie gasped. "That's not good."

"I figured that out on my own, thanks," came the sarcastic reply.

Ronnie spoke up. "He's on our radar Winnie. We are watching him. He needs space to process what he saw." He had guessed what Winnie said.

"You are in good hands now. I can feel a different energy between you two. I'll hang around for a bit, but I'll be out of sight," Winnie said carefully. She wondered if she went back to the gray if she could find another spirit that could find out more info.

"Thanks for checking on me, Winnie," she heard Airy say as she faded out.

Chapter Twelve

edan hung up his phone and stepped back in Jax's room to check on him. Nightmares terrorized him while he slept and Aedan began to wonder if permanent damage was done to him. He looked at his phone while he sat on the chair next to the foot of his bed.

He sent a text to Smitty and Ronnie. "Need to talk. Filming schedule revised. Going to do impromptu live show after this first shoot."

He had hung up with Tom, the studio had received a request addressed to Jax at the studio. That wasn't anything new, he got marriage proposals that way. Tom had said the letter described a family tormented by possession and driven to separation and they needed help. The money behind the show thought it was a great way to boost ratings to offset the hiring of Airiella.

It concerned Aedan because of Jax. Who knew how putting him into the vicinity of someone claiming to be possessed would play out. It could be extremely dangerous for Jax and he had reservations about it, and argued with the producers on speaker phone to rethink the decision.

Why did it have to be a live show? Why couldn't they film it and air it during the season?

They said it would be a great way to promote the new upcoming season with the live show ending in Washington. He shook his head, and woke Jax up. He needed to be a part of this conversation and they needed to have it sooner rather than later, given the prep time they had for this was next to nothing.

Unfortunately, it also meant putting him in the same room as Airiella, and Aedan didn't think that was the best of ideas either. Jax would just have to pull it together, some things couldn't be avoided if he wanted to the show to continue.

"Jax you need to get up. We have to have a meeting about a schedule change in the shoots. They just added a live show. Come on, get up," Aedan pushed.

Jax grumbled, looking like haunted shit, but got up and woodenly followed him downstairs. He didn't look anyone in the eye and sat himself as far away as possible from the others. Ronnie put a bottle of water in front of him and went back to sit by Airiella.

To her credit, Aedan thought she was handling it okay, though she looked uncomfortable. "I just hung up with Tom, who I argued with for fifteen minutes to try to get him to nix it, but the money men are insistent that this happens."

"Why?" Smitty questioned, leaning against the counter with one leg crossed over the other. His posture appearing casual, but Aedan saw he was tense.

"Ratings. Nothing more, nothing less. They are wanting to offset the cost of hiring an additional person," Aedan said without blame. "Tom saw reason in my arguments but he has no leg to stand on with them. They don't believe in the danger of the situation."

"What is the situation exactly?" Jax spoke up, his tone numb.

"Someone wrote a letter to you and sent it to the station. Whoever read it decided to show it up the line and the money men thought it would be a great live show. Some guy told a story about his family being possessed, and it drove them all apart and destroyed their lives. He insisted that you could help them because you understood," Aedan paraphrased.

"That's it? Hardly any different than others letters that have been sent." Jax was confused.

"The letter got shown to the right people to make it happen is my guess," Aedan simply stated.

"Did any of the crew research anything?" Smitty jumped in.

"Nothing more than seeing if this guy said he was who he said he was and not some crazed fan wanting to marry Jax." Aedan looked grim.

Airiella snorted, "That really happens?"

"More often than you think," Ronnie supplied. "People are nuts."

"We fly to Kansas after this shoot, no down time. We have no idea what we are walking into, and they are already hyping it up on TV. Shadow Seekers to the rescue of a destroyed family by evil spirits," Aedan grunted.

"Well, then let's start researching now, see what we can dig up about this guy, his family, the house, I'm assuming it's a house? People that know this guy, let's get invasive." Ronnie leaned forward, intent. "I'm not comfortable with this, same as you Aedan. I definitely don't want Airiella or Jax in danger on this. Knowledge is power."

"They give us the okay to spend money to dig?" Smitty added.

"Yes, though it's limited. Not as high of a budget as the other live show. Airiella, can you help Ronnie and Smitty with research? Also, you still need to train, this guy could be a loose cannon, and you'll have to help carry equipment on this first shoot. You will also be doing the preliminary walk through with us on both locations, especially the second. You'll have to be on essentially all the time."

"Got it, boss man," Airiella said.

"I'm the elephant in the room everyone is ignoring. What's the plan to make sure I don't lose my shit?" Jax gave Aedan a flat look.

"No one is ignoring you. Our best weapon is Airiella. In a perfect world, this shoot in a couple days goes perfectly and all is good with you so you are in top form for the live show. I haven't come up with a plan B," Aedan admitted. "Flying blind on this one, bro. It's part of our contract that when the backers say we need to do a show, we do it."

"You are hedging everyone's safety on me?" Airiella whispered.

Jax hung his head, unable to look at her and Aedan noted the position of his body was defeat. "Did last night help you?" Aedan dared to ask, watching Jax the whole time.

Jax's body went rigid but he didn't look up. Airiella shifted in her seat and Aedan saw Ronnie hold her hand and Smitty moved to stand behind her. "I know what I need to work on, if that's what you mean. If you are asking if it healed me, the answer is not yet, but I have a clearer path on what I need to do."

Jax was audibly breathing harder and Aedan moved his chair closer to him. "Look at me, Jax." He didn't, and Aedan knew he shouldn't push. "I know how you feel, but we don't have a choice. You need to get past this."

"Easier said than done," Jax said under his breath with a snarl. He looked up, directly at Airiella then. "You stripped my soul bare." His eyes shone with something Aedan hadn't seen in him before and he didn't know what to do.

"J-Jax," Airiella stuttered.

"No, don't." He stood. "I don't know how you smile, but I can't un-see that shit, the rage that I'm trying to keep down is only matched by the terror I feel. Just give me space. Please," he begged, his voice ragged, his body tremoring.

Aedan felt like he was watching a train wreck. "Go

do what you need to do, Jax. I'll take point on getting things lined up on this." Jax gave a small nod and walked off. "Don't take it personally." Aedan turned to Airiella.

"I don't. I know what he meant," she acknowledged in a small voice.

"Train with Ronnie, focus on self-defense moves," Aedan suggested. "I really don't have a good feeling about this."

"Just a minute," Airiella told him. "Whatever else happens," she pointed to his neck, "make sure that everyone keeps those on and against their skin. No matter what. If I have to pull his energy, I will."

Smitty started. "Baby girl…"

"No Smitty, I will do what I need to do. You don't need to be there for after." She put her hand on his arm to stop him from arguing.

"It's her call, Smitty," Ronnie said. "We don't have to like it; we just need to get her through it."

"Fuck," Smitty growled, his face stark white. "Go train her." He stalked off.

Airiella stood silently, "I'll go change, meet you out there," she told Ronnie.

Aedan dropped his head on the table. This was never going to work if the team was at odds. "Do an hour or so, then all of us guys need to go get the equipment put together for both shows. He needs to be out of the house a little bit."

Ronnie hummed in thought. "Let's do some gym time with him too. He can use the chance to lose some of the aggression, but not here."

Aedan agreed and got up to go talk to Smitty, then Mags, hoping like mad this all came together somehow. This rollercoaster was about to fall right off the rails if it didn't. He'd rather lose the show than Jax.

Smitty paced the TV room trying to control the fear that hit him when Airiella said she'd pull the energy. He felt like he was excreting it from his pores it was so heavy in him. There wasn't a damn thing he could do to stop anything from happening either.

He sat and pulled out his laptop and opened the email that Aedan forwarded with the info on this site for the live show. He was going to dig deep to find out all he could. Ronnie was right, knowledge was power. Aside from the feeling he had that something didn't feel right about it. Using logic wasn't going to get him answers on the feeling either.

He heard Aedan walk in and listened to him tell him about Ronnie's idea for them all to hit the gym and Aedan's about getting Jax out of the house. He liked it, just not the part about leaving which meant he wouldn't be researching.

If he was honest, he could use the gym time himself to lose some of the aggression that had built in him. Scott Elvis Franklin. What a name. He found a Facebook profile and he flipped through the pictures there saving a few to share with the others.

He entered the info into a background check site he used all the time, and searched on the address through public records online to download as much as he could before they left. It didn't seem like a lot to him, but it was a start and gave him the sense that he was doing something.

Ronnie's brain was spinning too fast to keep up with and he was on autopilot as he wrapped Airiella's hands before putting the gloves on her. He already had his wrapped and was putting the music on when she first came in. He got his gloves on and tried to mentally prepare himself for hitting her.

"Angel, I'm actually going to have to throw punches at you," Ronnie declared.

"I'm aware of what self-defense training is. You should know better than anyone else, I'm not fragile," she retorted, irritation lining her words. She looked exactly that though, fragile and very breakable.

Ronnie moved towards her so fast she stepped back. "When you sleep, all this," he waved his hand over her, "this you-can't-hurt-me persona you try to display, it melts. The you that you hide away from everyone shines through. You're right, I do know better than anyone else. I know that under it, you *are* fragile and extremely breakable in ways that only those that have been there know. Don't give me shit about it. We've both been punching bags, and while I've trained in this for years, it never gets easier throwing a punch at someone who has stood where I did."

Just like that she dropped her guard. "I'm sorry. You're right."

"Hands up!" Ronnie snapped at her, wincing internally at his tone. "Protect your face. I'm rather fond of it." He tried to soften his words. "Block me, anticipate my moves, look for weaknesses, don't stay still, keep moving and your hands up. If you spot an opening, take it, hit, kick, push, do whatever you have to do to throw me off."

Ronnie didn't put weight behind the punches, not enough to hurt, but he danced around her. His feet lightning quick, his body flowing like water. He shouted instructions at her as he pushed her to her limits, hard. He didn't let up and set a grueling pace she would probably hate him for later.

He praised her when she landed hits, grunted when she got a few powerful kicks in, corrected her form and after ninety minutes she was done. She was drenched in sweat, her skin red from the exertion and barely able to catch her breath or the bottle of water he threw her way.

"If you had to defend yourself against someone you knew was going to attack you, I think you'd do pretty good, at least be able to hold your own enough to get away. It's the surprise attacks that kept tripping you up, we will keep working at it when we have time while on the shoot. It won't be much time, though I'll try to work it in. Good job angel. I'm proud of you."

"I'm too tired to smile at you right now," she huffed.

"The guys and I are going to the studio to gather equipment and then to the gym to do what we just did, so you'll have some quiet time," he told her as he grabbed a towel and wiped it over her face.

"Does Aedan have reason to be so nervous about this live show?" she asked.

"Yes. It doesn't feel right, I agree with him on that. To me it feels like a trap," Ronnie admitted freely.

"How?" she drank half the bottle of water down.

"Gut feeling. The show has had some bad press because of the shit Jax is dealing with and a few of the money men want him out. To me, this smells of them, like they are trying to force something to happen." His tone was hard.

"Seems childish, putting people at risk for no good reason." She fiddled with the towel.

"We know their game," he said mildly. "Let's get as much info as we can before we get there."

"I'm at your disposal. After I shower." She smelled her armpit. "I stink."

"Relax for a bit. This will be the last chance you have for a couple weeks straight." He stood and held a hand out to her. He pulled her up and stuck his nose in the crook of her neck, "You smell fine to me angel."

"You need help, Ronnie." She laughed at him and headed for the house. "Have fun."

Ronnie cleaned up the mats and grabbed the dirty towels, locking up the garage behind him. Wasn't going to be fun, but it was necessary and he planned to work the guys just as hard as he worked her. They all needed a release.

Mags knocked on Airy's door but didn't get a response. She could hear music so she knew she was in there. She opened the door and heard the music coming from the bathroom. She called out to her to announce her presence.

"I'm in the bath, you can come in. You've already seen all of me, no need for me to be shy now," Airy answered.

Mags giggled. "You speak the truth, oh wise one.

How was the training?" She pushed herself onto the counter next to the sink.

"Brutal. Nothing this nice steamy bath couldn't fix though." Airy sighed in contentment.

"Baths are magical, and it smells divine, what is that?" Mags asked after taking a big breath in.

"Bath salts I made, or the soap I made, not sure which one you are smelling." She leaned her head back against the rim of the tub.

"I definitely need some of those," Mags said.

Airy pointed to the bag on the back of the toilet. "Help yourself."

Mags smiled. "Next time I take a bath you can bet your sweet ass I'm going to hit you up for some of those. Relaxing scent, is that jasmine?"

"Yeah, it's one of my favorite scents. Probably the only floral one I like," she murmured.

"Well you go on and relax. I've got a ton of errands to run. I just wanted to let you know that you will be alone in the house." She hopped off the counter. "Text me if you need anything."

"Will do, have fun," Airy said drowsily.

"Don't fall asleep in the tub," Mags warned, stopping by doorframe.

"You feel different." Airy's tone was distracted.

"You aren't touching me." Mags was confused. "Explain please."

"Your presence, it's you, but more." Airy's eyes were closed, her tone peaceful despite the confusing words.

"I'm more me?" Mags asked stupidly.

"No, you are just more, something extra there," Airy said again.

"That makes no sense at all." Mags sighed.

Airy bolted upright in the tub, splashing water everywhere. "You're pregnant!"

Mags was sure her jaw dropped open. "What? I can't be."

"You are," Airy breathed. "That's what is more. I

can sense the life in you. Holy shit. That's new."

"Airy, I can't be pregnant, doctors told me it would be almost impossible for that to happen, not to mention I am on birth control." Mags sounded sad.

"Well you just became a miracle then, you are pregnant. I'm sure of it," she insisted.

The smile on Mags' face lit up the room and her eyes shone with tears of happiness. "I'm afraid to get my hopes up. If it's true my heart will be complete. We tried for so long."

"It's true, Mags. I'm no doctor, I can't tell you how far along or anything else. I can just sense the life growing in you. It has a pure white energy to it. You've got a little bean in you." Airy sounded breathless.

Mags sunk to the floor and started bawling. Airy rushed to get out of the tub and Mags held out her hand, "They are happy tears, stay in your bath, I'm fine. Better than fine actually. Thank you Airy, for this beautiful gift. You have no idea what this means to me."

"As someone who won't ever get to experience this, I know how you felt thinking you couldn't. You are going to be one fucking awesome mom, Mags. I'm happy for you."

Mags stood and came over to the tub and brushed a kiss across Airy's lips. "My errands just got busier as I'm going to find a doctor fast, and then think of a way to tell Aedan. You magnificent girl, I love you."

Airy beamed at her. "Love you too Mags. Now go, I have more soaking to do."

Mags practically skipped out of the room searching her phone for the nearest medical clinic and praying for it to be true. Aedan was going to be ecstatic. Mags knew in her heart if it was true, it happened when all three of them were together, that connection bringing her a new life.

Jax had been shaken by Aedan's news and an odd feeling followed as they gathered their equipment and then headed to the gym. There hadn't been a lot of talking between any of them and unsaid worries hung in the air like ticking time bombs.

He knew they were worried about how he'd react, and Jax also knew he'd have to be the one to bring it up. "Okay, do you guys feel like this is a setup? This live show."

Ronnie answered immediately, "Yes."

Aedan was slower to respond, and a bit hesitant with his answer, "I'm hoping it's not, but I am leaning towards it being that way."

Smitty seconded Aedan's response and added, "Can they really be that cold?"

"It's not the first time they've done it deliberately," Jax pointed out.

"It wasn't as dangerous before. This is new levels of low," Smitty grumbled.

"Tom and the other producers are with us on this, Tom feels like we do. It's orchestrated for ratings. Feels vindictive as well." Aedan twisted in his seat to look back at Ronnie and Jax. "If I had to guess, the guy whose wife hit on you at the studio party a couple of years ago is behind this."

"Who are you talking to?" Ronnie pointed between himself and Jax.

"She hit on both of us," Jax muttered.

"Exactly." Aedan faced forward again.

"I'm not in a good place right now," Jax told them all honestly.

"We'll figure it out, we've got your back." Ronnie always his back, even when he was pissed at Jax.

"She scares the hell out of me." Jax looked down at his hands and picked at his stitches.

"I think Ronnie and I had the same reaction when we first met her," Smitty admitted as he parked the car.

"What I saw," Jax started, his voice catching, "I can't find words for what it did to me."

"It's why we are here." Ronnie nudged him. "I'm going to work you hard, let you get it out. You can't change it. She's working through it, and she's moved past a lot of it already. You can't dwell on it or let it change how you see her. I learned today that is a hot button issue and I for one do not want to see that woman unleash her full temper."

Jax rubbed his chest and gave a dry bark of laughter. "Let's go punch shit." He got out grabbing the bag Ronnie had put together for him of workout clothes and headed inside.

Ronnie didn't lie, he worked them into puddles of sweat, the echoing thuds of their blows on the pads and bags resounding through the gym. Grunts of pain and released frustrations bleeding out of Jax as he sparred with each of them, except Ronnie never fought back.

I finished my call with Father Roarke and hung up the phone feeling a little bit relieved that he would make himself available for the live show in Kansas, and found a church near the location that would allow him to use the space if necessary.

It didn't make me feel better knowing that he agreed with Ronnie about this being a trap. That put me on edge even though it was something I had no control over. I could only control my reactions, and Ronnie was right that we all needed to be informed before we got there.

I went over the information Smitty had been able to gather before leaving and jotted down a few more questions I thought we needed to look into if we had an avenue. I was sure Smitty had already thought of it, that was the way his brain worked. Still, it gave me somewhat of a sense of accomplishment.

I was mildly surprised that I wasn't sorer than I was after the mornings training and at the amount of energy I had firing me up. I needed to do something productive. I started laundry and checked the time. It was mid-afternoon, I figured they'd be gone for a little longer.

I decided to cook dinner as a distraction to everything, and roamed through the pantry to see what was stocked here. I loved this kitchen. It was huge, and had tons of counter space, even had that island that now held a special memory for me. I saw bottles of a variety of basic

Italian seasonings, so I decided on a pasta. Easy enough, and generally universally liked. No one was on any special diet that I knew of. I grabbed the spices, a clove of garlic and a few cans of tomato sauce out of the pantry and set them on the island and went back for a box of pasta.

I opened the fridge to see what was in there, and grabbed a couple of fresh tomatoes, and a package of beef I could stew, already knowing the guys all wanted meat. I saw some breakfast sausage and grabbed that too, I could squash that up for the sauce too. I took notice of a bag of fresh green beans and a head of lettuce too. I set it all on the island and started digging through the cupboards looking for pans to use, and pulling out what I needed, grabbing the utensils and a cutting board as well.

Smiling in satisfaction, I felt useful for a moment. Wanting music, I grabbed my purse out of the hall closet and dug around for my beat-up old iPod and ear buds. I glanced at the time again, noting that I had at least a couple hours before dinner time. I popped in my ear buds, set the music to random and got busy, briefly wondering how long the guys would be out and hoping they wouldn't eat before coming back.

I grabbed my phone and sent Ronnie a quick text to let him know I was making dinner and to tell the others not to eat, and then got back to work. Losing myself in the process of doing something inane and normal and the music swaying through my body, I was blissfully happy, closed off in my own little world for a bit.

The kitchen was filling with the comforting smell of the Italian food I had grown up with. I closed my eyes and let the music take my body, twisting, turning, swaying and gyrating myself across the ballroom sized kitchen. Sometimes, it was these quiet, simple moments that made my whole day. I went back over to the stove to add more spices to the meat I had searing in the pan for a few minutes before I added it to the sauce I had simmering.

I pulled the meat off the stove and added the whole chunk to the sauce, put the lid on it and went back to the island to crush up another clove of garlic for the beans. As I set it off to the side, I closed my eyes again, letting the lyrics of one of my favorite songs wash over me. I pushed myself forward and swayed to the music before I turned back around to clean up my mess.

Hand washing the prep stuff I used, I put it away, and started to prep for the pasta. Completely lost in what I was doing, I didn't hear them come in. I filled the pan with water, added some salt, and danced my way back to the stove to set the pan down, so all I had to do later was turn the water on. I stirred the sauce and dipped my finger in to taste to see if I had the seasoning right before I put those all away too. Happy with the taste, I grabbed the spices and danced my way back over to the pantry to put the stuff away. Never noticing the five people that stood in the hallway watching me.

I grabbed my phone again to text Mags this time, asking her to pick up a baguette while she was out at the store, and tossed the phone back down on the counter. Still under the illusion I was alone, I was probably more myself than I had been in a long time, and for that moment, I had no care in the world. I gave myself over to the music.

A faster pace song had come on, There's No Way by Lauv, and I danced my heart out, my hips swinging, body moving, head tipped back completely in the moment. I felt him before I saw him, and before I could freeze, Ronnie's body was pressed against my back, dancing with me, even though he couldn't hear the music. I kept dancing, a huge smile plastered on my face as I ground my hips back into him, and pulled my iPod out of my pocket and unplugged the earbuds so the music was out loud and he could hear the beat. He held the rhythm with me as we moved across the floor, his hands winding around from behind me as they skimmed down my belly and over my hips.

I laughed out loud as the lyrics of the song struck me with how we were dancing. It was true, I figured, and didn't care at all. Suddenly the music was coming from speakers in the kitchen, startled I swung around and

Ronnie caught me up in his arms, "We aren't done yet, angel, just relax." He smiled a wicked smile at me and I caught the blue outline of Winnie as she stood there smiling and clapping.

The song changed, and I found myself dancing with Smitty next. "Was that you? The music through the speakers?" I asked him grinning. He nodded at me and swung me around, and dipped me over his arm.

"Hell of a way to come home," he smirked.

"Don't get used to it," I fired back with an evil grin. I hip checked him, and pranced out of reach as he laughed. I danced back over to the stove to turn the heat down on the sauce.

"Sassy little Susie homemaker, aren't we," he teased as I danced back. I wove around him, dragging my fingers across his biceps as I was behind him.

"I'm a woman of many talents," I quipped in my best phone sex voice, my breath teasing his ear lobe. He burst out laughing as the song changed again. I bowed to him and spun in place. Feeling absolutely ridiculous, and loving it.

I felt someone behind me again, fully expecting Aedan or Mags, I spun around, my hair coming loose from its messy pony tail, I stopped in my tracks as I saw it was Jax. Feeling slightly dangerous, I raised my eyebrow at him.

"What? I don't get a turn?" He asked sarcastically. He was him, the air sizzled around us and I could tell he was holding himself tightly in check.

Fine with me, he wasn't going to win this round. I turned to look at Smitty who now had my iPod in his hand and said, "Smitty, give me a beat." He gave me an evil grin and within seconds, Ludacris was belting out Stand Up. I looked back at Jax with a challenge in my eyes and said, "In order to have a turn dancing, you actually have to move."

In perfect time with the lyrics, I mouthed, "When I move, you move..." as I shimmied up and down against his side. Ronnie and Smitty behind me, laughing hysterically and Jax stood there, his eyes following me, dark and deep. "It's easy, try it," I dared him, using my phone sex voice again.

His eyes darkened even more, and he reached out and tugged my hair the rest of the way loose and dropped my hair tie. He walked in a circle around me, so I moved my body to the beat in place, and swung my hips from side to side. I rotated down to the floor and moved slowly back up in front of him, my boobs barely touching him and I felt that weird chemistry we had flare up bright, hot and alive, and suddenly it wasn't a joke anymore.

I felt a fissure of fear trickle across my soul as I was in dangerous waters here and I knew it, but I refused to back down. He needed to see that I was okay. Despite the taunting and cat calls from the rest of the guys Jax hadn't moved, my body still brushing up against his as I let the music work me. I turned around and rubbed my ass all over his crotch, and I swear I heard him growl. I was almost happy the song was ending, but at the same time, I was horny as hell and had to tamp that shit down. Jax was not the turbulent sea I needed to jump in right now, even though it was all I wanted to do, I was likely to drown.

"Quite the eclectic mix of music you got goin' on here, baby girl," Smitty said as Tequila started to play. Jax stalked off and I saw Winnie glance after him, a worried look on her face. I shook my head gently so she left it alone.

Mags grabbed my hands and we swayed to the song together, as Aedan and Ronnie did a hilarious slow dance across the floor that had Smitty howling. We finished up dancing and I got back to fixing dinner, picking up my hair tie and winding my hair up again.

Everyone went to their rooms to relax a bit before dinner, except Ronnie. Even Winnie vanished. I was slightly out of breath, and a little sweaty, but Ronnie still hugged me from behind as I stirred the sauce. "You definitely won that round angel," he whispered in my ear. "I bet you anything he's in his room rubbing one out."

I blushed furiously at that thought, but broke out

laughing anyway. "Good, the bastard deserves blue balls." Damn it, I wanted to be the one rubbing it out for him. These men were hell on my libido.

"You might just be my favorite person alive angel," Ronnie chuckled into my ear. Yep, I was pretty sure I was going to end up tasting his goods too, sooner rather than later. I let the wave of lust wash over me, knowing he'd feel it. I smiled as his arms tightened around me.

Mags and Aedan left to go get the baguette I texted her about, and by the smiles on their faces I knew she told him some good news and tried to hide the grin that lit up my face. Ronnie noticed anyway and thankfully he didn't push me for an answer. We just hung out in the kitchen and talked about random things as I finished making dinner.

Happily, the dinner was a success. For the first time since we had all been together the group was relaxed and cohesive. It was a perfect night before the madness that was descending upon us. I stretched it out as long as I could for all of us, and was happy to clean up afterwards just so I could bask in it a little longer.

Chapter Thirteen

I walked the location with the guys, the trust they had in me implicit and humbling. It was off the charts in creepiness, but I didn't feel any bad energy. The old asylum was full of energy, just none that sent red flags off.

I was itching to get back outside of the hospital because it was wearing on my own energy, the sadness seeping deep into my bones. I could also see it getting to Jax. Confirmed for me that he did have some empath abilities, though I hadn't really doubted that.

Finally, as we went back outside to wait for the first interviewee to show up, I picked up on something odd and slowed down. I felt watched. I scanned the setting around me and only saw the forest and the lonely road to and from this place nestled into the hills.

Jax felt something too and I felt his energy shift though it didn't turn dark, it felt curious. That did send up a red flag for me. If that energy in him was curious then whatever I had felt was not something good.

I stopped fully and heard the beat of wings inside my head and reached out to separate the emotions around us, filtering them as I identified where they came from and what they were. Back to the left of the entrance to the hospital was a cement path that wound around the back for patients to walk around. Off that path was a worn trail in the grass leading to the forest. It almost looked like a game trail, though it wasn't. This was man made.

"What is it, angel?" came Ronnie's voice quietly from my side.

"Take Jax to the other side over there," I gestured to the opposite side of the hospital, "for the interview. I feel something out there." I nodded my head very slightly in front of me.

"Something bad?" he kept his tone low so it didn't carry.

"I can't tell." I glanced at his worried expression. "Whatever it is has that energy in Jax curious, and that can't be a good thing."

"What's your plan?" he shifted closer to me taking a protective stance.

I shot him a raised eyebrow, "I'm going to go look."

"The fuck you are," he growled in my ear. "If you don't know what it is, don't put yourself in danger, that's not the smart move."

"Remember our conversation about me not being fragile?" I pushed back, not about to be told I couldn't do it.

"Do you remember my answer?" he fired back, just as stubborn as me.

"He needs your protection right now, not me." I stood my ground. "I'll take the extra camera man with me. Go do your job and let me do mine."

"Your job is point out danger, not put yourself in it," he vehemently argued.

"Ronnie, I'm not backing down. Go. Send whoever that is standing there doing nothing over. All I'm going to do is walk over there and see if I can get a better read." I physically pushed him away from me.

"Airiella," he warned, an unmistakable edge to his tone.

I crossed my arms over my chest. "You might not like it, but you need to trust me. I can't be effective unless I can check something out."

His face thunderous, he swung away from me, snapping at the camera guy to go with me, and caught Smitty's attention. I turned my back on them both and headed directly to the little trail following the strange energy.

The camera man huffed up beside me carrying a camera. "I'm supposed to film this," he said apologetically.

"Film the trail then, not me," I said, my tone gruff. "Look for movement, like an animal or person."

He didn't question me, just propped the camera on his shoulder and did what he was told. "There's something glimmering, a reflection maybe, in that big tree right to your left with the branch that is low hanging."

I looked for what he was talking about but I didn't see any reflection or glimmer. He walked a bit ahead of me then pointed. I saw it then, sitting nestled between two branches almost invisible unless you were looking for it. "What is it?" I wondered if I could climb that tree.

"It's a camera," he said as he zoomed in on it with his camera. "Looks relatively new." He stepped to the side a bit. "There's a tie to it going around the tree." He moved a bit more. "It's connected to a battery pack."

"I wouldn't pick up on that, a camera doesn't have emotions, there has to be something else. Maybe whoever put it there is in the woods somewhere." I felt around a bit more as the guy got closer to the tree and filmed what he saw.

I felt curiosity and I figured there were some animals in the area because it didn't feel sinister in any way. There was a faint trace of something that went farther back in the woods and my instinct was to not follow it, something pricked at me telling me that was a bad idea.

"Do you pick up on residual energy or emotions?" he asked me. "Maybe you are feeling something that was left over from whoever put this up?"

It was a possibility. The raven in me wanted me to back off, which I found disconcerting. "Scan the area slowly with the camera, we can watch it later and look for anything that stands out," I suggested. "All information we had about this place says it's been abandoned for over forty years. No regularly scheduled maintenance or security, so the camera doesn't make sense."

He spent about fifteen minutes filming the area around us, zooming in and out when something caught his eye. He was observant, so it could be he caught something. We headed back and that tingling at the back of my neck hit again that I was being watched.

The closer we got to the guys the more I started picking up fear and I followed the thread to a stranger; he must have been the first interview. He was fidgeting noticeably, his eyes constantly darting around him and his fear was palpable.

I caught Aedan's eye who wasn't on camera at the moment and motioned him over. "This guy has some heavy fear rolling off him," I whispered to him.

"I first thought he was high on something, but he's talking to Jax right now about some satanic worshipping cult that is rumored to be out here doing rituals in the hospital," Aedan explained. "Do you pick up on anything like that?"

I told him about the feeling I had gotten of being watched, the camera and the unexplained emotion I picked up on, and Jax's response to it as well. Aedan tensed up, but nodded to me and went back over to the group.

I hung back and watched the rest of the interviews not picking up on anything else. Three more times though, I heard the flapping of the raven wings and felt the watching sensation. Something was going on, I just needed to figure out what.

Aedan, armed with the information Airiella had shared, paid closer attention to the guy Jax was interviewing. He saw the beads of sweat on his upper lip and that strain around his eyes. She was right, it wasn't drugs, it was just pure fear. Something had this guy spooked.

He sent the camera guy with the footage back to the little tent they had sent up to go over what he filmed and try to find something. She was also right in that a camera shouldn't have been there. It also meant that if the camera had its own battery pack that it had a memory card that was storing the footage of what it captured.

If it was a live feed there should have been more equipment, otherwise someone would have to be pretty close for a Bluetooth signal to relay it. Nothing was adding up. They finished the on-site interviews and left the tent and table there while they went back to town to film around the town and talk to local people.

He could tell by Ronnie's stiff posture that he wasn't happy about something, and he saw that Airiella was dragging. The amount of energy she was using to pick up on everything around her was draining her fast. He remembered Taklishim talking about the skin to skin contact with connections and wondered if that would help her now.

As they parked and got Ronnie and Jax set up with camera's he pulled Smitty off to the side. "I think Airiella needs to draw on our connections, she's dragging."

"I wondered about that too, but it's not like we can strip and have sex with her out in the middle of the street," Smitty drawled.

"We can hold her hands, isn't it just the skin to skin contact that ignites the connection we made permanent?" Aedan reminded him.

"Shit, you're right! Sorry, Ronnie is bent out of shape because she did what she was supposed to do and he didn't like it. I've been listening to him gripe at me." Smitty charged forward and gripped Airiella's hand, catching her off guard.

Aedan was a bit more subtle and walked up on her

other side, putting his hand around the bare skin of her arm. "Use the connection to refuel, you're looking a little drained," Aedan said in her ear so others couldn't hear.

She gave him a grateful look, though her eyes held a tired strain. "Being in public like this is hard with my senses open, it feels like a battlefield inside me," she whispered back.

"Just a few more hours," Aedan promised. She gave him a weak smile as he squeezed her arm and they followed Jax around.

"Something in him keeps shifting," she warned again as she caught a look that crossed Jax's face.

"Is it something to be worried about?" Smitty traced her palm with his thumb as they walked.

Aedan watched her face lose focus for a minute. "To me it feels, I don't know, studious? You know when you are teaching a kid something they want to know about, but it's more than just simple curiosity? That intent feeling that is on their face as they learn? It feels like that."

"Is that stuff inside him trying to learn?" Aedan asked sharply.

"Maybe? I can't say for certain. It hasn't become active in him in the way it does when it takes him over, but I can feel the energy shifts," she worded carefully.

"We need to wrap this up," Smitty said slowly looking around him. "There's a lot of people out here that could be in harm's way if that shit takes over. Thank fuck you are perceptive, baby girl."

"Exactly what I was thinking." Aedan steered them closer to Jax while staying out of the camera range.

Aedan felt Airiella stiffen and looked at her as she watched some female fling herself at Jax, professing her undying love and devotion to him. Interesting, she was jealous, Aedan filed that away for later dissection. It was something they were all used to when they went places. It had never bothered Mags, though she also knew that there was no one else for Aedan but her.

"By the way," Aedan whispered in Airiella's ear,

"thanks for the news."

"She got it confirmed?" Airiella's eyes were wide. Aedan nodded and smiled at the glee that lit her face.

"She said to me that our child was blessed by an angel, I agree." He looked at Airiella, his eyes shining with love. She blinked back tears and rested her head on his shoulder, it was enough. He knew what she was feeling.

Jax felt drained. Something was happening with that darkness inside him and it made him tired. He forced himself to eat dinner and then went straight back to him room. He needed quiet time. All those people today were exhausting.

The women who threw themselves at him left him feeling lonely in the worst way. He used to like the attention, often would bring one back to the hotel with him. It held zero interest for him now. He wanted Airiella.

He pulled out the notebook he'd been writing in and flipped to a blank page.

Today was her first time on location and I was impressed. She held her own, notified the others when something didn't feel right to her, and was so brave when she went to go check out that weird camera at the hospital.

I saw the guys holding on to her in the town, but I was too afraid to ask if something was wrong. She was honest about telling us she felt watched, and I noticed that it coincided with the weird feelings from the darkness in me.

Right now, I wish she was here with me in the room and we were just laying here decompressing and talking about the day. Those women made me feel lonely, and seeing Smitty and Aedan holding on to her made me hurt in a way that scares me. I'm terrified to love again, but I think that's what this is.

What if I lose her? I've said that before, but I

can't get over it. I have no idea how she faces the fears she has. After the things I saw, it baffles me how she can even be around people. I need to figure out how to protect her from me. I'm the biggest danger for her. It fucking sucks that I know it, too.

That right there was the problem Jax had. As much as his soul longed to be with her, he was afraid that he would ruin her. He was a broken record in his own head, the same fears just on repeat over and over until it defeated him. He wondered what she would say about that.

He rolled over and got up to put the notebook back in his bag and took a shower. Tomorrow would be another long day in the town while they filmed more interviews with historians and learned the history of the town and legends. Usually, his favorite parts of the shoots.

He dragged himself back to bed without putting anything on. He just didn't have the energy. He fell asleep dreaming of her smile and laugh, and the way that sun caught that dark hair and made it glow a wonderful cloud of curls around her tan face. The taste of her lips and tongue as he kissed her.

There was a fist around her throat and he couldn't save her. "Airiella!" he screamed but she never heard him. He watched her pass out and the guy dropped her to the floor, kicking her in the stomach as she laid there boneless and unmoving.

Rage tore at his heart as cruel laughter filled his ears and a voice taunted him. "You'll do this to her too." The tone was dark and sickening, making him retch. Suddenly, the guy that was kicking her had his face.

"No! Never!" Jax screamed in horror. Wake up! He told himself, it's a nightmare, wake up, Jax!

He smelled her scent, Jasmine on an ocean breeze. The terror flooding his veins slowed down and his heart sighed at the touch of her skin. Was he dreaming?

Jax cracked open an eye lid without moving. She

was in front of him, her hand on his chest as she stroked his face. "Sshh, I'm okay, Jax." She brushed a kiss over his forehead. He hauled her to him in a crushing grip.

"I need to save you from me," he sobbed into her neck.

"I don't need you to save me," she whispered. "And it's my choice to not want to be saved from you."

He let her soothe him, his body relaxing and skin buzzing as she ran her hands over his naked skin. He felt her pull the covers back over his body as she hummed softly, her siren song pulling him under its sweet spell as sleep took over. "I love you," he thought as he gave in to the pull, not realizing he'd said it out loud.

He never heard her reply, "I know. I love you too." She was gone when he woke up, he believed he had dreamt the whole thing. His heart ached for what he thought he couldn't have.

I was so tired. Ronnie was still aggravated with me, Jax was sullen, and I just wanted to sleep. I kept quiet on the drive back to the location and sent a message to one of my best friends, Chrissie, who now lived in Kansas.

I told her I'd be there in three days and gave her the location asking if she lived anywhere close in hopes that I'd get to see her again. I tucked my phone away and stared at the landscape. I did a quick scan of the guys before we got there to make sure that all was as okay as can be expected, and picked up on that same emotion again that I felt in the woods.

My attention became laser focused as I tried to pinpoint where it was coming from, and it wasn't from inside this vehicle. Of course, Ronnie noticed immediately and jumped on it. "What's wrong, angel?"

"Oh, now I'm angel again?" I sarcastically shot back at him.

"You never stopped being an angel," he threw back snidely.

"For fucks sake!" I cried. "Listen up! All of you! You

can't protect me from everything, and it's not your job to! I'm not a defenseless child. When I need something from you, I will ask for it. Do you understand?'

They were all shocked silent. Oops, I might have yelled that. "Sorry," came the muttered responses and sheepish looks.

"Good. Now that we are clear on that, I feel that same emotion I felt yesterday in the woods. It's somewhere around us, and it's human. Have we been followed?" I asked.

"I haven't paid attention to that," Aedan replied glancing in the rearview mirror as he talked. "I just looked to see if our crew was behind us. Should I start looking?"

"We all should," I said, taking in our surroundings more carefully.

"Why do you think it's human?" Jax asked. His posture was a little more relaxed than it had been yesterday. I was happy about that, at least one of us got a few hours of sleep. Though running my hands over his naked flesh was kind of worth it. If he was a drug, he would be my drug of choice.

"If it was residual or an animal it wouldn't be here around us now. An animal wouldn't have followed us, and a spirit can't put up a camera." I tried to focus on the job I had of keeping them safe from whatever this shit was.

"Are you sure it's not a spirit energy?" Ronnie broke in. "That can follow us, we'd not see it, and you usually don't detect it. It's possible maybe that a spirit spoke to someone, or possessed them to have the camera put up." Good suggestions, but it didn't feel right to me. God, these guys were a perfect complement to each other, the emotion and the logic.

"Right, on the not detecting spirits part, which leads me to believe it's human. Winnie is the only spirit I've picked up on," I argued. "Besides, my gut is saying human."

"That you know of," Ronnie added, mumbling.

"Have you identified the emotion yet?" Smitty interrupted, trying to keep the peace.

"I'm not sure. The closest I think I could come to naming it, would be passion. But I don't know what kind of passion. Or maybe manic." I thought for a minute. "You know how people say there's a thin line between love and hate? Oh wait, even better, between pain and pleasure?" I looked at all of them and Aedan in the rearview mirror.

Smitty and Aedan nodded. "Think of sex, people like it rough because it shows need, passion, desire, but not everyone likes it when you spank, because that's pain associated with bad behavior as a child. Well, not to everyone, but you get what I'm saying? A pleasure so intense that it becomes almost painful." The two emotional ones choked on coughs a little, while the logical ones made agreeing noises.

"It's like that. This emotion is some sort of mania or passion but it straddles that line between one or the other so I can't really tell which way it's going. Sometimes there is a tint of curiosity mixed in, though it shifts. My mom gets like that when she's having a bi-polar episode, though her emotions are more clearly defined. My instincts are telling me it's a person, and right now they are close to us. The direction I feel the tug from is behind, which makes sense if they are following us and watching."

Jax looked back at me and had a wild look in his eyes, heat pooled immediately, and I held his gaze not looking away. I saw the passion and hidden promise of pleasure and I fought the need to moan. Between that and the sudden lust rolling off of Ronnie coming from next to me, my senses were overwhelmed and my brain went straight in the gutter.

Smitty cleared his throat to get the attention back on track. "Do you have any suggestions?"

"On sex?" the words were out of my mouth before I even knew they were there. Blushing because I just gave away the direction my thoughts had taken, I shook my head. "On what?"

There was silence in all around me then as one, they all burst out laughing. Well shit. Glad I was the comedic relief. "Oh, fuck off," I muttered. "You guys screw with my head."

"Welcome to my life, siren," I heard Jax say.

"She's a unicorn, not a siren," Smitty corrected him.

"Right now, I have a horn," Ronnie joked.

This was getting out of hand fast. "My suggestion would be to watch who shows up at today's shoot." I tried changing the subject. "I noticed last time there was a crowd gathered."

"The cops kept them behind the line though," Aedan supplied, helping me out.

"They could have easily parked somewhere else if they had a truck or four-wheel drive vehicle," I pointed out. "It would have been easy to do that, or even if they parked with everyone else, they could have slipped off through the trees and hid."

"True," Smitty admitted winding his fingers through mine. "Maybe as a publicity stunt between takes, we could take turns flirting with the crowd and seeing if someone stands out."

"We invite the crazies to get close to us?" Jax argued. He did have a point there; I remembered the females that threw themselves at him and I fought back a wave of jealousy.

"What about the camera man that was with me?" I asked. "He was observant as hell. He is the one who spotted that camera, not me."

"That could work," Aedan said with a smile. "I don't want any marriage proposals today, so I like that idea better."

Perfect, that way no one put their hands on my men, I thought, then tried to erase that thought. Shit. What was wrong with me? They weren't mine. For someone with no hormones anymore mine were surely trying to make a comeback. Jeez.

Smitty squeezed my hand lightly. I'd gotten used to the zing of the connection from when he touched me. It no longer caught me off guard, instead now it wrapped around me like a bear hug. I threaded my other hand through Ronnie's to spread the connection between all of us, and as a way to let him know I forgave him for being an overbearing jerk.

We pulled up and climbed out of the vehicle, forcing me to let go of Smitty's hand, but Ronnie kept his grip on me and pulled me out after him. My phone started buzzing as soon as my feet hit ground and I used my free hand to pull it out of my pocket. It was Chrissie!

I answered, suddenly excited. I kept the call short since we were on site now, and we made plans to get together for dinner one of the nights I was in Kansas. I couldn't wait to see her and her three boys.

"Who was that?" Ronnie tugged me closer to him.

"My best friend," I answered honestly. "I haven't seen her in years, since she moved to Kansas."

"Can I come with you?" he asked tentatively.

I thought about it, wondering about the implications, and if it would affect my time with her. I must have taken too long to answer because he started to take a defensive posture. "As long as you don't tell me what to do, you can."

He sagged in relief. "I won't. Promise." He gave me a giant grin, kissed my cheek and went to join the others.

I set off to walk the area again, noted the same emotion as the last time and headed inside the building, a cameraman trailing after me. I made note of a few places where things felt strange, but not bad, and he marked them off on a map of areas to investigate.

The rest of the day went smoothly and we went back to get some rest before the nights filming of the location began. My room felt like someone had been in there and I shrugged it off as the cleaning crew and walled up my emotions. I needed to recharge.

Smitty laid back on the bed to call Jillian. "Hey babe, how's thing back home?"

"Okay; I miss you," she told him.

"I miss you too," he said as he got comfortable. "How about you come to Cali when we get back from the live show?"

"Weekend trip?" she speculated.

"Sure, however long you can spare. We should be back in town for at least five days before we head out again. I'd love you to meet Airiella, too," he told her.

"Still sleeping with her?" he thought there was a hint of jealousy in her voice.

"No, just the time I told you about. Things have been busy," he said carefully.

"Oh." He couldn't place the tone she was using.

"What's wrong?" he tried.

"I don't know, I just feel weird now knowing you were actually with someone else. I know I have no right to, we both agreed on that, it's just weird," she said fast, the words a jumble.

"That's why I want you to meet her," he said gently.

"I think that's why it's weird though. It makes me feel like she's more permanent in your life, or something else just as equally ridiculous that I can't explain," Jillian said angrily.

He understood that, he guessed. She'd never asked him to meet one of the hookups she had. She also had a point about it though, Airiella was permanent in his life. He knew that without a single shred of doubt. "Jilly, she is permanent. I'm not going to deny it, but I also can't explain it over the phone. It's just something you will understand once you meet her."

"I don't need to meet everyone you decide to sleep with!" she cried.

"Baby, it's not that. What we have is separate, no one will replace you. She's here for us as a group. Besides, I think Jax is her forever, if you believe in that stuff." Smitty used his most reasonable tone.

"Then why do I need to meet her?" she asked, mollified a bit.

"She will change your life." Simply put, he believed

that. "She changed mine. I don't want her to become a thing you hold between us. I won't ever ask for a three-way with her and us, nor will I suggest you sleep with her. She's mine," he said with care. "I don't want you to take that the wrong way either. I don't care how many people you sleep with, nor does that mean I will continue to have sex with her. It means that when I'm away from you, she keeps me grounded."

Jillian was quietly crying, "I don't understand how you don't get that is a threat to me."

"That's why I want you to meet her," he repeated.

"This won't be a goodbye between us after I do," she capitulated.

"Of course not." His voice was firm. "I love you."

"You love her too," she whispered.

"So will you." He sounded certain.

"I'll book a flight for that weekend," she finally agreed.

"Good, now tell me what you are wearing." Smitty's tone got husky.

"Well..." she played along, "if I take off this old t-shirt of yours that smells like you, then I will be wearing nothing."

Smitty growled deep in his throat, but before he could reply a scream shattered the air, and he flew to his feet. "Jilly..."

"Go," she said, her voice shaking. "That didn't sound good. Later, love."

Smitty dropped the phone and ran to the hallway.

The raven cawed at me frantically, wings flapping madly. I wasn't alone! Shit. I wasn't alone! I jolted awake and knew I wasn't alone; it wasn't a dream. I could hear breathing. Someone was moving, my instincts screaming danger.

I screamed. Ear splitting terror ripping from my throat as loud as I could make it. I felt the atmosphere shift that told me a storm was present and heard the raven's wings again at the same time. I screamed again and caught movement out of the corner of my eye.

On nothing but pure instinct, I rolled, dropping to the floor on the other side of the bed and belly crawled along the floor as something slammed into the bed where I had just been laying. Shouting from the hallway came as Ronnie pounded on my door trying to get it open.

I held absolutely still trying to gauge where the intruder was at, and as the air shifted in front of me, I rolled again then shot to my feet lunging to the door. I saw a shape moving toward me and jumped again, bashing my shoulder into the wall as I grasped for the door handle.

I sensed the atmosphere shift again, right as the power went out. Footsteps thudded across the room and out the balcony door as I got the door open. Ronnie came crashing into the room, followed by Smitty and Jax.

My knees shaking and heart racing I sank to the floor as phone flashlights clicked on. Even in the dark, I knew it was Jax that scooped me up and held me to him and stepped into the hallway where the emergency lights were flickering to life.

We were both shaking, and I clung to him, my arms around his neck and face turned into his chest. Someone had been in my room. Flashbacks slammed into my head as I fought off a panic attack and tried to get control of my emotions. The terror that gripped me wouldn't let go, and I couldn't breathe.

Jax carried me through an open door and sat down on the bed, holding me. He didn't say anything, and tremors were racking his body still. Someone had been in my room. He held me tight as my breathing grew more ragged. I was barely holding on to control.

The power came back on as Ronnie shouted my name from the hallway, only to be led by Smitty to where Jax held me. Jax surrendered to me to Smitty without a word and left the room, his face pale and haunted.

Smitty cradled me to him, his heart racing as fast as mine and my eyes sought out Ronnie. "Someone was in my room," I whispered and lost control, fear taking over completely as the panic attack hit hard. Silent tears streamed down my face and I shook so bad my teeth chattered.

"Angel." Ronnie was in front of me, kneeling on the floor. He reached for me and Smitty handed me over and stood up.

"I'm going to check on Jax," he said, his voice shaking in anger and fear, his face was redder than his hair. "Watch her, let no one in."

I wrapped myself around Ronnie like he was a lifeline and I was drowning, as Aedan came at a full run into the room. Smitty grabbed him and they went to find Jax leaving me with Ronnie and closing the door behind them.

"My dreams," I chattered, "someone was in my room. I wasn't alone. It's happening again." I couldn't stop the fear.

"I got you, angel. I got you," he chanted, standing up in one fluid move, he moved us to the bed and laid down with me still wrapped around him. He settled a blanket over us and held me. "You're safe. I got you."

Sobs broke free and I cried until I fell asleep, Ronnie never once letting go. I don't know how long I was out, but when I woke up, he was still holding me, but he was asleep too. His face soft in sleep, but a look of anger still present.

I kissed his jaw softly and he was awake in an instant. "Angel, are you okay?" his voice laced with worry.

"I am now, thanks to you," I told him with a weary smile, my voice still shook a little.

"Fuck," His face was raw with emotion. "I think I died twice when I heard you scream. I was about to break the damn door down."

A shiver ran through me and I tried to rein it in. "Someone was in there, Ronnie."

"Yeah, I know, sweetheart. They got out through the balcony. Smitty is getting you a new room, police were called, they want to talk to you, but I refused to let them see you until after you'd slept. You were pretty much in a full state of shock."

I know I was here to help them, but it seems like my being here kept bringing them shitty situations. "I'm sorry."

"For what?" he asked, astounded.

"Your lives have been totally disrupted because of me," I said, guilt setting in.

"Remember that stuff you drank? The crap you had to relive? Our talk afterward? You working on healing?" he listed off. Numbly, I nodded. I knew where he was headed.

"I get it." I resolved to push past this.

"You don't, though. This wasn't something that was in your control. You reacted far better than others would have. There is zero reason for you to blame this on yourself." He forced my chin up so I looked at him. "Your reaction was completely within reason. If you hadn't screamed, we would have never known you were in danger."

There was a knock at the door and I stiffened, my reactions clearly not under control yet. He called out, "Who is it?"

"Aedan," came the muffled voice. "Going to use my key." The door opened and all the guys came in. Even Jax. I unwound myself from Ronnie and immediately missed his body heat. I pulled up into a ball and rested against the headboard.

Jax searched my face as I read his. I don't know what mine showed, but by his tightening reaction I didn't think it was good. He stepped closer to me and reached out his hand, running his thumb under my eyes. He didn't say anything; he didn't need to. Those chestnut eyes were pools of concern, fear and anger.

"Darlin'," Smitty started, and I violently jolted and interrupted.

"Never call me that," I said, my voice hard. Ronnie raised his eyebrows at me, and Jax flinched at my tone. He saw the nightmares, he knew why.

Jax pulled Smitty back a little and whispered in his ear. For that, I was grateful, because I wouldn't have to explain. Contrite, he stepped back to me. "Baby girl, I'm sorry. I didn't know."

I guess the silver lining is that brought me right smack out of the fear that had frozen me since I woke to found someone in my room. "When do we need to leave for the filming?" I firmed up my nerves. This wouldn't beat me. I'd been through worse.

Aedan sighed and sat on the chair next to the bed. "The cops want a statement from you. You up to it?"

"Fine. Can someone grab my clothes for me?" I agreed, knowing there was no way out of it.

Smitty shifted. "Um, they're gone."

"My clothes are gone?" I repeated.

Jax stomped out of the room. "We think whoever was in your room took them," Smitty explained.

"My wallet? Phone? iPad?" I listed off.

"Just your clothes," Aedan replied gently.

"What the fuck?" I growled. Ronnie reached out and rubbed small circles on my arm.

Jax came back in the room, his face stormy and handed me one of his shirts, and a pair of sweats. "They'll be too big for you, but you can't meet the cops like that." He gestured to my tank top and pair of boy shorts.

I didn't even have a bra on, so there was no way I was turning him down or arguing. I slipped the shirt on and was surrounded by the smell of him. It aroused me, soothed me and made my insides hum. "Thank you, Jax."

Aedan spoke up, "If you can write down sizes, Jax and Ronnie can run to the chain store down the street and grab you some clothes so you at least have something to wear that fits while you give your statement."

I was suddenly furious at the thought of someone stealing my clothes. I snatched the pen and paper from the desk and wrote my info down handing it to Jax who simply nodded and left the room. Ronnie got up and pulled on his shoes and followed.

Smitty gently cupped my face. "Baby girl, whoever was in your room meant harm. This wasn't theft. I want you to know that before talking to the cops. They can be harsh and not take people's feelings into consideration sometimes."

"Not my first go around, Smitty, but thank you," I said as a gentle reminder.

"They are coming up to your room, we'll meet them there." Aedan steered me across the hall.

I sucked in a breath as I saw the shredded mattress where I had been laying. Note to self, never disregard instincts. Smitty put a hand in the small of my back. "They will assign you a new room."

"No. Can I stay with one of you instead? Please?" I hated the fear the crept into my voice.

"Thank God," Smitty breathed. "That's my preference. I don't even care who."

I leaned back into him and waited for the cops. I gave my statement and went back to Ronnie's room where I showered and waited for them to get back with clothes. Jax walked in and handed me the bag. "You get a new room?"

"I'd rather stay with one of you," I said softly.

He touched my face. "I'd rather that, too. Probably not me, though, I don't quite trust myself yet."

"Is this your room?" I'd thought it was Ronnie's.

"No, this one is Ronnie's. I just asked for a minute with you." Jax sounded unsure.

I opened the bag and started pulling clothes out and taking tags off. "Thanks for the clothes. And letting me wear yours." I felt suddenly shy.

"They look better on you than they do me." His voice was thick. "Witch."

I looked at him, his tone that gentle caress that did wicked things to my insides. "Thank you for taking care of me Jax." I stood and hugged him. "I know that wasn't easy."

"Caring for you isn't the problem," he said gruffly, but held me tight.

They pulled up to the location and everyone was subdued, Smitty included. Well, everyone except the gathering crowd half a mile back where the cops stopped them. They unloaded all their gear and got their base set up. While they did that Smitty walked back over to Airiella.

"Stay with me tonight, baby girl, please?" his voice was scratchy.

"Sure." She grabbed his hand.

He pulled her into a hug. "Those screams of yours take ten years off my life. I feel like an old man." His rough stubble scratched against her face. He hoped it wasn't hurting her, she had such soft skin.

"I need to walk the area, who is coming with me?" she asked, ignoring his statement.

"Ronnie. I'll go grab him, stay put." He dropped a kiss on her head and went to grab Ronnie.

"What's up?" Ronnie looked up as Smitty approached.

"She's ready for the walk thru. By the way, I asked her to stay with me tonight. You okay with that?" Smitty asked.

"Yeah. Those screams like the ones you heard her make in that chapel?" Ronnie's eyes were showing strain.

"Damn close. That's why I need her tonight." Smitty felt a shiver crawl up his spine.

"I'm getting a better picture, I understand. I'll go keep her safe right now." There was no hesitation in Ronnie's answer.

Smitty watched him walk away and checked on Jax. "You holding steady?"

"Yeah, I'm okay. If she doesn't sense anything let's focus on those spots she pointed out earlier and see if we can get evidence of activity there before we just go room to room. Between us, I just want this over with. I'm okay, but seeing her bed shredded rattled me." Jax had been more than rattled.

"Imagine how she feels," Smitty put it bluntly.

"I don't need to imagine it, I saw it. She was in my arms." Jax shifted. "I look like shit, don't I?"

"No. Just tired. Put your glasses on, it'll hide the worst of it." Smitty patted his shoulder and went back to the base to check the recording equipment on the feeds and the batteries on the cameras. Everything was good to go. He checked the walkie-talkies to make sure they worked. Since this wasn't live, she could radio them if she felt something off.

Smitty saw a tense Ronnie coming back towards him and he braced for bad news. "What?"

"She feels that energy again, coming from direction of the crowd. She said she's almost certain that it is the same as what was in her room." Tension rolled under Ronnie's skin.

"Where is she?" Smitty looked around.

"With Aedan. He thought it was a good idea she let the cops know that she thought the person is here. Not sure how she's going to convince a cop of that. Not a lot of people believe in what she can do, and since it was dark in her room, she can't exactly convince them they look the same. I thought it was pointless, but Aedan insisted."

"I can see both sides of it. It's not like they don't know what we are here doing, maybe the cops are fans." Smitty used logic with Ronnie, while wishing on the first star he saw that the cops found the psycho who tried to kill her.

"Hey Ron, why was she a lot more freaked out by someone being in her room than the shredded bed? You seemed to understand that part," Smitty asked him.

"I thought you knew her back story?" he evaded answering.

"I do, but she didn't give many in depth details. At least not about anything like that."

Ronnie mulled it over. "Her most recent ex gaslighted her. Like, bad. After he moved out, she kept waking up at night because she thought someone was in the room with her. Given how her instincts are dead on, if that's what she thought, it's probably what happened. She felt he was sneaking in after she went to sleep but doesn't know why. From the things she told me, it was a power game for him. Narcissist. He liked fucking with her head. She said she would wake up out of a dead sleep and feel like someone was right in front of her wearing all black."

"Okay. I can see why it would bother her. She's so calm usually, and that was full blown freak out. It doesn't add up." Smitty was trying to piece it together rationally.

"She said she didn't feel safe when it was happening before." Ronnie blew out a frustrated breath.

Smitty thought about it, there may be more to it than that, but tonight wasn't the time to push for answers. At least he now knew a trigger for panic attacks. To her credit, she didn't freak out until it was over, she got herself out first. Exactly as she had told them during the interview.

Those screams though. To his dying breath, her screams were going to haunt him.

Aedan hung up the phone with Mags after filling her in on everything and he looked around for Airiella. Filming was about to start and he wanted her to be with someone at all times. That attack was for her, not one of them, and it wasn't Jax that did it.

As he thought about it, he decided to let Taklishim know. Maybe he'd have some advice. Aedan tapped out a quick email giving brief descriptions and sent it. He scanned the area again looking for faces that didn't belong.

He finally spotted Airiella next to Ronnie, and they both looked tense. He headed over, but Ronnie met him halfway when he saw Aedan.

"She felt it again, coming from the direction the crowd is gathered," Ronnie started, his face hard.

"I'm going to take her and talk to one of the cops. They need to know," Aedan decided.

Ronnie looked like he was going to argue but then he backed off and headed back to Smitty. Aedan took

Airiella's hand and they went to find a cop to talk to. He looked for whoever was in charge, but he couldn't tell. It never crossed his mind that this could backfire on them.

Once he found one of the cops that was a senior member of the force, he started to explain what had happened in her room and how Airiella felt like that person was here in the crowd. To say the officer was a skeptic was an understatement. He didn't have time to try to convince him either, they needed to get the filming started.

At least he believed that Airiella was in danger and agreed to make sure no one got through, and for now, that would have to do. Aedan took her hand and they headed back to the base.

"Stay with someone at all times. Even if you have to pee, take someone with you. I'd prefer that you remain in the base tent where most people will be. If anything hits your radar, use the walkies that Smitty has set up. Each of us will have one. This isn't a live show, so feel free to interrupt as needed. We can always edit out stuff later."

"Alright," she agreed.

"Mags is worried about you. If you get bored, maybe text her." Aedan brushed her hair behind her ear. "Stay sharp. We will do our best to help you stay safe."

"I know, thank you." She gave a soft smile, but under it was fear. She kept a tight lid on it, but Aedan felt it. She was strong and capable, but rattled.

He kissed her cheek as he left strict instructions for no one to leave her by herself, and went to join the others as they prepared for the intro. They all did a walkie check with her before they went in, satisfied they had done as much as they could before they started filming.

It was uneventful for the remainder of the shoot, they got paranormal evidence in the spots that she had pointed out, the rest of the hospital was just eerie feeling. She didn't radio anything and when they came out, she was exactly where he had left her.

She looked tired and stressed, but unharmed. "You okay?" he asked.

"As well as can be expected. Whoever it was moved and is back behind the hospital where we found the camera at, but they never came closer. The energy never turned bad, it still straddles that line in the middle, and it's now over in this direction." She pointed off to the forest to the right. "Feels more distant now, like whoever it is, is moving away from us."

"We should tell that officer we talked to that." Aedan made to move but she stopped him.

"There's no point. He didn't believe us the first time; he's not going to start now." Her voice was slightly dead sounding.

He started to argue his point, but she just shook her head and he gave in. "We're wrapped for the most part, so we will start take down and go back to the hotel. We fly out in the morning, so if there is something we missed or need to add we can do it this evening after we get some sleep."

She nodded, "Tell me how I can help."

Aedan directed her to follow directions from the people in the tent on how to break down and put away the electronic gear and went to check with the others who were standing in the front of the hospital as they started to remove the static cameras from inside.

Aedan and the guys felt an odd prickle at the same time and he looked back to Airiella and saw her attention focused on the direction she had pointed. He felt the fear crawl up through the connection and he started back her direction with Smitty on his heels when they heard a sharp crack and she dropped.

Screams broke out, and he took off at a run. Smitty easily passed him up and he heard Jax and Ronnie's steps thundering behind him. Airiella suddenly stood up, blood soaking her arm and she held up her hand to halt them.

Aedan grabbed Jax by his shirt to make sure he didn't keep going. They felt all their hair stand on end and Aedan saw the thunderous look on her face. She was pissed. She was doing something with the energy around them, because not one person moved, and their faces echoed bewilderment.

Jax dropped to his knees, Ronnie staggering beside him but remained standing. "That was a gunshot," Jax gasped out.

Aedan's eyes flew back to Airiella as she swayed in the spot she was standing before breaking into a run, straight to where she had been looking. Lightning struck, charging the air around them, and she toppled to the ground, a raven cawing somewhere over her head.

She stood again, and not one of them was able to move. It felt like she had rooted them to the ground. Her hair was electrified around her face and Aedan swore he saw a halo. Logic failed him in that moment, he had no idea how to explain any of it.

The raven he heard cawing settled in front of her and she started walking again, headed right where lighting had struck, the trees burnt and hollowed out in one blast, glowing embers fizzling out. The bird hopped along with her, like they were communicating.

She got to where she needed to go, seemed satisfied with what she saw. She looked back at them and with a slight motion of her hands, they were all suddenly free. Commotion broke out all around them as cops came flying up the drive, sirens and lights going.

Aedan looked at his friends, not one of whom have moved. "Was that her?"

Smitty audibly swallowed, "Yeah. So's the bird."

Jax nodded, "The bird has been in my dreams, it's her."

"I should be scared," Aedan quietly said, "but I'm not."

"This happened on her interview," Smitty added.

Ronnie stood there shaking, pale and his eyes wide open, "She was shot. Someone shot her."

Smitty put a hand on his arm, "Well I think she just struck them with lightning, so they got theirs."

It shouldn't have been funny, it wasn't funny, yet they all laughed. It was either laugh or freak out. "Smitty, what if she did the energy thing, the pulling it that had you so whacked out?" Ronnie's tone was deathly quiet.

"I don't think she did, last time, she passed out afterwards," Smitty answered, hoping she hadn't done it.

"She's about to pass out," Aedan tossed in and made himself move towards her. She dropped right as one of the responding officers came up on her. He caught her before she hit the ground and called out for a medic.

That put speed in their feet. There was not one thing Aedan could explain about this. He thought the connection and other stuff they had seen was wild, this took it to a whole new level. While he was in awe of her, there was also a deeply rooted respect that blossomed in an entirely different way than it had before. He wasn't scared, he told himself.

Smitty was borderline panicked when they got to her and tried taking her from the cop, but he stood his ground, and held on to her. Aedan pulled him back and nodded to the pile of remains that lay just in front of them. A half melted and shredded rifle in the mix.

"Don't touch anything," the cop growled at them.

"Is she okay?" Ronnie asked, stepping closer.

"I don't know, she just passed out." The cop looked a little worried.

"Wake up, baby girl," Smitty was chanting at her while the cop glared at him.

Aedan saw her move and let go of a giant sigh he hadn't know he'd been holding back. "Smitty," she said weakly, "I think someone shot me."

Despite the fear of the situation, Aedan found himself chuckling again. "Airiella, you have a flair for the obvious."

The raven that had been watching them from a burnt branch cawed and took flight. Aedan followed its path with his eyes and just blinked when it disappeared into thin air. If there had been any doubt by any of them that they were in the presence of something special, it had been dispelled.

Chapter Fourteen

Smitty rode in the ambulance with Airiella to the closest hospital while the others stayed behind to give statements and finish packing up. Her hand was cold in his, but her skin tingled with electricity and he got a shock when he touched her. The paramedic got shocked too when he went to start an IV.

She opened her eyes a couple of times and locked on Smitty's gaze, a look of relief on her face at seeing him. He was downright terrified of what could happen at the live show in a few days. It felt even more dangerous now.

They got to the hospital, which wasn't all that close, and took her back into an exam room. They didn't try to keep Smitty away, but they didn't let him crowd them either. He was relegated to a chair and told to stay put.

The gunshot wound was a flesh wound, a deep one, but didn't require surgery. They stitched her up and were pumping fluids in her. The doctor said she was in shock, but he felt she would be fine. They'd release her in a couple of hours after they made sure that she wasn't exhibiting any other symptoms.

They wouldn't know about the energy stuff she did, and that's what Smitty needed to know. If she was in danger because she pulled some dark energy then he needed to get other stuff in motion fast, but he needed her to wake up so he could ask the questions.

He held her hand, squeezing it every so often and whispering to her to wake up. After about the longest hour of his life she finally did. "Smitty?"

"Shit, baby girl, thank god you are awake! Did you pull energy?" he asked quickly.

"No," came the weak response. "Did they drug me?"

"Yes, it will wear off soon. You might wish for more though. Your arm is going to hurt like a bitch."

"It's okay, pain and me are old friends." She swung her head to look at him. "I don't have to stay here, do I?"

"No, baby. We just need to wait for the guys to finish up back at the sight and they will come get us," Smitty reassured her.

"I killed her, didn't I?" She started shaking and tears rolled across her cheeks.

Smitty wanted to say no, but he couldn't. He was almost certain the lightning had been from her, though he couldn't prove it, and talking about it here might get them both on a psychiatric lockdown. "We'll talk about it later, I promise."

"Will you lay here with me?" she winced as she scooted over to make room for him.

He wasn't about to deny her request and he carefully moved stuff around so he could fit next to her. He pulled grass out of her hair with one hand and wrapped the other arm around her middle. "You are a mess," he told her, smiling softly. "Grass all up in your hair, even a twig." He held it out for her to see. "We aren't supposed to take souvenirs home with us."

Her gentle laughs eased his gut a little. The nurses scowled at him as they came in, but at Airiella's soft pleading voice to let him stay there next to her, they gave in. She had them wrapped around her finger.

The doctor came back in and told Airiella she would need to wear a sling for a few days so the muscle could stitch itself back together and she'd need to be seen in a week to get the stitches removed and check for signs of infection.

Smitty broke in at her lost look. "We'll be on another filming location in Kansas at that time. Can she just go to any urgent care in the area or is there somewhere else she can go since we won't be here?"

"You're in luck little lady, I have a friend in Kansas, in a small town near Independence. She runs a small family clinic there, I can call her and make an appointment for you so she can check over my work? Don't tell her I said this, but she's a better doctor than I am." He winked at her.

"Don't sell yourself short, Doc," she said with a small smile. "You did good."

Smitty knew the exact moment the doctor fell under her spell. It was written all over his face. He hadn't stood a chance. He asked if she needed more pain medicine, or a prescription to take with her and she refused. He wrote a prescription for antibiotics to ward off infection and told them both signs to watch for.

He left to make a call to his friend in Kansas for her and Smitty kissed her on the temple. "You never fail to amaze me, baby girl."

"I just want to leave. I don't like being in hospitals." Her weary voice broke Smitty's heart.

The doctor came back in with an appointment card and the doctor's contact info in Kansas. He handed Smitty the prescription to be filled for antibiotics. "There are officers here to see you. I've held them off for a bit, but they are pushing now." He looked at Smitty. "Stay where you are, even if they tell you to leave."

Smitty nodded. "Can you stay too, Doc?"

"No, but I'll send a nurse in here to make sure they don't get out of hand. The officers here are fantastic. But this is a small town, and we don't see a whole lot of gunshot wounds here, so they might be a little excitable," he warned.

"Thank you, doctor," Airiella said and held out her hand for him to shake.

"The pleasure was all mine Ms. Raven. You take care of yourself."

The officers came in asked the same questions about ten different ways and Airiella's answers never varied. It took about an hour, and the guys were waiting in the lobby. The nurse got her checked out and they left, much to Airiella's relief.

Smitty noted her face was tight with pain, though she refused anything for it and carried on as if nothing happened until they got in the vehicle to head back to the hotel. He got in first, and she slid in next to him. Ronnie sandwiched her between the two of them.

Aedan drove and Jax was in the front seat with him. As soon as the car moved, she sagged and started to cry. Jax was about to lose his shit and crawl back there until Aedan pushed him down. Smitty watched, feeling detached and exhausted.

She leaned against him, her left arm in the sling across her chest and her hip slid over against Ronnie. Smitty had his arm around her back and under the injured arm so he didn't jostle her. Ronnie had his hand on her thigh rubbing little circles.

Smitty had to admit, they all looked shell shocked. "Aedan, what did you find out from the cops on site?"

"They found an empty car. Registration was for some woman who they didn't find on the scene. They were checking to see if they could locate her at the address listed and find out if the car was stolen or not."

"I killed her," Airiella choked out. Smitty tightened his hold on her.

"Well the cops don't see it that way," Aedan said gently.

"She was going to kill you," Jax ground out. Smitty worried if the darkness in him was trying to take over and a fission of fear slid through him.

"He's okay, it's him," she told him softly.

"Do you want to tell us what happened?" Ronnie asked.

"No, but I will," she said bluntly.

"If you aren't ready to, that's okay," Smitty said soothingly into her ear.

"I'm fine." Her tone of voice said she was anything but fine.

"You aren't fine, you fucking got shot," Jax snarled.

She sat up and reached forward with her good arm and put her hand out to him. Smitty saw his face, he looked like a starving kid being given a five-course meal. He grasped her hand and kissed her knuckles. This was the Jax he knew.

Smitty saw Jax relax and he understood that she was calming him. Jax didn't even try to hide the tears tracking down his face. It gave Smitty renewed hope. No words were spoken between the two that anyone could hear. It was like they had a silent communication going on.

She leaned back against Smitty and got settled before she started. "You guys had just come out of the hospital when I felt the energy change. It went from borderline to pure crazy. I knew she was female. It just came across that way. Maybe that's part of this new stuff that's woken up in me, I don't know. In the next second, I was falling backward and hearing the crack afterwards. It took me a minute to realize that I'd been shot."

Smitty saw Ronnie tense up. "I felt around the wound and it didn't seem that bad, so I got up because her energy shifted again. It felt like she was going to come to us. There were so many people around that could have been hurt, that my instincts just took over when I got up. I was so angry."

"You ran towards the danger," Ronnie's voice was flat though his expression was cloudy.

"I did what I had to do to save lives. She was intent on harm. I was absolutely certain of it. The raven was telling me the same thing. I don't know how to make the lightning come. Maybe it only comes when my life is in danger? That happened last time too."

"It was you?" Aedan breathed and swerved a little. "The hotel, was it you then, too?"

"Lightning struck at the hotel?" she asked, distracted.

"That's why the power went out," Aedan told her.

"I guess that makes sense then, since my life was in danger there too," she puzzled out loud. "Anyway, I felt you guys on the move and I don't know what I did exactly, but I felt the fear from all of you and just used that to make you stay. The lightning slowed me down. Once I saw the danger was past, I took the extra fear back from you. That's the long and short of it."

Smitty was awestruck. "That was fear that stopped us? We were literally frozen in fear?"

"You didn't know?" she sounded surprised.

"I knew I was scared. I didn't know that you stopped us with it," he answered.

"I think that's why I passed out. It took a lot of energy in a short amount of time. I was terrified the crew or you guys were going to get hurt."

"The lightning pushed the darkness in me back, it felt like it was afraid of it," Jax mumbled.

"Good," Smitty heard her mutter quietly.

Aedan looked in the rearview mirror, catching her eye, "I felt your anger."

"I imagine you all did. I didn't have any walls up. I couldn't in order to keep watching for the bad energy," she said in a matter of fact way.

"The audio technician that was near you said you looked like an avenging angel," Aedan added.

"I read an old legend buried in some religious texts about some angels being gifted with the power of divine justice in order to 'smite' down the enemy of the dark ones." Ronnie looked over at them.

"Is that the lightning?" Smitty asked to clarify.

"I think so. Power of God and all that. Zeus, you

know." Ronnie got flustered.

"Was it dark, baby girl?" Smitty asked.

"Yes. Not at first, but after the gunshot it turned fast, hence my anger and fear for all the others. I didn't want to risk pulling it as I didn't know what it would do to Jax. The lightning just happened, I don't know how to do it, and it seems a little risky to try and practice something like that."

They pulled into the hotel and Smitty stood behind Airiella as each of the guys hugged her goodnight, Jax struggling the most to contain his emotions. He stepped back to give her a little space as she whispered something in his ear. Jax nodded and Smitty watched as his face became enraptured and he realized she was doing something for him.

Jax kissed her slowly, and tenderly and she swooned. Smitty stepped back closer to make sure she didn't fall but Jax wrapped an arm around her and whispered something back to her. This was the old Jax coming back, she did that for him.

Jax reluctantly went to his own room and Smitty took her to his. They'd gone through a drive through pharmacy to get her antibiotics and while they were waiting Smitty had ran in and gotten some medical tape and plastic wrap. He knew she'd want to shower.

He undressed her carefully and cleaned up around the wound and then wrapped it in plastic to keep it dry. He stripped down fully planning on getting in with her. She didn't argue with him. He washed her hair as she groaned in pleasure, his body reacting to the sound.

As he cleaned them off and got out to dry her, she pulled him back up and turned the water back on. "Let's take care of this." She wrapped her hand around his cock and stroked, all rational thought leaving head.

He stepped back under the spray, "This wasn't why I joined you in here." His voice was thick with need.

"I know." She took his hand and slid it between her legs. "That's not from the shower. I need you. Hard and fast please."

"Fuck," he growled, getting harder. He grabbed her beneath her ass and lifted her up, her back falling against the shower wall as she locked her legs around his waist, holding herself up. He kept one hand under her ass and used the other to rub it between her slick folds, pinching her bud between his finger and thumb, rolling it between them.

Her hips bucked and legs trembled. "Smitty," she moaned. He positioned his cock and drove it in. She anchored herself in the corner with her good arm and used her legs to pump herself as Smitty rode her hard. She locked her eyes on his, and he damn near came at the heat he saw in them.

He reached for her again, intent on making her come first and rolled the sensitive bud between his fingers, groaning deep in this throat as she tightened around him. "I'm so close," she mewled, "don't stop." He pinched her again and his hips jackhammered hers. He rolled the pad of his thumb in tight circles.

She exploded around him, squeezing him so tight he gritted his teeth and pounded into her finding his own release, the sexy sounds she was making as she came driving him right over the edge with her so hard he thought he was going to black out.

He held her there until his cock stopped twitching inside her then slowly lowered her back down. He kissed her slowly, and backed them up under the spray again and cleaned her up.

"Why me?" he asked her as he dried her off.

"You needed me the most." Her simple answer disarmed him. "And I needed you."

He picked her up and sat her down on the bed, her head lolling around as she tried to stay awake. He grabbed a clean t-shirt of his and helped her slip it on and he refastened the sling around her. She laid back and Smitty shut the lights off and made sure all the room darkening blinds were shut, then climbed in beside her.

He ran his fingers over her face and she snuggled into him. She might belong to Jax, but she was his too. "Love you, unicorn," he whispered.

"Love you Smitty," she whispered back.

He smiled and they both finally slept.

Chapter Fifteen

We landed in Kansas to a snowstorm. Thank God I didn't have to drive. I took the sling off on the plane and met four stony stares. I gave them all back one that defied them to argue with me. Each one backed down and they didn't argue. I knew my body best.

It hurt, but it wasn't the worst pain I'd ever felt. I swallowed some anti-inflammatories and tried to help get the luggage and was shut down firmly. Rolling my eyes, I pulled my phone out and sent Chrissie the address of where I had to go see the doctor before I left.

She responded that it was her family doctor and that was the town she lived in. I told her that we would meet there instead, since I had to go there anyway. I also let her know I'd have Ronnie with me. She didn't care.

The filming was the day after the doctor appointment, so we had time to get settled into the hotel, do research, scout around the town and get in some good interviews that they would use as background for the live segment.

The guys and the crew were even more on edge now

than they were before. The raven was ever present in my head, which told me they had reason to be so nervous. "Hey, did I tell you guys that Father Roarke was going to be here?"

As one, they all turned to look at me. "Guessing that's a no. Sorry. I reached out to him before we left for the first shoot, that night I made dinner. Because none of us knew what to expect, I asked him if there was a church or chapel that, uh, I could use, if needed," I said slowly, seeing the light click on in Smitty's face.

I didn't miss the look he shot me, but I wasn't going to acknowledge it. "And?" Aedan asked.

"He said he would be here and would have somewhere close by in case I needed him." I spoke more softly this time. The sad look on Jax's face was breaking my heart. "It's a precaution. It could be we are all overreacting."

"Did you tell him we think it's a trap?" Ronnie's eyes sought mine out.

"I did," I admitted. "For what it's worth, he agreed."

"That means he probably told Taklishim," Smitty added. They seemed to breathe easier after that little announcement I dropped on them.

"While we are being honest," Aedan started, then gave me a sheepish look. "You are going to be bunking with one of us every night."

"Fine." I almost laughed because they all looked like they were preparing to argue with me. I'd rather have had my own room, though I wasn't afraid to admit this last shoot had shaken me. I wasn't used to random strangers trying to kill me. Significant others, sadly, yes. Not strangers.

We got in the rental car, well SUV really, and headed to the boondocks of Kansas. It was flat here. I wasn't very impressed landscape wise. The flat did make it easier to drive in the snow. Unlike at home, where you were surrounded by hills set out to kill you if it snowed.

Smitty was driving and Ronnie was up front in the

passenger seat this time. That left Aedan and myself in the second row, and Jax behind me in the third row. I laid my head back over the seat and let my hair fall back over it. Jax shifted forward a bit and was winding it around his fingers.

It was relaxing to me, having my hair played with. Tended to make my brain numb and I was content with that. It seemed to make him happy too, so no complaints all around. Aedan cleared his throat, but I left my head right where it was and kept my eyes closed.

"Are you asleep?" he asked me.

"No, but I'm not moving either, so feel free to talk." Jax snorted behind me as he tugged lightly.

"I had a call while you were in the bathroom at the airport. The police were checking in with me. They suspect the remains of the lady are the same as that which the car is registered to," he informed me.

"Okay?" My brain was tingling. Jax had magic hands and he wasn't even touching my scalp.

"They found a Ronnie shrine in her house," Aedan finally spit out.

That got my attention. "Go on," I encouraged him.

"They also found your clothes," he added.

"Tell them to burn them. The ones Jax picked out are working fine except the bullet hole in the one."

"What do you mean a Ronnie shrine?" Came Ronnie's irritated voice from the front.

"Looks like she had an obsession with you. They found pictures of us going around town printed on paper with Airiella scribbled out in red marker," Aedan supplied.

"That makes no sense," I jumped in. "I felt the energy before we were in town."

"The camera," Smitty realized.

"So, I was the target of a crazy female fan in love with Ronnie?" I asked, stupefied.

"That's their official stance. Since the lightning strike killed her in what they are calling a freak accident, they are closing the case." Aedan tossed his hands up.

I laughed. "I'm the freak accident." They weren't

laughing. "Oh, come on, it was a joke."

"You aren't a freak," Ronnie said tersely.

"Hey, I took a bullet for you," I quipped. Dead silence. Even Jax stopped playing with my hair. "What? Too soon? Come on guys, lighten up, please?"

"You could have died," Jax said quietly in my ear. "I don't find that funny."

"Okay, fine. I'm sorry."

"Your hair is like silk," came the next whispered statement into my ear. His warm breath sliding over my skin.

"Smitty washed it last night, you can thank him for that," I fired back.

At least Smitty laughed at that. Jax resumed playing with my hair and I relaxed again. We remained quiet for the rest of the ride. Our hotel was in Wichita, and the site location was in some tiny little town called Fall River. My phone said it was an hour drive.

"They couldn't get us closer to the site?" I asked out of curiosity.

"That was my choice," Jax piped up. "I didn't want to be that close in case something was really off. A town that small and everyone would know where we are."

"Aren't they promoting the hell out of this live show though?" I was trying to piece together his logic.

"Yes, but we told them to leave the location off the promo's," Aedan said. "If we can keep a low enough profile, only a few people will know we are in Wichita. Then when it airs, the location will be given. I'm sure people in the town know if this guy told others."

"Can you guys keep a low profile? It wasn't advertised we would be where we were this last time."

Aedan conceded the point. "It's a show we are forced into and since Jax is who is being targeted, we think, we let him make the call on where we stay. He felt it would be safest for all of us."

"Fair enough. Now can any of you tell me why you think Jax is being targeted?" I wasn't going to let that go.

Jax sighed. "One of the backers of the show married a rich woman. She wanted to be a backer from the start when we pitched the idea. She had it in her head that I was easy prey for her. Broken hearted from losing my childhood sweetheart and in need of love and consolation."

"She wanted to fuck him," Ronnie broke in.

"Essentially yes, but she wrapped it up in pretty words. I knew her game, and I don't sleep with married people. It wasn't ever going to happen. Since we needed the money, my little friends here in the car were all too happy to use me as bait," Jax explained, darkly.

"Hey," Aedan protested.

"Stuff it, you went along. After the first season wrapped up, there was a party the studio provided, and of course her and her husband were there, along with the other money men. She kept bringing me drinks, little did I know she drugged one of them. If it hadn't been for Ronnie, she would have date raped me."

Chills ran up and down my spine. "She gave you Rohypnol?"

"Sure did. Tox screen proved it. She had me tied to a chair when Ronnie found me. Since the whole party saw her feeding me drinks, there was plenty of evidence against her. The husband didn't like it. The rest of the backers got her to agree to not be active, just her husband. He hates the show, thinks we are all hacks seeking Hollywood fame, and he's pissed he can't control his wife's deviant sexual behavior. If he divorces her, he loses the money. So instead he chooses to try to get rid of me in any way possible."

Jax's tone was bitter, and I didn't blame him. That was just plain fucked up. He leaned up to whisper in my ear, "You see, siren? I can identify with you more than you know."

I felt the warning of danger. "Jax," I spun around, "fight it. Fight back."

His jaw was clenched tight and I opened my senses and latched on to the growing anger and pushed love at him as fast as I could. As tired as I was, I didn't have a whole lot of energy to use and I blew through it fast as it fought me for control.

"Pull over," Aedan snapped. As soon as the car stopped moving Jax flung open the door and jumped out. I felt like a deflated balloon. Smitty grabbed my leg and moved my jeans to put his hand on my leg, and Aedan held on to the hand closest to him.

Ronnie had followed Jax out but kept his distance as Jax paced, fighting himself. "I'm so sorry." Guilt tore at me.

"It's not your fault, baby girl," Smitty told me gently. "He's been on the edge for a few days now."

I nodded mutely, and watched Ronnie approach and put his arm around Jax, saying something quietly to him. A few minutes later they started back to us, both covered in snow and shivering. Jax's desperate eyes clung to mine, but he didn't say anything.

Jax was just going through the motions on this. He felt like the whole shoot was a scam. He talked with Father Roarke briefly and Airiella was tailing him everywhere waiting for him to snap.

He didn't really think she wanted him to snap, that was the darkness in him trying to take over. He'd been so close. She'd told him she was proud of him for fighting it and he wanted to cry. He was a coward, it had been Ronnie that saved him, not himself.

The whole time they were doing interviews in this tiny town he felt off. He knew it was fake, these mysterious happenings were staged. None of the town could corroborate this guy's story, and nothing they dug up about the property hinted at a dark past.

They offered to let Father Roarke do a blessing of the land and exorcism, and were turned down flat. If this guy was really worried about his family being torn apart, he didn't show it. He hardly even mentioned them.

Airiella told them she felt something off about the guy. She was picking up vengeance from him, which told them this was fake. She did feel something in his house though, that had a dark tinge to it. Jax studied the house carefully.

It was certainly in rough shape, badly in need of repairs. It smelled like mold was growing in there, and faintly of blood. The floors creaked when they walked on them and the hand rail that followed the stair case up was barely held on by nails. It was a death trap, and should have been condemned.

Smitty had found that the background check had shown that this guy had been in trouble in the past with minor disturbances of the peace, and a few harassment charges. He'd been hospitalized for mental health as well. He found no evidence this guy even had a family.

After Airiella's assessment of him Smitty dug around looking for anything that could tie back to one of them and didn't find a thing there either. Smitty was positive this guy was unstable and up to something more than wanting his fifteen minutes of fame.

The hours' drive each way to this town was tiring, yet he had to admit Jax was right. It would have been mayhem if they stayed in one of these small towns, they wouldn't have gotten a moment's peace. There was no in between in how these people felt, they were either fans, or hated them.

Smitty leaned against the vehicle and watched as this guy tried to lure Jax in with his story that kept changing. Jax wasn't buying it. He didn't even bother trying to disguise his sarcastic comments. This little weaselly guy kept pushing, though. Airiella sat inside the vehicle, the guy creeped her out.

He wasn't too much taller than Airiella, which made him shorter than all the rest of the guys. He smelled like he hadn't showered in weeks, or brushed his teeth in a year. His hair was on the longish side of short, black and clumped together in greasy strands. His skin was sickly pale and pockmarked like he had a bad case of chicken pox at some point in his life. His eyes never stopped shifting around and were tinged red. He dressed like he thought he was a gangster, his pants sitting under his butt with his stained underwear showing. Baggy shirts and baggy coat, all dark colors.

Smitty shook his head, he felt like there was something he was missing. Maybe he should have listened to the guy ramble on more, but he couldn't help tuning out. His story kept changing and he suspected the guy was high on something.

He jumped as Airiella thumped on the window behind him. He opened the door. "What?"

"Get Jax out of there now," she frantically said, her voice borderline panic. "That guys energy just shifted."

Smitty launched himself across the yard. "Jax! We gotta go. Now!"

Smitty saw Jax turn and step, which saved him from getting hit, the guys fist sailing past Jax and throwing him off balance. Jax caught on and jogged over to Smitty.

"Airiella said his energy shifted," Smitty filled him in as they headed to the car. Aedan already had it started.

"Hey! Where are you guys going? We aren't done yet!" the guy called after them.

"Something came up. We'll see you tomorrow," Smitty yelled back slamming his door and locking it. "Drive, now."

Aedan drove off, the guy yelling something behind them. Smitty turned to Airiella, "Is he possessed?"

"I don't know," she said, her face pale. "I'm not qualified to answer that. I just felt his energy turn bad, fast."

Smitty looked at Jax who was just as confused as he was. "I don't know. He could be I guess, but none of the other signs are there," Jax thought out loud. "He's for sure not on this planet."

"Did you guys check with local churches to see if there was anything weird going on in the area?" Airiella checked.

"I did, well at least with that town," Aedan called back. "I didn't check the bordering towns though."

"We can do it tomorrow," Ronnie added. "I don't think we need to be back there until it's show time."

"I agree," Smitty seconded. He looked back at Airiella, "Thanks, baby girl."

She nodded. "I keep picking up on something in the house, but it's so faint, I keep thinking it's just residual energy."

"There is an off feel in there," Jax agreed.

"Is it centralized to a certain area?" came Ronnie's question.

She shrugged. "I can't tell that either. It just comes and goes."

"We've got a tail," Aedan informed them.

"Detour through the next town," Airiella told him. Smitty raised his eyebrows at her. "What? I've been stalked, remember?"

Jax stiffened next to him. He figured he remembered something from Airiella's dreamscape thing. Which meant it couldn't be good. Smitty nudged him with an elbow. "I'm fine," he muttered.

Airiella leaned as far forward as her seatbelt let her. "Take the next left, then take the next left after that."

"Do you know where you are going?" Ronnie asked, confused.

"No, but it should be random enough to be able to tell if they are following us. The map on my phone shows roads close together. If we see the car turn, then we take the next two lefts, another right and go straight for a couple miles. There are stores along that road that we can always pull into and park to try and hide the vehicle."

"Shit angel, you know way too much about this," Ronnie said uncomfortably. "It's not right."

"Maybe not, but it is what it is. The knowledge is coming in handy now." She sounded resolute.

Smitty silently agreed with both of them and

watched the car behind them. It followed, so they went with Airiella's directions and found a busy parking lot and parked in the midst of a bunch of similar looking vehicles. All of them ducking down below the window line except Aedan.

"Stay here for about fifteen minutes," she told Aedan. "If the car shows up, we go in the store, all of us. Together."

Smitty saw Ronnie flexing his arms, his fists clenching and unclenching. "We don't want to fight, bro."

"I will if I have to." Ronnie's tone was flat.

"No doubt, you can kick ass Ronnie, but take it from me, you can't beat a bullet. We don't know the end game of the person in the car," Airiella told him softly. "No confrontation. If I need to, I'll yank the energy out of them until they pass out."

Smitty looked back at her, her eyes dared him to argue. He knew she was right but he didn't have to like it. If this was part of the set-up, a physical confrontation wouldn't end well for them and would play right into the money man's hands. Smitty was willing to bet at this point, that this was all arranged by him.

Aedan called out the fifteen minutes when it was up and Airiella directed them through the backroads to the next town where they got back on the highway. Smitty noticed all of them watching the cars around them carefully.

Ronnie's room had a connecting door with Jax's, for obvious reasons. That was how he heard Airiella go in there when Jax cried out again, caught in another nightmare. Aedan was on the other side of Jax and that was where Airiella was staying that night.

Aedan had gotten a room with two beds, though why he didn't just sleep in the same one as Airiella he didn't understand. Him and Mags had already had sex with her, he didn't think sleeping would be a big deal. He got back into bed.

She would pull him out, Ronnie could go back to sleep. Except now he couldn't. He kept thinking about how calm she had been when that car was following them. It unnerved him how much she had been through. She didn't even have any fallout when it was over.

He thought back to when they pulled over for Jax to get control of himself. Jax had told him what she had said when they first talked. That for once she wished someone was willing to save her instead of her saving them all the time.

It had cut Ronnie deep, and he knew she wasn't talking about them, Jax did too, but it didn't ease the sting. Especially now. After she had repeatedly saved them. The bit she said about not being able to fight bullets hurt him too.

He and Jax were the only ones she hadn't connected with yet, and as far as he could tell, they were the ones that wanted her the most. She had told him that her connections with them were stronger than the others and he wondered if that was why she hadn't gone there yet.

Well, he knew why she hadn't with Jax, they all did. He wasn't quite ready for that yet, despite his need for her. Ronnie felt bad for wanting her when Jax did too, and he eased his conscious by telling himself that it was what she wanted.

Still made him feel guilty though. He knew Jax was the one for her. Hell, they all did. No one else had gotten through to Jax quite like she did. Ronnie rolled over and punched his pillows. He was taking her to the doctor tomorrow and to see her friend.

The guys were going to go check out the other little towns' libraries and churches. He hoped the days lesson in stalking stuck with them. He didn't hear any noise from Jax's room. He hated himself for it, but he got up to peek through the door. He told himself it was to make sure Jax was okay, but in reality, he knew he just wanted to see if it was more than just the nightmare.

She must have turned on the bathroom light and

left the door cracked open so she could see, because she was slightly illuminated. His breath caught in his throat at her beauty. She was glowing softly and sitting on the bed, her back up against the headboard and her head tilting forward so her hair cascaded over her face.

Jax's head was on her lap and she was humming so softly, at first, he thought it was noise coming from somewhere else. She ran her hands over his head, threading her fingers through his hair as he cried. Ronnie tried desperately to bite back the sob that rose in him, but a whimper escaped his lips.

"He's okay now, Ronnie," she said without looking up. "You can come in if you want."

Ronnie's feet led him forward before he even had time to think about it. The love he felt for these two swamped him and his heart broke for Jax. He couldn't imagine the shit that was going on inside him. He sat on the bed, Jax between them, and he put his hand on Jax's shoulder.

He knew Jax wasn't asleep, but Jax didn't care. He actually seemed to settle down more. Ronnie would give up any chance he had with Airiella to make Jax okay again. "He knows, Ronnie." She looked at him then.

He gave up all pretense and let his emotions go. He did the most unmanly thing he could possibly imagine and curled up behind Jax and cried with him. Airiella touching them both and giving her strength freely, filling them with the love she was never short of.

She started humming again, this angel he couldn't live without. No judgement came from her, no condemnation, no ridicule over two grown men spooning and crying on her. She had a hand on each of them, her fingers running along their scalps like she was seeking out the bad thoughts and zapping them with peace from her own soul. They both fell asleep, salty tears drying on their cheeks as she took care of them like she had been since she walked into their lives.

Ronnie woke up in the same position he fell asleep

in, feeling more refreshed than he had in a long time, and that felt wrong to him given their situation. He still felt his angel's hand in his hair but it was still, and she wasn't humming.

He glanced up and saw her somewhat slumped over, sleeping. She was going to be sore from sleeping like that. He tried to shift to ease out of the bed without waking them though it didn't work. The first movement had them both awake.

Airiella groaned and stretched while Jax shifted off her so she could move. Ronnie had thought it would have been awkward waking up like that but it wasn't. He felt a peace in him. Jax rolled, "Move to her other side so she can stretch out. I cramped her."

Ronnie stood and Jax scooted over to where he had been and pulled a protesting Airiella against him and Ronnie got slid in front of her. Ronnie glanced at his watch, they still had at least three hours before they had to be up. "We've got time for more sleep," he told them.

Jax spooned Airiella, who curled up against Ronnie's back. He was in heaven, everything else that was going on faded away as they fell back asleep for what felt like minutes, but was three hours. The knock on the door woke them.

Airiella was grumbling about fifteen more minutes when the door opened and Aedan flew in looking panicked. "Damn you! I woke up to no Airiella, checked with Smitty, she wasn't there, went in Ronnie's room find no Ronnie or no Airiella, only to find you all asleep here. You gave me a heart attack!"

"Jeez Dad, chill," came Airiella's muffled voice. "If you didn't sleep like the dead you would have heard me leave when Jax had a nightmare."

Ronnie heard Jax choke back a laugh that he tried to play off as a cough. "Ronnie and Airiella took care of me last night. It's fine, calm down."

"This is an interesting scene," came Smitty's voice.

"No different than when you and I fell asleep with

her," Ronnie shot back.

"Point to Ronnie," Jax mumbled.

"Clean up, we gotta leave soon," Aedan demanded then walked out with Smitty, closing the door behind him.

"Someone woke up cranky," Airiella groaned as she stretched that beautiful body behind him.

"Thanks for taking care of me again, siren," Ronnie heard Jax whisper. He climbed out of bed wanting to give Jax a moment.

"I'm going to shower, meet me in the dining room, Airiella," he said, nodding at Jax as he left.

"Ronnie, wait," Jax started, halfway sitting up.

"No man, we're good. I've always got you," Ronnie interrupted, knowing exactly where Jax was going to go. He gave Jax a smile to back up the words. In the grin Jax gave him, Ronnie saw who he had been missing for the past twelve years.

"Thanks," Jax said.

Ronnie left, understanding that Jax wanted to talk to Airiella, before he closed the door, he saw him kiss her, in a way he had always wanted to kiss Winnie.

Aedan had arranged another rental car for Ronnie and I to take to Independence. I was glad he thought about it, because the logistics hadn't even crossed my mind in my excitement to see Chrissie. It was about a two-hour drive, so we ate fast and left to make the doctor's appointment.

I fidgeted the whole way there, flipping between radio stations to find songs I liked. I was sure I was driving Ronnie crazy, though he never batted an eye. I couldn't wait to get the stitches out. They were itchy and I was having a hard time not pulling at them.

We finally got to the doctor's office and I was in the door in a flash, ready to get it done with so I could see Chrissie. "You're like a kid with too much sugar," Ronnie joked.

I flushed. It was accurate though. Shit. Kids. "We

need to find something for three boys before we see her. I don't want to show up empty handed."

Ronnie looked confused. "Doesn't she know we are coming?"

"Yes, it's an Italian thing. We never show up somewhere without something for the host," I tried to explain.

He looked blank then thoughtful. "Toys is the obvious answer, or candy."

"Sugar is what I usually do for my brother's kids and he doesn't like it so much. I'm not trying to drive her crazy like I do my brother. I'm thinking some sort of project toys."

"Like a science kit?" Ronnie suggested.

I laughed hard at that. "No, maybe if they were girls. Boys I would think would be inclined to find a way to blow something up."

"Good point," he agreed with a smile.

Ronnie fiddled with his phone looking for a store nearby as the doctor came in. "Hello Ms. Raven. I'm going to check for infection first and see how it's healing before I take these out."

She did her thing, asking questions along the way I didn't hesitate to answer. "It's not as far along as I hoped, though if you can't get to a doctor in the next few days, I'll just take them out now. I'll send you with some good bandages to keep them closed. You'll need to change them daily and clean the wound really good though."

I nodded my understanding and she got to work. It was an ugly wound though it could have been a lot worse so I wasn't going to complain. "Are you still using the sling?" she asked me casually. Damn.

Ronnie jumped all over that one. "No, she refused after the first night."

I glared at him. "I know my limits, I've been careful, kept it clean, haven't soaked it. I have other shoulder issues and keeping my arm still tends to make things hurt more."

"It's your body, you know it best," she said gently.

"Though I would recommend as little movement as possible so the wound heals faster. If you can do that, I won't harp on you about the sling."

"Deal," I agreed, knowing the man next to me was going to watch me like a hawk now.

She had the nurse make me up a take home kit of butterfly bandages and ointment that would last a couple of weeks. "If you start to notice a lot of seepage that has a smell or discoloration, or fresh blood, you are doing too much and the wound underneath has probably split again and might be infected. If that happens, you'll need to get back in to see someone."

"Got it," I told her, smiling.

She chuckled, "You're a stubborn one, I can tell."

Ronnie grunted from the chair and I shot him another look. "Just well acquainted with injuries."

She gave me a soft look. "Still?"

Oh, she knew. I must have given something away. "No, it's been a few years," I told her quietly. She nodded and touched my hand.

"Be gentle with yourself, healing takes time," she advised. "It was nice meeting you. Take care."

Ronnie stared after her with his jaw hanging open. I jumped up and tapped it close. "Keep it shut if you know what's good for you."

"How did she…" he started.

"People that have been there tend to know it in others," I reminded him. He followed me out of the office and we headed to the store.

"What about Legos, and some kind of outdoor foam toys like a nerf gun or something?" he suggested as we parked.

"Sounds perfect." I flew through the store letting Ronnie pick out the boy toys while I looked for something for Chrissie. I found an art kit that had enough supplies for whatever she wanted to do and we loaded up the car.

"You aren't a shopper, are you?" he asked as I texted her that we were on our way.

"No, I hate it," I replied.

"You shop like a guy," he laughed.

"That's not true," I smirked. "My brother loves shopping. And Jax did pretty well in the stuff he got for me."

"Maybe so, but he still flies in and out of the store like you do, none of the wandering around."

A wave of love washed over me and I glanced up from my phone and saw Ronnie staring at me. My heart melted a bit as I remembered how he came in last night. He was so close with Jax, it was pretty amazing. I cupped his cheek and gave him a soulful kiss that started a storm in other regions of my body. Didn't think that one through very well.

Totally worth it though to see his eyes darken like that. He took a minute to compose himself and we followed the GPS directions to Chrissie's. She must have heard the car because the front door opened and there she was. My best friend in the entire world.

I flew from the car, Ronnie laughing softly as I didn't even close my door. I practically bowled her over as I threw my arms around her, wincing slightly as I tugged at the bandages on my arms. Happy tears flooded down my face as I saw her three boys looking at me like I was an alien from behind her.

To be fair, she was crying too. Ronnie gave us a moment as he got the bags out of the car and closed it up. Joining us once we pulled apart. "Ronnie, this is Chrissie, Chrissie, Ronnie," I introduced them.

Judging by the look on her face she thought he was just as hot as I did. She introduced us to her boys who looked so much like her. Ronnie apparently had a knack with kids because they were on the floor playing in no time while Chrissie and I went and sat in the kitchen.

She filled me in on all the crap going on with her now ex-husband and I just listened. She had always believed that of the two of us I was stronger than her. Maybe it was true, though I tended to believe our strengths were just in opposite areas. We complemented each other.

Chrissie was just as beautiful as ever too. My heart was so happy to see her that I forgot all about the crap going on with the guys. That is until Ronnie popped in to say that the guys had found some weird references to occult activity in one of the bordering churches.

Reality came crashing back down as Ronnie filled me on what they found. References to sacrifices of this secret group in the basement of that house. Chrissie had a perplexed look on her face as she listened to Ronnie. He asked her permission to take the boys into the back yard to make snowmen and play with the nerf toys after he finished.

She bundled them up and sent them off while we watched from the warm kitchen. "He's good with them," she said offhandedly. I agreed. He was a natural. "Please tell me you are doing him so I can live through you."

I laughed. "No, not yet."

"Why the hell not? You have eyes, right?" she had an amazed look on her face.

"He's even better with no shirt on," I said wistfully.

"What the hell is wrong with you?" she demanded.

"It's complicated," I hedged.

"It's sex. It's not that complicated unless he's gay. Judging from the looks he's given you, he is definitely not gay."

"Nope. Not gay. It's a long story." I sighed.

"We've got time, those boys have energy to spare. I guarantee you he will tire before they do. Spill." She sat back in her chair and waited.

I gave her the condensed version of everything, including the angel and raven parts, and the sex and connections. Then I told her about the weird events, what happens when I release the energy, the crazy lady, all of it.

At the end she stared at me with her mouth hanging open. "You don't do things half way ever, do you?"

"Hey, be fair, it's not all my fault," I argued.

"Ells, none of it is your fault," she said, calling me

by my family nickname. "There's also not one part of that story that surprises me."

"You've got to be shitting me," I sputtered. "I still can't wrap my head around all of it."

"So instead, focus on the part where you get to have sex with all these fucking hot men," she said with a completely straight face.

I burst out laughing. "Out of all of that, you focus on the sex."

She grabbed my chin and turned my head to look out at Ronnie and the boys who were now making snow angels. "Look at that man, I'd strip now and do him."

Her tone had me pulling out her grip and looking at her. "Chris, do you feel something?" I asked her quietly.

"Maybe. I don't know," she admitted. "Even if I do, you still need to sleep with him."

"I still have the connection without the sex," I pointed out.

"It's better with it, though, right?" she pushed.

I nodded. "What did you feel?" Chrissie had always had a sense about people. Not to say she always made the right choice in them, but she always sensed things about them that I couldn't until their emotions revealed themselves.

"A future," she replied, her voice sad. "It's not possible. I live here, stuck, until I can get away from my ex's parents. He's over on the west coast somewhere, right?"

"Location doesn't matter, it's temporary. You know that. Look how he is with those boys, and he just met them." I pushed her to acknowledge it.

"For all I know, it's a reaction to how damn sexy he is." She had a fair point in that. "Regardless, even if we have a future, it's just that, in the future. He doesn't know me, and I don't know him. You need to sleep with him, even if it's just to test him out for me to see if I'll break him."

Full on belly laugh erupted from me. "How do you

know I won't break him?"

"If you do, then he will never work for me," she said deadpanned.

I loved this woman. "We need to get through this live show before I can think about any test drives."

"Is it safe?" she was serious now.

"I don't think so. Gut feeling I have." I hated voicing it too.

"Ells..." she worried.

I shrugged. "Not much I can do about it, Chris. I'm head over heels in love with him. I'll die as many times as I need to in order for him to be okay."

She winced and shuddered. "That's not easy to hear. Which one was with you when it happened last?"

"Smitty," I answered.

She took my hand. "How is he now?"

"It bothers him. It changed him." It made me sad to admit it, and it hurt me that he went through it.

"Ells, if you watched any of them die, and come back to life, what would it do to you?" Her quiet question grounded me.

"I don't want to hear logic," I gave her a look.

"It's not logic, it's truth." She gave me the same look back. "I've known you so long, and I can tell you that it would haunt me for the rest of my life to see you go through that. Shit, it's going to haunt me now and I didn't even see it. You've always been able to see things from all sides unless it comes to you."

"I'm not going to like this, am I?" I rolled my eyes at her.

"Nope," she said with snark then softened her tone. "You only see the worst in yourself. You need to see the other side of it." We both heard the raven's wings. She smiled. "Seems like I'm on to something here. Listen to them when they speak of you. Believe them. Believe me. Why do you think it's so easy for me to believe you are an angel?"

"Because you are crazy?" I fired off quickly.

"Really Ells? Sarcasm? You know I can see through that defense, right?" I shut up. I knew when I lost.

"Okay, fine, why do you believe it?" I huffed.

Neither of us heard Ronnie come in. "Because you always give, you never take. You always lift people up, never push them down." She took my hand again when she saw I was holding back. She gave me a sad smile. "You always hold back your pain and take on other's as well. Everywhere we ever went, people fell in love with you all the time, not once did you see it. You always believed the draw was whoever you were with."

"Chris, that's not true," I said. "Look at you."

"Ells, that's what I'm talking about. Why couldn't it have been you? It *was* you. If I went somewhere without you, I always ended up spending the time answering questions about where you were. When will you see that?" she asked.

"Maybe I'm not supposed to see it," I argued. "Aren't angels supposed to be humble?"

"There's humble," she held her hand out, then lowered it drastically, "then there's you."

"Ouch." I winced.

"Didn't you tell me the raven showed you what you needed to fix, and wasn't that on that list?"

"Fine, you made your point." I wiped my eyes.

"Yet, you still don't believe me." She handed me a tissue. "When have I lied to you?"

"Never," I whispered. "Why does believing hurt so much?"

"Because you will be admitting you are awful to yourself. It's an ugly truth." Chrissie smiled sadly.

"Shit, when did you get so wise?" I groaned.

She pointed to the backyard where the boys were playing. "It started after the first one."

I looked at the innocence on those beautiful faces. "Um, wait. Where's Ronnie?"

He stepped around the corner, and gave Chrissie a searching look. "I'm right here." He kneeled before me.

"Believing you are a good person hurts you?"

I shrugged, wondering how much he heard. "Maybe." My voice was soft. Chrissie glared at me. "Shit. Fine, yes."

He looked back at her to see her glaring and stifled a smile. "I like her. Angel, I'm assuming she knows you pretty well."

Chrissie piped up, "Better than anyone else."

He bit his lip. "If you don't believe her, you will never believe us. We are all saying the same thing."

Chrissie raised her eyebrow at me, and crossed her arms. "Healing takes time," I defended myself.

She snorted. "How old are you now? It takes thirty something years?"

"You guys are mean. Fine. It hurts me to think that I couldn't fix everything. If I was so special, why did all those people not heal from being with me. Why did they hurt me so bad? It makes me feel like I failed them, which in turn leads me to believe I'm not good enough, that what they did was just punishment for not being able to help them." I spit it all out in a rush.

Chrissie grabbed a tissue and held it to her eyes. "Ells. What do you tell others that have gone through even one of the things you've been through? What did you tell me?"

I avoided looking at Ronnie, I couldn't. I bared my soul in front of him once again and he could now see how ugly it was. The raven cawed loud in my head and I covered my ears. "I tell them, you, that it's not you, it's them."

"Why would it be different for you?" she cried and stood up walking into the kitchen and getting a drink of water to calm herself down.

"I'm supposed to be strong and help others," I said, my voice barely a whisper.

"Give me a minute," Ronnie growled and hauled me off the chair into his arms and dragged me into the other room. "Are you fucking kidding me right now? Why won't you look at me?"

"Because she thinks you will think she's ugly," Chrissie answered from the doorway, her eyes red.

Ronnie looked at me aghast. "Is that true?"

I couldn't answer, shame rolling through me. "Yes, it's true," Chrissie answered again, walking into the room. "Tell him the truth, Ells."

Ronnie sat down pulling me down on to his lap and wrapped his arms around me. They were shaking, I didn't know if it was anger, or if he was disgusted with me. I couldn't look at him.

Chrissie stepped into my line of sight. "Why do you think I don't know? Because I haven't seen you? I know it from the words you say and don't say, it doesn't matter if I can see your face or not. We are connected here." She gestured to her heart. "I felt the same way about myself until you pulled me up out of it. How long did it take you? I *know* why you are there. You pulled me out for those little monsters in the backyard. If you don't let others help you pull you out, will it be for nothing that you helped me? Is this evil shit that you are trying to beat back going to take over? Will it hurt my kids?"

The raven was flapping madly in my head and the guilt tore through me. What if she was right? Ronnie tightened his arms around me, and his whole body was shaking. He leaned his head against my shoulder.

Chrissie wasn't finished with her brutal onslaught though. "It won't kill you to ask for help. Consider this Ells, we might need to feel needed too. Even the helper needs help sometimes, right? God needs help, why do you think there are angels? How many times have I called you my guardian angel? *That's* why it's so easy for me to believe. You've always been different, and it's the best thing there is about you. I've never seen you turn someone away."

"God Chris, you're killing me." She shoved more tissues in my hand.

"Good, I'll give you a minute here before this beast holding you explodes." She walked away grabbing a coat and went outside with her kids.

"Angel if you don't look at me, I can't be held responsible for my actions," Ronnie warned me, his voice strained.

I looked at him and broke. His face was raw with pain, his eyes shining with tears. "I'm sorry."

"Stop apologizing! Is what she said true? You're afraid that me, that the others will see the pain in you as failures and think you are ugly?" he paraphrased Chrissie's words.

It sounded completely ridiculous when he said it like that. The trembling in his body still didn't give me a clue as to what he was feeling and I was too scared to try and figure it out. I just nodded.

He collapsed back on the couch pulling me along with him. "Do you think that little of me? Of Jax? Smitty? Aedan? Mags?"

Wait, what? "No," I choked out.

"Are we not doing enough to show you how we feel? Tell me how to make you understand." His voice cracked. "If you apologize, I'm going to get up and leave you here," he threatened.

I snapped my mouth closed. "You are infuriating with this steadfast belief that you disappoint others. It couldn't be farther from the truth. You've made each and every one of us a better person in the very short time we've known you. We are all madly in love with you and fight over who gets to spend time with you next. What would possibly make you believe that I would find anything about you remotely ugly? Do you think I'm ugly because my dad used to beat the shit out of me?" He held me away from him and forced my face to look at him.

I shook my head violently at him. "Do you get why I would find it insulting you would think we would feel that way about you?" I was slower to respond this time, but I did get it. I nodded.

"Do you know why I cried last night?" His tone gentled though he still shook. I shook my head no. "When I saw you there, taking care of Jax, how absolutely beautiful you were, I couldn't stop myself from being near you. When you touched me, the love that flowed was so much that I couldn't contain it. Everything I felt for you, for Jax, for everything that happened to us came out. You cleansed us. It's you, angel. Everything about you makes us whole. I don't care one damn bit about the assholes of your past. That's not you. Last night, that was you. I could no more have removed myself from that room than I could have transformed myself into a cow. Do you understand?"

I laid my head on his chest. "That's not an answer sweetheart. I need to hear you say that you understand."

Damn man. "I understand," I acquiesced. We sat there until Chrissie came back in with the boys and fed them a snack.

We visited for another hour or so and then we had to head back. As we said goodbye on her porch, I pulled Ronnie back close. "Hang on, let me see something." I held on to Ronnie's hand and grabbed Chrissie's. Just as I thought.

Ronnie and Chrissie gasped. "Wow, Ells. Um," she pulled her hand back, shocked, "that was different."

"She's good at shock value," Ronnie growled, looking confused.

Chrissie laughed, "That she is. We'll talk more about that later. For now, you know what I expect of you." She winked. "This too," she said and she tapped my heart. I hugged her tight and said goodbye. "I'll be watching the show tomorrow!" she called out as we got in. I loved her.

"Care to explain that little stunt you just pulled?" Ronnie started as we drove away. I missed her already.

"I miss her already," I said, my voice sad.

"Me too angel, so what was that?" He kept at me.

"She's yours," I answered.

"She's my what?" He sounded confused.

"Future," Why wasn't he following this?

"I need more." The confusion was replaced with disbelief.

"How much more? I thought I kept it pretty plain there. She's yours."

"How do you figure?" he snapped.

"Same way I knew you weren't mine, same way I knew Smitty wasn't mine, same way I knew Jax was. Also, coincidently, it's the same way I knew that you did have someone other than me."

"By touch?" his tone eased up a little.

"Yes, by touch. Chrissie and I have had a connection for years, not one from sex, so don't go there. Chris gets feelings about people. She sees things in a way. I saw the look she gets when that happens and she had it when she met you. Much like the you and Jax thing with me, she's the same with you and me with her. She wasn't going to explore it herself, so I tested it to see if I got anything. And I did." I felt like I was repeating myself.

"Still need more."

"Which part, Ronnie?" I was getting frustrated and I shouldn't be.

"The you and me part," he clarified.

"I told her there was no you and me, and she said there was, I just hadn't acted on it yet. Which is true. She won't even consider you, unless we do us first."

"Um, do I get a say in this?" I didn't understand the hurt tone he had.

"Sure, why not? What's your thoughts?" I gave up.

"I don't know her. I love her kids. She was a bit brutal with you, I guess it was necessary, and she hardly talked to me," Ronnie ticked off.

"She thinks you are ridiculously hot. She knows you love me. She thinks you were fantastic with her kids. She knows a lot just from that," I rebutted.

"She thinks I was good with her kids?" he asked, surprised.

I laughed. "That's what you are focusing on?"

"Angel, what if I think you are it for me? I mean, I know Jax is your forever, but what if this little brief time I get with you, what if I think that's it for me? It would be all

I'd ever need. I know that you'll be in my life forever," he told me and his tone was genuine and soft.

"Give it time, Ronnie. I'm not telling you to go marry her tomorrow, besides she'd probably kick you in the nuts and slam the door in your face if you did that. I'm just saying keep an open mind."

"I wasn't kidding when I said I was madly in love with you." He risked a glance at me.

I took his hand and kissed his knuckles. "I know. I'm in love with you too."

"Can you be though? I saw how you were with Jax, there was no denying how real that was." He sounded frustrated.

"I love you all differently, you know that. There is no competition." That was something I had to keep repeating with both of them.

"Does Jax know that?" he asked me.

"Yes, Ronnie. We had this discussion as well. Jax is by far the strongest connection out of you all. You are the second strongest. It's why I have saved you both for last. Aedan and Smitty were my voice of reason and logic, Mags was the free spirit and acceptance. You and Jax, you two are all the emotions I tell myself I don't deserve," I listed off.

He pulled over. "Angel, every time we talk you strip my soul bare. It's terrifying because you could destroy me, but it's absolutely amazing at the same time because you accept everything and you just give love." He reached for my face and gave me a panty melting kiss.

I moaned as his cell phone rang. Damn technology. He chuckled at my apparent frustration. And answered the phone and pulled back on the street.

"Here talk to the angel." He handed me the phone. I put it on speaker phone.

"When will you guys be back?" Aedan asked.

"I think we are about an hour away, why?" I checked my phone to see how much farther.

"Jax isn't doing so good." I could hear Aedan

shuffling around.

"What do you mean?" I responded immediately.

"He said he needs you, he's too close to the edge," Aedan answered, worried.

"I'll be there as soon as I can. We don't have plans tonight, right?" I asked.

"No," Aedan confirmed.

"Tell him to order room service and eat dinner. I'll go straight there when I get back," I instructed him.

"Okay. What did the doctor say?" Aedan abruptly changed the subject.

"That she should still be using the sling," Ronnie broke in.

"No, she didn't!" I exclaimed.

"Okay fine. She said that Airiella should use the arm as little as possible because it isn't mending together as fast as it should," he revised his statement.

"Is that true, or is Ronnie throwing his weight around?" Aedan asked.

"That part was true," I admitted.

"How was the rest of the day?" Aedan asked curiously.

"Enlightening," Ronnie answered again.

"You'll have to fill me in later," Aedan said.

"Bet your ass I will," Ronnie fired off, giving me a look. Uh oh. "And the subject of the talk will be with us speaking truth now that I know what it is."

"MMMMM, Okay! Go make Jax eat and give him my message. Thank you! Goodbye!" I hung up. "Damn you Ronnie. That was between us."

"No angel, that's between all of us," he admonished softly.

"Dangerous ground to be on," I warned.

"More dangerous than getting shot? Or falling apart because someone came in your room and tried to kill you?" he fired back.

"Fine, get through the filming first. Then you can all beat up on me."

"Angel, it's not..." Ronnie started.

"Don't. I know what it is, I know it's necessary, I know I'll do it. I don't have to like it," I interrupted him.

"Are you staying with Jax tonight?" he gave up.

"I don't know, if he needs me to, I guess I will. Otherwise, I'm homeless."

"If he doesn't need you, then I do," Ronnie stated.

"Okay." Chrissie's words ringing in my head about me never turning anyone away. I knew she was right. It's just who I was though. That didn't make me special.

"Angel, I don't need you for any reason other than my need to be close to you," Ronnie said, dangerously close to reading my mind.

"Oh," I breathed out. "I think you have it wrong though, it's you guys who can destroy me." I freely gave him my vulnerability.

Jax paced his room and eyed the food he hadn't had the stomach to eat yet. The darkness inside him was feeling like it was happy and it unsettled him. His stomach kept rolling and he was getting cold sweats. When he closed his eyes, he saw fire. It was consuming him, and burning with him was his hope and salvation laying on the floor, in the shape of Airiella.

He ground his fists into his eyes, refusing to give in to the dark thoughts trying to drown him. He checked his watch for the hundredth time wondering how close she was yet. And Ronnie, he was with her. The two people that he relied on to not let go of him.

He heard a soft knock on the door and tripped over his own feet to get there, flinging it open to see a startled Airiella. He dropped to his knees and buried his face in her belly, clinging to her. She was alive. "Oh, Jax." Her soft voice slid against him like velvet.

He felt someone else try to disengage him from her and he held tighter. "Bro, let's take it in the room, okay. We are drawing attention." Ronnie. It was Ronnie, he was here too. He let go and Ronnie helped him up, an arm supporting him like he had always done. "Why didn't you eat?" he asked spying the food Jax hadn't touched.

"I can't. It's doing something to me inside." Jax let Ronnie lead him to the little table.

"Can you try, please? You'll need the energy." The velvety voice of his siren wrapped around him again.

"Stay with me, don't leave me," Jax begged, not even caring how pathetic he sounded. She guided him to sit down at the small table and sat him down. He saw Ronnie nod to her and start to leave. "No! Don't go. I need you both."

He saw the naked hope on Ronnie's face, he didn't want to disappoint him. "I keep having visions when I close my eyes," Jax started, then stopped, the smell of smoke assailing his senses. He jumped up and spun around, looking for fire. "Can you smell it? The smoke?" He ran to the door to put his hand on it, feeling for heat. No heat, it was cool against his hand.

"Jax, man, sit down." Ronnie came back to him. "There's no smoke. Everything is okay." Ronnie sounded worried. Jax tried to calm down.

"Don't go," Jax repeated.

"I won't. I'm here as long as you want me here," Ronnie assured him.

Jax sagged in the chair and guzzled the water Airiella handed him, the coolness soothing the scratchiness of his throat. "You're alive," he whispered looking at her.

Alarm bloomed in her eyes at his words, and Jax wished he could take them back. "Of course, I am." Her soft hand on his arm pushed back the fear and he felt weak.

"I need to lay down," he mumbled. He found getting up was an effort and he tried to stand three times before Ronnie was there to help him. Concern etched in his face. "Don't go."

"We are both staying right here." She sat down on the bed, propping all the pillows behind her and she patted the bed between her legs. "Right here."

Ronnie led him to her and he lay face down resting

his face on her belly as she tried to find something to do with her legs. Jax wrapped his arms around her legs and she propped them on his back. Ronnie pulled her shoes off then sat on the other side of the bed.

The scent of jasmine on an ocean breeze enveloped him like a drug. He felt Ronnie move and heard the door open, and panic hit him. "No! Stay here!"

Jax felt her fingers in his hair. "He's just getting some pillows from his bed." Jax let go of her legs and snaked his arms around her back and held tight like he was afraid she would disappear from under him.

"I'm so scared," he mumbled into her belly.

"Of what?" He loved the sound of her voice.

"That I'm going to lose you both," he answered, his words muffled.

"I don't think either of us plan on letting you go, so you are stuck with us." He heard the tremor in her voice.

Ronnie settled back down on the bed. "I'm not going anywhere, bro."

Jax turned his head to see Airiella lift an arm and Ronnie settled under it so she was wrapped around them both. She buried her hand in Ronnie's hair, and the other was in Jax's. She shifted slightly to get more comfortable and started humming.

At the sound, Jax's world re-centered, and with his best friend and his woman surrounding him, he fell into sleep, the sound of fire crackling in the background.

Smitty woke up feeling unnaturally hot. Jax had been like a caged tiger yesterday growing more and more agitated. He felt bad for Airiella having to deal with it, and hoped she hadn't had to sleep sitting on the floor of his room while he had nightmares again.

He searched his dresser for the extra key to Jax's room. They all had one in case they needed to help with a nightmare. Finding it, he threw on some shorts and a shirt and knocked quietly before he opened the door.

His heart jumped to his throat as he saw Airiella

propped up by a ton of pillows with Jax sleeping between her legs, her shins locked around his back and Ronnie under her arm resting one of his on Jax's back. He swallowed back the feelings that rose up in him.

This was his family. She was their center. The heart of it. She had brought them closer together and wove some invisible thread between them all to bind them. The need to be with them overwhelmed him and he didn't care if he woke them up.

He heard Aedan come up behind him. "Damn," he heard Aedan say. "We need to be a part of that." Smitty was glad he wasn't the only one who thought so.

They gently closed the door behind them, and Smitty went to the side where Airiella was holding Jax. He had about a foot of space to wedge in there, and Aedan went behind Ronnie. Smitty angled in on his side and lifted her arm to settle around his shoulders as he slid up next to Jax. Aedan did the same on the other side.

Airiella was now touching each of them and the connection burst to life through them all, like a loop, it flowed through them. She opened her eyes wide at the contact. "Oh my God," she whispered sleepily.

"Imagine how strong this will be when you make those two permanent," Smitty breathed into her ear. "You made this, baby girl."

She kissed him on the forehead, and turned to do the same to Ronnie. Screw breakfast, Smitty thought. He wasn't moving from where he was until he had to. From the look on Aedan's face he felt the same way.

Chapter Sixteen

Jax watched as Smitty spliced together the interviews for the pre-show and then recorded a few intro scenes that would air while they were setting up for the live show. He had an uneasy feeling that had been following him since they got up this morning.

Airiella was never far from him and he knew she had his back and was watching out for him. For them all. He saw the strain on her a few times and they all kept pushing caffeine and energy bars at her. He was glad that they had managed to stay off the radar for the most part, less crowds made it easier for her.

People knew they were in town, but they didn't know where. Now, as they were loading up to head to the location, they were catching the interest of a few. Ronnie's stormy glare kept them at bay though. None of them liked the interest that was being shown in Airiella.

Father Roarke approached him looking concerned. "Jax, how are you feeling, son?"

"Uneasy, Father," Jax spoke honestly.

"Not out of control though?" the priest asked

specifically.

"No, not right now. Airiella has been pretty good about catching it before it gets that far and is able to warn the others."

"She's special, Jax," Father Roarke said. There was a warning in his tone that Jax couldn't place.

"I know." Jax studied the Father's face.

"Are you fighting for yourself yet? Or are you only using her as an anchor?" the question had barbs.

Jax bristled. More accurately, the energy in him bristled and Airiella appeared around the other side of the vehicle he'd been loading. "Everything okay, Father Roarke?" she stepped forward and pulled the priest back a little.

"Yes, lass. Just talking with Jax." He gave her a kind smile, patting her hand.

Jax felt it rise in him and she pushed the priest away hissing something at him, and was at Jax's side in the next instant. She hugged him and hummed something, running her hand up under his shirt making his skin tingle.

Jax struggled to regain control and wrapped his arms around her as he felt her energy sink into him. Maybe the priest had a point. He was only able to fight it when she was around. He released her and stepped away when he was back in control.

She gave him a look, and skimmed her fingers across his face. He loved it when she did that. She went back to loading the vehicles and Jax heard Ronnie bitching at her for doing too much. He walked around until he found Father Roarke again.

"Sorry Father. You were right, she has been the anchor. But when she is around, I do fight," Jax breathed the words out.

"Son, you aren't fighting for yourself though, you are fighting for her." The priest hit low and hard.

Jax sighed, "Isn't the end result the same?"

"No. You need to be able to control it when she isn't around too." There was more truth in there than Jax wanted to acknowledge.

"I get it. Hey Father, while I have you here, we found evidence in a church in one of the bordering towns of occult practices by some secret group. They referenced sacrifices in the basement of the house. We didn't see anything when we looked down there, how realistic do you think it is?" Jax deftly changed the subject.

"Anything is possible. Your subject doesn't exhibit any signs of possession, nor does the house or property. Demons would leave a trace of some sort." Father Roarke just confirmed Jax's own suspicions.

"I agree with you. But after we found that old journal and got back here, I started having weird visions every time I closed my eyes."

"Not to be indelicate, but have you closed the connection with Airiella?" Father Roarke looked intrigued by his statement.

"No, I'm, uh, too scared to do that yet," Jax floundered at the question.

"What are the visions?" Father Roarke asked, giving him an escape route.

"Fire. Consuming fire and her death." Jax felt the tremor run through him as it came flashing back through his mind in clear detail.

"Fire is often associated with some demons, or Satan, it still seems coincidental though. Perhaps it's just fear getting the better of you. Or maybe this energy in you is playing tricks on your mind," he suggested.

"Maybe. It seemed happy with those visions though. Really shook me up." Jax ran his hands through his hair in aggravation.

"Be on guard son. That's my best advice. I'll be on site with Airiella. Tom flew in as well. You have backup."

"Tom's here too? When did that happen?" Jax looked around.

"He's on site already, went straight there from the airport. He came in this morning. He's worried you are indeed being set up for something. He's here as a witness."

Father Roarke patted his shoulder.

"Great. I've gotta get this stuff loaded, so I'll see you there, Father. Thanks for the support."

"Anytime son. Don't worry so much about Airiella, she's far more capable than any of us realize," the priest declared quietly.

Jax nodded weakly. That didn't ease his fears. His heart was involved. What scared him straight through, was just how much. What he felt for Airiella was so much more than it had ever been with Winnie. He didn't know that he would survive losing Airiella.

Jax drove, he needed to have something to focus on other than the fucked-up thoughts that kept trying to pull him down. Aedan sat next to him in the passenger seat. The second row of the SUV was filled with equipment and bags of batteries and supplies. Also hidden there was the coat he had bought for Airiella as a surprise.

Squished into the third row of seating was Smitty, Airiella and Ronnie. Everyone was quiet and it caught his attention that Airiella was paying close attention to the cars around them. Her eyes missing nothing.

He forced his thoughts back to the road. Taking a trip back down her memory lane was not about to do him one damn bit of good. They arrived at the location safe, no one appearing to have followed them but their crew.

Airiella and Smitty went off to do a quick walk around, and Aedan and Ronnie went with him to set up the static cameras in spots they felt might be best. Jax felt an odd energy flow through him and he paused turning on his EMF device.

"Hey Aedan, EMF reading is pegged out right here, tape the floor so we can do something here later," Jax called out.

They went through the house marking spots and setting up the cameras and testing viewing angles. Once it was all set, they headed back out to the tents. Jax detoured to the SUV and grabbed the bag with the coat for Airiella.

She had been standing with Father Roarke and Tom

and huddled into herself wearing Smitty's old sweatshirt. They hadn't planned on snow, so when Jax had to replace her clothes a jacket hadn't crossed his mind.

"Airiella, could I have a moment please?" he called to her.

Father Roarke patted her on the back and she jogged over. "Everything okay? I haven't sensed anything alarming."

"What? Oh, yeah, it's fine. I just had something for you." Jax thrust the bag towards here, feeling like an awkward teenager.

She gave him a puzzled look and opened the bag. She squealed in delight and launched at him, throwing her arms around his neck. "Thank you!"

Jax grinned in success as she tore the tags off and bundled up in the coat. He reached behind her and settled the hood on her head. "Better?"

"Much. This is amazing! Thank you so much!" Love glowed in those eyes of hers that were mesmerizing to him.

"I'm trying to be the better man," he said, his voice quiet so that only she could hear him.

She cocked her head sideways, "You are Jax. Give us time. We've both got a long way to go." Her velvety voice reached his ears only. "Be careful tonight. While I don't feel anything alarming, I still feel something off."

"I do too," he agreed with her. "We can't use walkies on the live show, but we do have earpieces. Stay near Tom, he has one too. Relay through him."

"Smitty told me. Good luck." She touched his hand briefly before heading back over to Father Roarke and Tom.

Jax gathered the guys and they went and stood in position as the pre-show reels finished playing. He caught Airiella's eyes as they counted them down to live. She smiled at him and pushed love through to all of them. He knew because he felt the change in each of them as they stood there.

"Welcome to a special episode of Shadow Seekers. Tonight, we are doing a live show to help a man get to the bottom of why his family was torn apart by what he claims is a demonic force. Investigate with us, post on social media with the hashtag shadow seekers live if you see something." Jax spoke clearly, his voice strong and on point.

Aedan spoke next, "The first part of our investigation we will stay together as a group and go through the house testing areas we think we feel something. We have a priest on standby to aid us if we uncover a demon or one of us becomes possessed."

Smitty came next. "The second part of the investigation we will invite the man who lives here to join us to try and reveal the entity that has destroyed his family."

Ronnie ended the into. "Don't forget to follow along and keep giving us info on social media. We have crew following the posts that will relay messages to us of things we missed. Now, we get started revealing the secrets held in the shadows."

Jax led the guys into the house, a camera on Smitty, and one on Aedan. Smitty followed Jax, and Aedan filmed Ronnie. They moved from room to room using the various equipment calling out to any spirits, but receiving no evidence.

Jax felt no tingles, no cold spots, nothing close to anything he'd felt on any previous investigation. He had to wonder if this was the end game of the money man. A show so boring and hyped up that it fell flat and lost viewers. He mentally tried to find a way to spin it at the end to prove their worth.

It was time to bring in the phony possessed man. They paused for commercial and Jax checked in with command center to make sure all was okay. Airiella gave the all clear and they brought the guy in. Jax's skin crawled when he was around. Jax crossed his arms, to all that looked at him he seemed intimidating, when actually he was just creeped out. He wanted this over.

I thought they were fantastic. From everything I could see they tried to prove and disprove each statement the guy made, building a case that was showing him to be fake. Social media was all over it, and so far, all positive.

Each commercial break one of the guys checked in with me to make sure I still hadn't seen anything. I was happy to declare everything clear. They were heading down into the basement when I heard a screeching sound coming from the earpieces of those around me.

Everyone yelled and yanked them out. "Equipment failure," some called from behind me. Weird. Camera's still showed the guys. It didn't even look like they noticed anything. Was that just because they couldn't or didn't want to react due to it being live?

I watched the screens closely as Aedan and Ronnie headed back out of the basement and upstairs. There was a strange blip across the screen on Smitty's camera, though it only lasted a second. My eyes kept flicking between the monitors as I watched both teams, looking for signs of distress.

It took me a moment to realize I couldn't feel them. That's not right. They weren't far enough away for me to not feel them. I should be able to feel Smitty and Aedan regardless, because of the connection. That was why they split that way.

"Something's wrong," I said. Tom jolted and looked at me. At least he knew firsthand what I could do so I didn't have to explain everything. "I can't feel them anymore. Like a switch has been flipped."

Father Roarke stepped closer to me. "Are they blocking you?"

I spoke quietly to him, "Smitty and Aedan can't block me. I have a direct link with them."

Tom moved to my side. "Do you feel anything bad? Or another person on site?"

I couldn't feel anything, and that was the problem. I squatted down to the frozen ground and tried to dig my fingers into the earth. I wasn't getting far, I looked around and asked someone for keys. Tom handed me the ones he had and I dug out a little hole and handed them back.

I pushed my fingers in and felt for the natural energy around me. The raven started making noise in my head and I understood it was telling me something was wrong. The earth energy felt disturbed and unstable, I pulled my hand back, I couldn't draw on that. I didn't know what unstable energy would do.

Tom had been trying to reach the guys in side with no luck. Then something hit me hard and I fell back on the ground, the air knocked out of me. "Oh God. Get them out now." My voice shook.

Father Roarke pulled out his cell phone to try and call one of them to get through. He was shaking his head at me. My body started to shake as a sick feeling washed over me. I stood up and tore off the coat, looking at the screens. Jax was standing in a stiff posture, since Smitty was behind the camera I couldn't see what was happening with him. Ronnie and Aedan looked unaffected.

"Shit, it's Jax. Something is happening down there. Get them all out now!" I almost shouted.

Tom was reacting to my tone and got frantic, "I can't get through."

"Fuck it! I'm going in," I declared hotly.

"Airiella, no!" Father Roarke shouted.

I ran to the house and bolted up the stairs, Aedan swinging the camera around at me, "Get out, now!" I didn't wait to see what they did, but I heard them follow me. "Outside! Go!"

I thundered down the stairs to the basement, Smitty hearing someone coming did the same and pointed the camera at me. My face must have shown something because he came towards me fast. "Get out. Now. I've got Jax."

"Oh no, I'm sorry, no one is leaving here." The guy stepped from the shadows he'd been lurking in. "I'm so glad you could join us though."

The raven was going crazy in me. Danger was imminent. I kept pushing Smitty towards the stairs, and I felt a rabid energy growing in me. The atmosphere shifted, pressure building on me in a way I didn't understand.

I looked in Jax's eyes and saw his fear. The darkness in him starting to come to life. "Jax, look at me. Look in my eyes. Fight it." I pushed Smitty again, but his body felt wooden.

"Baby girl," his voice rasped.

"She's exactly what I need," the guy leered at me.

I felt around for Jax's energy and shoved love at him, flooding him with as much as I dared. I also looked around for what was coming from this guy, but I got nothing. He was the block. And he was advancing at me. The raven cawed loudly and the creep flinched.

"The bird can't save you. These useless tools can't save you, and now the world will see what you really are, thanks to that camera." He came closer. He was boxing me in.

Jax and Smitty were frozen in place. Fuck, I didn't know what to do. I was not about to let something happen to these two men. I touched Smitty, pulling from the connection we shared before the guy advanced on me again, forcing me away from Smitty.

I hoped it was enough to do whatever I needed to do. I couldn't pull from the guy because I couldn't find anything to pull. I hit the wall. I had nowhere else to back up to. I slid closer to Jax.

The guy lunged at me, an inhuman sound tearing from his lips as he bared his teeth and slammed into me. My head cracked against the wall making my eyes go out of focus. I could hear Ronnie in my head yelling at me to fight back.

I pushed, knocking him off balance, but I felt the energy in Jax growing bigger and I looked at him in panic. That slight distraction cost me. The guys hand was around my throat and my feet were no longer on the ground. Oxygen bleeding out of me, my vision swam.

Kick, Airiella! I heard a voice in my head screaming at me. I swung my feet but they couldn't get much movement. I started seeing spots before my eyes and the atmosphere shifted again. My throat was desperately seeking air. I let the fight go out of my body.

He thought he won, but I brought my elbow around and smashed it into his temple. He lost his grip and I fell to the floor in a heap, sucking air into my lungs. I felt the moment Jax lost control. It was the same moment that lightning struck the house.

The rickety, run down, wood house. "Smitty run! Go!" I pushed him, struggling to get to my feet. "Go! Get help!" He stumbled and fell backwards on the stairs. It was hurting me to talk, so I pushed him again. He ran. My heart sent out a thank you to whatever was looking out for us.

Jax wasn't Jax. Ice cold fear spread through my veins. I got between the guy and Jax, maybe not my best move, but it was all I could think of. The guy attacked me again, he was on top of me, both his hands around my throat squeezing with crushing force.

I didn't have long. In a move I have only ever seen Ronnie actually pull off, I swung my legs up trying to get them around this guy's head. It didn't work, though I managed to kick him in the side of the head with my heel. He lost his grip and I bucked him off and rolled.

I couldn't see Jax, but I could feel him, the anger suffocating in the basement that was mostly dark. I got up on my hands and knees, getting ready to stand when I got a kick to the head that stunned me. Dizziness was all I knew for a moment. My ears ringing and my lungs filling with smoke.

Smoke? Jax's vision of fire and death slammed into me with enough force to get me off the ground. "Jax!" I tried to scream, the damage in my throat keeping sound from coming out.

"He can't save you now. He'll die just like you. Returned to ashes. Whatever blasphemous thing you are deserves to die. You aren't good, you are no better than me," came the vicious snarl, foul breath blowing across my face.

Jax was close, the energy rolling off him far more malicious than the crazy man in front of me. The raven took flight. Right out of my head, up the stairs and out of the house. I could see through its eyes. Flashing lights, police, ambulance, the frantic crew. The house in flames.

Lightning struck the house again, and I knew it meant I was about to die. If I was going to die, then I was saving Jax. I closed my eyes and felt for the darkness in him, and I pulled. No time to be gentle, I could hear him scream and I begged his forgiveness as the energy filled me. I slammed my walls shut in a desperate attempt to keep it from invading me more than necessary.

I pulled, and pulled. I heard Jax hit the floor, out cold. The guy was trying to escape, I could hear his heavy footfalls on the wooden steps. I opened my eyes to the raven. Ronnie was coming. Save Jax, I tried to tell him with my mind.

I could feel the heat. I needed to move, I had to find Jax. My stomach heaved and I sucked in smoke. Dropping back to the ground I belly crawled until I felt him. My body screaming in pain I dragged him. Inch by inch close to the stairs.

I fought for consciousness with everything I had. The black energy in me fighting to take over. I had nothing left. I couldn't save him. I pulled one last time, feeling the bottom step. I felt the love I had for the guys give me one last push and I got Jax to the stairs. Then I felt nothing else.

The story continues in...

See Me Go

...coming April 2020